# FRIED GREEN TOMATOES at the WHISTLE STOP CAFE

# FRIED GREEN TOMATOES at the WHISTLE STOP CAFE

## Fannie Flagg

RANDOM HOUSE · NEW YORK

Published in the United States by Random House, an imprint of The Random House
Publishing Group, a division of Random House, Inc., New York.

RANDOM HOUSE and colophon are registered trademarks of Random House, Inc.

Originally published in 1987 by Random House, Inc.

Grateful acknowledgment is made to the following for permission to reprint
previously published material:

LEWIS MUSIC PUBLISHING CO., INC.: Excerpt from the lyrics to "Tuxedo Junction"
by Erskine Hawkins, William Johnson, and Julian Dash. Lyrics by Buddy Feyne.
Copyright © 1939 by Lewis Music Publishing Co., Inc. Copyright renewed.
All rights reserved.

MUSIC SALES CORPORATION AND WARNER BROS. MUSIC PUBLISHING:
Excerpt from "Smoke Rings," by Gene Gifford and Ned Washington.
Copyright © 1932 (renewed) by Onyx Music Corporation and EMI Mills Music, Inc.
All rights reserved for Onyx Music Corporation administered by
Music Sales Corporation. All rights outside of the United States controlled by
EMI Mills Music, Inc. International copyright secured. All rights reserved.
Reprinted by permission of Music Sales Corporation and Warner Bros.
Music Publishing, Miami, FL 33014.

THE SALVATION ARMY: Excerpt from *The Salvation Army Songbook*.
Copyright by the Salvation Army, New York, USA. Used by permission.

ISBN 1-4000-6462-7

Printed in the United States of America

DESIGN BY LILLY LANGOTSKY

FOR TOMMY THOMPSON

# Acknowledgments

I would like to acknowledge the following people, whose encouragement and support have been invaluable to me in the writing of this book: First and foremost, my agent, Wendy Weil, who never lost faith; my editor, Sam Vaughan, for the care and attention he has given me, and who kept me laughing, even through rewrites; and Martha Levin, my first friend at Random House. Thanks to Gloria Safier, Liz Hock, Margaret Cafarelli, Anne Howard Baily, Julie Florence, James "Daddy" Hatcher, Dr. John Nixon, Gerry Hannah, Jay Sawyer, and Frank Self. Thanks to DeThomas/Bobo & Associates, for sticking with me during the lean times. Thanks to Barnaby and Mary Conrad and the Santa Barbara Writers' Conference, Jo Roy and the Birmingham Public Library, Jeff Norell, Birmingham Southern College, Ann Harvey and John Loque, Oxmoor House Publishing. A grateful thank you to my typist and right hand, Lisa McDonald, and to her daughter, Jessaiah, for being quiet and watching *Sesame Street* while her mother and I were working. And my special thanks go to all the sweet people of Alabama, past and present. My Heart. My Home.

*I may be sitting here at the Rose Terrace Nursing Home, but in my mind I'm over at the Whistle Stop Cafe having a plate of fried green tomatoes.*

—MRS. CLEO THREADGOODE
JUNE 1986

# FRIED GREEN TOMATOES at the WHISTLE STOP CAFE

JUNE 12, 1929

## Cafe Opens

The Whistle Stop Cafe opened up last week, right next door to me at the post office, and owners Idgie Threadgoode and Ruth Jamison said business has been good ever since. Idgie says that for people who know her not to worry about getting poisoned, she is not cooking. All the cooking is being done by two colored women, Sipsey and Onzell, and the barbecue is being cooked by Big George, who is Onzell's husband.

If there is anybody that has not been there yet, Idgie says that the breakfast hours are from 5:30–7:30, and you can get eggs, grits, biscuits, bacon, sausage, ham and red-eye gravy, and coffee for 25¢.

For lunch and supper you can have: fried chicken; pork chops and gravy; catfish; chicken and dumplings; or a barbecue plate; and your choice of three vegetables, biscuits or cornbread, and your drink and dessert—for 35¢.

She said the vegetables are: creamed corn; fried green tomatoes; fried okra; collard or turnip greens; black-eyed peas; candied yams; butter beans or lima beans.

And pie for dessert.

My other half, Wilbur, and I ate there the other night, and it was so good he says he might not ever eat at home again. Ha. Ha. I wish this were true. I spend all my time cooking for the big lug, and still can't keep him filled up.

By the way, Idgie says that one of her hens laid an egg with a ten-dollar bill in it.

. . . Dot Weems . . .

# ROSE TERRACE
# NURSING HOME

OLD MONTGOMERY HIGHWAY
BIRMINGHAM, ALABAMA

## DECEMBER 15, 1985

Evelyn Couch had come to Rose Terrace with her husband, Ed, who was visiting his mother, Big Momma, a recent but reluctant arrival. Evelyn had just escaped them both and had gone into the visitors' lounge in the back, where she could enjoy her candy bar in peace and quiet. But the moment she sat down, the old woman beside her began to talk . . .

"Now, you ask me the year somebody got married . . . who they married . . . or what the bride's mother wore, and nine times out of ten I can tell you, but for the life of me, I cain't tell you when it was I got to be so old. It just sorta slipped up on me. The first time I noticed it was June of this year, when I was in the hospital for my gallbladder, which they still have, or maybe they threw it out by now . . . who knows. That heavyset nurse had just given me another one of those Fleet enemas they're so fond of over there when I noticed what they had on my arm. It was a white band that said: *Mrs. Cleo Threadgoode . . . an eighty-six-year-old woman.* Imagine that!

"When I got back home, I told my friend Mrs. Otis, I guess the only thing left for us to do is to sit around and get ready to croak. . . . She said she preferred the term *pass over to the other side.* Poor thing, I didn't have the heart to tell her that no matter what you call it, we're all gonna croak, just the same . . .

"It's funny, when you're a child you think time will never go by, but when you hit about twenty, time passes like you're on the fast train to Memphis. I guess life just slips up on everybody. It sure did on me. One day I was a little girl and the next I was a grown woman, with bosoms and hair on my private parts. I missed the whole thing. But then, I never was too smart in school or otherwise . . .

"Mrs. Otis and I are from Whistle Stop, a little town about ten miles from here, out by the railroad yards. . . . She's lived down the street from me for the past thirty years or so, and after her husband died, her son and daughter-in-law had a fit for her to come and live at the nursing home, and they asked me to come with her. I told them I'd stay with her for a while—she doesn't know it yet, but I'm going back home just as soon as she gets settled in good.

"It's not too bad out here. The other day, we all got Christmas corsages to wear on our coats. Mine had little shiny red Christmas balls on it, and Mrs. Otis had a Santy Claus face on hers. But I was sad to give up my kitty, though.

"They won't let you have one here, and I miss her. I've always had a kitty or two, my whole life. I gave her to that little girl next door, the one who's been watering my geraniums. I've got me four cement pots on the front porch, just full of geraniums.

"My friend Mrs. Otis is only seventy-eight and real sweet, but she's a nervous kind of person. I had my gallstones in a Mason jar by my bed, and she made me hide them. Said they made her depressed. Mrs. Otis is just a little bit of somethin', but as you can see, I'm a big woman. Big bones and all.

"But I never drove a car . . . I've been stranded most all my life. Always stayed close to home. Always had to wait for somebody to come and carry me to the store or to the doctor or down to the church. Years ago, you used to be able to take a trolley to Birmingham, but they stopped running a long time ago. The only thing I'd do different if I could go back would be to get myself a driver's license.

"You know, it's funny what you'll miss when you're away from home. Now me, I miss the smell of coffee . . . and bacon frying in the morning. You cain't smell anything they've got cooking out here, and you cain't get a thing that's fried. Everything here is boiled up, with not a piece of salt on it! I wouldn't give you a plugged nickel for anything boiled, would you?"

The old lady didn't wait for an answer. ". . . I used to love my crackers and buttermilk, or my buttermilk and cornbread, in the afternoon. I like to smash it all up in my glass and eat it with a spoon, but you cain't eat in public like you can at home . . . can you? . . . And I miss *wood*.

"My house is nothing but just a little old railroad shack of a house, with a living room, bedroom, and a kitchen. But it's wood, with pine walls inside. Just what I like. I don't like a plaster wall. They seem . . . oh, I don't know, kinda cold and stark-like.

"I brought a picture with me that I had at home, of a girl in a swing with a castle and pretty blue bubbles in the background, to hang in my room, but that nurse here said the girl was naked from the waist up and not appropriate. You know, I've had that picture for fifty years and I never knew she was naked. If you ask me, I don't think the old men they've got here can see well enough to notice that she's bare-breasted. But, this is a Methodist home, so she's in the closet with my gallstones.

"I'll be glad to get home. . . . Of course, my house is a mess. I haven't been able to sweep for a while. I went out and threw my broom at some old, noisy bluejays that were fighting and, wouldn't you know it, my broom stuck up there in the tree. I've got to get someone to get it down for me when I get back.

"Anyway, the other night, when Mrs. Otis's son took us home from the Christmas tea they had at the church, he drove us over the railroad tracks, out by where the cafe used to be, and on up First Street, right past the old Threadgoode place. Of course, most of the house is all boarded up and falling down now, but when we came down the street, the headlights hit the windows in such a way that, just for a minute, that house looked to me just like it had so many of those nights, some seventy years ago, all lit up and full of fun and noise. I could hear people laughing, and Essie Rue pounding away at the piano in the parlor; 'Buffalo Gal, Won't You Come Out To-night' or 'The Big Rock Candy Mountain,' and I could almost see Idgie Threadgoode sitting in the chinaberry tree, howling like a dog every time Essie Rue tried to sing. She always said that Essie Rue could sing about as well as a cow could dance. I guess, driving by that house and me being so homesick made me go back in my mind . . .

"I remember it just like it was yesterday, but then I don't think there's anything about the Threadgoode family I don't remember. Good Lord, I should, I've lived right next door to them from the day I was born, and I married one of the boys.

"There were nine children, and three of the girls, Essie Rue and the twins, were more or less my own age, so I was always over there playing and having spend-the-night parties. My own mother died of consumption when I was four, and when my daddy died, up in Nashville, I just stayed on for good. I guess you might say the spend-the-night party never ended . . ."

**THE WEEMS WEEKLY**

(WHISTLE STOP, ALABAMA'S WEEKLY BULLETIN)

OCTOBER 8, 1929

## Meteorite Hits Whistle Stop Residence

Mrs. Biddie Louise Otis, who lives at 401 1st Street, reported that on Thursday night a two-pound meteorite crashed through the roof of her house and just missed hitting her, but did hit the radio she was listening to at the time. She said that she was sitting on the couch because the dog was in the chair, and had just turned on "Fleischmann's Yeast Hour," when it happened. She said that there is a four-foot hole in her roof and that her radio is broken in half.

Bertha and Harold Vick celebrated their anniversary on the front lawn for all the neighbors to see. And congratulations to Mr. Earl Adcock Sr., an executive for the L & N Railroad, who has just been named Grand Exalted Ruler of the Benevolent and Protective Order of the Elks, Order No. 37, of which my other half is a member.

By the way, Idgie said if you want something bar-
becued, to send it over to the cafe and Big George
will do it for you. Chickens for 10¢ and hogs according
to your size.

. . . Dot Weems . . .

ROSE TERRACE
NURSING HOME

OLD MONTGOMERY HIGHWAY
BIRMINGHAM, ALABAMA

## DECEMBER 15, 1985

One hour later, Mrs. Threadgoode was still talking. Evelyn
Couch had finished three Milky Ways and was in the process
of unwrapping her second Butterfinger, wondering if the old
woman beside her was ever going to shut up.

"You know, it's a shame the Threadgoode house has fallen
into such disrepair. So much happened there, so many babies
born, we had so many happy times. It was a great big two-story
white-frame house with a big front porch that wrapped all the
way around to the side . . . and all the bedrooms had rose-
patterned wallpaper that looked so pretty when the lamps
were turned on at night.

"The railroad tracks ran right across the backyard, and on
summer nights that yard would be just full of lightning bugs
and the smell of honeysuckle that grew wild, right alongside
the tracks. Poppa had the back planted with fig trees and apple
trees, and he had built Momma the most beautiful white lattice
grape arbor that was full of wisteria vines . . . and little pink
sweetheart roses grew all over the back of the house. Oh, I
wish you could have seen it.

"Momma and Poppa Threadgoode raised me just like I was

one of their own, and I liked all the Threadgoodes. Especially Buddy. But I married Cleo, his older brother, the chiropractor, and wouldn't you know it, later on I turned out to have a bad back, so it worked out just fine.

"So you can see I've been keeping up with Idgie and the Threadgoodes all my life. And I'll tell you, it's been better than a picture show . . . yes it has. But then, I was always a tagalong sort of person. Believe it or not, I never did talk much until after I hit my fifties, and then I just couldn't stop. One time Cleo said to me, 'Ninny'—my name is Virginia but they called me Ninny—he said, 'Ninny, all I hear is Idgie said this and Idgie did that.' He said, 'Don't you have anything better to do than to hang around that cafe all day?'

"I thought long and hard and said, 'No, I don't' . . . not to downgrade Cleo in any way, but it was the truth.

"I buried Cleo thirty-one years ago last February, and I often wonder if I hurt his feelings when I said that, but I don't think so, because after all was said and done, he loved Idgie as much as the rest of us, and always got a good laugh out of some of her doings. She was his baby sister, and a real cutup. She and Ruth owned the Whistle Stop Cafe.

"Idgie used to do all kinds of crazy harebrained things just to get you to laugh. She put polker chips in the collection basket at the Baptist church once. She was a character all right, but how anybody ever could have thought that she killed that man is beyond me."

For the first time, Evelyn stopped eating and glanced over at the rather sweet-looking old lady in the faded blue flower-print dress, with the silver-gray fingerwaves, who didn't miss a beat:

"Some people thought it started the day she met Ruth, but I think it started that Sunday dinner, April the first, 1919, the same year Leona married John Justice. I can tell you it was April the first, because Idgie came to the dinner table that day and showed everybody this little white box she had with a human finger inside of it, resting on a piece of cotton. She claimed she'd found it out in the backyard. But it turned out to be her own finger she had poked through a hole in the bottom of the box. APRIL FOOL!!!

"Everybody thought it was funny except Leona. She was the oldest and the prettiest sister, and Poppa Threadgoode spoiled her rotten . . . everybody did, I guess.

"Idgie was about ten or eleven at the time and she had on a brand new white organdy dress that we'd all told her how pretty she looked in. We were having a fine time and starting in on our blueberry cobbler when all of a sudden, out of a clear blue sky, Idgie stood up and announced, just as loud . . . 'I'm never gonna wear another dress as long as I live!' And with that, honey, she marched upstairs and put on a pair of Buddy's old pants and a shirt. To this day, I don't have any idea what set her off. None of us had.

"But Leona, who knew Idgie never said a thing she didn't mean, began to wail. She said, 'Oh Poppa, Idgie's going to ruin my wedding, I just know it!'

"But Poppa said, 'Now, baby girl, that's just not so. You're gonna be the most beautiful bride in the entire state of Alabama.'

"Poppa had this great big handlebar moustache . . . then he looked at us and he said, 'Isn't that right, children?' . . . and we all put in our two cents' worth to make her feel better and to get her to shut up. All of us except Buddy, that is, who just sat there and giggled. Idgie was his pet, so anything she did was all right with him.

"So anyway, Leona was finishing her cobbler, and just when we thought she was all calmed down, she screamed so loud that Sipsey, the colored woman, dropped something in the kitchen. 'Oh Poppa,' Leona said, 'what's gonna happen if one of us dies?'

". . . Well, it was a thought, wasn't it?

"We all looked at Momma, who just put her fork down on the table. 'Now, children, I'm sure your sister will make that one small concession and wear a proper dress if and when that time ever comes. After all, she's stubborn, but she's not unreasonable.'

"Then, a couple of weeks later, I heard Momma tell Ida

Simms, the seamstress for the wedding, that she was gonna need a green velvet suit with a bow tie, for Idgie.

"Ida looked up at Momma kinda funny and said, 'A suit?' . . . And Momma said, 'Oh I know, Ida, I know. I tried my best to get her to wear something a little more weddinglike, but that child has a mind of her own.'

"And she did, even at that age. I think she wanted to be like Buddy, myself . . . oh, those two were a mess!" The old lady laughed.

"One time, they had this raccoon named Cookie, and I used to spend hours watching him try to wash a cracker. They'd put a little pan of water out in the backyard, and then they'd give him a soda cracker, and he'd wash cracker after cracker, and never could figure out what happened to it when it would disappear. Each time, he'd look at his little empty hands and be so surprised. Never did figure out where his cracker was going. He spent a good part of his life washing crackers. He'd wash cookies, too, but that wasn't as funny . . . he washed an ice cream cone once . . .

"Oh, I better quit thinking about that raccoon or they're gonna think I'm as crazy as Mrs. Philbeam, down the hall. Bless her heart, she thinks she's on the Love Boat, headed for Alaska. A lot of these poor souls out here don't even know who they are."

Evelyn's husband, Ed, came to the door of the lounge and motioned. Evelyn wadded up her candy wrappers and put them in her purse and got up.

"Excuse me, that was my husband. I think he's ready to go."

Mrs. Threadgoode looked up, surprised, and she said, "Oh? Do you hafto?"

Evelyn said, "Yes, I think I better. He's ready to leave."

"Well, I've enjoyed talking to you . . . what's your name, honey?"

"Evelyn."

"Well, you come back and see me, y'hear? I've enjoyed talkin' to you . . . bye-bye," she called after Evelyn, and waited for another visitor.

OCTOBER 15, 1929

## Ownership of Meteorite Questioned

Mrs. Vesta Adcock and her son, Earl Jr., have claimed that they are the rightful owner of the meteorite because she said that the Otises rented the house that the meteorite hit from her, and so it is her house and her meteorite.

Mrs. Biddie Louise Otis was questioned on the matter and it is her contention that the meteorite is hers because it was her radio that it hit. Her husband, Roy, who is a brakeman for the Southern Railroad, was working late shift and was not home at the time, but said it was not unusual because in 1833, 10,000 meteors fell in one night and that this was just one, and nothing to make a fuss about.

Biddie said she thought she'd keep it as a souvenir, anyhow.

By the way, is it just my imagination or are times

getting harder these days? My other half says that five new hobos showed up at the cafe last week, looking for something to eat.

... Dot Weems...

# DAVENPORT, IOWA

HOBO CAMP

OCTOBER 15, 1929

Five men sat huddled around a low-burning fire, orange and black shadows dancing on their faces as they drank weak coffee out of tin cans: Jim Smokey Phillips, Elmo Inky Williams, BoWeevil Jake, Crackshot Sackett, and Chattanooga Red Barker—five of the estimated two hundred thousand men and boys roaming the countryside that year.

Smokey Phillips looked up but said nothing; and the rest of them said the same. They were tired and weary that night, because that cold nip in the night air meant the start of another raw, heartless winter, and Smokey knew he would have to be starting south soon, with the great flocks of geese, just as he had done for so many years now.

He was born on a frosty morning, back up in the Smoky Mountains of Tennessee. His daddy, a knobby-legged man, a second-generation moonshiner who had fallen in love with his own product, made the fatal mistake of marrying a "good woman," a plain country girl whose life revolved around the Pine Grove Free Will Baptist Church.

Most of Smokey's childhood had been spent sitting on hard

wooden benches for hours, with his little sister, Bernice, at all-day singings and foot washings.

In the regular church services, his mother had been one of the women who would occasionally stand up and start babbling, out of her head, in an unknown tongue.

Eventually, as she became more and more filled with the Spirit, his father became less so and stopped going to church altogether. He told his children, "I believe in God, but I don't think you have to go crazy to prove it."

Then, one spring when Smokey was eight, things got worse. His mother said that the Lord had told her that her husband was evil and devil-possessed, and she turned him in to the revenue agents.

Smokey remembered the day they brought his daddy down the path from the still with a gun at his back. As he passed by his wife, he looked at her, dumbfounded, and said, "Woman, don't you know what you've done? You've done took the bread right out of your own mouth."

It was the last Smokey ever saw of him.

After his father left, his mother really went off the deep end and got mixed up with a bunch of backwoods Holy Roller snake handlers. One night, after an hour of ranting and beating the Bible, the red-faced, wild-haired preacher got his barefoot congregation all excited. They were all chanting and stomping their feet when suddenly he reached into a potato sack and pulled out two huge rattlesnakes and started waving them around in the air; lost in the Spirit.

Smokey froze in his seat and squeezed his sister's hand. The preacher was dancing around, calling out for believers to take up the serpent and cleanse their souls in the faith of Abraham when his mother ran up, grabbed one of the snakes away from him, and looked it right in the face. She began babbling in the unknown tongue, the whole time staring into the snake's yellow eyes. Everybody in the room began to sway and moan. As she started to walk around the room with it, people began falling down on the floor, jerking and screaming and rolling around under the pews and up and down the aisles. The place was in a frenzy, while she babbled on . . . "HOSSA . . . HELAMNA . . . HESSAMIA . . ."

Before he knew what was happening, his little sister, Bernice, broke away from him, and ran up to her mother and pulled her by the hem of her dress.

"Momma, don't . . . !"

Still wild-eyed and in a trance, she glanced down at her child for one split second, and in that second the rattler lunged and struck the woman in the side of her face. She looked back at the snake, stunned, and he struck again, fast and hard this time, striking her in the neck, the fangs puncturing her jugular vein. She dropped the angry serpent with a thud, and it crawled contemptuously away down the aisle.

His mother looked around the room that was now as silent as death, with a surprised look on her face, and as her eyes glazed over, she sank slowly to the floor. She was dead in less than a minute.

In that moment, his uncle had picked up Smokey and was headed out the door. Bernice went to live with a neighbor, and Smokey stayed at his uncle's house. Then, when he was thirteen, he headed down the railroad tracks toward nowhere, and never came back.

The only thing he took was a photograph of his sister and him. He would take it out every once in awhile. There they were in the fading photograph, with their lips and cheeks painted pink: a little chubby girl with bangs and a pink ribbon tied around her head, wearing a tiny string of pearls; and he sat just behind her, his brown hair slicked down, his cheek pressed close to hers.

He often wondered how Bernice was doing and thought he'd look her up one of these days, if he ever got back on his feet.

When he was about twenty or so, he lost the picture when some railroad bull detective kicked him off a freight, into a cold, yellow river somewhere in Georgia, and now he hardly ever thought about her; except when he happened to be on a train, passing through the Smoky Mountains at night, on his way to somewhere else . . .

This morning, Smokey Phillips was on a mixed train from Georgia, headed for Florida. He had not eaten anything for two days and remembered that his friend Elmo Williams had told him there were two women running a place right outside of Birmingham who were always good for a meal or two. On the way down he'd seen the name of the cafe written on the walls of several boxcars, so when he saw the sign WHISTLE STOP, ALABAMA, he jumped off.

He found the place across the tracks, just like Elmo had said. It was a small green building with a green-and-white awning under a Coca-Cola sign that said THE WISTLE STOP CAFE. He went around the back and knocked on the screen door. A little black woman was busy frying chicken and slicing green tomatoes. She glanced at him and called out, "Miz Idgie!"

Pretty soon, a good-looking, tall blonde with freckles and curly hair came to the door, wearing a clean white shirt and men's trousers. She looked to be in her early twenties.

He took off his hat. "Excuse me, ma'am, I was wondering if you had an odd job, or something I might do. I've had a run of some bad luck, lately."

Idgie looked at the man in the worn-out dirty jacket, frayed brown shirt, and cracked leather laceless shoes and knew he wasn't lying.

She opened the door and said, "Come on in, fella. I think we can find something for you."

Idgie asked what his name was.

"Smokey, ma'am."

She turned to the woman behind the counter. Smokey hadn't seen a neat and clean woman in months, and this one was the prettiest woman he had seen in his entire life. She was wearing a dotted swiss organdy dress and had her auburn hair pulled back with a red ribbon.

"Ruth, this is Smokey, and he's gonna be doing some work for us."

Ruth looked at him and smiled. "That will be fine. Nice to meet you."

Idgie pointed to the men's room. "Why don't you go in there and freshen up, and then come have a bite to eat."

"Yes ma'am."

The bathroom was big and had a light bulb hanging down from the ceiling, and when he pulled it he saw that there was a big stand-up claw-foot tub over in the corner, with a black rubber stopper on a chain. On the sink, already laid out, was a razor and a dish of shaving soap with a brush.

As he looked at himself in the mirror, he felt ashamed that they had seen him so dirty, but he had not had more than a speaking acquaintance with soap for quite a while now. He took the big bar of brown Oxydol soap and tried to scrub all the grime and coal dust off his face and hands. He had not had a drink in twenty-four hours, and his hands shook so bad he was not able to get a clean shave, but he did the best he could. After he had splashed himself with the Old Spice shaving lotion and combed his hair with the Ace comb he had found on the shelf above the sink, he came back out into the cafe.

Idgie and Ruth had set a place for him at a table. He sat down to a plate of fried chicken, black-eyed peas, turnip greens, fried green tomatoes, cornbread, and iced tea.

He picked up his fork and tried to eat. His hands were still shaking and he was not able to get the food to his mouth. He spilled his tea all over his shirt.

He had been hoping they were not watching, but in a minute the blond woman said, "Smokey, come on, let's take a walk outside."

He got his hat and used his napkin, thinking he was being thrown out. "Yes'm."

She walked him out behind the cafe, where there was a field.

"You're a pretty nervous fella, aren't you?"

"I'm sorry about spilling my food in there, ma'am, but to tell you the honest to God truth . . . well . . . I'll just head on, but thank you anyway . . ."

Idgie reached in her apron pocket and pulled out a half-pint bottle of Old Joe Whiskey and handed it to him.

He was a mighty appreciative man. He said, "God bless you for a saint, ma'am," and they sat down on a log out by the shed.

While Smokey was calming his nerves, she talked to him.

"See that big plot of empty land over there?"

He looked over. "Yes'm."

"Years ago, that used to be the most beautiful little lake in Whistle Stop . . . in the summer, we'd swim in it and fish, and you could go for a boat ride if you wanted to." She shook her head sadly. "I sure do miss it, I sure do."

Smokey looked at the vacant land.

"What happened to it, did it dry up?"

She lit a cigarette for him. "Naw, it was worse than that. One November, a big flock of ducks, oh, about forty or more, landed right smack in the middle of that lake, and while they were sitting there, that afternoon, a fluke thing happened. The temperature dropped so fast that the whole lake froze over, as solid as a rock, in a matter of three seconds. One, two, three, just like that."

Smokey was amazed at the thought. "You don't mean it?"

"Yep."

"Well, I reckon it must have killed them ducks."

Idgie said, "Why, hell no. They just flew off and took the lake with 'em. That lake's somewhere in Georgia, to this very day . . ."

He turned and looked at her, and when he realized she was pulling his leg, his blue eyes crinkled up and he started laughing so hard that he started to cough at the same time, and she had to bang him on the back.

He was still wiping his eyes when they went back in the cafe, where his dinner was waiting. When he sat back down to eat, it was warm. Someone had kept it in the oven for him.

> *Oh, where is my wandering boy tonight*
> *The boy of his mother's pride. . .*
> *Oh, he's counting the ties*
> *With a bed on his back*
> *Or else he's dinging a ride . . .*
> *Oh, where is my boy tonight?*

THE WEEMS WEEKLY

(WHISTLE STOP, ALABAMA'S WEEKLY BULLETIN)

OCTOBER 22, 1929

# Meteorite to Be on Display at Cafe

Mrs. Biddie Louise Otis announced today that she was going to take the meteorite that came through her roof last week down to the cafe so people would stop calling her up about it, because she is busy moving. She said that it is nothing but a big gray rock, but if anyone wants to look at it they can.

Idgie says to come on in the cafe whenever you want to and she will have it on the counter.

Sorry I don't have more news this week, but my other half, Wilbur, has the flu and I've had to wait on him hand and foot all week.

Is there anything worse than a man that's sick?

We are sorry to report that our beloved 98-year-old Bessie Vick, Bertha's mother-in-law, died yesterday, of what was thought to be old age.

. . . Dot Weems . . .

DECEMBER 22, 1985

The next Sunday, when Evelyn came to the visitors' lounge, Mrs. Threadgoode was sitting in the same chair, wearing the same dress, waiting for her.

Happy as a lark, she continued the conversation about the Threadgoode house as if they had never been apart, and there was nothing Evelyn could do about it but unwrap her Almond Joy candy bar and sit there for the duration.

"The front yard had a great big old chinaberry tree. I remember, we'd pick those little chinaberries all year long, and at Christmas, we'd string them and wrap them all around the tree from top to bottom. Momma was always warning us not to put chinaberries up our nose, and of course the first thing Idgie did, as soon as she learned to walk, was to go out in the yard and put chinaberries up her nose and in her ears as well. To the point that Dr. Hadley had to be called! He told Momma, 'Mrs. Threadgoode, it looks like you've got yourself a little scalawag on your hands.'

"Well, of course Buddy just loved to hear that. He encouraged her every step of the way. But that's how it is in big families. Everybody has their favorite. Her real name was Imogene, but Buddy started calling her Idgie. Buddy was eight when she was born, and he used to carry her all over town, just like she was a doll. When she got old enough to walk, she'd paddle around after him like a little duck, dragging that little wooden rooster behind her.

"That Buddy had a million-dollar personality, with those dark eyes and those white teeth . . . he could charm you within an inch of your life. I don't know of a girl in Whistle Stop that wasn't in love with him at some time or another.

"They say you never forget your sweet sixteen party, and that's true. I still can remember that pink-and-white cake with the carousel on top, and that pale lime-green punch Momma had in her crystal punch bowl. And those paper lanterns hanging all around the yard. But what stands out the most in my mind was Buddy Threadgoode stealin' a kiss from me, over behind the grape arbor. Oh, he did! But I was just one of the many . . .

"Idgie was kept busy delivering love notes to and from Buddy, night and day. We even started calling her Cupid. Idgie was a towhead; had short, curly blond hair, blue eyes, and freckles. She took after Momma's side of the family. Momma's maiden name had been Alice Lee Cloud. She'd always say, 'I was a Cloud before I married.' She was the sweetest thing. Almost everybody in the family had blue eyes, except Buddy and poor Essie Rue, who had one brown eye and one blue one. Momma told her that was the reason she had so much musical talent. She saw the good in everything. One time, when Idgie and Buddy stole four big watermelons from old man Sockwell, they hid them in her blackberry patch. And, honey, the next morning, before they could get out there and get them, Momma found them and was convinced they had grown overnight. Cleo said there wasn't a year that went by she wasn't disappointed they didn't grow back. Nobody had the heart to tell her those melons had been stolen goods.

"Momma was Baptist and Poppa was a Methodist. He said he had an aversion to being dipped underwater. So every Sunday, Poppa would go off to the left to the First Methodist church and the rest of us would go off to the right to the Baptist church. Every once in a while Buddy would go with Poppa, but he stopped after a while. Said Baptist girls were prettier.

"Everybody was always staying at the Threadgoode house. One summer, Momma had this big fat Baptist preacher, who was in town for a camp meeting, staying with us, and when he was out somewhere, the twins went into his room and got to playing in a pair of his trousers. Patsy Ruth got in one leg and Mildred got in the other. They were having a fine time, until they heard him comin' up the stairs . . . They got so scared that Mildred took off in one direction and Patsy Ruth took off in the other. Split those pants right in two. Momma said the only reason Poppa didn't give them a spanking is because that preacher was a Baptist. But it never caused a serious rift, because after church we'd all meet back home for our Sunday dinner.

"Poppa Threadgoode wasn't rich, but it seemed to us at the time he was. He owned the only store in town. You could get anything you needed in there. You could buy a National washboard or shoestrings or get yourself a corset or a dill pickle right out of the barrel.

"Buddy used to work in the drugstore part. And I'd give all the tea in China for a strawberry ice cream soda like Buddy used to make. Everybody in Whistle Stop traded there. That's why we were so surprised when the store closed down in 'twenty-two.

"Cleo said the reason the store failed was because Poppa couldn't say no to anybody, white or colored. Whatever people wanted or needed, he just put in a sack and let them have it on credit. Cleo said Poppa's fortune had walked right out the door on him in paper bags. But then, none of the Threadgoodes could ever say no to anybody. Honey, they would give you the shirt off their backs, if you asked for it. And Cleo was no better. Cleo and I never did have a lot of fancy things, but the good Lord provided, and we had everything we ever needed. I believe poor people are good people, except the ones that are mean . . . and they'd be mean even if they were rich. Most of the people who are living out here at Rose Terrace are poor. Just have their Social Security, and most of them are on Medicaid."

She turned to Evelyn. "Honey, that's one thing you be sure and you get on right away, is your Medicaid, you don't want to be caught without that.

"There's a few rich women out here. A couple of weeks ago, Mrs. Vesta Adcock, this little bird-breasted woman I know who's from Whistle Stop, came in, wearing her fox furs and her diamond dinner rings. She's one of the rich ones. But the rich ones don't seem happy to me. And I'll tell you something else—their children don't come to see them any more often than the rest.

"Norris and Francis, Mrs. Otis's son and daughter-in-law, come to see her every week, rain or shine. That's why I come back here in the lounge on Sundays, to give them a little privacy, so they can visit . . . but oh, it would just break your heart to see some of them waiting for their visitors. They get their hair all done up on Saturday, and on Sunday morning they get themselves all dressed and ready, and after all that, nobody comes to see them. I feel so bad, but what can you do? Having children is no guarantee that you'll get visitors . . . No, it isn't."

# THE WEEMS WEEKLY

(WHISTLE STOP, ALABAMA'S WEEKLY BULLETIN)

JULY 12, 1930

## Whistle Stop Growing by Leaps and Bounds

Opal Threadgoode, Julian's wife, has rented the building two doors down from me at the post office, and is opening up a beauty shop of her own. She had been fixing people's hair in her kitchen, but Julian said for her to stop doing that because so many women were coming in and out the back door all day that it was causing their hens not to lay.

Opal said the prices would still be the same: shampoo and set for 50¢, and a permanent for $1.50.

I, for one, am delighted at the new addition to our busy street. Just think, now you can mail a letter, have a meal, and get your hair done all on the same block. All we need now is a picture show to open up, then none of us would ever need to go over to Birmingham again.

Mr. and Mrs. Roy Glass had the Glass family annual

reunion in their backyard, and all the Glasses came from all over the state to be there, and Wilma said the cake tasted better than it looked.

By the way, my other half hooked his own finger the other day when he was fishing, so I've had him at home again, moaning and groaning.

. . . Dot Weems . . .

# WHISTLE STOP CAFE

## NOVEMBER 18, 1931

By now, the name of the cafe was written on the walls of hundreds of boxcars, from Seattle to Florida. Splinter Belly Jones said he had seen it as far away as Canada.

Things were especially bad that year, and at night the woods all around Whistle Stop twinkled from the fires at the hobo camps, and there wasn't a single man there that Idgie and Ruth had not fed at one time or another.

Cleo, Idgie's brother, was concerned about it. He had come over to the cafe to pick up his wife, Ninny, and their little boy, Albert. He was having a cup of coffee and eating peanuts.

"Idgie, I'm telling you, you don't need to feed everybody that shows up at your door. You've got a business to run here. Julian told me that he came by here the other day and there were seven of them in here eating. He says he thinks you'd let Ruth and the baby go without to feed those bums."

Idgie dismissed the thought. "Oh Cleo, what does Julian know? He'd starve to death himself if Opal didn't have the beauty shop. What are you listening to him for? He doesn't have the sense God gave a billy goat."

Cleo couldn't disagree with her on that point.

"Well, it's not only Julian, honey. I worry about you.

"I know."

"Well, I just want you to be smart and not be a fool and give away all your profits."

Idgie looked at him and smiled. "Now, Cleo, I know for a fact that half the people in this town have not paid you for five years. I don't see you throwing them out the door."

Ninny, who was usually quiet, piped up, "That's right, Cleo."

Cleo ate a peanut. Idgie got up and grabbed him around the neck, playing with him. "Listen, you old bone cracker, you've never turned a hungry man away from your door in your life."

"I never had to. They were all over here," he said and cleared his throat. "Now, seriously, Idgie, I'm not trying to run your business or anything, but I just want to know if you're saving any money, that's all."

"What for?" Idgie said. "Listen, money will kill you, you know that. Why, just today, a man came here and told me about his uncle, who had a *good*-paying job working up in Kentucky at the national mint, making money for the government, and everything was going fine until one day he pulled the wrong lever and was crushed to death by seven hundred pounds of dimes."

Ninny was horrified. "Oh no. How awful."

Cleo looked at his wife like she was crazy. "Good Lord, woman, I think you'd believe anything this nutty sister of mine told you."

"Well, it could have happened, couldn't it? Was he really killed by dimes, Idgie?"

"Sure was. It was either dimes or three hundred pounds of quarters, I forget which, but in any case, he was killed all right."

Cleo shook his head at Idgie and had to laugh.

JANUARY 29, 1986

Every Sunday on visiting day, Ed Couch and his mother, Big Momma, would just sit in her cramped little room all afternoon and look at television. Today, Evelyn thought if she didn't get out of there soon, she would scream. She excused herself and said she was going to the bathroom down the hall. She had really planned to go sit in the car but had forgotten that Ed had the car keys; so there she was—back again . . . in the lounge with Mrs. Threadgoode, unwrapping a package of coconut Sno Balls from the Hostess company while Mrs. Threadgoode was telling her about last night's dinner at Rose Terrace.

"So there she was, honey, sitting at the head of the table . . . all puffed up and braggin'."

"Who?"

"Mrs. Adcock."

"Mrs. Adcock?"

"Mrs. Adcock! You remember Mrs. Adcock—with the fox furs—Mrs. Adcock!"

Evelyn thought for a minute. "Oh, the rich one."

"That's right, Mrs. Adcock, with the dinner rings."

"That's right."

Evelyn handed her the open package.

"Oh, thank you. I love a Sno Ball." She took a bite and after a while she said, "Evelyn, don't you want a Coca-Cola to wash it down with? I've got some change in my room, and I'll get you a cold drink if you want one. They've got a machine down the hall."

Evelyn said, "No, Mrs. Threadgoode, I'm all right, but would you like one?"

"Oh no, honey. Normally I would, but today I've got a kinda gassy-like feeling, so I'd just as soon have some water, if you don't mind."

Evelyn went outside the door and got them both little white cone cups of cold water.

"Thank you kindly."

"What about Mrs. Adcock?"

Mrs. Threadgoode looked at her. "Mrs. Adcock? Do you know her?"

"No, I don't know her, you were just saying that she was bragging about something."

"Oh, that's right, I was . . . well, Mrs. Adcock was telling us at the dinner table last night that everything in her house is a genuine antique . . . over fifty years old . . . said everything she owned was worth a lot of money. I told Mrs. Otis, 'Here I started out in life not worth much of anything, and I've turned out to be a priceless antique. Probably worth a fortune on the market.' " She laughed, tickled at the idea, and then thought for a moment.

"I wonder whatever happened to all those little china-doll dishes and that little goat cart we used to play with?

"On Saturdays, we'd go for a ride in this goat cart that Poppa had made for us girls, and we thought it was better than a trip to Paris. I wouldn't be surprised if that old goat was still alive. His name was Harry . . . Harry the goat! He'd eat anything!" She laughed. "One time, Idgie fed him a whole jar of Leona's Mum underarm deodorant, and he lapped it up just like it was ice cream . . .

"We played all kinds of games—but nobody loved to play dress-up any more than the Threadgoodes. One year, Momma dressed us four girls up as the four different suits in a pack of cards for the contest they were having over at the church. I was the clubs, the twins were hearts and diamonds, and Essie Rue was spades, and here comes Idgie, tagging along after us, as the joker in the pack. We took first prize!

"I remember one Fourth of July, all of us girls had on our stars-and-stripes dresses, with our paper crowns. We were all out in the backyard, having our dish of homemade ice cream, waiting for the fireworks to start, when here comes Buddy Threadgoode down the back stairs, all dressed up in one of Leona's middy dresses, with a big bow tied on his head, and he commenced to prissing and mincing. He was imitating Leona, don't you see? Then, to make matters worse, Edward or Julian or one of the boys had carried the Victrola out in the yard and was winding away on it, playing 'The Sheik of Araby' while Buddy hootchy-kootchied all around the yard. We've laughed over that for years. Later, Buddy gave Leona a big kiss. You could forgive Buddy anything.

"After it got dark, Poppa would hire these fireworks people to come and put on a show for the whole town . . . and all the colored people from Troutville would come. What a sight! Those fireworks would explode and light up the whole sky. And, of course, all the boys would go crazy popping their firecrackers. Then, after it was all over, we'd go back in and sit in the parlor and listen to Essie Rue pound away on the piano. She'd play 'Listen to the Mockingbird,' 'Nola,' or whatever song was popular that year . . . while Idgie sat in the tree and howled at her.

"Seems like Idgie was always in overalls and barefooted. It's a good thing, too. She would have ruined any nice dresses, going up and down trees like she did, and she was always going hunting or fishing with Buddy and her brothers. Buddy said that she could shoot as good as any of the boys. She was a pretty little thing, except after Buddy got her hair all bobbed off, you'd swear she was a little boy.

"But all the Threadgoode girls were pretty. Oh, not that they didn't work at it. Especially Leona. She was the vainest one of the girls, and she didn't have a sense of humor about it, either.

"Course, my looks were always just passing, because I was so tall. I used to want to hunch over a little because of it, but Momma Threadgoode used to say, 'Ninny, the good Lord made you tall so you could be closer to heaven . . .' But I'm not as tall now as I used to be. When you get old, you shrink.

"Isn't hair a funny thing? So many people are just crazy about their hair. Of course, I guess it's just natural. The mention of hair runs all through the Bible: Samson, and that Sheba woman, and that girl that washed Jesus' feet with her hair. . . . Isn't it odd, the colored want straight hair and we're always wanting curly hair. I had brown hair at one time, but now I use Silk and Silver Number Fifteen . . . I used to use Number Sixteen, but it made my hair too dark, and it looked kinda dyed-lookin'.

"Back then, I just twisted it up in a knot and went on about my business. Not Miss Leona. Her hair was always a sore spot between her and Idgie. I guess Idgie was around nine or ten, and she'd been over in Troutville, playing with the children there, and came home with a case of head lice. So we all had to wash our hair with this mixture of sulphur, kerosene, and lard. I never heard so much screaming and hollering. You would have thought that Leona was being burned at the stake. Leona wouldn't speak to poor Idgie after that.

"During that time, Buddy came home from school and saw that Idgie was pretty low. He had a football game to go to and when he was leaving the house that night, he said, 'Come on, Little Bit,' and he took her down to the football game and let her sit right on the bench with the rest of the players. That was Buddy for you . . .

"I don't think Leona ever really forgave Idgie until after she married. Leona was vain about her looks until the day she died. One time, she read an article in the *McCall's* magazine that said anger and hate could cause wrinkles. She was always threatening Idgie she was going to kill her, but she kept a smile on her face while she was doing it.

"Of course, Leona did get the richest husband, and her wedding was exquisite. She had been so scared that Idgie was going to ruin her wedding, but she needn't have been, because Idgie spent most of the day with the groom's family and charmed them so, that by the end of the day, they thought she was the grandest thing on bush or tree. Even at that age, she had that Threadgoode charm. And nobody in the world had charm like Buddy Threadgoode."

Mrs. Threadgoode stopped for a moment to take a sip from her cup, and reflected, "You know, this little coconut cake reminds me of the picnic, that awful day.

"I was already engaged to Cleo, so I must have been seventeen at the time. It was a Saturday afternoon in June, and we had just had the best time at our BYO church picnic. The young people's group from the Andalusia Baptist Church had ridden the train over for the day, and Momma and Sipsey had baked about ten coconut cakes for the occasion. The boys were wearing their white summer suits and Cleo had just gotten himself a brand-new straw hat from Poppa's store, but for some reason, Buddy had talked Cleo into letting him wear his new hat on that day.

"After the picnic, Essie Rue and I came home with the cake plates, and all the Threadgoode boys went down to the train station to see the group from Andalusia off, like they always did. Momma was out in the backyard with a pan, picking figs off her tree, and I was out there with her when it happened . . .

"We heard the train start up, and just as it pulled out, the whistle blew. Then we heard the train screech and grind to a halt, and at the same moment we heard the girls screaming.

"I looked at Momma, who all of a sudden clutched at her heart and fell down on her knees and cried out, 'Oh no, not one of my babies! Dear God, not one of my babies!'

"Poppa Threadgoode had heard the noise from the store and ran over to the station. I was on the front porch with Momma when the men came up the walk. The minute I saw that straw hat Edward was carrying, I knew it was Buddy.

"He had been flirting around with that pretty Marie Miller

that day, and as the train pulled away, he'd stepped on the track, tipped his hat, and flashed his lady's smile at her; just as the whistle blew. They say he never even heard the train that was coming up behind him. Oh, how I wish to this day Cleo had never lent him that straw hat."

She shook her head. "You just don't know, it liked to have killed us all. But the one that took it the hardest was Idgie. She must have been twelve or thirteen at the time, and had been over in Troutville playing ball when it happened. Cleo had to go over and get her.

"You never saw anybody hurt so much. I thought she would die right along with him. It would break your heart to look at her. She ran away the day of the funeral. Just couldn't stand it. And when she did come home, all she did was go upstairs and sit in Buddy's room for hours on end, just sit up there in the dark. And when she couldn't bear to be home any longer, she'd just take off and go stay with Sipsey over in Troutville . . . but she never did cry. She was too hurt to cry. . . . You know, a heart can be broken, but it keeps on beating, just the same.

"Momma Threadgoode was worried sick over her, but Poppa said to let her go and do what she had to do. Course, she was never the same after that, not until she met Ruth, then she started getting back to her old self. But I know she never really got over Buddy . . . none of us did.

"But, I don't want to dwell on sad times. That wouldn't be right. Besides, just like Idgie meeting Ruth, God never shuts a door unless he opens another, and I believe He must have sent Ruth over to stay with us that summer for a reason . . . 'His Eye Is on the Sparrow, so I Know He Watches Me.' "

DECEMBER 1, 1931

## Radio Star in Whistle Stop

Hollywood has nothing on us. Our own Essie Rue Limeway, who is the organist for the Baptist church and the accompanist for the Jolly Belles Ladies' Barber Shop Quartet, can be heard every morning at 6:30, this month, on "King Biscuit Time," on W.A.P.I. radio, playing the piano on a commercial that she made for the Stanley Charles Organ and Piano Company. When Mr. Charles says, "Remember, folks, I'll hold your organ or piano till Christmas," that's Essie Rue playing "Jingle Bells" in the background. So be sure and listen.

Essie told me that Stanley Charles has entirely too many organs and pianos in stock this year, and needs to sell them in a hurry. Essie says, if you go in and mention her name, that he will give you a discount. The store is located in downtown Birmingham, right at the streetcar stop, across from Gus's Hot Dogs.

By the way, the *O* fell off Opal's Beauty Shop sign, and just missed hitting Biddie Louise Otis in the head. Opal says she is glad that she wasn't hurt, but wasn't it a coincidence that Mrs. Otis's name started with an *O* too? Julian says he is fixing it sometime this week, but Biddie says she is going in the back door from now on.

. . . Dot Weems . . .

P.S. Opal says she's just got in a consignment of human hair ringlets . . . So if you have any place that needs a little more hair . . . she says to come on in . . .

# 212 RHODES CIRCLE

BIRMINGHAM, ALABAMA

### JANUARY 5, 1986

Evelyn Couch had locked herself in her sewing room and was eating a second pint of Baskin-Robbins chocolate chip ice cream and staring at the table, piled high with the Butterick sewing patterns she had not touched since the day she had bought them in a fit of good intentions. Ed was in his den, busy watching his football game, and that was fine with her because, lately, he always looked at her whenever she had anything fattening to eat and said in mock surprise, "Is that on your diet?"

She had lied to the boy at Baskin-Robbins. She told him the ice cream was for a party for her grandchildren. She didn't even have grandchildren.

Evelyn was forty-eight years old and she had gotten lost somewhere along the way.

Things had changed so fast. While she had been raising the required two children—"a boy for him and a girl for me"—the world had become a different place, a place she didn't know at all.

She didn't get the jokes anymore. They all seemed so mean, and she was still shocked at the language. Here she was, at her age, and she'd never said the *f* word. So she mostly watched old movies and reruns of *The Lucy Show*. When the Vietnam War was going on, she'd believed what Ed had told her, that it was a good and necessary war, and that anyone against it was a communist. But then, much later, when she finally decided that it may not have been such a good war, Jane Fonda had already moved on to her exercise class and nobody cared what Evelyn thought, anyway. She still held a grudge against Jane Fonda and wished she'd get off TV and stop slinging her skinny legs around all the time.

Not that Evelyn hadn't tried along the way. She had tried to raise her son to be sensitive, but Ed had scared her so bad, telling her that he would turn out to be a queer, she had backed off and lost contact with him. Even now her son seemed like a stranger to her.

Both her children had passed her by. Her daughter, Janice, had known more about sex at fifteen than Evelyn did at this very minute. Something had gone wrong.

When she was in high school, things had been so simple. There were the good girls and the bad girls, and everyone knew who was who. You were either a member of the "in" group or you were not. Evelyn had been in the golden circle; a cheerleader. She had not known the name of one person who was in the high school band or the boys in the pegged pants and their girl friends with the nylon see-through blouses and ankle bracelets. Her crowd had been the crew-cut, button-down madras shirt and pressed khakis for boys, and Ship 'n Shore blouses with circle pins for girls set. She and her girl friends smoked one Kent cigarette at their sorority meetings, and at a pajama party they maybe had a beer, but that was it. No petting below the neck.

Later, she had felt like a fool going with her daughter to get her fitted for a diaphragm. Evelyn had waited until her wedding night.

And what a shock. Nobody had told her how much it would hurt. She still didn't enjoy sex. Every time she would start to relax, the bad-girl image would pop into her head.

She had been a good girl, had always acted like a lady, never raised her voice, always deferred to everybody and every-thing. She had assumed that somewhere down the line there would be a reward for that; a prize. But when her daughter had asked her if she'd ever had sex with anyone but her hus-band and she'd answered, "No, of course not," her daughter's reply had been, "Oh Mother, how dumb. You don't even know if he's any good or not. How awful."

It was true. She didn't know.

So in the long run, it didn't matter at all if you had been good or not. The girls in high school who had "gone all the way" had not wound up living in back alleys in shame and disgrace, like she thought they would; they wound up happily or unhappily married, just like the rest of them. So all that struggle to stay pure, the fear of being touched, the fear of driving a boy mad with passion by any gesture, and the ultimate fear—getting pregnant—all that wasted energy was for nothing. Now, movie stars were having children out of wedlock by the carload, and naming them names like Moonbeam or Sunfeather.

And what was the reward for staying sober? She had always heard, There's nothing worse than a woman drunk, and she never allowed herself more than one whiskey sour. Now, all the best people were waltzing into the Betty Ford Center, getting their pictures made, and having lots of parties thrown for them when they came out. She often wondered if Betty would take people who needed to lose twenty-five pounds.

Her daughter had given her a puff of a marijuana cigarette once, but after all the hot pads on the counter started walking toward her, she got scared and never tried it again. So dope was out.

Evelyn wondered where her group was, the place where she fit in . . .

About ten years ago, when Ed had started seeing a woman he worked with down at the insurance company, she had at-tended a group called the Complete Woman, to try and save her marriage. She wasn't sure she loved Ed all that much, but she loved him just enough to not want to lose him. Besides, what would she do? She had lived with him as long as she had lived with her parents. The organization believed that women could find complete happiness if they, in turn, would dedicate their entire lives to just making their man happy.

Their leader had informed them that all the rich and successful career women out there who appeared to be so happy were, in reality, terribly lonely and miserable and secretly envied them their happy Christian homes.

It was a stretch to imagine that Barbara Walters might want to give it all up for Ed Couch, but Evelyn tried her hardest. Of course, even though she was not religious, it was a comfort to know that the Bible backed her up in being a doormat. Hadn't the apostle St. Paul said for women not to usurp power over the men but to be in silence?

So, hoping she was on the right track, she started up the ladder on *The Ten Steps to Complete Happiness.* She tried step number one and met Ed at the front door nude, wrapped in Saran wrap. But Ed had been horrified: He'd jumped inside the house and slammed the door. "Jesus Christ, Evelyn! What if I had been the paper boy! Have you gone insane?"

So she never tried step number two: going to his office dressed as a prostitute.

But pretty soon, the group leader, Nadine Fingerhutt, got a divorce and had to go to work, so the group just sort of fizzled out. Then, after a while, Ed stopped seeing that woman and things settled down.

Later on, still looking, she had tried to get involved with the Women's Community Center. She liked what they stood for but secretly wished they would wear just a little lipstick and shave their legs. She had been the only one in the room in full makeup, wearing pantyhose and earrings. She had wanted to belong, but when the woman suggested that next week they bring a mirror so they could all study their vaginas, she never went back.

Ed said that those women were nothing but a bunch of frustrated old maids and too ugly to get a man anyway. So there she was, too bored for Tupperware parties and too scared to look at her own vagina.

The night she and Ed went to their thirtieth high school reunion, she had been hoping she'd find someone to talk to about what she was feeling. But all the other women there were just as confused as she was, and held on to their husbands and their drinks to keep themselves from disappearing. Their generation seemed to be on a fence, not knowing which way to jump.

After the reunion, she would sit for hours looking at all her school pictures, and she began to drive by the places where she used to live, over and over.

Ed was no help. Lately, he had started acting more and more like his daddy, trying to behave like he thought the man of the house should. He had become more closed off as the years went by, and on Saturdays he would wander around the Home Improvement Center alone, for hours; looking for something, but he didn't know what. He hunted and fished and watched his football games like the other men, but she began to suspect that he, too, was just playing a part.

Evelyn stared into the empty ice cream carton and wondered where the smiling girl in the school pictures had gone.

# THE WEEMS WEEKLY

(WHISTLE STOP, ALABAMA'S WEEKLY BULLETIN)

NOVEMBER 2, 1932

## Whistle Stop Pig Club Started

Due to the encouragement of the Alabama Extension Service, a local pig club has been formed. Anyone wanting information is to call Mrs. Bertha Vick at home. Bertha said that a Miss Zula Hight of Kittrel, North Carolina, earned a pure-bred Registered China Pig in just seven days, and Bertha said that you could do the same thing if you just put your mind to it. She said to own a pure-bred pig is a mark of distinction for you and your community and will start you on the road to prosperity. It will mean the laying of a foundation for a comfortable income for you all of your life, and when old age overtakes you.

Idgie just got her brand-new Philco radio at the cafe, and says anybody wanting to hear "Amos 'n' Andy," or any other program, is welcome to come in and need not order anything to eat. She says the sound is good at night especially.

By the way, does anybody know how to get rid of dog tracks in cement? If so, call me up or come by the post office and tell me.

. . . Dot Weems . . .

# ROSE TERRACE
# NURSING HOME

OLD MONTGOMERY HIGHWAY
BIRMINGHAM, ALABAMA

JANUARY 12, 1986

Evelyn opened her purse and gave Mrs. Threadgoode one of the pimiento-cheese sandwiches she had wrapped in wax paper, and brought from home.

Mrs. Threadgoode was delighted. "Oh, thank you! I love a good pimiento-cheese sandwich. In fact, I love anything to eat that's a pretty color. Don't you think pimiento cheese has a pretty color? It's so cheery. I like a red pepper, too, and I used to love candied apples, but I cain't eat them anymore, because of my teeth. Come to think of it, I like anything that's red." She thought for a minute.

"We had a red hen named Sister, once, and every time I'd go in the backyard, I'd say, 'Sister, don't you peck my toes, girl, or I'll fry you up with dumplings,' and she'd cock her head and walk sideways away from me. She'd peck everybody else except me and my little boy, Albert. We never could eat that hen, even during the Depression. She died of old age. When I get to heaven, with all my people, I hope Sister and Cookie the raccoon is gonna be there. I know old Sipsey's gonna be there.

"I don't have any idea where Sipsey came from . . . you never know where colored people come from. She was about ten or eleven when she started working for Momma Threadgoode. She'd walked over from Troutville, the colored quarters across the tracks, and said her name was Sipsey Peavey and she was lookin' for a job, and Momma just kept her. She helped raise all the Threadgoode children.

"Sipsey was a skinny little thing, and funny. She had all those old-timy colored superstitions. Her mother'd been a slave, and she was scared to death of spells . . . told Momma that her neighbor in Troutville had put yellow conjure powder in this man's shoes every night, and had caused him to lose his functions. But the thing she was the most deathly afraid of in the world was the heads of animals. If you brought her a chicken or a fish or if Big George killed a hog, she wouldn't touch it or cook it until she'd buried the head out in the garden. She said that if you didn't bury the head, the spirit of that animal would enter your body and cause you to go completely insane. One time, Poppa forgot and brought some hog's-head cheese in the house, and Sipsey ran home, screaming like a banshee, and wouldn't come back until the place had been conjured by a friend of hers. She must have buried hundreds of heads out in the garden. But you know, we got the biggest tomatoes and okra and squash in town because of it!" She laughed. "Buddy used to call it the fish-head garden.

"But, with all of her spooky ways, there wasn't a better cook in the state of Alabama. Even at eleven, they say she could make the most delicious biscuits and gravy, cobbler, fried chicken, turnip greens, and black-eyed peas. And her dumplings were so light they would float in the air and you'd have to catch 'em to eat 'em. All the recipes that were used at the cafe were hers. She taught Idgie and Ruth everything they knew about cooking.

"I don't know why Sipsey never had any children of her own. You never saw anybody love babies more than Sipsey did. All the colored women in Troutville would leave their babies with Sipsey overnight when they wanted to go out and have a good time. They knew she'd take good care of them. Sipsey said nothing made her happier than to have a little baby to rock. She'd rock those little babies and sing to them all night long, sometimes two at a time, and just pine away for one of her own.

"Then, one afternoon in November, right around Thanksgiving—Momma said it was freezing cold outside and all the trees were bare—Sipsey was upstairs making the beds, when a friend of hers from the colored church came in the backyard, hollering up to her. Her friend was all excited and told her that there was a girl from Birmingham down at the train station that was giving away a baby. And she said to hurry up 'cause the train was fixin' to leave.

"With that, Sipsey ran downstairs as fast as she could with nothing on but a thin dress and her apron. When she ran through the back door, Momma Threadgoode said she yelled at her to put her coat on, but she called back, 'I don' have time, Miz Threadgoode. I got to go get me that baby,' and was gone in a flash. Momma stood on the back porch and waited, and pretty soon she saw the train pull away, and here came Sipsey, grinning from ear to ear, her legs all scratched and bleeding from running through the briars, carrying the fattest, blackest little baby boy, all wrapped up in a towel that said HOTEL DIXIE, MEMPHIS, TENNESSEE. Sipsey said that gal had been on her way back home and had told Sipsey she didn't dare show up with a baby, 'cause her husband had been in jail for three years.

"So we never did know the baby's real name. Sipsey said since he came off the train, she would just call him George Pullman Peavey, after the man that invented the pullman car. But whoever his real daddy was, he must have been a big man, because George grew up to be a six-foot-four, two-hundred-fifty-pounder.

"When he was a little boy, Poppa took him over to the store and taught him how to be a butcher. He was slaughtering hogs when he was only ten, and Sipsey was so proud of him . . . she couldn't have loved him any more if he had been her very own. She used to hug him and she would say, 'Honey, just 'cause we ain't no kin don' mean you don' belong to me.'

"And later, when Big George was on trial, she dressed up and went to that courtroom, come rain or come shine . . . she must have been close to ninety years old. Course, you can never really tell how old colored people are.

"She was always singing her gospel songs . . . 'In the Baggage Car Ahead,' and 'I'm Going Home on the Morning Train' . . . always singing about trains. The night before she died, she told George that she had a dream where she saw Jesus all dressed in white. He was the conductor of a ghost train and he was coming to get her and take her to heaven.

"But I would venture to say she was still cooking over at the cafe well up into her eighties. That's the reason most people came, because of her cooking. It sure wasn't for the look of the place. When Idgie and Ruth bought it, it wasn't nothing more but one big old room. It sat just across the street from the railroad tracks, down from the post office, where Dot Weems worked.

"I remember the day they moved in the cafe. We were all down there helping, and Sipsey was busy sweeping the floor when she noticed that Ruth was hanging her picture of the Last Supper. Sipsey stopped sweeping and studied that picture for a while, and then she asked, 'Miz Ruth, who's that sitting up there at the table with Mr. Jesus?'

"Ruth, who was trying to be sweet, said, 'Why, Sipsey, that's Mr. Jesus and the Brethren.' Sipsey looked back at her and she said, 'Oh. Uh-huh. I thought Miz Mary just had the one boy,' and went on sweeping. We 'bout died laughing. Sipsey knew exactly who that was in the picture. She just liked to play with people.

"Julian and Cleo had built four wooden booths and built the room in the back, so Idgie and Ruth would have a place to live. The cafe part had walls that were knotty Georgia pine, and the floor was just plain old wood.

"Ruth tried to fix the place up. She put a picture of a ship sailing in the moonlight, but Idgie came right along behind her and took it down and stuck up a picture she found of a bunch of dogs sitting around a card table, smoking cigars and playing polker. And she wrote underneath it, *The Dill Pickle Club.* That was the name of this crazy club that she and her friend Grady Kilgore had started. Other than the Christmas decorations they put up the first year that Idgie never did take down, and an old railroad calendar. That was it.

"There was only about four tables and a bunch of uncertain chairs." She laughed. "You never knew for certain if they was gonna hold you up or not. And they never did have a cash register. They just kept the money in a Roy Tan Cigar box and made your change out of that. At the counter they had potato chips and pig skins on a rack, combs and chewin' tobacco, fishing lures and little corncob pipes.

"Idgie opened the place at daybreak and didn't close the place until, as she said, 'the last dog was hung.'

"The big L & N switching yard was only two blocks down the street, and all the railroad people ate there, colored and white alike. She'd serve the colored out the back door. Of course, a lot of people didn't like the idea of her selling food to the coloreds, and she got into some trouble doing it, but she said that nobody was gonna tell her what she could and could not do. Cleo said she stood right up to the Ku Klux Klan all by herself, and wouldn't let them stop her. As good-natured as she was, Idgie turned out to be brave when push came to shove . . ."

# THE WHISTLE STOP CAFE

MARCH 22, 1933

Idgie was drinking coffee and talking about not much of anything with her hobo friend Smokey. Back in the kitchen, Sipsey and Onzell were busy frying up a batch of green tomatoes for the lunch crowd, due in about 11:30, and listening to the "Wings Over Jordan Gospel Hour," over W.A.P.I. radio when Ocie Smith knocked at the kitchen door.

Sipsey came out into the cafe, wiping her hands on her apron. "Miz Idgie, there's a colored boy who's axing to speak wid you."

Idgie went to the screen door and immediately recognized Ocie Smith, a friend of hers from Troutville, who worked at the railroad yard.

"Well hey there, Ocie. How are you?"

"I's fine, Miz Idgie."

"What can I do for you?"

"Miz Idgie, they's a whole bunch of us boys over at the yard, and we's been smelling barbecue every day for 'bout two months and it's 'bout to drive us out of our heads, and we's wonderin' if you wouldn't be willing to sell us some of them barbecue sandwiches. I's got money."

Idgie sighed and shook her head. "Let me tell you something, Ocie. You know that if it was up to me, I'd have you come on in the front door and sit at a table, but you know I cain't do that."

"Yes'm."

"There's a bunch in town that would burn me down in a minute, and I've got to make a living."

"Yes'm, I knows you do."

"But I want you to go back over to the yard and tell your friends, anytime they want anything, just to come on around to the kitchen door."

He grinned. "Yes'm."

"Tell Sipsey what you want, and she'll fix you up."

"Yes'm. Thank you, ma'am."

"Sipsey, give him his barbecue and anything else he wants. Give him some pie, too."

Sipsey mumbled under her breath, "You gonna get yourself in a whole lot of trouble wid them Ku Kluxes, and I'm gonna be gone. You ain't gwine see me aroun' no more, no ma'am."

But she fixed the sandwiches and got grape drinks and pie and put them in a paper sack with a napkin for him.

About three days later, Grady Kilgore, the local sheriff and part-time railroad detective, came in all puffed up. He was a big bear of a man who had been a friend of her brother, Buddy.

He put his hat on the hat rack, like he always did, and told Idgie he had some serious business to discuss. She brought his coffee to the booth and sat down. Grady leaned across the table and started his unpleasant task.

"Now, Idgie, you ought not to be selling those niggers food, you know better than that. And there's some boys in this town that's not too happy about it. Nobody wants to eat in the same place that niggers come, it's not right and you just ought not be doin' it."

Idgie thought it over for a moment and shook her head in agreement.

"You're right, Grady, I know better and I just ought not be doing it."

Grady sat back and seemed pleased.

She continued, "Yeah, Grady, it's funny how people do things they ought not to do. Take yourself, for instance. I guess a lot of people might think that after church on Sunday you ought not to go over to the river and see Eva Bates. I reckon Gladys might think you ought not be doing that."

Grady, who was at the present time a deacon in the Baptist church and had married the former Gladys Moats, who was known to have a temper, got flustered.

"Oh come on, Idgie, that's not funny."

"I think it is. Just like I think a bunch of grown men getting liquored up and putting sheets on their heads is pretty damn funny."

Grady called out to Ruth, who was behind the counter, "Ruth, will you come over here and try to talk some sense into her? She ain't gonna listen to me. I'm just trying to keep her out of trouble, that's all. Now, I'm not saying who, but there's some people in town that don't like her selling to niggers."

Idgie lit her Camel and smiled. "Well, Grady, tell you what. The next time those 'some people' come in here, like Jack Butts and Wilbur Weems and Pete Tidwell, I'll ask 'em if they don't want anybody to know who they are when they go marching around in one of those stupid parades you boys have, why don't they have enough sense to change their shoes?"

"Now, wait a minute, Idgie—"

"Oh hell, Grady, y'all ain't fooling anybody. Why, I'd recognize those size-fourteen clodhoppers you got on anywhere."

Grady looked down at his feet. He was losing this battle in a hurry.

"Aw now, Idgie, I've got to tell them something. Are you gonna stop it or not? Ruth, come over here and help me with this stubborn mule."

Ruth went to the table. "Oh Grady, what harm can it be to sell a few sandwiches out the back door? It's not like they're coming in and sitting down."

"Well, I don't know, Ruth . . . I'll have to talk to the boys."

"They're not hurting anybody, Grady."

He thought for a minute. "Well . . . okay for now, I guess."

He pointed his finger at Idgie. "But you make sure you keep them at the back door, you hear me?"

He got up to leave and put his hat on, and then turned back to Idgie.

"We still playing polker Friday?"

"Yep. Eight o'clock. And bring plenty of money, I feel lucky."

"I'll tell Jack and them . . . 'bye, Ruth."

" 'Bye, Grady."

Idgie shook her head as she watched him go on down the street.

"Ruth, I wish you could have seen that big ox, down at the river for three days, drunk as a dog, crying like a baby, 'cause Joe, that old colored man that raised him, died. I swear, I don't know what people are using for brains anymore. Imagine those boys: They're terrified to sit next to a nigger and have a meal, but they'll eat eggs that came right out of a chicken's ass."

"Oh, Idgie!"

Idgie laughed. "I'm sorry, but it just makes me mad sometimes."

"I know, honey, but you shouldn't get yourself so upset. That's just the way people are and there's not a thing in the world you can do to change them. That's just how it is."

Idgie smiled at her and wondered what would happen if she didn't have Ruth to let off steam with. Ruth smiled back.

They both knew they had to make a decision about what to do. And they did. After that day, the only thing that changed was on the menu that hung on the back door; everything was a nickel or a dime cheaper. They figured fair was fair . . .

THE WEEMS WEEKLY

(WHISTLE STOP, ALABAMA'S WEEKLY BULLETIN)

APRIL 6, 1933

## Change of Menu at Cafe

Patrons of the cafe got quite a surprise when they read the menu last week that featured, among other things: Fillet of Possom . . . Prime Rib of Polecat . . . Goat's Liver and Onions . . . Bull Frog Pudding and Turkey Buzzard Pie Ala Mode.

An unsuspecting couple, who had come all the way from Gate City for dinner, read the menu and were halfway down the block when Idgie opened the door and yelled April Fool's at them.

The couple from Gate City then ordered from the regular menu and got some free coconut cream pie.

By the way, my other half let one of his old hunting dogs in the house the other day, and he brought his bone with him, and wouldn't you know it, I tripped on it and broke my toe. Doctor Hadley wrapped it up for me, but I'm having to wear house shoes to work and can't get out and gather news, like I want to. So if you have any news, just bring it on over to me at the post office.

... Dot Weems ...

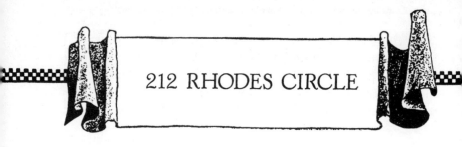

## 212 RHODES CIRCLE

### JANUARY 19, 1986

It was Sunday again. Evelyn and Ed Couch were getting ready to leave for the nursing home. She turned off the coffeepot and wished that she didn't have to go, but Ed was so sensitive where his mother was concerned that she dare not refuse to go and at least say hello to her whiny, demanding mother-in-law. Going out there was like torture to her; she hated the smell of sickness and Lysol and death. It reminded her of her mother, of doctors and hospitals.

Evelyn had been forty when her mother died, and after that, the fear started. Now, when she read the morning paper, she turned immediately to the obituary column, even before she read her horoscope. She was always pleased when the person who had died had been in their seventies or eighties, and she loved it when the dear departed had been over ninety; it made her feel safe somehow. But when she read that they had died in their forties or fifties, it disturbed her all day, especially if, at the end of the obituary, the family had requested that a donation be sent to the cancer society. But what disturbed her the most was when the cause of death was not listed.

A short illness of *what*?

Died suddenly of *what*?

What kind of accident?

She wanted all the details in black and white. No guessing. And she loathed it when the family asked that a donation be made to the humane society. What did that mean? Rabies . . . dog bite . . . cat fever?

But lately, it had been mostly donations to the cancer society. She wondered why she had to live in a body that would get old and break down and feel pain. Why couldn't she have been living inside a desk, a big sturdy desk? Or a stove? Or a washing machine? She would much rather have an ordinary repairman, like an electrician or a plumber, than a doctor work on her. While she had been in the throes of labor pains, Dr. Clyde, her obstetrician, had stood there and lied to her face. "Mrs. Couch, you're going to forget these pains as soon as you see that baby of yours. So push a little harder. You won't even remember this, trust me."

WRONG! She remembered every pain, right down the line, and would not have had the second child if Ed had not insisted on trying for a boy. . . . Another lie exposed: The second one hurt as much as the first, maybe even more, because this time she knew what to expect. She was mad at Ed the whole nine months, and thank God she had Tommy, because this was it, as far as she was concerned.

Her whole life she'd been afraid of doctors. Then, wary, but now she hated, loathed, and despised them. Ever since that doctor had come swaggering into her mother's hospital room with his chart that day . . .

This little tin God in the polyester suit and the three-pound shoes. So smug, so self-important, with the nurses fluttering around him like geisha girls. He had not even been her mother's doctor; he was only making some other doctor's rounds that morning. Evelyn had been standing there, holding her mother's hand. When he came in, he did not bother to introduce himself.

She said, "Hello, Doctor. I'm her daughter, Evelyn Couch,"

Without taking his eyes off the chart, he said in a loud voice, "Your mother has a rapidly progressing cancer of the lung that has metastasized itself in the liver, pancreas, and spleen, with some indication of invasion into the bone marrow."

Up until that very moment, her mother had not even known that she had cancer. Evelyn had not wanted her to know because her mother had been so scared. She would remember the look of sheer terror on her mother's face as long as she lived, and that doctor, who continued on down the hall with his entourage.

Two days later, her mother went into a coma.

She could also never forget that gray, sterile, concrete-walled intensive care waiting room where she had spent all those weeks, frightened and confused, just like the rest of the ones waiting there; knowing that their loved one was lying just down the hall in a cold, sunless room, waiting to die.

Here they were, perfect strangers, in this small space, sharing what was probably the most intimate and painful moment of their lives, not knowing how to act or what to say. There were no rules of etiquette. Nobody had prepared them for this ordeal. Poor people, terrified like herself, trying to be brave, chatting on about their everyday lives, completely in shock, pretending everything was all right.

One family had been so frightened that they couldn't bring themselves to accept the fact that the woman down the hall, dying, was their mother. They would always refer to her as "their patient," and ask Evelyn how "her patient" was doing: to put the truth as far away from them as possible and try to ease the pain.

Every day they waited together, knowing the moment would come, that awful moment when they would be called upon to make "the decision" whether or not to turn the machines off . . .

"It's for the best."

"They'll be much better off."

"It's what they would want."

"The doctor says they're already gone."

"This is only a technicality."

A *technicality?*

All those calm, adult discussions. When all she really wanted to do was scream for her momma, her sweet momma, the one person in the world who loved her better than anyone ever would or ever could.

That Saturday the doctor came to the waiting room and looked in. All eyes were on him and the conversation stopped. He glanced around the room.

"Mrs. Couch, may I see you in my office for a moment, please?"

As she gathered her purse with shaky hands and pounding heart, the others looked at her in sympathy, and one woman touched her arm; but they were secretly relieved that it had not been them.

She felt as if she were in a dream and listened carefully to what he said. He made it seem so simple and so natural. "No point in prolonging it . . ."

He made perfect sense. She got up like a zombie and went home.

She thought she was ready to accept it, to let her go.

But then, nobody was ever really ready to turn off their mother's machine, no matter what they thought; to turn off the light of their childhood and walk away, just as if they were turning out a light and leaving a room.

She could never forgive herself for not having the courage to go back over to the hospital and be with her mother. She still woke up crying over the guilt, and there was not a way in the world she could ever make up for it.

Maybe having gone through this had been the start of Evelyn's fear of anything having to do with doctors or hospitals. She didn't know; all she knew was that the thought of going to a doctor made her literally break out in a cold sweat and start to shake all over. And just the sound of the word *cancer* caused the hair on the back of her arms to stand up. She had stopped touching her breasts at all, anymore, because one time she had felt a lump and almost fainted. Fortunately, it turned out to be Kleenex that had stuck to her bra in the wash. She knew it was an unreasonable fear and that she really should go in for a checkup. They say you should have one every year. She knew she should do it, if not for her sake, for her children's sake. She knew all that, but it didn't make any difference. She'd had a few moments of bravery and made appointments for a checkup, but she always canceled them at the last minute.

The last time she had been to a doctor was six years ago, for a bladder infection. All she wanted was for the doctor to prescribe some antibiotics over the phone, but he made her come in and insisted on giving her a pelvic exam. Lying there with her feet in the stirrups, she wondered if there was anything worse than having some man you didn't know reach inside of you, looking for things, like you were a grab-bag.

The doctor asked how long it had been since her last breast exam. Evelyn lied and said, "Three months ago."

He said, "Well, as long as you're here, I might as well do another one."

She started talking a mile a minute to try and distract him, but in the middle of it, he said, "Uh-oh, I don't like the feel of this."

The days of waiting for the test results had been almost unbearable. She'd walked around in a nightmarish fog, praying and bargaining with a God she was not even sure she believed in. She promised, if he would only let her not have cancer, she would never complain about anything again. She would spend the rest of her life just being happy to be alive, doing good works for the poor, and going to church every day.

But the day after she found out she was fine and would not be dead soon, as she had imagined, she went back to being just like she was. Only now, after that scare, she was convinced that every pain was cancer, and if she went to the doctor to see if it was, she was sure that not only would it be true, but that he would listen with a stethoscope to her heart and rush her to the hospital for open-heart surgery before she could escape. She began living with one foot in the grave. When she looked at her palm, she even imagined that her life line was getting shorter.

She knew she couldn't go through any more days of waiting for test results, and decided that she really did not want to know if anything was wrong, and preferred to drop dead in her tracks, never knowing.

This morning, as they drove out to the nursing home, she realized that her life was becoming unbearable. Every morning she would play games with herself, just to get her through the day. Like telling herself that today something wonderful was going to happen . . . that the next time the phone would ring, it would be good news that would change her life . . . or that she was going to get a surprise in the mail. But it was never anything but junk mail, a wrong number, a neighbor wanting something.

The quiet hysteria and awful despair had started when she finally began to realize that nothing was ever going to change, that nobody would be coming for her to take her away. She began to feel as if she were at the bottom of a well, screaming, no one to hear.

Lately, it had been an endless procession of long, black nights and gray mornings, when her sense of failure swept over her like a five-hundred-pound wave; and she was scared. But it wasn't death that she feared. She had looked down into that black pit of death and had wanted to jump in, once too often. As a matter of fact, the thought began to appeal to her more and more.

She even knew how she would kill herself. It would be with a silver bullet. As round and as smooth as an ice-cold blue martini. She would place the gun in the freezer for a few hours before she did it, so it would feel frosty and cold against her head. She could almost feel the ice-cold bullet shooting through her hot, troubled brain, freezing the pain for good. The sound of the gun blast would be the last sound she would ever hear. And then . . . nothing. Maybe just the silent sound that a bird might hear, flying in the clean, cool air, high above the earth. The sweet, pure air of freedom.

No, it wasn't death she was afraid of. It was this life of hers that was beginning to remind her of that gray intensive care waiting room.

MAY 16, 1934

## Gopher Bite Report

Bertha Vick reported that Friday night, at about 2 A.M. in the morning, she went to the bathroom and was bitten by a gopher rat that had come up through the pipes and into her toilet. She said she ran and woke up Harold, who did not believe her, but he went in and looked, and sure enough, there it was swimming around in the toilet.

My other half said that the floods must have been the reason it came up through the pipes. Bertha said she did not care what caused it, that she would always be sure to look before she sat down anywhere.

Harold is having the gopher rat stuffed.

Was anybody else's light bill high this month? Mine was very high, which I think is strange, but my other half was off for a week, fishing with his brother Alton, and he is the one who always leaves the lights on. Let me know.

By the way, Essie Rue has a job over in Birmingham, playing the Protective Life organ for the "Protective Life Insurance Company Radio Show" on W.A.P.I., so be sure and listen.

. . . Dot Weems . . .

JANUARY 19, 1986

Mrs. Threadgoode guessed that Evelyn hadn't come out to the nursing home that Sunday, and she was taking a walk on the side corridor, where they keep the walkers and the wheelchairs. As she turned the corner, there was Evelyn, sitting all by herself in one of the wheelchairs, eating a Baby Ruth candy bar, with big tears streaming down her face. Mrs. Threadgoode went over to her.

"Honey, what in the world is the matter?"

Evelyn glanced up at Mrs. Threadgoode and said, "I don't know," and continued to cry and eat her candy.

"Come on, honey, get your purse, let's walk a little." Mrs. Threadgoode took her hand and pulled her up from the chair, and began to walk her up the corridor and back.

"Now, tell me, honey, what is it? What's the matter? What are you so sad over?"

Evelyn said, "I don't know," and burst into tears all over again.

"Oh sugar, things cain't be all that bad. Let's start one by one, and you tell me some of the things that are bothering you."

"Well . . . it just seems like since my children went off to college, I just feel useless."

Mrs. Threadgoode said, "That's perfectly understandable, honey, everybody goes through that."

Evelyn continued, "And . . . and I just cain't seem to stop eating. I've tried and tried, every day I wake up and think that today I'm gonna stay on my diet, and every day I go off. I hide candy bars all over the house and in the garage. I don't know what's the matter with me."

Mrs. Threadgoode said, "Well, honey, a candy bar's not gonna hurt you."

Evelyn said, "One's all right; not six or eight. I just wish I had the guts to get really fat and be done with it, or to have the willpower to lose weight and be really thin. I just feel stuck . . . stuck right in the middle. Women's lib came too late for me . . . I was already married with two children when I found out that I didn't have to get married. I thought you had to. What did I know? And now it's too late to change . . . I feel like life has just passed me by." Then she turned to Mrs. Threadgoode, tears still running down her face. "Oh Mrs. Threadgoode, I'm too young to be old and too old to be young. I just don't fit anywhere. I wish I could kill myself, but I don't have the courage."

Mrs. Threadgoode was appalled. "Why, Evelyn Couch, you mustn't even think such a thing. That's like sticking a sword in the side of Jesus! That's just silly talk, honey—you've just got to pull yourself together and open your heart to the Lord. He'll help you. Now, let me ask you this. Are your breasts sore?"

Evelyn looked at her. "Well, sometimes."

"Does your back and legs ache?"

"Yes. How did you know?"

"Simple, honey. You're just going through a bad case of menapause, that's all that's the matter with you. What you need is to take your hormones and to get out every day and walk in the fresh air and walk yourself right through it. That's what I did when I was in it. I used to burst into tears eating a steak, just thinkin' about that poor cow. I like to have drove Cleo crazy, crying all time, thinking nobody loved me. And whenever I'd get to pestering him so bad, he'd say, 'Now, Ninny, it's time for your B-12 shot.' And he'd give me a B-12 shot right in the backside.

"I got out and walked every day, alongside the railroad tracks, up and down, just like we're doing now, and pretty soon I had walked my way right through it and I was back to normal."

"But I thought I was too young to be going through it," Evelyn said. "I just turned forty-eight."

"Oh no, honey, lots of women go through it early. Why, there was this woman over in Georgia who was only thirty-six years old, and one day she got in her car and drove right up the stairs of the county courthouse, rolled down her window, and tossed her mother's head, that she had just chopped off in her kitchen, at a state policeman, and hollered, 'Here, this is what you wanted,' and drove right back down the courthouse stairs. Now, that's what an early menapause will do for you if you're not careful."

"Do you really think that's what's the matter with me? Is that why I've been so irritable?"

"Sure it is. Oh, it's worse than a merry-go-round . . . up and down, down and up . . . and as far as your weight goes, you don't want to be skinny. Why, just take a look at all these old people out here, most of them are just skin and bones. Or just go to the Baptist hospital and visit the cancer ward. Those people would love to have a few extra pounds. Those poor souls are struggling to keep weight on. So, stop worrying about your weight and be thankful you're healthy! What you need to do is to read your daily Word, along with Psalm Ninety, every morning, and it will help you just like it did me."

Evelyn asked Mrs. Threadgoode if she ever got depressed.

Mrs. Threadgoode answered truthfully. "No honey, I cain't say I have been lately, I'm too busy being grateful for His blessings—why, I've had so many blessings I cain't even count them. Now, don't get me wrong, everybody's got their sorrows, and some more than most."

"But you seem so happy, like you never had a care in the world."

Mrs. Threadgoode laughed at the thought. "Oh honey, I've buried my share, and each one hurt as bad as the last one. And there have been times when I've wondered why the good Lord handed me so many sorrowful burdens, to the point where I thought I just couldn't stand it one more day. But He only gives you what you can handle and no more . . . and I'll tell you this: You cain't dwell on sadness, oh, it'll make you sick faster than anything in this world."

Evelyn said, "You're right. I know you're right. Ed said maybe I should go and see a psychiatrist or something."

"Honey, you don't need to go and do that. Anytime you want to talk to someone, you just come and see me. I'd be happy to talk to you. Be more than happy to have the company."

"Thank you, Mrs. Threadgoode, I will." She looked at her watch. "Well, I'd better go, Ed's gonna be mad at me."

She opened her purse and blew her nose with a Kleenex that earlier had been full of chocolate-covered peanuts. "You know, I feel better, I really do!"

"Well, I'm glad, and I'm gonna pray for your nerves, honey. You need to go to church and ask the Lord to lighten your burdens and see you through this bad period, just like He's done for me so many times."

Evelyn said, "Thank you . . . well, I'll see you next week," and headed down the hall.

Mrs. Threadgoode called out after her, "And in the meantime, you get yourself some Stresstabs Number Ten!"

"Number Ten!"

"Yes! Number Ten!"

JUNE 8, 1935

## Drama Club Has Hit

The Whistle Stop Drama Club put on their annual play Friday night, and I want to say, Good work, girls. The name of the play was *Hamlet,* by the English playwright Mr. William Shakespeare, who is no stranger to Whistle Stop because he also wrote last year's play.

Hamlet was played by Earl Adcock, Jr., and his sweetheart was played by Dr. Hadley's niece, Mary Bess, who is visiting us from out of town. In case you missed the play, she ends up killing herself in the end. I am sorry to report that I had trouble hearing her, but then, I think the child is too young to travel, anyway.

The roles of Hamlet's mother and daddy were played by Reverend Scroggins and Vesta Adcock, who is president of the Drama Club and, as we all know, Earl Jr.'s real mother.

Music for the production was provided by our own Essie Rue Limeway, who made the sword fighting scene all the more exciting.

By the way, Vesta says that next year's show will be a pageant that she is writing, entitled, *The History of Whistle Stop,* so if anyone has any, send it to her.

... Dot Weems ...

## ROSE TERRACE NURSING HOME

OLD MONTGOMERY HIGHWAY
BIRMINGHAM, ALABAMA

### JANUARY 26, 1986

Evelyn stopped just long enough to say a polite hello to her mother-in-law and headed on back to the lounge, where her friend was waiting.

"Well, how are you today, honey?"

"Fine, Mrs. Threadgoode. How are you?"

"Well, I'm fine. Did you ever get yourself some of those Stresstabs like I told you?"

"I sure did."

"Did they help?"

"You know, Mrs. Threadgoode, I think they have."

"Well, I'm glad to hear it."

Evelyn started digging in her purse.

"Well, what you got in there today?"

"Three boxes of Raisinettes for us, if I can find them."

"Raisinettes? Well, that ought to be good."

She watched Evelyn as she searched. "Honey, aren't you afraid you'll get ants in your purse, carrying all those sugary, sweet things in there?"

"Well, I never really thought about it," Evelyn said, and found what she was looking for, plus a box of Junior Mints.

"Thank you, honey, I just love candy. I used to love Tootsie Rolls, but, you know, those things can pull your teeth out if you're not careful—a Bit-O-Honey will do the same thing!"

A black nurse named Geneene came in, looking for Mr. Dunaway to give him his tranquilizers, but there were only the two women sitting in the room, as usual.

After she left, Mrs. Threadgoode made the observation of how peculiar it seemed to her that colored people came in so many different shades.

"Now, you take Onzell, Big George's wife . . . she was a pecan-colored woman, with red hair and freckles. She said it nearly broke her momma's heart when she married George, because he was so black. But she couldn't help it, said she loved a big black man and George was sure the biggest and blackest man you ever saw. Then Onzell had the twin boys and Jasper was light like her, and Artis was so black he had blue gums. Onzell said she couldn't believe that something that black had come out of her."

"Blue gums?"

"Oh yes, honey, and you cain't get any blacker than that! And then next, here comes Willie Boy, as light as she was, with green eyes. Of course, his real name was Wonderful Counselor, named right out of the Bible, but we called him Willie Boy."

"Wonderful Counselor? I don't remember that. Are you sure that's from the Bible?"

"Oh yes . . . it's in there. Onzell showed us the very quote: 'And he shall be called wonderful counselor.' Onzell was a very religious person. She always said if anything was starting to get her down, all she had to do was to think of her sweet Jesus, and her spirit would rise, just like those buttermilk biscuits she baked. And then came Naughty Bird, as black as her daddy, with that funny nappy hair, but she didn't have blue gums . . ."

"Don't tell me *that* name came out of the Bible!"

Mrs. Threadgoode laughed. "Oh, Lord no, honey. Sipsey used to say that she looked like a skinny little bird, and when she was little she would always run in the kitchen and steal a couple of those buttermilk biscuits her mother was making and run under the cafe and eat them. So Sipsey started calling her Naughty Bird. Come to think of it, she did look like a little blackbird. . . . But, there they were, two black ones and two light ones, in the same family.

"It's funny, now that I think about it, there aren't any colored people here at Rose Terrace at all, except the ones that clean up and some of the nurses . . . and one of them is just as smart, she's a full-blown registered nurse. Geneene's her name, a cute and sassy little thing, and talks as smart and big as you please. She reminds me a bit of Sipsey, independent-like.

"Old Sipsey lived at home by herself until the day she died. That's where I want to be when I go, in my own house. I don't ever want to go back into the hospital. When you get to be my age, every time you go in, you wonder if you're ever gonna get back out. I don't think hospitals are safe, anyway.

"My neighbor Mrs. Hartman said she had a cousin in the hospital over in Atlanta that told her that a patient there went out of his room to get a breath of fresh air, and they didn't find him until six months later, locked out on the sixth-floor roof. Said by the time they found him, there wasn't anything left but a skeleton in a hospital gown. Mr. Dunaway told me that when he was in the hospital, they stole his false teeth right out of the glass when he was being operated on. Now, what kind of a person would steal an old man's teeth?"

"I don't know," Evelyn said.

"Well, I don't know either."

# TROUTVILLE, ALABAMA

## JUNE 2, 1917

When Sipsey handed Onzell the twin boys she had just given birth to, she couldn't believe her eyes. The oldest son, whom she named Jasper, was the color of a creamy cup of coffee, and the other one, named Artis, was black as coal.

Later, when Big George saw them, he about laughed his head off.

Sipsey was looking inside Artis's mouth. "Lookie here, George, dis baby done got blue gums," and she shook her head in dismay. "God help us."

But Big George, who was not superstitious, was still laughing . . .

Ten years later, he didn't think it was so funny. He had just whipped Artis within an inch of his life for stabbing his brother Jasper with a penknife. Artis had stabbed him five times in the arm before an older boy had pulled him off and thrown him across the yard.

Jasper had gotten up and had run down to the cafe, holding his bleeding arm and calling for his momma. Big George was out in the back, barbecuing, and saw Jasper first and carried him down to the doctor's house.

Dr. Hadley cleaned him up and bandaged him, and when Jasper told the doctor that his brother had been the one who had done it, Big George was humiliated.

That night, both boys were in pain and couldn't sleep. They were lying in bed, looking out the window at the full moon and listening to the night sounds of frogs and crickets.

Artis turned to his brother, who looked almost white in the moonlight. "I knowed I shouldn'ta done it . . . but it felt so good, I jes couldn't stop."

# THE WEEMS WEEKLY

(WHISTLE STOP, ALABAMA'S WEEKLY BULLETIN)

JULY 1, 1935

## Bible Group Meets

The Whistle Stop Baptist Church Ladies' Bible Study Group met Wednesday morning, last week, at the home of Mrs. Vesta Adcock and discussed ways to study the Bible and make it easier to understand. "Noah and the Ark," was the topic, and "Why Did Noah Let Two Snakes on the Boat When He Had a Chance to Get Rid of Them Once and for All?" If anyone has an explanation, they are asked to please call Vesta.

Saturday, Ruth and Idgie had a birthday party for their little boy. All the guests enjoyed pinning the tail on the donkey and eating cake and ice cream, and they all got glass locomotives with little candy pellets inside.

Idgie says they are going to the picture show again Friday night, if anyone wants to go.

Speaking of shows, the other night when I came in

from the post office, my other half was in such a hurry to get over to Birmingham and get to the picture show before the prices changed that he grabbed his coat and ran out the door with me. And then, when we got there, all he did was complain about his back hurting him so bad all through the movie. When we got home, he found out he had been in such a rush, he had forgotten to take the coat hanger out of his coat. I told him, the next time we'd pay the extra money for the ticket, because he ruined the picture for me, jerking around in his seat.

By the way, does anybody out there want to buy a slightly used husband, cheap?

Just kidding, Wilbur.

. . . Dot Weems . . .

# ROSE TERRACE
# NURSING HOME

OLD MONTGOMERY HIGHWAY
BIRMINGHAM, ALABAMA

FEBRUARY 2, 1986

When Evelyn walked in, her friend said, "Oh Evelyn, I wish you had been here ten minutes earlier. You just missed seeing my neighbor Mrs. Hartman. She came out and brought me this." She showed Evelyn a tiny mother-in-law tongue plant in a small ceramic white cocker-spaniel pot.

"And she brought Mrs. Otis the prettiest spider lily. I wanted you to meet her so bad, you would just love her. Her daughter's the one that's been watering my geraniums for me. I told her all about you . . ."

Evelyn said that she was sorry she'd missed her, and gave Mrs. Threadgoode the pink cupcake she had gotten over at Waites Bakery earlier this morning.

Mrs. Threadgoode thanked her kindly and sat there eating and admiring her planter.

"I love a cocker spaniel, don't you? There's nothing in the world happier to see you than a cocker spaniel. Ruth's and Idgie's little boy used to have one, and every time he'd see you, he'd zigzag and bang his tail all over the place like you'd been gone for years, even if you had just been to the corner and back. Now, a kitty will act like they don't care a thing in the world about you. Some people are like that, you know . . . run from you, won't let you love them. Idgie used to be like that."

Evelyn was surprised. "Really?" she said and bit into her cupcake.

"Oh yes, honey. When she was in high school, she gave everybody fits. Most of the time she wouldn't even go to school, and when she did, she would only wear that ratty old pair of overalls that had belonged to Buddy. But half of the time she would be off in the woods with Julian and his friends, hunting and fishing. But you know, everybody liked her. Boys and girls, colored and white alike, everybody wanted to be around Idgie. She had that big Threadgoode smile, and when she wanted to, oh, she could make you laugh! Like I said, she had Buddy's charm . . .

"But there was something about Idgie that was like a wild animal. She wouldn't let anybody get too close to her. When she thought that somebody liked her too much, she'd just take off in the woods. She broke hearts right and left. Sipsey said she was like that because Momma had eaten wild game when she was pregnant with Idgie, and that's what caused her to act like a heathen!

"But when Ruth came to live with us, you never saw a change in anybody so fast in all your life.

"Ruth was from Valdosta, Georgia, and she had come over to be in charge of all the BYO activities at Momma's church that summer. She couldn't have been more than twenty-one or twenty-two years old. She had light auburn hair and brown eyes with long lashes, and was so sweet and soft-spoken that people just fell in love with her on first sight. You just couldn't help yourself, she was just one of those sweet-to-the-bone girls, and the more you knew her, the prettier she got.

"She'd never been away from home before, and at first she was shy with everybody and a little afraid. Of course, she didn't have any brothers or sisters. Her mother and daddy had been real old when they had her. Her daddy had been a preacher, over there in Georgia, and I think she was raised real strict-like.

"But as soon as they saw her, all the boys in town, who never went to church, started going every Sunday. I don't think she had any idea how pretty she was. She was kind to everybody, and ol' Idgie was just fascinated with her . . . Idgie must have been around fifteen or sixteen at the time.

"The first week Ruth was there, Idgie just hung around in the chinaberry tree, staring at her whenever she went in or out of the house. Then, pretty soon she took to showing off; hanging upside down, throwing the football in the yard, and coming home with a huge string of fish over her shoulder at the same time that Ruth would be coming across the street from church.

"Julian said she hadn't been fishing at all and had bought those fish off some colored boys down at the river. He made the mistake of saying that in front of Ruth, and it cost him a good pair of his shoes that Idgie filled with cow manure that night.

"Then, one day, Momma said to Ruth, 'Will you please go and see if you can get my youngest child to sit down like a human being and have her supper?'

"Ruth went out and asked Idgie, who was in the tree reading her *True Detective* magazine at the time, if she wouldn't please come and have supper at the table tonight. Idgie didn't look at her, but said she'd think about it. We'd been seated and had already finished saying grace when Idgie came in the house and went upstairs. We could hear her upstairs in the bathroom running water, and in about five minutes, Idgie, who almost never ate with us, started down the stairs.

"Momma looked at us and whispered, 'Now, children, your sister has a crush, and I don't want one person to laugh at her. Is that understood?'

"We said we wouldn't, and in comes Idgie, with her face all scrubbed and she had her hair all slicked down with some old grease that she'd found up there in the medicine cabinet. We tried not to laugh, but she was a sight to see. All Ruth asked her was if she cared for some more string beans, and she blushed so bad that her ears turned as red as a tomato. . . . Patsy Ruth started it first, just a snicker, then Mildred. And like I say, I always was a tagalong, so I started and then Julian, who couldn't control himself a minute longer, spit his mashed potatoes all over poor Essie Rue, who was sitting across from him.

"It was terrible to have that happen, but it was just one of those things. Momma said, 'You may be excused, children,' and all of us ran in the parlor and fell on the floor and about killed ourselves laughing. Patsy Ruth peed her pants. But the really funny thing is Idgie was struck so dumb at sitting next to Ruth that she never even knew what we'd been laughing at, because when she passed by the parlor, she looked in and said, 'That's a fine way to act when we have company.' And of course, we all just collapsed again . . .

"Pretty soon after that, Idgie started acting like a tame puppy. I think Ruth was lonesome, herself, that summer . . . Idgie could make her laugh, and, oh, Idgie would do anything to entertain her. Momma said it was the only time in Idgie's life that she could get her to do anything she wanted—all she had to do was to ask Ruth to get her to do it. Momma said Idgie would have jumped off a mountain backwards if Ruth had asked her to. And I believe that! It was the first time since Buddy died that she even went to church.

"Everywhere Ruth was, that's where Idgie would be. It was a mutual thing. They just took to each other, and you could hear them, sittin' on the swing on the porch, gigglin' all night. Even Sipsey razzed her. She'd see Idgie by herself and say, 'That ol' love bug done bit Idgie.'

"We had a fine time that summer. Ruth, who tended to be a little reserved, at first learned to cut up and play games. And pretty soon when Essie Rue would play the piano, she joined in the singing just like the rest of us.

"We were all happy, but Momma said to me one afternoon that she dreaded what was going to happen when the summer ended and Ruth went back home."

# WHISTLE STOP, ALABAMA

JULY 18, 1924

Ruth had been in Whistle Stop for about two months, and this Saturday morning, someone knocked at her bedroom window at 6 A.M. Ruth opened her eyes and saw Idgie sitting in the chinaberry tree and motioning for her to open the window.

Ruth got up, half asleep. "What are you up so early for?"

"You promised we could go on a picnic today."

"I know, but does it have to be this early? It's Saturday."

"Please. You promised you would. If you don't come right now, I'll jump off the roof and kill myself. Then what would you do?"

Ruth laughed. "Well, what about Patsy Ruth and Mildred and Essie Rue, aren't they going to come with us?"

"No."

"Don't you think we should ask them?"

"No. Please, I want you to myself. Please. I want to show you something."

"Idgie, I don't want to hurt their feelings."

"Oh, you won't hurt their feelings. They don't want to come anyhow. I asked them already, and they want to stay home in case their old stupid boyfriends come by."

"Are you sure?"

"Sure I'm sure," she lied.

"What about Ninny and Julian?"

"They said they've got things to do today. Come on, Ruth, Sipsey's already made us a lunch, just for the two of us. If you don't come, I'll jump and then you'll have my death on your hands. I'll be dead in my grave and you'll wish you'd have come to just one little picnic."

"Well, all right. Let me get dressed, at least."

"Hurry up! Don't get all dressed up, just come on out—I'll meet you in the car."

"Are we going in the car?"

"Sure. Why not?"

"Okay."

Idgie had failed to mention that she had sneaked into Julian's room at 5 A.M. and had stolen the keys to his Model T out of his pants pockets, and it was extremely important to get going before he woke up.

They drove way out to this place that Idgie had found years ago, by Double Springs Lake, where there was a waterfall that flowed into this crystal clear stream that was filled with beautiful brown and gray stones, as round and smooth as eggs.

Idgie spread the blanket out and got the basket out of the car. She was being very mysterious.

Finally, she said, "Ruth, if I show you something, do you swear that you will never tell another living soul?"

"Show me what? What is it?"

"Do you swear? You won't tell?"

"I swear. What is it?"

"I'll show you."

Idgie reached into the picnic basket and got out an empty glass jar, said, "Let's go," and they walked about a mile back up into the woods.

Idgie pointed to a tree and said, "There it is!"

"There is what?"

"That big oak tree over there."

"Oh."

She took Ruth by the hand and walked her over to the left, about one hundred feet away, behind a tree, and said, "Now, Ruth, you stay right here, and no matter what happens, don't move."

"What are you going to do?"

"Never mind, you just watch me, all right? And be quiet. Don't make any noise, whatever you do."

Idgie, who was barefoot, started walking over to the big oak tree and about halfway there, turned to see if Ruth was watching. When she got about ten feet from the tree, she made sure again that Ruth was still watching. Then she did the most amazing thing. She very slowly tiptoed up to it, humming very softly, and stuck her hand with the jar in it, right in the hole in the middle of the oak.

All of a sudden, Ruth heard a sound like a buzz saw, and the sky went black as hordes of angry bees swarmed out of the hole.

In seconds, Idgie was covered from head to foot with thousands of bees. Idgie just stood there, and in a minute, carefully pulled her hand out of the tree and started walking slowly back toward Ruth, still humming. By the time she had gotten back, almost all the bees had flown away and what had been a completely black figure was now Idgie, standing there, grinning from ear to ear, with a jar of wild honey.

She held it up, offering the jar to Ruth. "Here you are, madame, this is for you."

Ruth, who had been scared out of her wits, slid down the tree onto the ground, and burst into tears. "I thought you were dead! Why did you do that? You could have been killed!"

Idgie said, "Oh, don't cry. I'm sorry. Here, don't you want the honey? I got it just for you . . . please don't cry. It's all right, I do it all the time. I never get stung. Honest. Here, let me help you up, you're getting yourself all dirty."

She handed Ruth the old blue bandanna she had in her overalls pocket. Ruth was still shaky, but she got up and blew her nose and wiped off her dress.

Idgie tried to cheer her up. "Just think, Ruth, I never did it for anybody else before. Now nobody in the whole world knows I can do that but you. I just wanted for us to have a secret together, that's all."

Ruth didn't respond.

"I'm sorry, Ruth, please don't be mad at me."

"Mad?" Ruth put her arms around Idgie and said, "Oh Idgie, I'm not mad at you. It's just that I don't know what I'd do if anything ever happened to you. I really don't."

Idgie's heart started pounding so hard it almost knocked her over.

After they had eaten the chicken and potato salad and all the biscuits and most of the honey, Ruth leaned back against the tree and Idgie put her head in her lap. "You know, Ruth, I'd kill for you. Anybody that would ever hurt you, I'd kill them in a minute and never think twice about it."

"Oh Idgie, that's a terrible thing to say."

"No it isn't. I'd rather kill for love than kill for hate. Wouldn't you?"

"Well, I don't think we should ever kill for any reason."

"All right, then, I'd die for you. How about that? Don't you think somebody could die for love?"

"No."

"The Bible says Jesus Christ did."

"That's different."

"No it isn't. I could die right now, and I wouldn't mind. I'd be the only corpse with a smile on my face."

"Don't be silly."

"I could have been killed today, couldn't I have?"

Ruth took her hand and smiled down at her. "My Idgie's a bee charmer."

"Is that what I am?"

"That's what you are. I've heard there were people who could do it, but I'd never seen one before today."

"Is it bad?"

"Nooo. It's wonderful. Don't you know that?"

"Naw, I thought it was crazy or something."

"No—it's a wonderful thing to be."

Ruth leaned down and whispered in her ear, "You're an old bee charmer, Idgie Threadgoode, that's what you are . . ."

Idgie smiled back at her and looked up into the clear blue sky that reflected in her eyes, and she was as happy as anybody who is in love in the summertime can be.

AUGUST 29, 1924

It's funny, most people can be around someone and then gradually begin to love them and never know exactly when it happened; but Ruth knew the very second it happened to her. When Idgie had grinned at her and tried to hand her that jar of honey, all these feelings that she had been trying to hold back came flooding through her, and it was at that second in time that she knew she loved Idgie with all her heart. That's why she had been crying, that day. She had never felt that way before and she knew she probably would never feel that way again.

And now, a month later, it was because she loved her so much that she had to leave. Idgie was a sixteen-year-old kid with a crush and couldn't possibly understand what she was saying. She had no idea when she was begging Ruth to stay and live with them what she was asking; but Ruth knew, and she realized she had to get away.

She had no idea why she wanted to be with Idgie more than anybody else on this earth, but she did. She had prayed about it, she had cried about it; but there was no answer except to go back home and marry Frank Bennett, the young man she was engaged to marry, and to try to be a good wife and mother. Ruth was sure that no matter what Idgie said, she would get over her crush and get on with her life. Ruth was doing the only thing she could do.

When she told Idgie she was leaving for home the next morning, Idgie had gone completely crazy. She was in her room breaking things and carrying on so loud that you could hear her all over the house.

Ruth was sitting on her bed, wringing her hands, when Momma came in.

"Ruth, please go in there and talk to her. She won't let me or her daddy in the room, and everyone else is afraid to go in there. Please, honey, I'm scared she's gonna hurt herself."

They heard another crash.

Momma looked at Ruth and pleaded, "Oh Ruth, she's just like a wounded animal, down there. Won't you please go and see if you can calm her down a little?"

Ninny came to the door. "Momma, Essie Rue says that now she's broken the lamp," and then she looked at Ruth apologetically. "I think she's upset because you're leaving."

Ruth took the long walk down the hall. Julian, Mildred, Patsy Ruth, and Essie Rue were all hiding behind their bedroom doors, with nothing but their heads poked out, staring bug-eyed at her as she passed them by.

Momma and Ninny stood way down at the end of the hall. Ninny had her fingers in her ears.

Ruth tapped gently on Idgie's door.

From inside the room, Idgie yelled, "LEAVE ME ALONE, GODDAMMIT!" and threw something that crashed against the door.

Momma cleared her throat and said in a sweet voice, "Children, why don't we all go wait in the parlor and give Ruth some privacy."

All six of them went downstairs in a hurry.

Ruth continued to knock at the door. "Idgie, it's me."

"Get away!"

"I want to talk to you."

"No! Leave me alone!"

"Please, don't be like this."

"Get the hell away from the door and I mean it!" And something else crashed against the door.

"Please let me in."

"NO!"

"Please, honey."

"NO!"

"IDGIE, OPEN THIS GODDAMNED DOOR RIGHT THIS MINUTE, AND I MEAN IT! DO YOU HEAR ME?"

There was a moment of silence. The door slowly opened.

Ruth walked in and closed it behind her. She saw that Idgie had broken everything in the room. Some things twice.

"Why are you acting like this? You knew I was going to have to leave sometime."

"Then why cain't you let me go with you?"

"I told you why."

"Then stay here."

"I cain't."

Idgie yelled at the top of her lungs, "WHY NOT?"

"Would you quit that yelling? You're embarrassing me and your mother. The whole house can hear you."

"I don't care."

"Well, I do. Why are you acting like such a baby?"

"BECAUSE I LOVE YOU AND I DON'T WANT YOU TO GO!"

"Idgie, have you lost your mind? What are people gonna think of a big grown girl like you acting like an I-don't-know-what?"

"I DON'T CARE!"

Ruth started picking things up.

"Why are you gonna marry that man?"

"I told you why."

"WHY?"

"Because I want to, that's why."

"You don't love him."

"Yes I do."

"Oh no you don't. You love me . . . you know you do. You know you do!"

"Idgie, I love him and I'm going to marry him."

Then Idgie went really crazy and started crying and screaming in a rage, "YOU'RE A LIAR AND I HATE YOU! I HOPE YOU DIE! I DON'T EVER WANT TO SEE YOU AGAIN AS LONG AS I LIVE! I HATE YOU!"

Ruth took her by the shoulders and shook her as hard as she could. Tears were streaming down Idgie's face as she kept yelling, "I HATE YOU! I HOPE YOU ROT IN HELL!"

Ruth said, "Stop it! Do you hear me!" And before she knew what had happened, she had slapped Idgie across the face with all her might.

Idgie looked at Ruth, speechless and stunned. They just stood there, looking at each other, and in that moment Ruth wished more than anything in the world that she could just grab her and hold her as tight as she could; but if she had, she knew she would never let go.

So Ruth did the hardest thing she had ever done in her life; she just turned around and left, and closed the door behind her.

### FEBRUARY 9, 1986

Evelyn had brought a box of tacos from Taco Bell, three blocks from where she lived, and Mrs. Threadgoode was fascinated.

"This is the first foreign food I've ever had except for Franco-American spaghetti, and I like it." She looked at her taco. "This is about the size of a Chrystal burger, isn't it?"

Evelyn was anxious to find out more about Ruth and tried to change the subject. "Mrs. Threadgoode, did Ruth leave Whistle Stop that summer or did she stay?"

"They were the size of a biscuit, and had little chopped-up onions on them."

"What?"

"The Chrystal burgers."

"Oh, that's right, they did have little onions on them, but what about Ruth?"

"What about her?"

"I know she must have come back, but did she go back home that summer?"

"Oh yes indeed, she did. You know, you could get five of them for a quarter. Can you still do that?"

"I don't think so. When did she leave?"

"When? Oh let's see, it was July or August. No, it was August, that's right. I remember now. Are you sure you want to hear about her? I never give you a chance to say anything. I just talk and talk."

"No, Mrs. Threadgoode, it's fine. Go ahead."

"Are you sure you want to hear about these old-timy things?"

"Yes."

"Well, when the end of August came around, Momma and Poppa pleaded with Ruth to stay and help them get Idgie through her senior year of high school. They told her they'd pay her anything she asked. But Ruth said she couldn't. Said she was engaged to be married to a man over in Valdosta, that fall. But Sipsey told Momma and I that no matter what that girl said, she didn't want to go back over there to Georgia. Sipsey said every morning her pillow would be soaking wet with tears where she'd cried all night.

"I don't know what Ruth told Idgie the night before she left, but we heard Idgie go into her room, and a few minutes later, you never heard such a racket—it sounded like a jackass in a tin stall. She had taken one of Buddy's football trophies and broke out all of her windows, and anything else she could find. It was awful.

"I wouldn't have gone near that room, not for love nor money. . . . The next morning, she didn't even come out on the porch to tell Ruth goodbye. First Buddy, then Ruth. She just couldn't take it. The next day, Idgie was gone. She never did go back to school. She lacked one year of finishing.

"Oh, she would show up at the house every once in a while . . . when Poppa had his heart attack and when Julian and the girls got married.

"Big George was the only one who knew where she was and he would never betray her. Whenever Momma needed her, she'd tell Big George and he'd say to Momma that he'd pass it on if he happened to run into her. But she always got the message and would come home.

"Of course, I have my theories as to where she was . . ."

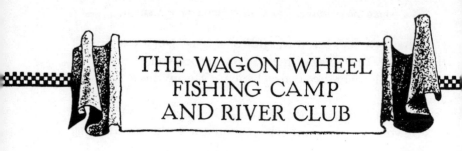

# THE WAGON WHEEL FISHING CAMP AND RIVER CLUB

WARRIOR RIVER, ALABAMA

J. BATES, PROPRIETOR

AUGUST 30, 1924

If you drove eight miles south of Whistle Stop, turned left on the river road, and went two more miles, you'd see a board nailed to a tree, that had been all shot up with buckshot. It read WAGON WHEEL CAMP AND CLUB, with an arrow pointing down a sandy road.

Idgie had been going down there with Buddy since she was eight. As a matter of fact, she was the one who had come down there to tell Eva that Buddy had been killed, because Idgie knew that Buddy loved her.

Buddy first met Eva when he was seventeen and she was nineteen. He knew that she had slept with a lot of men since she was twelve and had enjoyed it every time, but he didn't care. Eva was as easy with her body as she was with everything else, not at all like the Baptist girls at Whistle Stop. The first time she took him to bed, she made him feel like a man.

A big, buxom girl with a shock of rust-colored hair and apple-green eyes, Eva always wore colored beads and bright red lipstick, even when she went fishing. She didn't know the meaning of the word shame, and was indeed a friend to man.

She was not the sort of girl that most men would take home to Momma, but Buddy decided he would.

One Sunday, he brought her over to Whistle Stop for dinner, and afterward he took her over and showed her his poppa's store and made her an ice cream soda. Buddy was not a snob, but Leona was, and she nearly fainted at the table when she saw Eva. Eva, who was not a fool, told Buddy later that she had enjoyed seeing where he lived, but that she liked it better down at the river.

All the boys in town made jokes about her and said dirty things whenever her name was mentioned, but not while Buddy was around. It was true that she had slept with whomever she pleased, whenever she pleased; but no matter what anybody thought or said, when she loved you, she was strictly a one-man woman. Eva belonged to Buddy, and as much as Buddy liked to flirt around, he belonged to Eva. She knew it and he knew it, and that's all that mattered.

Eva had the extreme luxury in life of not caring about what people thought of her. She had gotten that from her daddy, Big Jack Bates, a part-time bootlegger who weighed in at about three hundred pounds and loved to have a good time. He could eat and drink every other man in the county under the table.

Idgie used to beg Buddy to take her to the river with him, and sometimes he would. The Fishing Camp and River Club was just an old wooden shack with blue lights strung all around the porch, with a couple of rusty Royal Crown Cola signs and a faded ad for Goodyear tires stuck up by the door, and, around the back, a bunch of cabins with screened-in porches—but Idgie had fun when he brought her.

There was always a big gang of people out there on the weekends, and they'd play hillbilly music and dance and drink all night. Idgie would sit with Buddy and Big Jack and watch Eva, who could dance the tail off of a monkey.

One time, Buddy pointed to Eva and said, "Look at her, Idgie. Now, that's a woman. That's what makes life worth living, that redheaded woman."

Big Jack, who was crazy about Buddy, laughed and slapped

him on the back and said, "You think you're man enough to handle that girl of mine, boy?"

"I'm trying, Big Jack," Buddy said. "I may die trying, but I'm sure trying."

Pretty soon Eva would come over and get Buddy and they would go over to her cabin, and Idgie would sit with Big Jack and wait and watch him eat. One night he ate seven country-fried steaks and four bowls of mashed potatoes.

Then, after a while, Buddy and Eva would come back and he'd take Idgie home. Going back, he'd always say, "I love that woman, Idgie, don't ever doubt that I do," and Idgie never did.

But that was nine years ago, and on this particular day, Idgie hitched a ride with some fishermen and had been let out by the sign nailed to the tree. Yesterday, Ruth had left to go back to Georgia, and Idgie couldn't stand to be at home anymore.

It was almost dark when she got to the white gate with the two big wagon wheels. She could hear the music as she walked down the road and there were about five or six cars parked outside and the blue lights were already turned on.

A little three-legged dog came running up to her, jumping up and down. Idgie was sure it belonged to Eva; she could never turn anything away. There were always about twenty stray cats hanging around that Eva would feed. She'd open the back door and throw food out in the backyard for them. Buddy used to say if there was a stray anywhere within fifty miles, it wound up at Eva's.

Idgie hadn't been down at the river for a while, but everything looked about the same. The tin signs were a little rustier and a couple of the blue lights were burned out, but she could hear the people inside laughing, just like always.

When she walked in, Eva, who was sitting at a table drinking beer with some men, saw her right off and screamed, "My God! Look what the cat drug in!"

Eva had on a pink angora sweater with beads and earbobs to match, and bright red lipstick. She hollered to her daddy in the kitchen, "Daddy! It's Idgie!

"Come here, you hound dog, you." She jumped up and grabbed Idgie and just about squeezed the life out of her.

"Where have you been all this time? Girl, we thought the dogs had eat you!"

Big Jack came out of the kitchen and was about fifty pounds heavier than the last time Idgie had seen him. "Well, look who's here. If it ain't Little Bit. Glad to see you."

Eva held her out by the shoulders and looked at her. "Well, hell, if you ain't gone and got tall and skinny on me. We've gotta fatten you up, pal, ain't we, Daddy?"

Big Jack, who had been looking at her, said, "Damn, if she don't look more and more like Buddy every day. Look at her, Eva, don't she?"

"Damned if she don't!" Eva said.

Then she pulled Idgie over to the table. "Boys, this is a friend of mine. I want you to meet Idgie Threadgoode, Buddy's little sister. Sit down, honey, and have a drink."

Then Eva said, "Wait a minute, are you even old enough to have a drink?" She thought better. "Oh, what the hell! A little drink never hurt nobody none, did it, boys?"

They agreed.

As soon as Eva got over the excitement of seeing Idgie, she saw that something was wrong. After a while she said, "Hey, boys, why don't you go over to the other table for a spell. I need to talk to my pal, here. . . . Honey, what's the matter? You look like you just lost your best friend."

Idgie denied that there was anything the matter, and started ordering more drinks and trying to be funny. She got all liquored up and wound up dancing all over the place and acting like a fool. Eva just watched her.

Big Jack made her sit down and eat, around nine o'clock, but by ten she was off and running again.

Eva turned to her daddy, who was concerned. "We might as well just let her alone, let her do what she wants to."

About five hours later, Idgie, who had made a roomful of new friends, was holding court and telling funny stories. Then somebody played a sad hillbilly song about lost love, and Idgie stopped right in the middle of her story, put her head down on the table, and cried. Eva, who was pretty well liquored up, herself, by this time and had been thinking about Buddy all night, started to cry right along with her. The group moved on away from them to a happier table.

At about three o'clock that morning, Eva said, "Come on," and, putting Idgie's arm around her shoulder, she took her over to her cabin and put her in the bed.

Eva couldn't stand to see anything hurt that bad. She sat down beside Idgie, who was still crying, and said, "Now, sugar, I don't know who you're crying over, and it doesn't really matter, 'cause you're gonna be all right. Hush up, now . . . you just need somebody to love you, that's all . . . it's gonna be all right . . . Eva's here . . ." and she turned off the lights.

Eva didn't know about a lot of things, but she knew about love.

Idgie would live down at the river, on and off, for the next five years. Eva was always there when needed, just like she had been for Buddy.

NOVEMBER 28, 1935

## A Friend Indeed

Railroad Bill threw 17 hams off the government supply train the other night, and I understand our friends in Troutville had a wonderful Thanksgiving.

The pageant *The History of Whistle Stop* that was presented over at the school was a reminder that the Indians who used to live around here were a brave and fierce-like people, especially as portrayed by Vesta Adcock, who was Chief Syacagga, the Blackfoot Indian Chief whose land this was.

My other half claims that he is one-third Blackfoot Indian, but he ain't so fierce . . . just kidding, Wilbur.

P.S. In case you wondered who was inside that cardboard train that came across the stage, it was none other than Peanut Limeway.

Idgie says that Sipsey, her colored woman, grew a stalk of okra six feet, ten inches tall, in the garden over by the Threadgoode place, and that she has that over at the cafe.

Everyone here is still heartbroken over the death of Will Rogers. We all loved him so much, and wonder who can replace our beloved Doctor of Applesauce. How many of us remember those happy evenings at the cafe, listening to him on the radio? In these hard times, he made us forget our trouble for a little while, and gave us a smile. We are sending his wife and children our sympathy and good wishes, and Sipsey is sending one of her pecan pies, so you all come by the post office and sign the card that's going with it.

. . . Dot Weems . . .

FEBRUARY 16, 1986

Evelyn had brought an assortment of cookies from the Nabisco company, hoping to cheer her mother-in-law up, but Big Mama had said no thank you, that she didn't care for any, so Evelyn took them down the hall to Mrs. Threadgoode, who was delighted. "I could eat ginger snaps and vanilla wafers all day long, couldn't you?"

Evelyn unfortunately had to nod yes. Chewing on her cookie, Mrs. Threadgoode looked down at the floor.

"You know, Evelyn, I hate a linoleum floor. This place is just full of ugly gray linoleum floors. You'd think with so many old people out here, running around in their felt slippers, that are prone to slippin' and slidin' and breaking their hips, they'd put down some rugs. I have a hooked rug in my living room. I made Norris take my black tie-up shoes down to the shoe shop and get me a rubber Cat's Paw sole put on them, and I don't take them off from the time I get up until the time I go to bed at night. I'm not gonna break my hip. Once you do that, it's goodbye, Charlie.

"These old people out here are all in bed by seven-thirty or eight o'clock. I'm not used to that. I never went to bed before the ten-twenty to Atlanta passed by my house. Oh, I get into bed by eight and turn out the lights so I won't disturb Mrs. Otis, but I can never get to sleep good until I hear the ten-twenty blow his whistle. You can hear it all the way across town. Or maybe I just think I hear it, but it doesn't matter. I still don't go off until I do.

"It's a good thing I love trains, because Whistle Stop wasn't never nothing more than a railroad town, and Troutville was just a bunch of shacks, with one church, the Mount Zion Primitive Baptist Church, where Sipsey and them went.

"The railroad tracks run right along the side of my house. If I had me a fishin' pole, I could reach out and touch the trains with it, that's how close I am. So, I've been sitting on my glider swing on the front porch for the past fifty years, watching those trains go by, and I never get tired of looking at them. Just like the raccoon washing the cracker. I like to look at them at night the best. My favorite thing was the dining car. Now, they just have a snack bar where people sit and drink their beer and smoke their cigarettes, but back before they took the good trains off, the seven-forty *Silver Crescent* from New York, on its way to New Orleans, would pass by right at suppertime, and, oh, you should have seen it, with the colored waiters dressed up in their starched white jackets and black leather bow ties, with the finest flatware and silver coffeepots, and a fresh rose with baby's breath on each table. And each table had its own little lamp with a little shade on it.

"Of course, those were the days when the women would dress in their finest, with hats and furs, and the men looked so handsome in their blue suits. The *Silver Crescent* even had little tiny venetian blinds for each window. There you could sit, just like you were in a restaurant, rolling through the night. I used to tell Cleo, eating and getting somewhere at the same time appealed to me.

"Idgie always said, 'Ninny, I think you ride that train just to eat' . . . and she was right, too. I loved that porterhouse steak they used to serve, and you've never had a better plate of ham and eggs than what you could get on the train. Whenever the train stopped in those small towns along the way, people would sell the cooks fresh eggs and ham and fresh trout. Everything was fresh back then.

"I don't cook that much anymore . . . oh, I'll heat up a can of Campbell's tomato soup, now and then. Not that I don't enjoy a good meal. I do. But it's hard to find one nowadays. One time, Mrs. Otis signed us up for this Meals on Wheels program they got down at the church, but they were so terrible that I just stopped them from coming. They may have been on wheels, but they weren't anything like the meals you could get on the trains.

"Of course, living so close to the tracks had its bad side. My dishes got all cracked, even that green set I won when we all went to the picture show over in Birmingham during the Depression. I can tell you what was playin': it was *Hello Everybody*, with Kate Smith." She looked at Evelyn. "Now, you probably don't remember her, but she was known as the Songbird of the South. A big fat girl with a good personality. Don't you think fat people have a good disposition?"

Evelyn smiled weakly, hoping this was true, since she was already on her second bag of Lorna Doones.

"But I wouldn't take anything for the trains. What would I have done all those years? They didn't have television yet. I used to try and guess where people were comin' from and goin' to. Every once in a while, when Cleo could scrape together a few dollars, he'd take me and the baby on the train and we'd go as far as Memphis and back. Jasper, Big George and Onzell's son, was a pullman porter at the time, and he'd treat us like we were the king and queen of Rumania. Jasper went on to become the president of the Brotherhood of the Sleeping-Car Porter's Union. He and his brother Artis moved to Birmingham when they were very young . . . but Artis wound up in jail two or three times. It's funny, you never know how a child will turn out. . . . Take Ruth and Idgie's little boy, for instance. Having to go through life like that could have ruined some people, but not him. You never know what's in a person's heart until they're tested, do you?"

## WHISTLE STOP CAFE

### JUNE 16, 1936

The minute Idgie heard the voices outside by the tracks, she knew that somebody had been hurt. She looked out and saw Biddie Louise Otis running for the cafe.

Sipsey and Onzell had walked out of the kitchen, just as Biddie threw open the door and screamed, "It's your little boy, he's been run over by the train!"

Idgie's heart stopped for a moment.

Sipsey threw her hands up to her mouth, "Oh Lord Jesus!"

Idgie turned to Onzell: "Keep Ruth in the back," and started running over to the tracks. When she got there, the six-year-old boy was lying on his back with his eyes wide open, staring at the group of people who were looking down on him in horror.

When he saw her, he smiled, and she almost smiled back, thinking he was all right, until she saw his arm lying in a pool of blood three feet away.

Big George, who had been out in the back of the cafe, barbecuing, had come running right up behind her and saw the blood at the same time. He picked him up and started running as fast as he could toward Dr. Hadley's house.

Onzell was standing in the door, blocking Ruth from leaving the back room.

"No, now, Miz Ruth, you cain't go. You jus' stay put right here, sugar."

Ruth was scared and confused. "What's the matter? What's happened? Is it the baby?"

Onzell took her over to the couch and sat her down and held her hands with a death grip.

"Hush, sugar . . . you jus' sit here and wait now, honey, it's gonna be all right."

Ruth was terrified. "What is it?"

Sipsey was still in the cafe, wagging her finger up to the ceiling. "Don't you do dis, Lord . . . don't you do dis to Miz Idgie and Miz Ruth . . . don't you do dis thang! You hear me, God? Don't do it!"

Idgie was running right behind Big George and they were both yelling at the house, three blocks away, "Doctor Hadley! Doctor Hadley!"

The doctor's wife, Margaret, heard them first and came out on the front porch. She spotted them just as they came around the corner, and she shouted for her husband, "Get out here quick! It's Idgie and she's got Buddy Jr.!"

Dr. Hadley jumped up from the table and met them on the sidewalk, with his napkin still in his hand. When he saw the blood spurting from the boy's arm, he threw the napkin down and said, "Get in the car. We've got to get him to Birmingham. He's gonna need transfusions."

As he was running to the old Dodge, he told his wife to call the hospital and tell them they were coming. She ran inside to call, and Big George, who was by this time completely covered with blood, got in the backseat and held the boy in his arms. Idgie sat in the front seat and talked to him all the way there, telling him stories to keep him calm, although her own legs were shaking.

When they arrived at the Emergency entrance, the nurse and the attendant were waiting for them at the door.

As they started in, the nurse said to Idgie, "I'm sorry, but you'll have to have your man wait outside, this is a white hospital."

The boy, who hadn't said a word, kept watching Big George as they took him down the hall, and until they turned the corridor, out of sight . . .

Still covered with blood, Big George sat outside on the brick wall and put his head in his hands and waited.

Two pimply-faced boys walked by, and one snarled over at Big George.

"Look, there's another nigger that's got hisself all cut up in a knife fight." The other called out, "Hey! You better get yourself over to the nigger hospital, boy."

His friend with the missing front tooth and the crossed eye spit, hitched up his pants, and swaggered on down the street.

JUNE 24, 1936

## Tragedy Strikes in Front of Cafe

I am sorry to report that Idgie's and Ruth's little boy lost his arm last week while playing on the tracks in front of the cafe. He was running alongside of the train when he slipped and fell on the tracks. The train was traveling about forty miles an hour, Conductor Barney Cross said.

He is still over at the hospital in Birmingham, and although he lost a lot of blood, he is fine and will be home soon.

That makes a foot, an arm, and an index finger we have lost right here in Whistle Stop this year. And also, the colored man that was killed, which just says one thing to us, and that is that we need to be more careful in the future. We are tired of our loved ones losing limbs and other things.

And I, for one, am tired of writing about it.

. . . Dot Weems . . .

ROSE TERRACE
NURSING HOME

OLD MONTGOMERY HIGHWAY
BIRMINGHAM, ALABAMA

FEBRUARY 23, 1986

Mrs. Threadgoode was enjoying the Reese's Peanut Butter Cup that Evelyn had brought and reflecting back to what seemed to be her favorite period, the time when all the trains were running past her house.

But something she had said the week before interested Evelyn, and her curiosity got the best of her.

"Mrs. Threadgoode, did you say that Idgie and Ruth had a little boy?"

"Oh yes, Stump, and you never saw a more manly little fella. Even when he lost his arm."

"Good Lord, what happened?"

"He fell off one of the trains and had his arm cut off, right above the elbow. His real name was Buddy Threadgoode, Jr., but they called him Stump 'cause all he had left was a little stump of an arm. Cleo and I went to see him in the hospital, and he was just as brave, didn't cry, didn't feel sorry for himself. But then Idgie raised him that way, to be tough and take hard knocks.

"She went over to see her friend who owned the tombstone

place and had him make up a baby tombstone that had carved on it:

HERE LIES BUDDY JR'S ARM
1929–1936
SO LONG OLD PAL

"She put it out in the field behind the cafe, and when he got home, she took him out there and they made a big to-do about having this funeral for his arm. Everybody came. Onzell and Big George's children, Artis and Jasper, little Willie Boy and Naughty Bird, and all the neighborhood kids. Idgie had some Eagle Scout come out there and play 'Taps' on the bugle.

"Idgie was the first one to start calling him Stump, and Ruth near had a fit, said it was a mean thing to do. But Idgie said it was the best thing, so nobody would call him anything about it behind his back. She thought he might as well face up to the fact that he had an arm missing and not be sensitive about it. And she turned out to be right, because you never saw anybody that could do more with one arm . . . why, he could shoot marbles, hunt and fish, anything he wanted to. He was the best shot in Whistle Stop.

"When he was little and there was somebody new in the cafe, Idgie would bring him in and have him tell this long, tall tale about going fishing for catfish down on the Warrior River, and he'd get them all caught up in the story and then Idgie would say, 'How big was the catfish, Stump?'

"And he'd put out his arm, like the grown fisherman used to do to show how long the fish was, and he'd say, 'Oh, about that big.' And Idgie and Stump would laugh over the expressions on the people's faces, trying to figure out how long that fish was.

"Of course, now, I'm not saying he was a saint, he had his little temper fits, just like the other little boys. But in his whole life, the only time I ever knew him to complain or be upset is that one Christmas afternoon when we were all sitting around the cafe, drinking coffee and having fruitcake, when all of a sudden he started carrying on like a crazy person, just a-mashing up all of his toys. Ruth and Idgie went in the back room where he was, and in as little time as it takes you to say 'butter the biscuits,' Idgie had him in his coat and out the door. Ruth was upset and worried and ran after them and asked where they were going, but Idgie said, never mind that, they would be back in a little while.

"And, sure enough, they were back in about an hour, and Stump was laughing and in a good mood.

"Years later, when he was down at my house cutting my yard, I had him come up on the porch and handed him a glass of iced tea. I said, 'Stump, do you remember that Christmas when you got so mad and stomped your Erector set that Cleo and I gave you?'

"Well, he just laughed and said, 'Oh Aunt Ninny'—that's what he called me—he said, 'Aunt Ninny, I sure do.'

"I said, 'Where did Idgie take you that afternoon?'

"He said, 'Aw, I cain't tell you, Aunt Ninny, I promised I wouldn't.'

"So I still don't know where he went, but Idgie must have said something to him, because he never worried about his arm being missing again. He was the nineteen forty-six Champion Wild Turkey Hunter . . . and do you know how hard it is to shoot a wild turkey?"

Evelyn said, no, she didn't.

"Well honey, let me tell you, you have to shoot those turkeys right between the eyes, and their heads are no bigger than my fist! Now, that's a good shot!

"He even went on to play all kinds of sports . . . never let that arm stop him in any way. . . . And sweet. You never met a sweeter boy.

"Course, Ruth was a good mother, and he adored her. We all did. But Stump and Idgie were special. They'd take off hunting or fishing and leave us all behind. They enjoyed each other's company more than anyone else, I guess.

"One time, I remember, Stump put a piece of pecan pie in his pocket and ruined his good pants, and Ruth was just afussin' at him, but Idgie thought it was the funniest thing in the world.

"Now, Idgie could be rough with him. She was the one that threw him in the river when he was five, and taught him how to swim. But I tell you one thing, he never sassed his mother like some boys will do. At least not when Idgie was around. She just wouldn't allow it. Not at all. No sir. He minded his momma, not like Onzell's boy Artis. They couldn't do a thing with him, could they?"

Evelyn said, "I guess not," and noticed Mrs. Threadgoode had her dress on inside out.

### CHRISTMAS DAY, 1937

Almost everyone in town had gotten a cap pistol for Christmas, and most of them had gathered in Dr. Hadley's backyard that afternoon for a shoot-out. The whole yard smelled of sulphur from the caps that had been cracking in the cold air all afternoon. They had all been killed a hundred times over. Pow! Pow! Pow! You're dead!

Pow! Pow!

"Augh! You got me! . . . Auggh!"

Eight-year-old Dwane Kilgore grabbed his chest, fell to the ground, and took three minutes to die. When he had jerked his last jerk, he jumped up and unrolled another red strip of caps and reloaded in a frenzy.

Stump Threadgoode was a late arrival to the shoot-out, and had just finished his Christmas dinner up at the cafe with the family and Smokey Lonesome. He hit the yard running, and he had timed it just right, because everyone was loaded and ready to go. He ran behind a tree and took aim at Vernon Hadley. POW! POW!

CRACK CRACK CRACK . . . Vernon, who was behind a bush, jumped up and yelled, "You missed, you dirty varmit!"

Stump, who had shot all his caps, was busy trying to reload when Bobby Lee Scroggins, an older boy, ran up to him and let him have it.

CRACK CRACK CRACK . . . POW POW POW . . . "Got ya!"

And before he knew it, Stump was dead . . .

But Stump was game. He reloaded time and time again, only to be killed in the process, over and over again.

Peggy Hadley, Vernon's little sister, who was in the same class as Stump, came out, all bundled up in her new maroon coat, with her new doll, and sat on the back steps to watch. All of a sudden it wasn't so much fun to be getting killed over and over, and Stump started desperately trying to get one of them, but there were too many of them and he couldn't reload fast enough to protect himself.

CRACK CRACK CRACK . . . killed again! But he kept trying. He made a desperate run and got behind a big oak tree in the middle of the yard, where he could dart out and shoot and jump back behind the tree. He had already killed Dwane with a lucky shot and was working on Vernon when Bobby Lee jumped up behind him from behind a stack of bricks—Stump turned, but it was too late.

Bobby Lee had pulled two guns on him and let him have it with both barrels.

CRACK CRACK CRACK CRACK CRACK CRACK CRACK CRACK CRACK CRACK

Bobby Lee shouted, "You're dead! You're double dead! Die!"

Stump had no choice but to die in front of Peggy.

It was a quick, quiet death. He got right up and said, "I've gotta go home and get some more caps. I'll be right back."

He had plenty of caps, but he wanted to die for real. Peggy had seen him get killed over and over.

After he left, Peggy stood up and yelled at her brother, "Ya'll aren't playing fair. Poor Stump has only one arm and that's not fair. I'm gonna tell Mother on you, Vernon!"

Stump ran in the back room and threw his cap pistol across the floor and then kicked his electric train set against the wall, mad and crying with frustration. When Ruth and Idgie came back, there he was stomping his Erector set that he'd already smashed flat.

When he saw them, he started crying and screaming at the same time, "I cain't do anything with this thing," and he began hitting at his missing arm.

Ruth grabbed him. "What's the matter, honey? What happened?"

"Everybody's got double holsters but me! I cain't beat 'em, they've killed me all afternoon!"

"Who?"

"Dwane and Vernon and Bobby Lee Scroggins."

Ruth said, stricken, "Oh honey . . ."

She knew this day would come, but now that it had, she didn't know what to say. What was there to say? How do you tell a seven-year-old boy that it would be all right? She looked to Idgie for help.

Idgie stared at Stump for a minute and then got her coat, picked him up off the bed, put his coat on, and took him outside to the car.

"Come on, mister, you're going with me."

"Where are we going?"

"Never mind."

He sat there in silence while she drove him down to the river road. When they came to a sign that said WAGON WHEEL CAMP AND CLUB, she made a turn. Pretty soon they came to a gate made out of two big white wagon wheels. Idgie got out and opened the gates and then drove on through, down to a cabin by the river. When she got there, she blew the horn, and after a minute, a redheaded woman opened the door.

Idgie told Stump to stay in the car and she got out and went up to talk with the woman. The dog inside the house was beside itself, jumping up and down, yapping, it was so excited to see her.

Idgie talked for a few minutes, and then the lady went away for a second and came back and handed Idgie a rubber ball. When she opened the screen door, the little dog flew out and was about to wiggle itself to death, so glad to see her.

Idgie walked down off the porch, and said, "Come on, Lady!

Come on, girl!" and threw the ball up in the air. The little
white rat terrier jumped at least four feet and caught the ball
in midair, and then ran back to Idgie and gave it back to her.
Then Idgie threw the ball up against the house and Lady
jumped straight up and caught it again.

That's when Stump noticed that the little dog only had three
legs.

That dog jumped and ran after that ball for about ten minutes and never once lost its balance. After a while, Idgie took
the little dog back up to the house and went inside to say
goodbye to the redheaded woman.

Then she came back out to the car and drove down a little
road, where she parked by the river.

"Stump, I want to ask you something, son."

"Yes ma'am."

"Did that dog look like it was having a good time?"

"Yes ma'am."

"Did it look like she was happy to be alive?"

"Yes."

"Did it look to you like she felt sorry for herself?"

"No ma'am."

"Now, you're my son and I love you no matter what. You
know that, don't you?"

"Yes ma'am."

"But you know, Stump, I'd hate like the devil to think that
you didn't have any more sense than that poor, little dumb dog
we saw today."

He looked down at the car floor. "Yes ma'am."

"So I don't want to hear any more about what you can and
cain't do, okay?"

"Okay."

Idgie opened up the glove compartment and pulled out a
bottle of Green River Whiskey. "And besides, your Uncle
Julian and I are going to take you out next week and teach you
how to shoot a real gun."

"Really?"

"Really!" She removed the bottle cap and took a swallow.
"We're gonna make you the best goddamned shot in the state,

and just let one of them try and beat you at anything . . . here, have a drink."

Stump's eyes got big as he reached for the bottle. "Really?"

"Yes, really. But don't tell your mother. We'll make those boys wish they hadn't got up in the morning."

Stump took a sip and tried to act as if it hadn't tasted like gasoline on fire and asked, "Who was that woman?"

"A friend of mine."

"You've been here before, haven't you?"

"Yeah, a couple of times. But don't tell your mother."

"Okay."

# BIRMINGHAM, ALABAMA

(SLAGTOWN)

DECEMBER 30, 1934

Onzell had told her son Artis over and over again that she did not want him going over to Birmingham, ever; but tonight, he went anyway.

He jumped off the back of the freight that arrived at the L & N terminal station at about eight o'clock. When he went inside, his mouth dropped open.

The station seemed as large, to him, as Whistle Stop and Troutville put together, with its rows and rows of thick, rich mahogany benches and the multicolored tile that covered the floor and the walls of the huge building.

SHOE SHINE . . . SANDWICH COUNTER . . . CIGAR STAND . . . BEAUTY SHOP . . . MAGAZINES . . . BARBERSHOP . . . DONUTS AND CANDY . . . CIGARETTES . . . WHISKEY BAR . . . COFFEE . . . BOOKSTORE . . . HAVE YOUR SUITS PRESSED . . . GIFT SHOP . . . COLD DRINKS . . . ICE CREAM . . .

Here was a *city*, teeming with redcaps, porters, and train passengers, all under the seventy-five-foot glass ceiling. It was all too much for the seventeen-year-old black boy in overalls who had never been out of Whistle Stop. He thought he had seen the whole world inside that one building, and he staggered out the front door, dazed.

And then he saw it. There it was, the largest electric light sign in the world—twenty stories high, with ten thousand golden light bulbs glowing against the black sky: WELCOME TO BIRMINGHAM . . . THE MAGIC CITY . . .

And it was magic; billed as the "fastest growing city in the South," and even now, Pittsburgh was being called the Birmingham of the North . . . Birmingham, with its towering skyscrapers and steel mills that lit up the sky with red and purple hues, and its busy streets buzzing with hundreds of automobiles and the streetcars on wires, whisking back and forth, day and night.

Artis walked down the street in a trance, past the St. Clair (Birmingham's Up-to-the-Minute Hotel), on by the L & N Cafe, and the Terminal Hotel. He peered in between the venetian blinds on the window of the coffee shop and saw all the white men sitting there, enjoying their blue-plate specials, and knew that this was not the place for him. He made his way past the Red Top Bar and Grill, and over the Rainbow Viaduct, on by the Melba Cafe, and, as if by some primeval instinct, he found 4th Avenue North, where all of a sudden the complexion began to change.

He had found it: Here it was, those twelve square blocks, better known as Slagtown . . . Birmingham's own Harlem of the South, the place he had dreamed about.

Couples began moving past him, all dressed up, talking and laughing on their way to somewhere; and he was being pulled along with them, like a whitecap floating on the crest of a wave. Music throbbed out of every door and window and spilled down flights of stairs into the streets. The voice of Bessie Smith wailed from an upstairs window, "Oh, careless love . . . Oh, careless love . . ."

Hot jazz and blues were melting together as he passed by the Frolic Theater, which boasted to be the finest colored theater in the South, featuring only musicals and high comedy.

And the people kept on moving. . . . Down the block, Ethel Waters sang and asked the musical question, "What did I do to be so black and blue?" While next door, Ma Rainey shouted out "Hey, Jailor, tell me what have I done?" . . . And people in the Silver Moon Blue Note Club were doing the shimmy-sham-shimmy to Art Tatum's "Red Hot Pepper Stomp."

He was here—Slagtown on a Saturday night—and just one block away, white Birmingham was completely unaware that this exotic sepia spot even existed. Slagtown, where the Highland Avenue maid of that afternoon could be tonight's Queen of the Avenue, and redcaps and shoeshine boys were the leaders of Slagtown's after-dark fashion show. They were all here, with black shiny patent-leather slick hair and gold teeth that glistened and sparkled as they passed under the colored lights that flashed and traveled around the signs. Blacks, tans, cinnamons, octoroons, reds and dukes mixtures, moving Artis down the street, all dressed in suits of lime green and purple, sporting two-toned yellow-and-tan brogans and thin red-and-white silk ties, while the ladies, with gleaming deep maroon and tangerine lips and swinging hips, were promenading in spectator pumps and red fox furs . . .

Lights blinked away at him. THE MAGIC CITY BILLIARDS PARLOR FOR GENTLEMEN; THE ST. JAMES GRILL; BLUE HEAVEN BAR-B-CUE; ALMA MAE JONES SCHOOL OF BEAUTY CULTURE . . . on past the Champion Theater, Where Happiness Costs So Little, ¢10 . . . Two doors down, he saw dancing couples through the window of the Black and Tan Ballroom, where amber spotlights lazily searched the room, turning the couples a pale purple as they floated by. He turned the corner and was carried along, faster and faster, down the teeming street, past The Clouds of Joy Used Clothing Exchange, the Little Delilah Cafe, Pandora Billiards, and the Stairway to the Stars Cocktail Lounge, advertised as *The Home of the Mixed Drink*, and the Pastime Theater, this week featuring *Edna Mae Harris in an All-Colored Revue*. Next door, at the Grand Theater, Mary Marble and Little Chips were appearing. He went on by the Little Savoy Cafe, past more dancing couples, silhouetted through the windows of the Hotel Dixie Carlton Ballroom, with its large revolving mirrored ball shooting silver sparkles of light all over the room. . . . Foxtrotting couples inside were unaware of the young black boy in overalls, wide-eyed with wonder, being swept by the Busy Bee Bar-b-cue Shop, for Ladies and Gents that offered *Electrically Cooked Waffles and Hot Cakes at All Hours and Your Favorite Sandwiches Toasted, Served with the Best Coffee in the City, Hot Dogs for ¢5, Homemade Chili, Hamburger, Pork, Ham, Swiss Cheese Sandwiches, All for a Dime* ... past the Viola Crumbely Over the Rainbow Insurance Co., which specialized in burial policies, with a sign in the window that urged her potential customers to *Get a Lot While You're Young*, on by the De Luxe Hotel and Rooms for Gentlemen.

Near the Casino Club at the Masonic Temple, a large-breasted beauty behind him, resplendent in a corn-colored satin dress, wearing a lemon-yellow feather boa, squealed and swung her purse at a fleet-footed gentleman and missed. The gentleman laughed, and Artis laughed, too, as he continued on down the street with the crowd; he knew he was home at last.

# SLAGTOWN NEWS
# FLOTSAM & JETSAM

(BIRMINGHAM'S SEPIA NEWSPAPER)
BY MR. MILTON JAMES

MAY 6, 1937

Mr. Artis O. Peavey was admitted to the University Hospital late Saturday evening, suffering from multiple self-inflicted accidental injuries he received while attempting to open a particularly expensive bottle of wine, his female companion said; the year and the label unknown.

Is it just my imagination, or did I see Miss Ida Doizer on the midnight streetcar the other night headed out to Ensley to Tuxedo Junction for a few dances with Bennie Upshaw, only to see her ride home with Mr. G. T. Williams?

We must have two or three Birmingham boys in every one of the popular bands around the country, thanks to the expert musicianship of our own beloved Professor Fess Watley. We are well received on the music scene. Don't forget our old friend Cab Calloway is due to grace our magic city soon.

Fine fare over at the Frolic Theater this week . . .

Monday-Thursday: A 5-Star Program
Erskine Hawkins, "The Twentieth Century Gabriel,"
in
"DEVILLED HAMS"
Also—ALL COLORED SPORTS REEL

## ROSE TERRACE
## NURSING HOME

OLD MONTGOMERY HIGHWAY
BIRMINGHAM, ALABAMA

### MARCH 2, 1986

Eating a cup of vanilla ice cream with a wooden spoon, Mrs. Threadgoode was reminiscing to Evelyn about the Depression . . .

"A lot of people died, one way or the other. It hit hard. Especially the colored, who never did have much to begin with. Sipsey said that half the people over there in Troutville would have froze or starved to death if it hadn't been for Railroad Bill."

This was a new name to Evelyn. "Who was Railroad Bill?"

Mrs. Threadgoode seemed surprised, "Didn't I ever tell you about Railroad Bill?"

"No, I don't believe you have."

"Well, he was a famous bandit. They say he was a colored man that would sneak on the trains and throw food and coal off the government supply trains at night, and the colored people that lived along the tracks would come and get the stuff at daybreak and run home with it as fast as they could.

"I don't believe they ever did catch him . . . never did find out who he was . . . Grady Kilgore, who was a railroad detective friend of Idgie's, used to come in the cafe every day, and Idgie would laugh and say, 'I hear ol' Railroad Bill is still on the loose. What's the matter with you boys?' He used to get so mad, they must have put twenty extra men on the trains, at one time or another, and they offered a lifetime pass on the L & N Railroad to whoever had information about him to come forth, but nobody did. Idgie just razzed him to death over that one! But they were always good friends. He was in that Dill Pickle Club . . ."

"That what?"

Mrs. Threadgoode laughed. "The Dill Pickle Club, this crazy club Idgie and Grady and Jack Butts started."

"What kind of a club was it?"

"Well, they claimed it was a breakfast and social club, but it was really just a bunch of Idgie's ragtag friends that would all get together, she and some of the railroad men and Eva Bates and Smokey Lonesome. About all they did was drink whiskey and make up lies. They'd look you right in the eye and tell you a lie when the truth would have served them better.

"That was their fun, making up tales. Crazy tales. One time, Ruth had just come in from church and Idgie was sitting around with them and she said, 'Ruth, I'm sorry to have to tell this, but while you were gone, Stump swallowed a 22-caliber bullet.'

"When Ruth got all excited, Idgie said, 'Don't worry, he's just fine. I just took him over to Doc Hadley's and he gave him a half a bottle of castor oil, and said it was all right to bring him home but just be careful not to point him at anyone.' "

Evelyn laughed. Mrs. Threadgoode said, "Well, you can imagine that Ruth didn't care much for the idea of that club. Idgie was the president and she was always calling secret meetings. Cleo said those secret meetings were nothing more than hot poker games. But he said the club did some good things, but they would never tell you about it if they did, they'd deny it every time.

"They didn't care anything about the Baptist preacher, Reverend Scroggins, 'cause he was a teetotaler, and every time some poor fool would ask where he could buy whiskey or live bait, they'd sent him over to the preacher's house. Like to have driven him crazy.

"Sipsey was the only colored member, because she could tell lies right along with the rest of them. She told them about this woman she was helping who has having trouble giving birth, and how she gave her a tablespoon of snuff and she said that woman sneezed so hard that she shot that baby clear across the end of the bed and into the other room . . ."

Evelyn said, "Oh no!"

"Oh yes! Then she told them this tale about her friend Lizzy, over in Troutville, that was expecting a baby and started craving starch. Said that Lizzy took to eating it right out of the box by the handfuls, and sure enough, when that baby came, it was white as snow and stiff as a board . . ."

"Oh for heaven's sake."

"But you know, Evelyn, that could have been true. I know for a fact some of those colored women ate clay right out of the ground."

"I can't believe that."

"Well, honey, that's what I heard. Or maybe it was sticks of chalk. I forget which one. But it was either clay or chalk."

Evelyn shook her head, smiling at her friend. "Oh Mrs. Threadgoode, you are funny."

Mrs. Threadgoode thought about it and was pleased with herself and said, "Well, yes. I guess I am at that."

DECEMBER 1, 1938

## Snow Comes to Whistle Stop

What a treat for us, real snow. Whistle Stop could have passed for the North Pole last week. Is there anything prettier than seeing the red holly bushes covered with snow? I think not, but thank heavens it only snows once every ten years. My other half, who thinks he can drive in any sort of weather, was determined to take his old hunting dogs for a ride and skidded into a ditch on 1st Street. So the little lady you see bumming a ride for the next month, until we can get the car fixed, will be me.

Yes, my other half is the same one who went for a ride when we had that hailstorm with hail as big as baseballs and it took us three weeks to get the windshield replaced. He's the same one that got struck by lightning, fishing down on the river in a rowboat. So the next time you see bad weather coming and you see Wilbur, send him home and I'm gonna put him in the closet and lock him up. I'm afraid a tornado is liable to pick him up and take him on off somewhere . . . then who would I have to fight with?

I hear through the grapevine that Railroad Bill has hit five trains in one week. I ran into Gladys Kilgore over at the beauty shop, and she says that her husband, Grady, who works for the railroad, is hopping mad.

By the way, if Railroad Bill reads this, how about throwing a brand-new car off one of those trains before Grady catches you . . . I need one!

. . . Dot Weems . . .

# WHISTLE STOP CAFE

## DECEMBER 1, 1938

The sun had just come up behind the cafe, and Idgie shook him awake, shouting, "Get up, Stump! Get up! Look!" She pulled him to the window to look out.

The entire field was covered with white.

His mouth flew open. "What is it?"

Idgie laughed. "It's snow."

"It is?"

"Yes."

He was in the third grade and this was the first time in his life he had ever seen real snow.

Ruth came up behind them in her nightgown and looked out, just as surprised.

All three of them got dressed as fast as they could and were out in the yard five minutes later. It was only two inches deep, but they rolled in it and made snowballs. You could hear the doors opening all over town and children shouting with excitement. By seven o'clock that morning, Stump and Idgie had already built a short, fat snowman and Ruth made them snow ice cream with milk and sugar.

Idgie decided to walk Stump to school, and as they looked

up the railroad tracks, there was nothing but white for as far as they could see. Stump was still so excited, he was jumping around and fell twice. Idgie decided to tell him a story to calm him down.

"Did I ever tell you the time me and Smokey played poker with Pig Iron Sam?"

"No. Who's Pig Iron Sam?"

"You mean to tell me you never heard of Pig Iron, the meanest poker player in Alabama?"

"No ma'am."

"Well, me and Smokey was sitting in this all-night poker game over in Gate City, and I started winning. I guess I won every pot for an hour or so, and Pig Iron was getting madder and madder, but what could I do? I couldn't quit, not while I was winning like that . . . that's not etiquette. And the more I won, the madder he got, and pretty soon he was in a rage and pulled this gun out and put it on the table and said that he was going to kill the next man that dealt him a bad hand."

Stump was totally engrossed by this time. "Whose turn was it to deal?"

"Well, that's the irony of it. He forgot it was his turn, and lo and behold, he dealt his own self a pair of two's. So he just picked up the gun and shot himself to death, right there at the table . . . a man of his word to the end."

"Wow. Did you see it?"

"Sure I did. It was a pair of two's, big as life."

Stump was thinking it over when he spied something sticking out of the snow beside the track. He ran over and picked it up. "Look, Aunt Idgie, it's a can of Deer Brand sauerkraut, and it hasn't even been opened!"

Then it hit him like a ton of bricks. He held the can up with awe and whispered, "Aunt Idgie, I'll bet this is one of the cans that Railroad Bill threw off the train. Do you think it is?"

Idgie examined the can. "It could be, son, it very well could be. Put it back where you found it, so the folks that are supposed to find it will."

Stump placed the can back down on the exact place he'd found it, like it was a sacred thing.

"Wow."

His first snow and now a tin can that could have been from Railroad Bill. It was all too much.

They continued walking, and after a few minutes Stump said, "I guess that Railroad Bill is about the bravest man that ever lived, huh, Aunt Idgie?"

"He's brave all right."

"Don't you think he's the bravest man we know of in our whole lives?"

Idgie thought. "Well now, I wouldn't say the bravest person I know. I don't think I'd say that. One of the bravest, but not the bravest."

Stump was taken aback. "Who could be braver than Railroad Bill?"

"Big George."

"Our Big George?"

"Yeah."

"What he ever do?"

"Well, for one thing, I wouldn't be here if it hadn't been for him."

"You mean, here today?"

"No, I mean here at all. I would have been eaten up by hogs."

"Are you serious?"

"Yes sir. When I was about two or three, I guess, me and Buddy and Julian were all hanging around the hog pens, and I climbed up on the fence and fell head first right into the hog trough."

"You did?"

"I did. Well, those hogs all started running over towards me—you know a hog will eat anything . . . they've been known to eat lots of babies."

"Really?"

"Sure. Anyhow, I jumped out of the trough and started running, but I fell down, and they almost had me before I could get out, when Big George saw me and jumped in that pen, right in the middle of those hogs, and started knocking them out of the way. Now, I'm talking about three-hundred-pound hogs. He would grab 'em and sling 'em across the pen, one by one, like they were sacks of potatoes. He was able to keep them off me long enough for Buddy to crawl under the fence and pull me out."

"Really!"

"Really. Did you ever notice those scars on Big George's arms?"

"Yeah."

"Well, that's where those hogs bit him. But Big George never said a word to Poppa, because he knew Poppa would kill Buddy for bringing me down there."

"I never knew that."

"I know you didn't."

"Wow. . . . Do you know any other brave people? What about Uncle Julian shooting that twelve-point deer last week? That took a lot of courage."

"Well now, there's courage and then there's courage," Idgie said. "You don't have to be too brave to shoot some poor dumb animal with a twenty-gauge shotgun."

"Who else do you know that's brave besides Big George?"

"Well, let's see," she said, musing. "Besides Big George, I'd have to say that your mother was one of the bravest people I know."

"Momma?"

"Yes. Your momma."

"Oh, I don't believe that. Why, she's scared of everything, even a little bug. What'd she ever do?"

"Something. She did something once."

"What?"

"It doesn't matter what. You asked me and I told you. Your mother and Big George are the two bravest people I know."

"*Really?*"

"I promise you so."

Stump was amazed. "Well, I'll be . . ."

"That's right. And there's something else I want you always to remember. There are magnificent beings on this earth, son, that are walking around posing as humans. And I don't ever want you to forget that. You hear me?"

Stump looked at her sincerely and said, "No ma'am, I won't."

As they continued on down the tracks, a bright red cardinal swooped out of a snow-covered tree and made a Christmas flight across the white horizon.

### MARCH 9, 1986

Before, during those long endless black nights when Evelyn had been awake sweating with fear and fighting visions of death and tubes and tumors growing, she had wanted to scream out for help while Ed slept beside her. But she had just lain there in that dark pit of her own personal hell until morning.

Lately, to get her mind off that cold gun and pulling the trigger, she would close her eyes and force herself to hear Mrs. Threadgoode's voice and if she breathed deep and concentrated she would soon see herself in Whistle Stop. She would walk down the street and go in Opal's beauty shop and could actually feel her hair being washed with warm water, then cool, then cooler. After a comb-out she would stop by to visit with Dot Weems at the post office and then on to the cafe where she could see everyone so clearly, Stump and Ruth and Idgie. She would order lunch and Wilbur Weems and Grady Kilgore would wave to her. Sipsey and Onzell would smile at her and she could hear the radio from the kitchen. Everyone would ask her how she was and the sun was always shining and there would always be a tomorrow . . . Lately she slept more and more and thought of the gun less and less . . .

When she woke this morning, Evelyn realized that she was actually looking forward to going to the nursing home. Sitting there all these weeks listening to stories about the cafe and Whistle Stop had become more of a reality than her own life with Ed in Birmingham.

When she arrived, her friend was in a good mood, as usual, and was happy to get the Hershey bar without almonds, a special request.

Halfway through it, Mrs. Threadgoode was busy wondering about a hobo she had known years ago.

"Lord, I wonder whatever happened to Smokey Lonesome. It's no telling where he is now, probably dead somewhere, I guess.

"I remember the first time he ever came in the cafe. I was having a plate of fried green tomatoes, and he knocked on the back door, looking for food. Idgie went in the kitchen and pretty soon she came back in with this poor fella that was filthy dirty from riding the rails, and told him to go into the bathroom and wash up and she'd give him a bite to eat. Idgie went to fix him a plate and said that was the lonesomest-looking character she'd ever seen. He said his name was Smokey Phillips, but Idgie named him Smokey Lonesome, and after that, every time she'd see him coming in off the road, she'd say, 'Here comes ol' Smokey Lonesome.'

"Poor ol' thing, I don't think he had a family, and Ruth and Idgie felt sorry for him 'cause he was 'bout half dead, and let him stay in that old shed they had out in back of the cafe. Oh, he'd get the wanderlust every once in a while and take off two or three times a year, but sooner or later he'd show back up, usually drunk and run-down, and, he'd go out back in his shed and stay awhile. He never owned a thing in his life. All he had was a knife and a fork and a spoon that he carried inside his coat pocket, and this can opener that he kept in his hatband. Said he didn't want to be burdened down. I think that shed out back was the only place he ever had to call home, and if it hadn't been for Ruth and Idgie, he might have starved to death.

"But I think the real reason he kept coming back was because he was in love with Ruth. He never said so, but you could tell by the way he looked at her.

"You know, I'm thankful that my Cleo passed on first. It seems like a man cain't live without a woman. That's why most of them die right after their wives do. They just get lost. It's pitiful . . . you take Old Man Dunaway who's out here. His wife hasn't even been dead over a month yet, and he's already started goosing all the women . . . that's why they're giving him those tranquilizers, to calm him down. Thinks he's a Romeo, can you imagine? And you should see what he looks like, just like an old turkey buzzard, with big floppy ears and all. But who am I to say? No matter what you look like, there's somebody who's gonna think you're the handsomest man in the world. Well, maybe he'll catch one of these old women yet . . ."

# WEST MADISON STREET

CHICAGO, ILLINOIS

## DECEMBER 3, 1938

West Madison Street, Chicago, was no different from Pratt Street in Baltimore, South Main Street in Los Angeles, or Third Street in San Francisco; a street of gospel missions, cheap rooming houses, and hotels, secondhand clothes stores, greasy-spoon soup lines, pawn shops, liquor stores, and whorehouses, teeming with what were kindly referred to as "disappointed men."

The only thing that made that year in Chicago different from any other was that Smokey Lonesome, who usually traveled alone, had picked up a friend. Just a kid, really, but he was company. They'd met over a month ago, in Michigan.

He was a good-looking, fresh-faced kid, wearing a thin blue-gray slipover sweater over a brown frayed shirt and ragged brown pants, with skin like a baby's ass. Still wet behind the ears, he'd had a lot of trouble over in Detroit with guys trying to bugger him, and he'd asked Smokey if he could travel with him for a while.

Smokey had told him the same thing that an old guy once said: "Go home now, kid, while you can. Get away from this life, 'cause once you piss out of a boxcar, you're hooked."

But it didn't do any good, just like it hadn't done any good with him, so Smokey decided to let him tag along.

He was a funny kid. He had about pulled his own britches off, digging so hard for a dime. He wanted to see Sally Rand do her fan dance to "White Birds in the Moonlight," as it said on the poster. He never did find a dime, but the woman in the glass ticket booth felt so sorry for him that she let him in free.

Smokey had hustled up a quarter while he was waiting for him to come out of the show, and thought they'd go get them a ten-cent steak over at the Tile Grill. They had not had anything to eat that day except for a can of Vienna sausages and some stale crackers. He was smoking a Lucky Strike that he had found mashed in a cigarette package someone had thrown away when the kid came bursting out of the theater, flying high.

"Oh Smokey, you should have seen her! She's the most beautiful and delicate thing I've ever seen. She was like an angel, a real live angel come down from heaven."

All through dinner he couldn't stop talking about her.

After they had their steaks, they were thirty cents short of a hotel room, so they headed on over to Grant's Park, where they hoped to grab a sleep in one of the shacks, made out of tar paper and cardboard and a few scraps of lumber, that you could sometimes find if you were lucky; and they were lucky that night.

Before they went to sleep, the kid said, as he had every night, "Tell me about where all you've been and what all you've done, Smokey."

"I told you that once."

"I know, but tell me again."

Smokey told him about the time he'd been in Baltimore and had a job at the White Tower hamburger place, and how it had been so shiny and clean you could eat right off the black and white tiles on the floor; and about the time he had been a coal miner, outside of Pittsburgh.

"You know, a lot of these fellows will eat a rat, but as for me,

I couldn't do it. I've seen 'em save too many lives. Saved mine, once. Rats are the first ones to smell gas in a mine . . .

"One time, me and this old boy was deep down in this mine, picking away, when all of a sudden here comes two hundred rats running past us, going more than sixty miles an hour. I didn't know what to think, and this old colored boy throws his pick down and shouts, 'Run!'

"I did, and it saved my life. If I see one, to this day, I just let him go on about his rat business. Yes sir, they're tops in my book."

The kid, who was almost asleep, mumbled, "What's the worst job you ever had, Smokey?"

"Worst job? Well, let's see . . . I've done a lot of things a decent man wouldn't do, but I guess the worst was back in 'twenty-eight, when I took that job in the turpentine mill, down at Vinegar Bend, Alabama. I hadn't had nothing to eat but pork and beans in two months, and I was so busted that a nickel looked as big as a pancake, or I'd of never took the job. The only white people they could get to work down there were the Cajuns, and they called them turpentine niggers. That job would kill a white man; I only lasted five days and was sick as a dog for three weeks from the smell; it gets in your hair, your skin . . . I had to burn my clothes . . ."

Suddenly, Smokey stopped talking and sat up. The minute he heard the sound of men running and shouting, he knew it was the Legion. In the past couple of months, the American Legion had been raiding the hobo camps, knocking down everything in their path, determined to clean up the riffraff that had descended on their city.

Smokey shouted to the kid, "Let's go! Let's get out of here!"

And they started running, just like the hundred and twenty-two other residents of that particular Hooverville that night. All you could hear was the sound of men crashing through the woods and the sound of the tar-paper shacks being ripped apart and struck down with crowbars and iron pipes.

Smokey ran to the left, and as soon as he hit thick under-brush, he lay down, because he knew, with his weak lungs, he could never outrun them. He went flat to the ground and stayed there until it was over. The kid could run and he'd catch up with him somewhere down the line.

Later, he went back over to the camp to see if there was anything left standing. What had once been a little town of shacks was now just loose piles of tar paper, cardboard, and wood, scattered and smashed flatter than pancakes. He turned and was leaving when he heard a voice.

"Smokey?"

The kid was lying about twenty feet from where their shack had been. Surprised, Smokey went over to him. "What happened?"

"I know you told me not to ever untie my shoes, but they was tight. I tripped."

"You hurt?"

"I think I'm killed."

Smokey squatted beside him and saw that the right side of his head had been beaten in. The kid looked up at him.

"You know, Smokey . . . I thought tramping would be fun . . . but it ain't . . ."

Then he closed his eyes and died.

The next day, Smokey got a couple of guys he knew and they buried him out in the tramps' graveyard they had outside of Chicago, and Elmo Williams read a selection he found on page 301 of the little red Salvation Army songbook he always carried with him.

> *Rejoice for a comrade deceased,*
> *Our loss is his infinite gain,*
> *A soul out of prison released,*
> *And free from its bodily chain.*

They never did know his name, so they just put up a wooden marker, made out of a crate. It said, THE KID.

When the other men left, Smokey stayed behind for a minute to say goodbye.

"Well, pal," he said, "at least you got to see Sally Rand. That was something . . ."

Then he turned around and headed for the yard to hop a train south, to Alabama. He wanted to get out of Chicago; the wind that whipped around the buildings was so cold that it sometimes brought a tear to a man's eye.

## THE WEEMS WEEKLY

(WHISTLE STOP, ALABAMA'S WEEKLY BULLETIN)

DECEMBER 8, 1938

## Beware of Blasting Caps

Tell your kids not to play out by the railroad yards where they are dynamiting. My other half tells me that when he was on his run to Nashville a few days ago, he heard tell of a fellow who bit down on a blasting cap by mistake and blew his lips off.

Opal says that there was such a rush in the shop the other day, with everyone getting ready for the Eastern Star Banquet, that a blue woman's coat was taken by mistake. So if you have it, bring it back.

A hayride was sponsored by the Baptist church and Peggy Hadley was left in the parking lot by mistake, but caught up with the gang later on.

Idgie and Ruth made a group of our kids happy last Saturday by taking them over to Avondale Park to pay a visit to Miss Fancy, the famous elephant who is so popular with young and old alike. Everyone had their picture made with Miss Fancy, and can have them as soon as they come back from the drugstore, Thursday.

Dr. Cleo Threadgoode returned home last Friday night from a visit to the Mayo Clinic, where he had taken little Albert for some tests. We are sorry he did not come home with good news for Ninny. We can only hope the doctors are wrong. Cleo will be back in his office on Monday.

. . . Dot Weems . . .

MARCH 15, 1986

Today they were busy eating Cracker Jack and talking. Or at least Mrs. Threadgoode was.

"You know, I was sure hoping I would be home by Easter, but it doesn't look like I'm gonna make it. Mrs. Otis is still having a hard time, but she did sign up for this arts and crafts class they have out here. Your mother-in-law joined up, too. Geneene said that Easter, they were going to hide Easter eggs and invite some schoolchildren to come out and look for them. That should be fun . . .

"I've always loved Easter, from the time I was a little girl. Loved everything that went with it. Back when we were kids, every Saturday night before Easter, we would all be out in the kitchen dyeing eggs. But Momma Threadgoode was always in charge of dyeing the golden Easter egg.

"Easter morning, we'd all have on new outfits and brand new Buster Brown shoes from Poppa's store. After church, Momma and Poppa would put us on the trolley car and we'd take a ride to Birmingham and back, while they hid about two hundred Easter eggs all over the backyard. There was all kinds of prizes—but the grand prize was for the one who found the golden egg.

"I was thirteen the year I found the golden egg. We'd been running around the yard for two whole hours, and not one person had found the golden egg. I was standing in the middle of the backyard, resting a minute, when I happened to glance over and saw something shiny under the seesaw. And sure enough, there it was, the golden egg, hidden in the grass, just sitting there waiting for me. Essie Rue was mad as a wet hen. She had wanted to find it, herself, that year, 'cause the grand prize was this big lemon-colored see-through china Easter egg, with the most delicate sparkle dust sprinkled on it. And if you looked inside the egg, you could see a miniature scene of a tiny little family: a mother, a father, and two little girls and a dog, standing in front of a house that looked just like ours. I could look inside that egg for hours. . . . I wonder whatever happened to that egg. I think it got sold in the porch sale we had during World War One.

"Easter was always a lucky day for me. That was the day the good Lord let me know I was going to have Albert.

"Sometimes when I think of other people's troubles, I realize how lucky I was to have gotten Cleo. I couldn't have asked for a better husband. Didn't have a roving eye, didn't drink, and was he smart. I'm not bragging, because I don't do that, but it's the truth. Just had a naturally keen mind. Never had to dig for anything. I used to call him my dictionary. Whenever I was struggling, trying to write something or other, I'd call out to him, 'Daddy, how do you spell this word or that word?' He could spell anything. And he knew history. You could ask him any date and there it would be, right on the tip of his tongue. And I never saw anybody who wanted to be a doctor more than he did . . . wanted to be a surgeon. I know it like to broke his heart when Poppa died and he had to come out of medical school, but I never heard him say a word about it, not once.

"And he was loved. You ask anybody that knew him, and they will tell you that there wasn't a sweeter man on earth than Cleo Threadgoode.

"But young girls are funny. They want dash and sparkle and

romance. Cleo was kinda quiet. He wasn't the one I wanted at first, but I was the one he wanted. He said he made up his mind the first night he came back home from college and saw me out in the kitchen helping Sipsey cut the biscuits on that big white tin table.

He walked into the parlor, where Momma and Poppa Threadgoode were, and he said, 'I'm going to marry that big girl out in the kitchen cuttin' biscuits.' Made his mind up in just a flash. But then, all the Threadgoodes were like that. I was only fifteen at the time, and I told him I wasn't interested in getting married to anyone, that I was too young. He said he'd try again the next year, and he did, and I still wasn't ready. I married him at eighteen, and I still wasn't ready.

"Oh, at first I was afraid Cleo wasn't the right one, and I cried to Momma Threadgoode that I thought I had married the wrong man. Momma said not to worry, that I would learn to love him." She turned to Evelyn. "I just wonder how many people never get the one they want, and wind up with the one they're supposed to be with. Anyhow, when I look back on all the years of happiness I had with Cleo and I think that I could have turned him away, it just makes me shudder.

"Of course, when I married Cleo I was green." She chuckled. "I'm not gonna tell you how green I was. I didn't know a thing about sex or what was in back of it or anything, and I'd never seen a man before, and, honey, that'll scare you to death if you're not prepared for it. But Cleo was so sweet with me, and by and by, I got the hang of it.

"And in all those years of marriage I can honestly say that there was never an unkind word passed between us. He was my mother, father, husband, teacher. Everything you could possibly want in a man. Oh, and it was so hard the times we had to be separated. First, the world war, and then, I had to stay home again with Momma when he was putting himself through chiropractic school. Cleo was a self-made man. Didn't get help from anyone. Didn't complain, just did it. That was Cleo.

"And all those years we tried to have a baby and couldn't, he never said a word to make me feel bad, and I know how much he wanted children. Finally, when the doctor told me that my problem was a tipped uterus and that I would never have a baby, Cleo just put his arm around me and said, 'That's all right, honey, you're all I need in this world.' And he never made me feel any different. But, oh, how I wanted to give him a baby. I'd pray and pray and I'd say, 'Oh Lord, if it's something I've done, if that's why you've made me barren, please don't make Cleo suffer for it.' Oh, I agonized over it for years.

"Then, one Easter Sunday I was sitting in church and Reverend Scroggins was telling us the story of our Lord ascending into heaven, and I closed my eyes and thought how wonderful it would be if I could raise up my arms and ascend into heaven with Jesus and bring home a little angel for Cleo. Just as I was thinking so hard, a beam of sunlight shot right through the top of the stained glass window and hit me like a spotlight. That light was so bright that it blinded my eyes, and that stream of light stayed shining on me for the rest of the sermon. Reverend Scroggins said afterwards that he couldn't take his eyes off me while he was talking, that my hair lit up like fire and I simply glowed. He said, 'You sure picked the right seat this Sunday, Mrs. Threadgoode.'

"But I knew right away that that was God's way of telling me that he had answered my prayers. Alleluia. Christ is risen. The Lord is risen, indeed.

"I was thirty-two years old when Albert was born. And you never saw a happier daddy than Cleo Threadgoode.

"Albert was a big baby. He weighed twelve and a half pounds. We were still living at the big house at the time, and Momma Threadgoode and Sipsey were upstairs with me and Cleo was downstairs in the kitchen with everybody else, waiting. That afternoon, Idgie and Ruth came over from the cafe and Idgie brought a bottle of Wild Turkey whiskey and was sneaking it to Cleo in a teacup to help calm him down. That was the only time I know of that Cleo took a drink. Idgie said she knew just how he felt. She had been through the same thing when Ruth had her baby.

"They said when Sipsey handed Albert to Cleo for the first

time, he just burst into tears. It wasn't until later that we found out there was anything the matter.

"We noticed that the baby was having such a hard time sitting up. He'd try so hard, then he'd just topple over. And he didn't walk until he was twenty-one months old. We took him to all the doctors, all over Birmingham, and they didn't know what the trouble was. Finally, Cleo said that he thought he ought to carry Albert up to the Mayo Clinic, to see if there wasn't something that could be done. I dressed him in his navy suit and his little cap, and I remember it was a cold, wet day in January, and when Cleo and the baby got on the train and it pulled out, little Albert turned around in Cleo's arms, looking for me.

"It hurt me so to see them go. When I walked home I felt like somebody had just pulled the very heart out of me. They kept Albert up there for three weeks, giving him test after test, and I prayed every minute they were gone, 'Please, God, don't let them find anything wrong with my baby.'

"When Cleo and Albert came back home, the first day, Cleo didn't say a word to me about what they found out, and I didn't ask. I guess I didn't want to know. He brought me the cutest picture that he had made up there in a penny arcade of he and Albert sitting on a half moon, with stars in the background. I still have that picture on my dresser and I wouldn't take a million dollars for it.

"It wasn't until after supper, when he sat me down on the sofa. He held my hand and said, 'Momma, I want you to be brave.' And I felt my heart drop to my knees. He told me that the doctors found out that our baby suffered a brain hemorrhage at birth. I asked him, 'Is he gonna die?' Cleo said, 'Oh no, honey, he's physically as healthy as he can be. They checked him from top to bottom.' When I heard that I felt as if a hundred-pound weight had been lifted off my chest. I said, 'Thank God,' and got up, but Cleo said, 'Now, wait a minute, honey, there's something else you have to know.' I told him that as long as the baby was healthy, I didn't care about anything else. He made me sit back down and he said, 'Now, Momma, this is something very serious that you and I are going to have to discuss.' Then he went on to tell me that the doctors up to the clinic said, although Albert may very well be physically sound and live a long and healthy life, that most likely he will never develop mentally past the age of four or five years. That he would remain a child all his life. And sometimes the burden of having a child like that, one that required constant attention, was too great. Cleo said that there are special places that . . . I stopped him right in midsentence. 'Burden!' I said. 'How could that precious, sweet baby ever be a burden?' How could anybody ever think such a thing? Why, from the minute he was born, Albert was the joy of my life. There wasn't a purer soul that ever lived on this earth. And years later, whenever I would get to feeling a little down, I would just look at Albert. I had to work every day of my life to be good, and it was just a natural thing with him. He never had an unkind thought. Didn't even know the meaning of the word *evil*.

"A lot of people might have been sad to have a birth-injured child, but I think the good Lord made him like that so he wouldn't have to suffer. He never even knew there were mean people on this earth. He just loved everybody and everybody loved him. I truly believe in my heart that he was an angel that God sent down to me, and sometimes I cain't wait to get to heaven to see him again. He was my pal, and I miss him . . . especially at Easter." Mrs. Threadgoode looked down at her hands.

"Well, now that it looks like I'm gonna be here for a little while yet, I've been thinking about that picture I have in my bedroom at home, of that Indian maiden paddling her canoe down the river in the moonlight. She's fully clothed, so I'm gonna see if Norris will go over and bring it to me whenever he gets the chance."

Mrs. Threadgoode pulled something out of the Cracker Jack box and all of a sudden her eyes lit up. "Oh Evelyn, look! Here's my prize. It's a little miniature chicken . . . just what I like!" and she held it out for her friend to see.

DECEMBER 30, 1939

## Religious Sewing Machines a Fraud

The man that was in town a couple of weeks ago, selling those religious sewing machines that were supposed to heal you as you sewed, was arrested in Birmingham. It seems that the machines were not from France, but were made outside of Chattanooga, Tennessee, and were not religious at all. Biddie Louise Otis is very upset, because she thought the one she bought had helped her arthritis a lot.

Whistle Stop's Boy Scouts, Duane Glass and Vernon Hadley, all received their merit badges, and Bobby Lee Scroggins moved up to Eagle Scout. Scout leader Julian Threadgoode treated them to a visit to the iron statue of Vulcan, over in Birmingham, *Atop Red Mountain. . . .*

Julian said that the statue of Vulcan is so big that a man can stand inside of his ear.

Who would want to stand in a man's ear, is my question.

Vesta Adcock had an afternoon party for her Eastern Star ladies, and served petit fours.

By the way, Opal asks that the neighbors not feed her cat, Boots, even though she acts like she's hungry and begs. She has plenty to eat at home and is on a diet, because the doctor said she was too fat.

. . . Dot Weems . . .

P.S. Has anybody seen my other half's December *National Geographic*? He claims he lost it somewhere in town and he is having a fit because he hasn't finished it yet.

## JANUARY 8, 1938

Ever since Idgie had put the picture of Miss Fancy the Elephant up at the cafe, Onzell and George's youngest child, Naughty Bird, had been fascinated. She would beg her daddy to take her to Avondale Park so she could see the elephant; and today, that's all Naughty Bird had on her mind.

She had been sick for over a month now. Dr. Hadley had just told them that pneumonia had set in, and if they couldn't get her to eat, he didn't see how she could live out another week.

Big George was leaning over the bed with an uneaten bowl of oatmeal, pleading with her. "Please, won't you eat a bite for Poppa? Just one little bite for Poppa, baby. What you want, baby? You want Poppa to get you a sweet kitten?"

Naughty Bird, who was six and weighed only thirty pounds, just lay there, listless, with her eyes glazed over, and shook her head.

"You want Momma to fix you some biscuits?" Onzell said. "You want some biscuits and honey, baby?"

"No ma'am."

"Miz Idgie and Miz Ruth's here. They done brung you some candy . . . won't you eat a bite?"

The little girl turned her head toward the wall covered with magazine pictures and mumbled something.

Onzell leaned down. "What, baby? You say you want some biscuits?"

Naughty Bird said, weakly, "I wanna see Miz Fancy."

Onzell turned, with tears in her eyes. "See what I mean, Miz Ruth. She got it in her head to go see that elephant, and ain't nothin' else gonna do, and she ain't gonna eat till she does."

Idgie and Big George went out on the porch and sat on the faded green tin chairs. He stared out in the yard.

"Miz Idgie, I cain't let my baby die before she sees dat elephant."

"Now, George, you know you cain't go in Avondale Park, they just had a big Klan meeting over there the other night. As soon as you set one foot in that gate, they'd shoot your head off in a minute."

Big George thought it over and said, "Well then, they's gonna hafta kill me, cause dat's my baby girl in dere and I'd rather be dead in my grave than let anything happen to her."

Idgie knew he meant it.

This six-foot-five giant of a man, who could pick up a full-grown hog and carry it like it was a sack of potatoes, had such a soft spot for his little girl that he would leave the house whenever Onzell gave her a whipping. And when he came home at night, it was Naughty Bird who would run and crawl up him like a tree and hug his neck. She could twist him around her little finger like he was the red on a barber pole.

That year, he had ridden the streetcar over to Birmingham to buy her a snow-white Easter dress, with shoes to match. Easter morning, Onzell had managed to get Naughty Bird's nappy hair all up in pigtails and tied them with white ribbons. When Sipsey saw her in that white dress, she had laughed and said she looked just like a fly in a pan of milk. But Big George didn't care if she was black as midnight and had nappy hair: he'd carried her to church with him and sat her on his lap, like she was Princess Margaret Rose.

So the sicker Naughty Bird became, the more Idgie worried about Big George and what he would do.

. . .

Two days later, it was cold and wet after a hard rain. Stump was walking home from school down the railroad tracks, smelling the strong wet pine smoke rising up from the houses along the way. He was wearing brown corduroy pants and a leather jacket that had seen better days. He was chilled to the bone.

When he got home to the cafe, he sat by the wood stove in the back, his ears burning as they thawed out, listening to his mother.

"Honey, why didn't you wear your hat?"

"I forgot."

"You don't want to get sick, do you?"

"No ma'am."

He was glad to see Idgie come in. She went over to the closet and got her coat and asked him if he wanted to drive over to Birmingham, to Avondale Park, with Smokey and her. He jumped at the chance. "Yes ma'am."

"Well, come on then."

Ruth said, "Wait a minute. Do you have homework?"

"Just a little."

"Do you promise to do it when you get back, if I let you go?"

"Yes ma'am."

"Idgie, you're coming right back, aren't you?"

"Sure. Why not? I'm just gonna talk to the man."

"Well, all right, but get your hat, Stump."

He ran out the door. " 'Bye, Momma."

Ruth handed Idgie his hat. "Try to get back before dark."

"I will. Don't worry."

They piled into the car and headed to Birmingham.

At twelve o'clock that night, a frantic Ruth received a phone call from Smokey, saying not to worry, that they were all right. He hung up before Ruth had a chance to ask where they were.

At five forty-five the next morning, Ruth and Sipsey were in the kitchen getting ready for the breakfast crowd. Onzell had stayed home with Naughty Bird, who was getting worse. Ruth was a nervous wreck, worrying over Stump, Idgie, and Smokey, who had not come home yet.

"She's gonna be back," Sipsey said. "Dat's jest her way, she's always runnin' off. You know she ain't gwine let nothin' happen to dat boy."

An hour later, while Grady Kilgore and the boys were having their morning coffee, they heard a horn blowing, coming toward the cafe. Then, from far off, they heard the sound of Christmas bells jangling, getting louder and louder. They all got up to look out the window and couldn't believe their eyes.

Next door, at the beauty shop, Opal, who had just slung a teacup of bright green Palmolive shampoo at her six-thirty customer's head, looked out the window and screamed so loud that it scared poor Biddie Louise Otis nearly half to death.

Miss Fancy, all decked out in her leather ankle bracelets, with her bells and her bright purple feather plume, was happily strolling by the cafe, her snout waving in the air, thoroughly enjoying the scenery. She headed over the tracks to Troutville.

When Sipsey came out of the kitchen and saw the huge animal floating past the window, she ran into the ladies room and locked the door behind her.

A second later, Stump burst into the cafe. "Momma! Momma! Come on!" And he ran out, pulling Ruth behind him.

As Miss Fancy sauntered down the red dirt roads of Troutville, doors started flying open and the air became filled with the sounds of children screaming with delight. Their dumbfounded parents, many still in robes and pajamas, with their hair still done up in rags, were speechless.

J. W. Moldwater, Miss Fancy's trainer, was walking beside her. He had been in a bout with old man whiskey last night and had come out the loser. He was now wishing that the children, who were running along beside him and jumping up and down like Mexican jumping beans, screaming in loud, ear-piercing squeals, would be quiet.

He turned to Idgie, walking along with him. "Where's she live at?"

"Just follow me."

Onzell, still in her apron, ran out of the house and yelled for Big George. He came around the side of the house holding the hatchet he'd been chopping wood with, and stood there for a minute, not believing what he was seeing. Then he looked at Idgie and said softly, "Thank ya, Miss Idgie. Thank ya."

He put his hatchet against the side of the house and went inside. Carefully, he began wrapping the thin little girl up in a quilt. "Der's somebody dat come all the way from Birmingham to see you dis morning, baby . . ." And he carried her onto the front porch.

When they came out, J. W. Moldwater nudged his wrinkled friend with a stick, and the old circus veteran sat up on her hind legs and greeted Naughty Bird with a loud trumpet.

Naughty Bird's eyes lit up and filled with wonder at the sight in the yard. She said, "Ohhhh, it's Miz Fancy, Daddy . . . it's *Miz Fancy.*"

Ruth put her arm in Onzell's and watched as the trainer with the hangover led the elephant to the edge of the porch. He gave Naughty Bird a five-cent bag of peanuts and told her she could feed them to her if she wanted to.

Willie Boy could only be seen peeking through the window. The other children had also kept their distance from this big, gray thing, the size of a house. But Naughty Bird had no fear and fed her the peanuts, one by one, while she talked to Miss Fancy like an old friend, telling her how old she was and what grade she was in.

Miss Fancy blinked her eyes and seemed to be listening. She took the peanuts from the little girl, one at a time, as gently as a gloved woman getting a dime out of a change purse.

Twenty minutes later, Naughty Bird waved goodbye to the elephant and J. W. Moldwater began the long walk home to Birmingham. He vowed that he would never take another drink and would never, ever get involved in an all-night poker game with strangers.

Naughty Bird went inside and ate three buttermilk biscuits with honey.

# VALDOSTA, GEORGIA

## SEPTEMBER 15, 1924

Two weeks after Ruth Jamison left to go home and get married, Idgie drove into Valdosta and parked on the main street, in front of the newspaper office, next to the barbershop. About an hour later, she got out and walked across the street into the grocery store on the corner. It looked very much like her poppa's store, only bigger, with a wooden floor and high ceilings.

She wandered around, looking at all the stuff. Soon, a balding man in a white apron said, "Can I help you, miss? What you gonna need today?"

Idgie told him she'd have some saltine crackers and a couple of slices of that cheese he had out on the counter. While he was slicing the cheese, Idgie said, "You don't happen to know if Frank Bennett is in town today, do you?"

"Who?"

"Frank Bennett."

"Oh, Frank. Naw, he usually just comes on up here on Wednesday to the bank, or sometimes he gets a haircut across the street. Why? You need to see him?"

"No, I don't even know him. I was just wondering what he looked like."

"Who?"

"Frank Bennett."

He handed Idgie her crackers and cheese. "You want anything to drink with that?"

"No, this is fine."

He took her money. "What does he look like? Well, let's see. . . . Oh, I don't know, just like anybody, I guess. He's kind of a big fellow . . . got black hair, blue eyes . . . of course, he's got that one glass eye."

"A glass eye?"

"Yeah, he lost it in the war. Other than that, I'd say he's a nice-looking fellow."

"How old is he?"

"Oh, I guess he's about thirty-four or thirty-five, somewhere around in there. His daddy left him about eight hundred acres of land about ten miles south of town, so he doesn't come in much anymore."

"Is he nice? I mean, is he well liked?"

"Frank? Oh, I'd say so. Why do you ask?"

"I was just wondering. My cousin is engaged to him and I was just wondering."

"You're Ruth's cousin? Oh! Now, there's a fine person. Now, she's well thought of. I've known Ruth Jamison since she was a little girl. Always so polite. . . . She teaches my granddaughter Sunday School. Are you visiting her?"

Idgie changed the subject. "I think I'd better have me something to drink with these crackers."

"I thought you would. What you want? Milk?"

"Naw, I don't like milk."

"You want a cold drink?"

"Do you have a strawberry drink?"

"Sure do."

"Give me one of them."

He went to the drink box to get her drink. "We're all pleased Ruth is going to marry Frank. She and her mother have had such a hard time of it since her daddy died. Last year, some of us over at the church tried to help out, but she won't take a cent. Proud. . . . But then, I'm not telling you anything you don't know. Are you staying with them?"

"No. I haven't seen them yet."

"Well, you know where the house is, don't you? It's just two blocks down. I can run you over there if you like. Did she know you were coming?"

"No, that's all right. I'll tell you the truth, mister, it would be better if they didn't know I was here. I'm just passing through on business, I'm a traveling saleswoman for the Rosebud Perfume Company."

"You are?"

"Yes. And I've got a few more stops to make before I get back home, so I better be going. . . . I just wanted to be sure that this Frank was okay, and I don't want her to know that the family was worried about her. It might upset her. So, I'm just gonna go home and tell her aunt and uncle, my momma and daddy, that everything is fine, and most likely we'll all be back for the wedding and it would just upset her to know and to think that we were asking around, so I'm just gonna head on home now, and thanks."

The storekeeper watched the strange young woman in the railroad overalls back out of the store.

He called out, "Hey! You didn't finish your cold drink!"

NOVEMBER 2, 1924

## Bennett-Jamison Nuptials Told

Sunday, Miss Ruth Anne Jamison became the bride of Mr. Frank Corley Bennett, the Reverend James Dodds officiating. The bride wore a white lace dress and carried a bouquet of tiny sweetheart roses. The groom's brother, Gerald Bennett, stood as best man.

The bride is the daughter of Mrs. Elizabeth Jamison and the late Reverend Charles Jamison. The former Miss Jamison was graduated from Valdosta High School with honors, and attended the Baptist Seminary for young women in Augusta, and is a well-known and respected church worker in this area. The groom, Mr. Frank Corley Bennett, was graduated from Valdosta High School, and later served four years in the military, where he received a wound and was awarded a Purple Heart.

After enjoying a two-week honeymoon in Tallulah Falls, Georgia, the couple will reside at the family home of the groom, ten miles south of town. Mrs. Bennett will continue to teach her Sunday School class when she returns.

# VALDOSTA, GEORGIA

## NOVEMBER 1, 1924

It was the morning of Ruth's wedding; Idgie had borrowed Julian's car and had been parked across the street from the Morning Dove Baptist Church since seven o'clock. Four hours later, she saw Ruth and her mother go into the side door of the church. Ruth looked as beautiful in her wedding gown as Idgie thought she would.

Later, she saw Frank Bennett and his brother arrive. She sat there watching the guests go in, one by one, until the church was full. When the usher, in his white gloves, closed the doors, her heart sank, but she could still hear the organ from inside the church when the "Wedding March" started, and she felt sick.

Idgie had been drinking a bottle of rotgut rye since six o'clock that morning, and just before the bride said "I do," everyone in the church was wondering who was outside in the car blowing their horn like that.

After a minute, Idgie heard the organ start up again, and all of a sudden, the church doors burst open and Ruth and Frank came running down the steps, laughing, with people cheering and throwing rice. They jumped into the back of the waiting car and drove off.

Idgie blew her horn once more. Ruth looked around just as they turned the corner, a second too late to see who it was.

Idgie threw up on the side of Julian's car, all the way home to Alabama.

## ROSE TERRACE NURSING HOME

OLD MONTGOMERY HIGHWAY
BIRMINGHAM, ALABAMA

### MARCH 30, 1986

Ed Couch had picked up Big Momma from the nursing home on Easter morning, and she had spent the day with them. Evelyn had wanted to invite Mrs. Threadgoode, but Ed said that it might upset Big Momma, and God knows we didn't want Big Momma upset; as it was, she might not go back. So Evelyn had cooked this huge meal for just the three of them, and after dinner, Ed and Big Momma went in the den and watched television.

Evelyn had planned to ride back to the nursing home with them so she could at least say hello to Mrs. Threadgoode, but her son had called her long distance, just as they were headed out the door. Big Momma, who had whined all through dinner about how she hated Rose Terrace, was dressed and ready to go, so Evelyn told Ed to go on without her.

Consequently, it had been two weeks since she had seen her friend, and when she did, she got a surprise . . .

"I went to the beauty shop and got my hair fixed for Easter. How do you like it?"

Evelyn didn't know what to say; someone had dyed Mrs. Threadgoode's hair bright purple.

"Well, you got your hair fixed."

"Yes. I always want to look my best for Easter."

Evelyn sat down and smiled like nothing was wrong. "Who did it for you, darling?"

Mrs. Threadgoode said, "Well, believe it or not, it was a student from the beauty college over in Birmingham. Sometimes they come out here and do our hair for free, just to get a little practice. Mine was a tiny little thing and she worked so hard, I tipped her fifty cents. Now, where else in the world can you get your hair shampooed, colored, and set for fifty cents?"

Evelyn was curious. "How old was the girl?"

"Oh, she was a full-grown woman, only she was tiny, she had to stand on a box while she did my hair. I'd say she was about two inches away from being a midget. Of course, I don't let any handicap like that bother me, and I love a midget. . . . I wonder whatever happened to that little midget that sold cigarettes?"

"Where?"

"On the radio and TV. They used to dress him up like a bellboy, sold Phillip Morris cigarettes. You remember!"

"Oh yes. I know who you're talking about now."

"Oh, I used to get the biggest kick out of him. I always wished he would come to Whistle Stop so I could sit him on my lap and play with him."

Evelyn had brought dyed eggs, candy corn, and Easter chocolates, and told Mrs. Threadgoode that they would celebrate all over again this week since she had not been with her on the actual day. Mrs. Threadgoode thought that was a fine idea, and told Evelyn that candy corn was her favorite and that she liked to bite the white tips off first and save the rest for later, and she proceeded to do so as she reported on Easter.

"Oh Evelyn, I wish you could have been out here. The nurses hid eggs all over. We put some in our pockets and in our rooms and the entire third grade from Woodlawn came out and they were the cutest things, running up and down the hall. Oh, they had the grandest time! And it meant so much for these old people out here, most of them are just starved to see youngsters. I think it cheered everybody up. Old people need to see children every once in a while," she whispered confidentially. "It lifts their spirits. Some of these real old ladies they have out here just sit in their wheelchairs all hunched over . . . but when the nurses give them a baby doll to hold, you'd be surprised at how they just sit right up, holding on to their dolls. Most of them think it's their own babies they've got.

"And guess who else came out here Easter?"

"Who?"

"That weather girl from the television station . . . I forget her name, but she's famous."

"Well, that must have been very nice."

"Oh, it was . . . but, you know what?"

"What?"

"It just dawned on me. Not one famous person ever came to Whistle Stop . . . except Franklin Roosevelt and Mr. Pinto, the criminal, but they were both dead at the time, so it doesn't count. Poor old Dot Weems never did have anything exciting to write about."

"Who was he?"

Mrs. Threadgoode was surprised. "You never heard of Franklin Roosevelt?"

"No, Mr. Pinto."

"You never heard of Mr. Pinto?"

"Pinto? You mean like a pinto pony?"

"No honey, like a pinto bean. Seymore Pinto. He was a famous murderer!"

"Oh . . . no, well, I guess he was before my time."

"Well, you're lucky, because he was a mean somebody. I think he was half Indian, or maybe he was Eye-talian, but whatever he was, you wouldn't want to meet up with him on a dark night, I can tell you that."

Mrs. Threadgoode finished her candy corn and bit the head off one of her chocolate bunnies. She looked at it. "Sorry, mister." Then she said, "You know, Evelyn, I guess I'm the only one out here that's having myself two Easters. It may be a sin, but I won't tell anyone if you won't."

## THE WEEMS WEEKLY

(WHISTLE STOP, ALABAMA'S WEEKLY BULLETIN)

MARCH 28, 1940

## Famous Criminal Comes to Whistle Stop

Mr. Pinto, the famous murderer, passed through Whistle Stop on the 7:15 from Mobile. The train stopped for only ten minutes, and Stump Threadgoode and Peggy Hadley got a picture of the dead man, and when it is developed, Idgie will put it up in the cafe.

Idgie took her Cub Scout troop over to Birmingham, to Kiddyland Park, and then to the Five Points Theater to see *I Was a Fugitive from a Chain Gang,* which they all enjoyed.

Idgie says that she has a genuine shrunken head from headhunters in South America, and it is on the counter at the cafe, if you want to see it.

Is there anybody out there that can cure snoring? If so, come over to my house. My other half is about to drive me insane. I might send him out to the dogs.

Even one of his old hounds snores, just like he does. I told him the other day, it must run in the family. Ha. Ha.

The reward for Railroad Bill just went up again. Some people think he may be from around here. The big question is: Who is Railroad Bill? I would even suspect Wilbur, but he's too lazy to get up in the middle of the night.

The Elks Club named Rev. and Mrs. Scroggins's son, Bobby, Boy of the Year and we know they are proud.

. . . Dot Weems . . .

P.S. My other half came home from the Dill Pickle Club fishing trip without any fish again and with poison ivy to boot. He said it was Idgie's fault because she told him to sit there. Ruth said Idgie had a bad case of it too.

# WHISTLE STOP, ALABAMA

MARCH 25, 1940

Stump turned off all the lights in the back room and was lying on the floor by the radio, listening to "The Shadow." He was admiring the ring he had sent off for, the way it shone in the dark, and was waving his hand around, fascinated with the eerie green glow.

The man on the radio with the deep voice was saying, *"The weeds of crime bear . . . bitter fruit . . . crime does not pay . . ."* Followed by the maniacal laugh, *"Ha! ha! ha!!!"*

Just then, Idgie came in from the cafe and threw on the lights, nearly scaring him to death.

"Guess what, Stump? Grady just told me that Mr. Pinto is coming through here in the morning, on the seven-fifteen, on his way to be buried, and they're gonna change trains over at the yard."

Stump jumped up, his heart still pounding. "Mr. Pinto? The real Mr. Pinto?"

"Yes. Grady said he was only gonna be here for a few minutes, just long enough to put him on the other train. I'd go with you, but I've got to drive your mother over to Birmingham for this church thing she's got to go to. But if you want to see him,

Grady said you should be down there by six-thirty, and he said for you not to tell anyone, because everyone in town is likely to show up."

"Okay, I won't."

"And Stump, for God's sake, don't tell your mother I told you."

"Okay."

Since Stump had received a Brownie camera for his birthday, he asked Idgie if he could take a picture of Mr. Pinto.

"You're not gonna see anything but his coffin, but if you want a picture of it, I guess you can. Ask Grady first, do you hear me?"

"Yes ma'am."

He ran over to Peggy's house to impress her with this privileged information about Mr. Pinto, who had been captured only after a long and hard gun battle at a cabin in north Alabama, where three policemen had been shot. He had been apprehended with his girl friend, billed as Hazel, the Flame-Haired Murderess with the Heart of Steel, who had personally knocked off a lawman in Baldwin County. When he got the death sentence, headlines blazed all over Alabama: "MR. PINTO TO TAKE A SEAT IN 'BIG YELLOW MOMMA.'"

That was the name given to the huge iron electric chair down at Folsom Prison that had claimed hundreds of lives over the years. But this was something special.

When he got to the house, Dr. Hadley was sitting on the front glider and told Stump that Peggy was inside, helping her mother with the dishes. So he went in the backyard and waited.

When Peggy came out, Stump told her the news, and she was duly impressed, like he'd hoped she would be. Then he proceeded to give her instructions.

"In the morning, I'll come to this tree, right here, and I'll signal you like this . . ."

He then made a bobwhite bird whistle, three times.

"When you hear me, come on out, but be ready about five o'clock, because I want to be there in case the train is early."

The next morning, Peggy was already dressed and outside

waiting for him at the tree when he got there, a fact that irritated him because he liked the idea of a bird signal. He had gotten the idea out of a book he was reading at the time, *The Talking Sparrows Murder Mystery*. Besides, he had been up all night, practicing his bobwhite whistle; that is, until Idgie told him she would kill him if he didn't shut up.

That was the first thing that went wrong with the plan. The second was that the train was an hour late, so they had been at the railroad station for three hours now, waiting.

Stump must have loaded and unloaded his camera a hundred times, just to make sure it was in working order.

In another half hour, the big black train finally came rumbling on in and stopped. Grady and a crew of four railroad men came out of the switching house and pulled open the boxcar and lifted the large white-pine box in which the state had seen fit to ship Mr. Pinto.

The train rumbled off again, leaving the box on the loading platform, while the other men went to bring in the other train, and Grady stood guard, looking important in his khaki shirt and pants, with his leather gun-holster strapped to his side.

He saw Stump and Peggy running down the platform toward him and said, "Hi, kids!" and kicked the box. "Well, here he is, just like I told Idgie—Mr. Seymore Pinto, as big as life and as dead as they come."

Stump asked if he could take a picture.

"Sure, go right ahead."

Stump began taking pictures from every angle possible, while Grady reminisced about the time he had once been a guard at Kilbey Prison, in Atmore, Alabama.

Peggy, who was in charge of holding the extra rolls of film, asked him if he had ever seen any real murderers.

"Oh sure, lot's of them. Even had a couple working for me and Gladys up at the house when we lived in Atmore."

"You had real live murderers in your house?"

Grady looked at her, surprised. "Why sure. Why not? Some of your best people are murderers." He pushed his hat off his forehead and said sincerely, "Yes sir. I wouldn't give you nickel for a thief. Now, a murder is usually just a one-time thing—

mostly over some woman, not a repeat crime. But a thief is a thief until the day he dies."

Stump was already on his second roll of film, and Grady continued talking to a fascinated Peggy. "Naw, I don't mind murderers. Most of 'em are pretty mild-mannered, pleasant folks, as a rule."

Stump was snapping away, and threw in a question. "Did you ever see one of them electrocuted, Grady?"

He laughed. "Only about three hundred. . . . Now, *that's* a sight to see. Before they go to the Big Yellow Momma, they shave 'em as bald as a billiard, not an ounce of hair is left on their bodies, bald as the day they were born. Then they dip these sponges in cold salt water and put it under the cap. That water, there, conducts the electricity faster. Last one I saw fry, it took 'em seven tries. Everybody in Atmore was mad 'cause it interfered with the electricity in town and messed up their radio show. And then the doctor had to stick a needle in his heart to make sure that nigger was dead . . ."

Grady looked at his watch and said, "What the hell is taking them so long? I better go over there and see what they're doing," and he left them alone with the box.

Stump lost no time. "Help me pull this lid off, I want a picture of his face."

Peggy was horrified. "You cain't fool with that, it's a dead body! You have to honor the dead!"

"No we don't, he's a criminal, so it doesn't count. Move out of the way if you don't want to look."

Stump was busy opening the lid and Peggy went over and hid behind a post, saying, "You're gonna get in trouble." After he got the lid off, Stump just stood there, staring into the box. "Come here."

"No, I'm scared."

"Come here. You cain't see nothing, it's got a sheet over it."

Peggy walked over and very carefully peeked in at the body that was, in fact, all covered up.

Stump, desperate for time, said, "You've got to help me. I want you to pull the sheet off his face so I can get a picture."

"No, Stump, I don't want to look at him."

Stump did not really want to look at Mr. Pinto's face, either, but he was determined to get a picture of him, one way or another; and so he devised a plan on the spot that would save them both from having to look.

He handed her the camera, "Here, you point the camera right where his head is, and I'll count to three. You close your eyes and I'll count to three, pull the sheet back, you take the picture, and I'll cover him back up and you won't have to see him at all. Come on, please? Grady's gonna be back in a minute . . ."

"No, I'm scared to."

"Please . . . you're the only person in town I told he was gonna be here."

Peggy said reluctantly, "Well, all right, but don't you *dare* pull that sheet back until my eyes are closed. Do you promise me, Stump Threadgoode?"

Stump gave the Boy Scout signal for Truth and Honor. "I promise. Now, hurry."

Peggy aimed the shaking camera at the sheet-covered head. "Are you ready?"

"Yes."

"Okay. Now, close your eyes and when I count three, you take the picture and don't look until I tell you."

Peggy shut her eyes and so did Stump. He carefully lifted and pulled the sheet back and said, "Okay, one, two, three, *now!*"

Peggy snapped the picture on command, as planned, and Grady came up behind them and yelled in a loud voice, "HEY! WHAT ARE YOU KIDS DOING!"

They both opened their eyes with a jolt and stared right into the face of Mr. Seymore Pinto, still warm from The Big Yellow Momma.

Peggy screamed, dropped the camera in the coffin, and ran off in one direction—and Stump squealed like a girl and ran off in the other.

Mr. Pinto just lay there, burned to a crisp, with his mouth and eyes wide open, and if he'd had any hair left, it would have been standing straight up on his head.

Later that afternoon, Peggy was still in bed, under the covers, with Mr. Pinto's face looming before her, and Stump sat in the back room, in the closet, wearing his Lone Ranger glow-in-the-dark belt, still shaking, knowing he would never forget that man's face for as long as he lived.

Grady came into the cafe about six that night, and he brought Stump's camera back.

He laughed. "You're not gonna believe this," and told them what had happened, "but they broke that poor dead bastard's nose!"

Ruth was appalled. Smokey stared down in his coffee to keep from breaking up; and Idgie, who was taking a grape drink to the back door for her friend Ocie Smith, spilled it all over herself, she was laughing so hard.

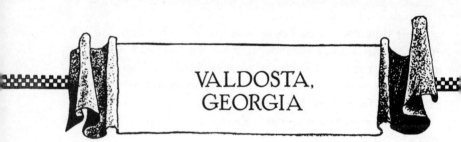

# VALDOSTA, GEORGIA

SEPTEMBER 30, 1924

When Frank Bennett was growing up, he had adored his mother, to the point that it had disgusted his father, a bull of a man who thought nothing of knocking Frank out of a chair or kicking him down the stairs. His mother had been the only softness and sweetness he had known as a child and he loved her with all of his heart.

When he came home from school early one day, with some feigned illness, and found his mother and his father's brother on the floor in the kitchen, all that love turned to hate in the five seconds before he screamed and ran out of the room: the five seconds that would haunt him for as long as he lived.

At thirty-four, Frank Bennett was a vain man. His black shoes were always shined to a high spit polish, his hair was always brushed, his clothes were perfect, and he was one of the few men who received a manicure at the barbershop every week.

You could say he was a dandy. You could say he was handsome, in a black Irish sort of way, with that head of thick hair and the steel-blue eyes; and although one was made of glass and the other was just as cold as shiny, it was hard to tell which was which.

But above all things, he was a man who got what he wanted, and he wanted Ruth Jamison. He'd had just about every available girl around, including, and preferring, the black girls he would take by force while his friends held them down. Once he had them, he was not one to want them again. One pale-blond woman, who lived on the outskirts of town now, had a little girl that looked like him, but after he had blackened her eyes and threatened her child, she no longer made any claims on him. It was clear he did not have much interest in used women. Particularly if he had been the one who'd used them.

But in town, he was known as a hale and hearty fellow, and he decided that he needed to have sons to carry on the Bennett name; a name that didn't mean anything to anybody, except that he was a man who owned a lot of land south of town.

Ruth was young, pretty, certainly untouched, and needed a place for herself and her mother. What could be better? Ruth was flattered; she couldn't help but be. Wasn't he the most eligible man around? Hadn't he courted her like a gentleman and charmed her mother?

Ruth had come to believe that this handsome young man loved her, and that she should and therefore did love him.

But who could have known that all the shiny shoes and flashy three-piece suits could never cover up the bitterness that had been growing in his heart all these years . . .

Certainly no one in town guessed; it took a complete stranger. On the night of Frank's bachelor party, he and a group of men had stopped by a bar for a few drinks, on the way to a cabin where three whores from Atlanta had been hired for the night. An old bum, passing through, had wandered into the bar, off the street, and was watching the party of young men from across the room. Frank did what he did to all strangers: He walked over to the man, who was obviously in need of a drink, and slapped him on the back. "I'll tell you what, old-timer, if you can tell me which one of these eyes of mine is glass, I'll buy you a drink."

His friends laughed because it was impossible to tell, but the old man looked at him and without a beat said, "The left."

His friends roared, and although Frank was taken aback, he laughed it off as luck and threw a half dollar on the bar.

The bartender watched the party of men leave, and then said to the old man, "What'll it be, mister?"

"Whiskey."

He poured the old man his shot. A little later, the bartender said, "Hey, old friend, how were you able to tell his left eye was glass right off the bat like that?"

The old man drank his whiskey and said, "Easy. The left one was the only one with even a glimmer of human compassion in it."

# VALDOSTA, GEORGIA

APRIL 28, 1926

Idgie, who was now nineteen, had driven over to Valdosta almost every month for over two and a half years to watch Ruth going to and from church. She just wanted to make sure she was all right, and Ruth never knew she'd been there.

Then one Sunday, quite unexpectedly, she drove up to Ruth's house and went to the front door and knocked. Idgie herself had not known she was going to do it.

Ruth's mother, a frail woman, came to the door, smiling. "Yes?"

"Is Ruth home?"

"She's upstairs."

"Would you tell her that a bee charmer from Alabama is here to see her?"

"Who?"

"Just tell her that a friend of hers from Alabama is here."

"Oh, won't you come in?"

"No, that's all right. I'll just wait out here."

Ruth's mother went in and called up the stairs, "Ruth, there is some kind of a bee person here to see you."

"What?"

"You've got company on the porch."

When Ruth came down, she was taken completely by surprise. She walked out on the porch and Idgie, who was trying to act casual even though her palms were sweaty and she could feel her ears burning, said, "Look, I don't want to bother you. I know you're probably very happy and all . . . I mean, I'm sure you are, but I just wanted you to know that I don't hate you and I never did. I still want you to come back and I'm not a kid anymore, so I'm not gonna change. I still love you and I always will and I still don't care what anybody thinks—"

Frank called down from the bedroom, "Who is it?"

Idgie started backing down the porch stairs. "I just wanted you to know that—well, I gotta go."

Ruth, who had not said a word, watched her get into the car and drive off.

There had not been a day when Ruth had not thought about her.

Frank came down the stairs and out on the porch. "Who was that?"

Ruth, still watching the car that was now a black dot down the road, said, "Just a friend of mine, someone I used to know," and walked back into the house.

ROSE TERRACE
NURSING HOME

OLD MONTGOMERY HIGHWAY
BIRMINGHAM, ALABAMA

APRIL 6, 1986

Mrs. Threadgoode started talking the minute Evelyn set one foot in the room.

"Well, honey, Vesta Adcock has lost it. She came into our room about four o'clock this afternoon and grabbed up this little milk-glass slipper that Mrs. Otis keeps her hairpins in, and said, 'The Lord said if the eye offends thee, pluck it out,' and with that, she slung it out the window, hairpins and all, and then she left.

"It upset Mrs. Otis something awful. After a while, that little colored nurse, Geneene, came in with Mrs. Otis's slipper she had gotten out of the yard and told her not to be upset, that Mrs. Adcock had been throwing stuff out of everybody's room all day . . . said Mrs. Adcock was as crazy as a betsy bug and not to pay attention to her.

"I tell you, I'm lucky to have the mind I do have, with all that's going on out here . . . I'm just living from day to day. Just doing the best I can, and that's all I can do."

Evelyn handed her the box of chocolate-covered cherries.

"Oh thank you, honey, aren't you sweet." She sat there eating for a moment, pondering a question.

"Do you reckon betsy bugs are crazy, or do people just think they are?"

Evelyn said she didn't know.

"Well, I know where the expression *cute as a bug* comes from, because I happen to think there is nothing cuter than a bug . . . do you?"

"What?"

"Think there's anything cuter than a bug?"

"I cain't say I've looked at too many bugs to know if they're cute or not."

"Well, I have! Albert and I would spend hours and hours looking at them. Cleo had this big magnifying glass on his desk, and we'd find centipedes and grasshoppers and beatles and potato bugs, ants . . . and put them in a jar and look at them. They have the sweetest little faces and the cutest expressions. After we'd looked at them all we wanted to, we'd put them in the yard and let them go on about their business.

"One time, Cleo caught a bumblebee and put it in the jar for us, and he was a precious thing to look at. Idgie loved bees, but my favorite is the ladybug. That's a lucky bug. Every bug has a different personality, you know. Spiders are kind of nervous and grumpy, with teeny heads. And I always liked the praying mantis. He's a very religious bug.

"I could never kill a bug, not after seeing them up close like that. I believe they have thoughts, just like us. Of course, that has its bad side. My snowballs around my house were all dog-eared and eaten up. And all my gardenia bushes are chewed down to the nub. Norris said he wanted to come over there and spray, but I didn't have the heart to let him do it. I'll tell you one thing, a bug wouldn't stand a chance at Rose Terrace. A germ would be hard pressed to survive in this place. Their motto here is: 'It's not enough to look clean, it's got to be clean.' Sometimes I feel like I'm living in one of those cellophane sandwich bags, like the ones they used to sell on the trains.

"As for me, I'll be glad to get home to my nasty old bugs. Even an ant would be a welcome sight. I'll tell you one thing, honey, I'm glad I'm on the going-out end, instead of coming-in . . . 'My Father's house has many mansions and I'm ready to go.' . . .

"The only thing I ask is, please, Lord, get rid of all the lineoleum floors before I get there."

# WHISTLE STOP, ALABAMA

OCTOBER 17, 1940

When Vesta Adcock was younger, someone had told her to speak up, and she never forgot it. You could hear Vesta through brick walls. The booming voice from that little woman traveled for blocks.

Cleo Threadgoode made the remark that it was a shame that Earl Adcock had to pay his telephone bills since Vesta could just as well have opened the door and aimed at whoever's house she was calling.

Considering that, and the fact that she had appointed herself president of the "I'm Better Than Anyone Else Club," it was not surprising that Earl did what he did.

Earl Adcock was a quiet, decent man who had always done the right thing—one of the unsung heroes of life who had married the girl just because she had picked him out and he didn't want to hurt her feelings. And so he had just remained quiet while Vesta and his mother-in-law-to-be had arranged everything from the wedding to the honeymoon to where they would live.

After the one child, Earl Jr., had been born, a soft, pudgy, pasty little boy with brown ringlets who screamed for his mother whenever his father got near him, Earl realized he had made a big mistake, but he did the gentlemanly, manly thing: He stayed married and raised this son, who lived in the same house, had the same blood, but was a stranger to him.

Earl was in charge of over two hundred men down at L & N Railroad, where he worked, and commanded great respect and was extremely capable. He had served bravely in the First World War, killing two Germans, but in his own home he had been reduced to just another child of Vesta's, and not even a favorite child: He came in second to Earl Jr.

"WIPE YOUR FEET BEFORE YOU COME IN HERE! DON'T SIT IN THAT CHAIR!"

"HOW DARE YOU SMOKE IN MY HOUSE . . . GO OUT ON THE PORCH!"

"YOU CAIN'T BRING THOSE NASTY FISH IN HERE. TAKE THEM OUT IN THE BACKYARD AND CLEAN THEM!"

"EITHER YOU GET RID OF THOSE DOGS OR I'M TAKING THE BABY AND LEAVING!"

"MY GOD, IS THAT ALL YOU HAVE ON YOUR MIND? YOU MEN ARE NOTHING BUT A BUNCH OF ANIMALS!"

She picked out his clothes, she picked out their friends, and flew at him like an enraged wild turkey the few times that he had tried to swat little Earl; eventually, he gave up.

Thus, throughout the years, Earl had worn the correct blue suit, carved the meat, gone to church, been the husband and father, and never said one word against Vesta. But Earl Jr. was grown now, and the L & N had retired him with a nice pension that he immediately signed over to Vesta, and had given him a gold Rockford railroad watch. And so, as quietly as he had lived, he slipped out of town, leaving only a note behind:

Well, that's that. I'm off, and if you don't believe I'm leaving, just count the days I'm gone. When you hear the phone not ringing, it'll be me that's not calling.

Goodbye, old girl, and good luck.

Yours truly,
Earl Adcock

P.S. I'm not deaf.

Vesta smacked a surprised Earl Jr. in the face and went to bed for a week with a cold rag on her head, while everyone in town secretly cheered Earl on. If good wishes had been ten-dollar bills, he would have left a rich man.

OCTOBER 18, 1940

## Warning to Wives

It's that time of the year again, and my other half is chomping at the bit to get out with the gang and hunt. He's been cleaning his guns and fooling with his old hounds and doing everything short of baying at the moon. So, get ready to say goodbye to the boys for a while. Nothing that moves is safe . . . Remember last year, when Jack Butts shot a hole in the bottom of the rowboat? Idgie said they all sunk to the bottom of the lake while ten flocks of ducks flew right over their heads.

Congratulations to Stump Threadgoode for winning the first prize at the school Science Fair, with his project, "The Lima Bean . . . What Is It?"

Second prize went to Vernon Hadley, whose project was "Experimenting with Soap."

Idgie has a big jar of dried lima beans on the counter, down at the cafe, and says anyone who guesses how many lima beans are in the jar gets a prize.

The photograph of Mr. Pinto did not turn out as well as expected, and is just a blur.

Ruth said to tell everybody that she has thrown the shrunken head out, because it was making people sick to see it on the counter while they were trying to eat. Ruth said it was nothing but a rubber head that Idgie had bought at the Magic Shop in Birmingham, anyway.

By the way, my other half says that somebody asked us over for supper, but he can't remember who it was. So, whoever asked us, we will be happy to come, just call me and let me know.

. . . Dot Weems . . .

P.S. Opal says again to please stop feeding Boots.

# VALDOSTA, GEORGIA

## AUGUST 4, 1928

It had been two years since Idgie had seen Ruth, but every once in a while, Idgie went over to Valdosta on Wednesdays, because that was the day that Frank Bennett would come into town and go to the barbershop. She would usually hang around Puckett's Drug Store, because she had a good view of the front door of the barbershop and could see Frank sitting in the barber's chair.

She wished she could hear what he was saying, but it was enough just to see him. He was her only link to Ruth, and as long as she saw him, she knew that Ruth was still there.

This Wednesday, Mrs. Puckett, the thin little old lady in black-framed glasses, was busy as usual, moving around the store, arranging things as if life depended on everything being neat and in its place.

Idgie was sitting at the counter, looking across the street; watching.

"That Frank Bennett sure does talk a lot, doesn't he? A real friendly fella, huh?"

Mrs. Puckett was on the first step of a ladder, arranging jars of Stillman's Freckle Cream, her back to Idgie. "Some might say so, I guess."

Idgie heard a strange tone in her voice.

"What do you mean?"

"I just said, some may think so, that's all." She came down off the stepladder.

"Don't you think so?"

"It doesn't matter what I think."

"Don't you think he's friendly?"

"I didn't say I didn't think he was friendly, did I? I guess he's friendly enough."

Mrs. Puckett was now poking at the boxes of Carter's Liver Pills on the counter. Idgie got off the stool and went over to her.

"What do you mean, friendly enough? Do you know something about him? Has he ever not been friendly?"

"No, he's always pleasant enough," she said, arranging the boxes in a row. "It's just that I don't like any man that'll beat his wife."

Idgie's heart went cold.

"What do you mean?"

"Just what I said."

"How do you know that?"

Mrs. Puckett was now busy restacking the tins of toothpaste. "Oh, Mr. Puckett's had to go out there and take that poor little thing medicine—more than once, I'll tell you. He's blackened her eye and knocked her down the stairs, and once, he broke her arm. She teaches Sunday School and you never met a nicer person." She moved on to torment the Sal Hepatica bottles. "That's what liquor will do to a man, make them do crazy things they wouldn't ordinarily do. Mr. Puckett and I are Temperance, ourselves . . ."

Idgie was out the door and didn't hear the last sentence.

The barber was brushing off the back of Frank's neck with sweet-smelling talcum powder when Idgie burst into the shop. She was in a rage. She stuck her finger in Frank's face. "LISTEN, YOU MEALY-MOUTHED, MOLE-FACED, GLASS-EYED SON OF A BITCHING BASTARD! IF YOU EVER HIT

RUTH AGAIN, I'LL KILL YOU! YOU BASTARD! I SWEAR I'LL CUT YOUR DAMN HEART OUT! YOU HEAR ME, YOU ASSHOLE BASTARD!"

And with that, she took her arm and knocked everything off the marble counter. Dozens of bottles of shampoo, hair tonics, hair oils, shaving lotions, and powders crashed to the floor. Before they knew what had hit them, Idgie was back in her car, screeching out of town.

The barber stood there with his mouth open. It had happened so fast. He looked at Frank in the mirror and said, "That boy must be crazy."

The minute Idgie got home to the Wagon Wheel Fishing Camp, she told Eva what had happened, and was still in a rage, vowing that she was going back over there and get him.

Eva listened carefully. "You're gonna go over there and get yourself killed, is what you're gonna do. Now, you cain't go interfering with somebody's marriage, that's their business. Honey, there are things between a man and a woman that you don't go fooling with."

Poor Idgie was in agony and asked Eva, "Why does she stay with him? What's the matter with her?"

"That's not any of your business. Now honey, you have to forget all about it. She is a grown woman and she is doing what she wants, as much as you don't like to hear it. You're still a baby, sugar, and if that man is as mean as you say, you could get yourself hurt."

"I don't care what you say, Eva, I'm gonna kill that son of a bitch someday, you wait and see."

Eva poured Idgie another drink. "No you're not. You're not gonna kill anyone and you're not going back over there. You promise?"

Idgie promised. Both of them knew she was lying.

APRIL 27, 1986

Mrs. Threadgoode was especially happy today because she had fried chicken and coleslaw on a paper plate, and Evelyn was down the hall at this very minute, getting her a grape drink to go with it.

"Oh thank you, honey. You're spoiling me, bringing me all these treats each week. I told Mrs. Otis, I said that Evelyn couldn't be any sweeter to me if she was my own daughter . . . and I appreciate it so much—I never had a daughter of my own. . . . Does your mother-in-law enjoy good things to eat?"

Evelyn said, "No, not at all. I brought her some chicken, but she didn't want it. She or Ed could care less about food, they just eat to keep alive. Can you imagine?"

Mrs. Threadgoode said she certainly could not imagine such a thing.

Evelyn started her off. "Now, Ruth left Whistle Stop and went off to Valdosta to get married . . ."

"That's right. Oh, and it liked to have killed Idgie. She pitched such a fit."

"I know, you told me about that. But what I want to know is, when did Ruth come back to Whistle Stop?"

Evelyn settled in her chair, ate her chicken, and listened.

"Oh yes, honey, I remember the very day that letter came. It must have been in 'twenty-eight or 'twenty-nine. Or was it 'thirty? Oh well. . . . I was in the kitchen with Sipsey when Momma came running back in with it in her hand. She threw open the back door and hollered for Big George, who was out in the garden with Jasper and Artis. She said, 'George, go get Idgie right away and tell her she's got a letter from Miss Ruth!'

"George took off running to get her. About an hour later, Idgie came into the kitchen. Momma, who was shelling peas at the time, just pointed to the letter on the table, without a word. Idgie opened it, but the funny thing was, it wasn't a letter at all.

"It was just a page torn out of the Bible, King James Version. Ruth 1:16–20:

And Ruth said, Intreat me not to leave thee, *or* to return from following after thee: for whither thou goest, I will go; and where thou lodgest, I will lodge: thy people *shall be* my people, and thy God my God.

"Idgie just stood there, reading that quotation over and over and then she handed it to Momma and asked her what she thought it meant.

"Momma read it, put it down on the table, and continued shelling her peas. She said, 'Well, honey, it means just what it says. I think tomorrow you and your brothers and Big George better go over there and get that girl, don't you? You know you're not going to be fit to live with till you do. You know that.'

"And it was true. She wouldn't have been.

"So the next day, they went over to Georgia and got her.

"I admired Ruth for having the courage to walk away like that. It took real courage in those days, not like today, honey. Back then, if you were married, you stayed married. But she was a lot stronger than people knew. Everybody was always treating Ruth like a china doll, but you know, she was a lot stronger than Idgie in many ways."

"Did Ruth ever get a divorce?"

"Oh, I don't know that. That's something I never asked. I just figured that was Ruth's business. I never met her husband, but they say that he was handsome, all except that glass eye. Ruth told me he had come from a nice family, but just had a mean streak where women were concerned. Said on their wedding night, he got drunk and forced her, while the whole time she was begging him to stop."

"How awful."

"Yes, it was. She bled for three days, and after that, she never could relax and enjoy herself. And, of course, that just made him madder. And she said he kicked her down a flight of stairs once."

"Good Lord!"

"Then he started forcing himself on the poor colored girls he had working for him. Ruth said one little girl was only twelve years old. But by the time she found out what kind of a man he was, it was too late. Ruth's mother was sick, and she couldn't leave. She said that on the nights he would come home mean and drunk and force her, she'd lie there and pray to God and think about us to keep herself from going crazy."

Evelyn said, "They say you never know a man until you live with him."

"That's right. Sipsey used to say, 'You never know what kind of fish you've got till you pull it out of the water'—so it's best that Stump never met his daddy. Ruth left before he was born. As a matter of fact, she didn't even know she was pregnant at the time. She'd been over there with Idgie about two months before she noticed that her stomach was just a-pooching out. Went to the doctor and found out she was expecting. He was born over at the big house, and he was the cutest little blond baby, weighed seven pounds and had brown eyes and blond hair.

"Momma said, the first time she saw him, 'Oh look, Idgie, he's got your hair!'

"And he did. He was just as blond as could be. That's when Poppa Threadgoode sat Idgie down and told her that now that she was going to be responsible for Ruth and a baby, she'd better figure out what she wanted to do, and gave her five hundred dollars to start a business with. That's what she bought the cafe with."

Evelyn asked if Frank Bennett had known he had a child.

"I don't know if he did or not."

"He never saw her at all after she left Georgia?"

"Well, I cain't say for a fact if he ever did or not, but one thing's for sure, he came over to Whistle Stop at least once, and it may have been one time too many, as far as he was concerned."

"Why do you say that?"

" 'Cause he was the one that was murdered."

"Murdered!"

"Oh yes, honey. Deader than a doornail."

### SEPTEMBER 18, 1928

When Ruth had gone home that summer to marry, Frank Bennett and her mother had been at the station to meet her. Ruth had forgotten how handsome he was and how happy it had made her mother that she had made such an important catch.

Almost immediately, the parties started, and she tried to shut out any thoughts of Whistle Stop. But sometimes, in the middle of a crowd or alone at night, she never knew when it was going to happen, Idgie would suddenly come to mind, and she would want to see her so bad that the pain of longing for her sometimes took her breath away.

Whenever it happened, she would pray to God and beg Him to take such thoughts out of her head. She knew that she must be where she should be and doing the right thing. She would get over missing Idgie. Surely, He would help her . . . surely, this feeling would pass in time . . . with His help, she would make it pass.

She had gone to her wedding bed determined to be a good, loving wife, no matter what, holding nothing back. That's why it had been such a shock when he had taken her with so much violence—almost as if he were punishing her. After he was finished, she lay there in her own blood and he got up and went into the other room to sleep. He never came back to her bed unless he wanted sex; and then, nine times out of ten, it had been because he was too drunk or too lazy to go into town.

Ruth couldn't help but think that something inside of her had caused him to hate her; that somehow, no matter how hard she tried to suppress it, Frank felt the love inside she had for Idgie. It had slipped out somehow, in her voice, her touch; she didn't know how, but she believed he must have known and that's why he despised her. So she had lived with that guilt and taken the beatings and the insults because she thought she deserved them.

The doctor came out of her mother's room. "Mrs. Bennett, she's started to talk a little, you might want to go in for a while."

Ruth went in and sat down.

Her mother, who hadn't spoken in a week, opened her eyes and saw her daughter. She whispered, "You get away from him. . . . Ruth, promise me. He's the devil. I've seen God, and he's the devil. I hear things, Ruth . . . you get away . . . promise me . . ."

It was the first time this shy woman had ever said anything about Frank. Ruth nodded and held her hand. That afternoon, the doctor closed her mother's eyes for good.

Ruth cried for her mother and, an hour later, went upstairs, washed her face, and addressed the envelope to Idgie.

After she sealed it, she went over to the window and looked up at the blue sky. She took a deep breath of fresh air and felt her heart rising like a kite that some child had just released to the heavens.

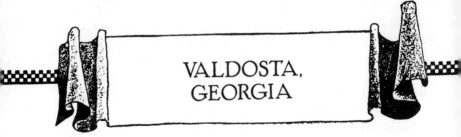

# VALDOSTA, GEORGIA

## SEPTEMBER 21, 1928

A car and a truck pulled up in front of the house. Big George and Idgie were in the truck; Cleo and Julian and two of their friends, Wilbur Weems and Billy Limeway, were in the Model T.

Ruth, who had been dressed and waiting since early that morning, hoping they would come today, stepped out the door.

The boys and Big George got out and waited in the yard, and Idgie went up on the front porch.

Ruth looked at her and said, "I'm ready."

Frank had been taking a nap when he heard them driving up. He came down the stairs and recognized Idgie through the screen.

"What the hell are you doing here?"

He threw open the door and was heading for her when he saw the five men standing in the yard.

Idgie, who had not taken her eyes off Ruth, said quietly, "Where's your trunk?"

"Upstairs."

Idgie called to Cleo, "It's upstairs."

As four men marched by him, Frank spluttered, "What the hell's going on?"

Julian, the last one, said, "I think your wife's leaving you, mister."

Ruth had gotten into the truck with Idgie, and Frank started toward them when he saw Big George, who was leaning against the truck, calmly pull a knife out of his pocket and core the apple he had in his hand with one swift movement, and throw it over his shoulder.

Julian yelled down from the top of the stairs, "I wouldn't get that nigger mad, mister. He's crazy!"

Ruth's trunk was in the back of the truck, and they were headed down the driveway before Frank knew what had happened. But as an afterthought, and for the benefit of Jake Box, his hired hand, who had witnessed the exit, Frank Bennett screamed at the dust the cars had stirred up, "And don't you come back, you frigid bitch! You whore! You coldhearted whore!"

The next day, he went into town and told everyone that Ruth had gone completely out of her mind with grief after her mother died. He had been forced to have her committed to an insane asylum, outside of Atlanta.

# WHISTLE STOP, ALABAMA

SEPTEMBER 21, 1928

Momma and Poppa Threadgoode were on the front porch waiting. Momma and Sipsey had been fixing up Ruth's room all morning, and now Sipsey was in the kitchen with Ninny, baking biscuits for supper.

"Now, Alice, don't jump at her and scare her off. Just be calm and wait and see. Don't make her think she has to stay. Don't put any pressure on her."

Momma was fidgeting with her handkerchief and pulling at her hair, a sure sign that she was nervous. "I won't, Poppa. I'll just say how glad we are to see her . . . that's all right, isn't it? Let her know she's welcome? You're going to say how glad you are to see her, aren't you?"

"Of course I will," Poppa said. "But I just don't want you getting your hopes up too much, that's all."

After a minute of silence, he asked, "Alice . . . do you think she'll stay?"

"I pray to the Lord she does."

At that moment, the truck, with Ruth and Idgie, turned the corner.

Poppa said, "They're here! Ninny and Sipsey, they're here!"

Momma jumped up and flew down the front steps, with Poppa right behind her.

When they saw Ruth get out of the car and how thin and weary she looked, they forgot their plan and grabbed her and hugged her, both talking to her at the same time.

"I'm so glad you're home, honey. We're not gonna let you run off from us this time."

"We got your old room ready, and Sipsey and Ninny have been cooking all morning."

As they walked Ruth up the stairs, Momma turned and looked back down at Idgie.

"You better behave yourself this time, young lady! Do you hear me?"

Idgie looked baffled and said to herself as she followed them inside, "What'd I do?"

After supper, Ruth went into the parlor with Momma and Poppa and closed the door. She sat across from them with her hands in her lap, and began, "I don't have any money, I really don't have anything but my clothes. But I can work. I want you both to know that I'll never leave again. I should never have left her four years ago, I know that now. But I'm going to try and make it up to her and never hurt her again. You have my word on that."

Poppa, who was embarrassed at any sort of sentiment, shifted in his chair. "Well, I hope you're aware of what you're in for. Idgie's a handful, you know."

Momma shushed him. "Oh Poppa, Ruth knows that. Don't you, dear? It's just that she has a wild streak . . . Sipsey says it's because I ate wild game when I was carrying Idgie. Remember, Poppa, you and the boys brought home some quail and wild turkeys that year?"

"Mother, you have eaten wild game every year of your life."

"Well, that's true, too. Anyhow, that's beside the point. Poppa and I just want you to know that we think of you as one of the family now, and we couldn't be happier for our little girl to have such a sweet companion as you."

Ruth got up and kissed both of them and went outside, where Idgie was waiting in the backyard, lying in the grass, listening to crickets, and wondering why she felt so drunk when she had not had a drop to drink.

After Ruth left the room, Poppa said, "See, I told you you didn't have anything to worry about."

"Me? You were the one who was worried, Poppa, not me," Momma said, and went back to her needlework.

The next day, Ruth changed her name back to Jamison and Idgie went all over town and told everybody about poor Ruth's husband, how a Brinks armored truck had turned over on him and squashed him to death. At first, Ruth was horrified that Idgie had told such a lie, but later, after the baby was born, she was glad she had.

# THE WEEMS WEEKLY

(WHISTLE STOP, ALABAMA'S WEEKLY BULLETIN)

AUGUST 31, 1940

## Yard Man Run Over by Car

Vesta Adcock ran over her colored yard man, Jesse Thiggins, on her way to her Eastern Star meeting on Tuesday. Jesse had been napping under a tree when Vesta made a turn around in her front yard and the wheel rolled over his head and pushed it into the mud. When she heard him holler, she stopped the car on his chest and got out to see who it was. Some neighbors nearby came running over and picked the car up off of him.

Grady Kilgore came over and said thank God it had been raining a lot lately, because if it had not been for the mud, Jesse might have been killed, being run over like that.

At this report, Jesse is fine except for the tire marks, but Vesta said that he should not have been napping, because she pays him good money.

I guess by now most of you know that fool of a

husband of mine burned down our garage the other day. He was so busy trying to fix the radio, so he and his railroad gang could listen to the baseball game, that he threw his cigarette on my pile of *Ladies' Home Companions* that I'd been saving, and it was down to the ground in minutes. My other half was so busy trying to save his precious buzz saw I got him for his birthday that he forgot to back the car out.

I didn't feel so bad about the car as I did my magazines. The car didn't run anyhow.

Essie Rue's little boy, whose size has earned him the name of Pee Wee, won the $10 prize in the lima bean contest. His guess was 83 lima beans off, but Idgie says he was the closest.

By the way, Boots died and Opal says she hopes you're satisfied.

. . . Dot Weems . . .

# WHISTLE STOP CAFE

WHISTLE STOP, ALABAMA

## NOVEMBER 22, 1930

It was a cold, crystal-clear day outside, and inside it was almost time for one of their radio programs to come on. Grady Kilgore was just finishing his second cup of coffee, and Sipsey, who was sweeping up the cigarette butts left over from the breakfast crowd, was the first one to see them out the window.

Quietly, two black pickup trucks had parked in front of the cafe and about twelve members of the Klan, dressed in full regalia, had slowly but deliberately gotten out and lined up outside the cafe.

Sipsey said, "Oh Lord, here dey is . . . I knowed it, I just knowed it."

Ruth, who was working behind the counter, asked Sipsey, "What is it?" and then went over to look for herself.

The minute she saw them, she called back, "Onzell, lock the back door and bring me the baby."

The men were just standing there on the sidewalk, facing the front of the cafe like white statues. One had a sign that had written on it, in bloodred letters: BEWARE OF THE INVISIBLE EMPIRE . . . THE TORCH AND THE ROPE ARE HUNGRY.

Grady Kilgore stood up and went over, looked out and

picked his teeth with a toothpick while he scrutinized the men in the pointed hoods.

The radio announcer said, "And now, to the many friends who wait for him, we present, 'Just Plain Bill, Barber of Har-ville' . . . the story of a man who might be living right next door to you . . ."

Idgie, who had been in the bathroom, came out and saw everybody looking out of the window.

"What's going on?"

Ruth said, "Come here, Idgie."

Idgie looked out. "Oh shit!"

Onzell handed Ruth the baby and did not leave her side.

Idgie said to Grady, "What the hell is this all about?"

Grady, who was still picking his teeth, said with certainty, "Them's not our boys."

"Well, who are they?"

Grady dropped his nickel on the table. "You stay here. I'm gonna damn well find out."

Sipsey was over in the corner with her broom, muttering to nobody, "I ain't scared of no white men's ghosties. No suh."

Grady went out and talked to a couple of the men. After a few minutes, one man nodded and said something to the others, and one by one, the men began to leave, as quietly as they had come.

Ruth couldn't be sure, but it seemed to her that one of the men had been staring right at her and the baby. Then she remembered something that Idgie had once said, and she looked down at the man's shoes as he was climbing into the truck. When she saw the shiny, black-polished shoes, she was suddenly terrified.

Grady came back into the cafe, unconcerned. "They didn't want nothing. They was just a bunch of old boys out to throw a little scare in you, that's all. One of them was over here the other day for something or another and saw you was selling to niggers out the back door and thought he'd try to shake you up a little bit. That's all."

Idgie asked him what he had said to get them to leave so fast.

Grady got his hat off the hat rack, "Oh, I just told them that these are our niggers and we sure as hell don't need a bunch from Georgia coming over here telling us what we can and cain't do."

He looked Idgie right in the eye. "And I'll guaran-damn-tee you they won't be back," and he put his hat on and left.

Even though Grady was a charter member of the Dill Pickle Club and a confirmed liar, that day he had told the truth. What Idgie and Ruth didn't know was that although these Georgia boys were mean, they were not stupid enough to ever fool around with the Klan in Alabama and were smart enough to leave in a hurry and stay gone.

That's why when Frank Bennett did come back, he came alone . . . and he came at night.

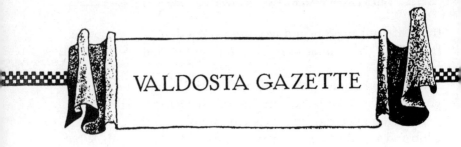

VALDOSTA GAZETTE

DECEMBER 15, 1930

## Local Man Missing

Frank Bennett, 38, lifelong resident of Valdosta, was reported missing today by his younger brother, Gerald, after Jake Box, an employee of the elder Bennett, informed him of Bennett's failure to return home from a hunting trip.

He was last seen on the morning of December 13, when he left home and told Mr. Box that he would be returning that evening. Anyone having any information as to his whereabouts is asked to please inform the local authorities.

# WHISTLE STOP, ALABAMA

### DECEMBER 18, 1930

It was another ice-cold Alabama afternoon, and the hogs were boiling in the big iron pot out in back of the cafe. The pot was bubbling over the top, full of long-gone hogs that would soon be smothered with Big George's special barbecue sauce.

Big George was standing by the pot with Artis, when he looked up and saw three men with guns strapped to their sides walking toward him.

Grady Kilgore, the local sheriff and part-time railroad detective, usually called him George. Today, he was showing off in front of the other two men, "Hey, boy! Come here and take a look at this." He held out a photograph. "You seen this man around here?"

Artis, whose job it was to stir the pot with a long stick, began to sweat.

Big George looked at the picture of the white man in the derby hat and shook his head. "No suh . . . I shore ain't," and handed it back to Grady.

One of the other men walked over and looked in the pot at the pink and white hogs bobbing up and down like a carousel.

Grady put the photograph back in his vest pocket, his official duty over, and said, "Hey, when are we gonna get some of that barbecue, Big George?"

Big George looked in the pot and studied it a moment. "You come 'round 'bout noon tomorrah . . . yes suh, 'bout noon it's gonna be ready."

"You save us some, y'hear?"

Big George smiled. "Yes suh, I will, I shore 'nuff will."

As the men headed to the cafe, Grady bragged to the others. "That nigger makes the best goddamned barbecue in the state. You've gotta get yourselves some of that, then you'll know what good barbecue is. I don't think you Georgia boys know what good barbecue is."

Smokey and Idgie were sitting in the cafe, smoking cigarettes and drinking coffee. Grady came in and put his hat on the rack by the door and walked over to where they were sitting.

"Idgie, Smokey, meet Officer Curtis Smoote and Officer Wendell Riggins. They're over here from Georgia, looking for a fella."

They all nodded hello and sat down.

Idgie said, "What can I get you boys? How 'bout some coffee?"

They all agreed that would be fine.

Idgie hollered to the kitchen, "Sipsey!"

Sipsey stuck her head out of the kitchen door.

"Sipsey, we need three coffees."

Then she said to them, "How 'bout some pie?"

Grady said, "Naw, we better not, we're here on official business."

The younger, heavier-set man seemed disappointed.

"These two boys are over here lookin' for a fella, and I've agreed to cooperate." He had only agreed to cooperate if he could be in charge of the photograph.

He cleared his throat and pulled the picture out, trying to look important and nonchalant at the same time. "Has either one of you seen this man, here, in the past couple of days?"

Idgie looked at it, said, no, she had not seen him, and passed it on to Smokey.

"What's he done?"

Sipsey brought the coffee, and Curtis Smoote, the wiry, skinny one with the neck that looked like a wrinkled arm sticking out of a white shirt, said in a high-pitched, tight little voice, "He ain't done nothing that we know of. We're trying to find out what's been did to him."

Smokey handed the picture back. "Naw, I ain't never see'd him. What you looking for him over here for?"

"He told some old boy who worked for him, over in Georgia, that he was coming over here, a couple of days ago, and he never did come back home."

Smokey asked whereabouts in Georgia.

"Valdosta."

"Well, I wonder what he was a-coming over here for." Smokey said.

Idgie turned around and called out to the kitchen, "Sipsey, bring us a couple of pieces of that chocolate pie, out here." Then she said to Officer Riggins, "I want you to try a piece of this for me. Tell me what you think. We just made it a few minutes ago, have a piece on me."

Officer Riggins protested, "No, I couldn't really, I . . ."

Idgie said, "Oh, come on, just a bite. I need an expert opinion."

"Well, okay, just a bite then."

The skinny one squinted at Idgie. "I told these boys that he most likely is on a drunk somewhere and gonna show up in the next day or so. What I cain't figure out is what he was coming over here for. There ain't nothing here . . ."

Wendell said, between bites, "We figure maybe he had a girl friend around here, or something."

Grady exploded with laughter. "Hell, ain't no woman in Whistle Stop that somebody would come all the way from Georgia for!" Then he paused. "Except maybe Eva Bates."

Then all three of them laughed, and Smokey, who also had had the pleasure of knowing Eva in the biblical sense, said, "That's the God's truth."

Grady started in on the other piece of pie, still amused at his own joke. But the skinny man was serious, and he leaned over the table to Grady.

"Who's Eva Bates?"

"Oh, she's just an old redheaded gal that runs a joint over by the river," Grady said. "A friend of ours."

"You think this Eva woman might be the one he came over for?"

Grady, eating his pie, glanced over at the photo on the table and dismissed the thought. "Naw. Not in a million years."

The skinny one persisted. "Why not?"

"Well, for one thing, he ain't her type."

They all three laughed again.

Wendell Riggins chuckled along with them, although he didn't know why.

Officer Smoote said, "What do you mean, not her type?"

Grady put his fork down. "Now, I don't want to hurt your feelings or nothing, and I don't even know this old boy in the picture here, but he looks a little sissified to me. Wouldn't you say so, Smokey?"

Smokey agreed.

"Naw, the truth is, boys, Eva would take one look at him and throw him back in the water."

They all laughed again.

Smoote said, "Well, I guess you know what you're talking about," and squinted his eyes at Idgie again.

"Yeah, well, that's just the facts of life!" Grady continued. He winked at Idgie and Smokey. "From what I hear, all you boys over in Georgia is a little light on your feet."

Smokey sat there giggling. "That's the way I heard it."

Grady leaned back in his chair and patted his stomach. "Well, I guess we better head on out of here. We got a few more stops to make before dark," and put the picture back in his pocket.

As they all got up to go, Officer Riggins said, "Thanks for the pie, Mrs. . . ."

"Idgie."

"Mrs. Idgie, it sure was delicious, thank you again."

"You're welcome."

Grady got his hat. "You're gonna see them again. I'm gonna bring 'em back tomorrow for some barbecue."

"Good. Be happy to see you."

Grady looked around to the back. "By the way, where's Ruth?"

"She's over at Momma's house. Momma's been real sick."

Grady said, "Yeah, that's what I heard. I'm real sorry to hear that. Well, see you tomorrow."

And they headed out the door.

Although it was only four-thirty in the afternoon, the sky was already a gunmetal gray, with silver streaks shooting across the north, and the winter rain that had just started was as thin and cold as ice water. Next door, the windows of Opal's beauty shop had already been decorated with blinking Christmas lights that reflected on the wet sidewalk. Inside, Opal's shampoo girl was sweeping up and Christmas music was playing on the radio. Opal was finishing up her last customer, Mrs. Vesta Adcock, who was going to an L & N banquet in Birmingham that night. The bells on the door jangled as Grady and the men came in, and Grady put on his official voice.

"Opal, can we speak to you for a minute?"

Vesta Adcock looked up horrified and clutched her flowered smock around her, screaming, "WHAT IN THE WORLD!"

Opal looked up, equally horrified, and rushed over to Grady with a green comb in her hand. "You cain't come in here, Grady Kilgore, this here is a beauty shop! We don't let men in here. What is the matter with you? Have you lost your mind? Now, go on, get out! The very idea!"

The six-foot four-inch Grady and the two men stumbled all over each other trying to get out the door and wound up back on the sidewalk, with Opal glaring at them through the foggy window.

Grady put the photograph of Frank Bennett back in his pocket and said, "Well, that's one place he ain't been in, that's for damn sure."

The three men pulled up their collars and headed across the tracks.

# WHISTLE STOP CAFE

### DECEMBER 21, 1930

Three days after the two men from Georgia had first arrived in town asking questions about Frank Bennett, the skinny one, Curtis Smoote, came in by himself and ordered another barbecue and an Orange Crush.

When Idgie brought it over to the booth, she said, "Between Grady and your partner, ya'll are about to eat up all my barbecue. That makes ten you three have had today!"

He squinted at her and said, in his high nasal little voice, "Have a seat."

Idgie looked around the room and saw that it wasn't busy, and then sat down across from him.

He took a bite of his sandwich and looked at her, hard.

"How ya doing?" Idgie said. "Found that man you was looking for yet?"

This time he glanced around the room and then leaned across the table, his face like a razor. "You're not fooling me, girlie girl. I know who you are. Don't think for a minute you're fooling me. . . . You gotta get up early in the morning to put one over on Curtis Smoote. Yes sir, the first time I come in here, I knowed I'd seen you somewhere before, but I couldn't place you. So I made a few phone calls, and last night it come to me who you were."

He sat back and continued eating, never taking his eyes off her. Idgie, not batting an eye, waited for him to continue.

"Now, I got me a sworn statement from this fellow Jake, that works out at the Bennett place, that someone answering the description of you and that big black buck you got out in the back, there, come over with a bunch and took Bennett's wife off, and that nigger threatened Bennett with a knife."

He picked a piece of dark meat out of his sandwich and put it on his plate and looked at it. "Besides that, I was in the back of the barbershop that day, and me and a whole bunch heard you threaten to kill him. Now, if I can remember, you can be damn sure the rest of them will."

He took a swig of his cold drink and wiped his mouth with the paper napkin. "Now, I cain't say Frank Bennett was no particular friend of mine . . . no sir. I got my oldest girl living in a shack, outside of town, with a kid, because of him, and I heard tell of what was going on out at his place. And I would venture a guess that there's others that wouldn't shed a tear if he was to show up dead. But it looks to me, girlie girl, that you would be in a whole passel of trouble if he did, 'cause the fact that you threatened him twice is in the official record, and I can tell you right now, that don't look too good in black and white.

"What we're talking about here, girlie, is murder . . . running afoul of the law. And nobody can get away with that."

He leaned back in the booth and took on a casual air. "Now, of course, just hypothetically speaking, of course, if it was me in your shoes, why, I'd figure it would do me a whole lot of good if that body didn't show up at all. Yes, a whole lot of good . . . or if anything that belonged to him was to be found, for that matter. I'd figure it wouldn't bode well if anybody could prove that Frank Bennett had been over here at all, you understand, and I'd figure, if I was smart, that is, it would be real important to make sure there wasn't nothing to find."

He glanced up at Idgie to make sure she was listening. She was.

"Yes sir, that would be too bad, 'cause I'd have to come back over here and arrest you and your colored man on suspicion. Now, I'd hate to come back over here after you, but I will, 'cause I'm the law and I'm sworn to uphold it. You cain't beat the law. Do you understand that?"

Idgie said, "Yes sir."

Having made his point, he pulled a quarter out of his pocket and threw it on the table, put his hat on, and said as he was leaving, "Of course, Grady may be right. He may just show back up at home one of these days. But I ain't gonna hold my breath."

JANUARY 7, 1931

## Local Man Feared Dead

The search for Frank Bennett, 38, a lifelong resident of Valdosta, missing from his home since early morning December 13 of last year, has officially ended. The extensive search, conducted by Detective Curtis Smoote, and Detective Wendell Riggins, led to people being questioned as to Bennett's whereabouts as far away as Tennessee and Alabama. However, neither Bennett nor the truck in which he was traveling at the time of the disappearance has been recovered.

"We left no stone unturned," said Officer Smoote in an interview early today. "He just seems to have vanished off the face of the earth."

MARCH 19, 1931

## Sad News for All of Us

After having lost their daddy a year before, it was another sad trip home for Leona, Mildred, Patsy Ruth, and Edward Threadgoode, who all came back home for their mother's funeral.

After the service, we all went over to the Threadgoode house, and everyone in town must have been there to pay their respects to Momma Threadgoode. Half the people here practically grew up over at the Threadgoode house with she and Poppa. I can never forget the good times we had over there and how she always made us feel so welcome. As for me, I met my better half over there at one of their big Fourth of July parties. We courted with Cleo and Ninny, and many an hour was spent sitting on that front porch after church.

Everybody is going to miss her and the place is not going to seem the same without her.

. . . Dot Weems . . .

MAY 11, 1986

Evelyn Couch opened the plastic Baggie full of carrot sticks and celery she had brought for herself and offered them to her friend. Mrs. Threadgoode declined, but went on eating her orange-marshmallow peanuts. "No thank you, honey, raw food just doesn't sit well with me. Why're you eating raw food, anyway?"

"It's Weight Watchers, well, kind of. I can eat anything I want as long as it doesn't have fat or sugar in it."

"Are you trying to slim down again?"

"Yes. I'm going to try. But it's hard. I've gotten so fat."

"Well, you do what you want to, but I still say you look fine to me."

"Oh Mrs. Threadgoode, you're sweet to say so, but I've gotten up to a size sixteen."

"You don't look heavy to me. Essie Rue . . . now, *she* was heavyset. But then, she was always inclined in that direction, ever since she was a little girl. But I guess at one time she got up to well over two hundred pounds."

"She did?"

"Oh yes, but she never let it bother her, and she always

dressed up in the best-looking outfits and always had a little flower in her hair to match. Everybody used to say that Essie Rue looked like she had just stepped out of a bandbox, and she had the cutest little hands and feet. Everybody in Birmingham used to talk about what cute little feet she had when she got her job playing the mighty Wurlitzer . . ."

"The what?"

"The mighty Wurlitzer organ. They had it down at the Alabama Theater for years. They said it was the largest organ in the south, and I believe they were right. We'd all get on the streetcar and go over and see the picture show. I'd always go when Ginger Rogers was playing. She was my favorite player. That girl is the most talented one they got out there in Hollywood. I don't even care to see a picture if she's not in it . . . she can do it all: dance, sing, act . . . what have you . . .

"But anyhow, between shows, the lights would go down and you'd hear this man's voice saying, 'And now, the Alabama Theater is proud to present . . .' he'd always say that, 'proud to present' Miss Essie Rue Limeway, performing on the mighty Wurlitzer. And from far away you'd hear this music . . . and then, all of a sudden, here would come this huge organ, rising up from the floor, and there would be Essie Rue, playing her theme song, 'I'm in Love with the Man in the Moon.' And all the spotlights would hit her and the sound of that organ would fill the theater and shake the rafters. Then she'd turn around and smile and never miss a note; and move into another song. Before you knew it, she'd be playing 'Stars Fell on Alabama' or 'Life Is Just a Bowl of Cherries,' and her tiny little feet would just fly over those pedals like butterflies! She wore ankle straps that she ordered especially from Loveman's department store.

"You'd think she'd put weight on everywhere, but she never did, just her body.

"Everybody has their good points, and she knew hers and played them up. That's why I hate to see you so down on yourself. I was telling Mrs. Otis the other day, I said, 'Evelyn Couch has got the prettiest skin I ever saw,' I said. 'She looks like her mother has just kept her wrapped up in cotton all her life.' "

"Why, thank you, Mrs. Threadgoode."

"Well, it's true. You don't have a wrinkle on you. I also told Mrs. Otis that I thought you ought to think about selling some of that Mary Kay cosmetics. With your skin and personality, why I bet you could get yourself a pink Cadillac in no time. My neighbor Mrs. Hartman has a niece who sells it and she made a bundle, and Mary Kay gave her a pink Cadillac as a bonus. And she's not half as pretty as you are."

Evelyn said, "Oh Mrs. Threadgoode, thank you for saying that, but I'm too old to start anything like that. They want young women."

"Evelyn Couch, how can you say that, you are still a young woman. Forty-eight years old is just a baby! You've got half your life left to live yet! Mary Kay doesn't care how old you are. She's no spring chicken herself. Now, if it was me and I had that skin and was your age, I'd make a try at that Cadillac. Of course, I'd have to get me a driver's license, but I'd try for it anyway.

"Just think, Evelyn, if you live to be as old as I am, you've got thirty-seven more years to go . . ."

Evelyn laughed. "What does it feel like to be eighty-six, Mrs. Threadgoode?"

"Well, I don't feel any different. Like I say, it just creeps up on you. One day you're young and the next day your bosoms and your chin drops and you're wearing a rubber girdle. But you don't know you're old. Course, I can tell when I look in the mirror . . . sometimes it nearly scares me to death. My neck looks just like old crepe paper, and I've got so many wrinkles and there's nothing you can do about it. Oh, I used to have something from Avon for wrinkles, but it didn't last but about an hour and they all came back, so I finally stopped fooling with it. I don't even put on a face anymore, just a little lotion and eyebrow pencil, so you can tell I've got eyebrows . . . they're white now, honey . . . and I'm full of liver spots." She looked at her hands. "You wonder where all those little fellows come from." Then she laughed. "I'm even to old to make a good picture. Francis wanted to snap a picture of me and Mrs. Otis, but I hid my head. Said I might break the camera."

Evelyn asked if she ever got lonesome out there.

"Well, yes, sometimes I do. Of course, all my people are gone . . . but once in a while, some of the ones from the church come to see me, but it's just hello and goodbye. That's just the way it is, hello and goodbye.

"Sometimes I look at my picture of Cleo and little Albert and wonder what they're up to . . . and dream about the old days."

She smiled at Evelyn. "That's what I'm living on now, honey, dreams, dreams of what I used to do."

# WHISTLE STOP CAFE

NOVEMBER 18, 1940

Stump was in the back room shooting at cardboard blackbirds with a rubber-band gun and Ruth was correcting papers when Idgie came banging in the back door from the annual Dill Pickle Club fishing trip.

He ran and jumped up on her and nearly knocked her down.

Ruth was glad to see her because she always worried whenever Idgie went off for a week or more, especially when she knew she was down at the river with Eva Bates. Stump ran out to look on the back steps.

"Where's the fish?"

"Well, Stump," Idgie said, "the truth is, we caught a fish, it was so big we couldn't get it out of the water. We took a picture of it, though, and the picture alone weighs twenty pounds . . ."

"Oh Aunt Idgie, you didn't catch any fish!"

About that time, they heard, "*Whooo-ooo,* it's me . . . me and Albert, come to visit . . ." and in came a tall, sweet-looking woman, with her hair twisted back in a knot, and a little re- tarded boy, about Stump's age, coming to visit just like they had every day for the past ten years; and they were always glad to see her.

Idgie said, "Well hey there, gal, how you doing today?"

"Just fine," she said, and sat down. "How are you girls doing?"

Ruth said, "Well, Ninny, we almost had some catfish for supper, but they must not have been biting." She laughed. "We're having photographs instead."

Ninny was disappointed. "Oooh, Idgie, I wish you had brought me a good ol' catfish tonight . . . I love a good catfish. What a shame, I can just taste him."

"Ninny," Idgie said, "catfish don't bite in the dead of winter."

"They don't? Well, you'd think they would be just as hungry in the winter as they are in the summer, wouldn't you?"

Ruth agreed. "That's true, Idgie. Why don't they bite this time of year?"

"Oh, it's not that they're not hungry, it has to do with the temperature of the worm. A catfish won't eat a cold worm, no matter how hungry it gets."

Ruth looked at Idgie and shook her head, always amazed at the tales she could come up with.

Ninny said, "Well, that makes sense. I hate my food to get cold, myself, and I guess even if you were to heat up the worms, they would be cold by the time they got to the bottom of the river, wouldn't they? And speaking of cold, hasn't it been a cold old winter? It's as cold as blitzen out there."

Albert was across the room playing with Stump and shooting at the cardboard blackbirds. While Ninny was having her coffee, she had a thought. "Stump, do you reckon you could come over to my house and shoot your gun at these old blackbirds that are sitting on my telephone wires? I don't want you to hurt them, I just want you to scare them off . . . I think they're up there listening to my telephone calls, through their feet."

Ruth, who adored Ninny, said, "Oh Ninny, you don't think that's true, do you?"

"Well, honey, that's what Cleo told me."

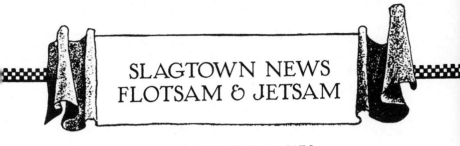

NOVEMBER 19, 1940

## Faith Act Used to Fleece Woman Out of $50 in Cash

Mrs. Sallie Jinx, of 68-C Howell Street, S.E., was the victim of flimflam, she reported to police yesterday. Mrs. Jinx said a woman, known to her as Sister Bell, came to her home and, through a faith act, pretended to tie $50 of her money in a napkin and put it in a trunk with instructions not to open the napkin until four hours later. When the napkin was opened, the money was gone, the victim stated.

Toncille Robinson and E. C. Robinson are telling their friends they don't care what the other does.

## Missing from Our Alley

8th Avenue just doesn't seem the same. Artis O. Peavey, that well-known fellow around town, has seen fit to exit to the Windy City. He is sorely missed by the female population, of that fact you can be sure.

We hear that Miss Helen Reid had to call the law over a late-night prowler trying to enter her home on Avenue F, and do her bodily harm . . . and when the officers of the law arrived, they apprehended a gentleman hiding under the house with an ice pick in his hand, who claimed that he was the iceman.

Could that gentleman have been Mr. Baby Shephard, who heretofore had been sweet on Miss Reid?

. . . The Esquire Club is preparing for its annual Limb Loosener . . .

## Platter News

Ellington's "Black and Tan Fantasy" is a new Decca release of considerable interest and novelty. The pianist in "Creole" gets on a boogie-woogie kick that's odd but effective.

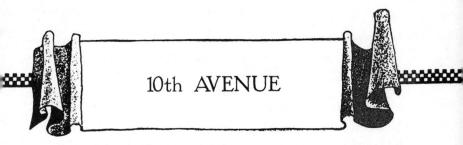

# 10th AVENUE

CHICAGO, ILLINOIS

NOVEMBER 20, 1940

It was raining in Chicago, and Artis O. Peavey was running down the street. He ducked into a doorway, under a sign that read SEA FOOD LUNCH, FRIED FISH 35¢. Across the street, at the RKO Alhambra, *Dealers in Crime* and *Hoodlum Empire* were showing. He felt like a fugitive, himself, up here, away from home, hiding out from a dusky damsel named Electra Greene.

He stood there, smoking a Chesterfield cigarette and contemplating life and its turmoils. His mother had said, whenever she was down, that just the thought of her sweet Jesus could always make her spirits rise.

But it hadn't been such thoughts that made Artis rise. It was the sight of a certain high-hipped, thick-lipped black beauty; and it hadn't been just his spirits that would rise and stay risen, much to the delight of said beauty. His main problem in life, at the moment, was that he loved too well and not too wisely.

He had always played a dangerous game where the lovely ladies' husbands were concerned, for Artis knew no boundaries. Every living female was his particular domain, and because of that lack of respect for territorial rights, he had often been forced to search his own body for stab wounds and broken bones, and on too many occasions had found them. After being caught with the wrong woman at the wrong time, one bronze amazon stuck him with a corkscrew. He was much more careful after that unhappy affair, the result of which was an interesting scar, to say the least, and a natural hesitation to fool with any more women who were bigger than he was. Still, he was a heartbreaker. He had told one too many to look for him the next night, and that's just what they wound up doing—looking . . .

This skinny little man, so black he was a deep royal blue, had caused a lot of trouble for the opposite sex. One gal drank a can of floor wax and topped it off with a cup of Clorox, trying to separate herself from the same world he was in. When she survived, claiming that the liquids had ruined her complexion for life, he became continually uneasy after dark, because she had snuck up behind him more than once and cracked him in the head with a purseful of rocks.

But this situation with Electra Greene was more serious than a purseful of rocks. Electra was packing a .38 revolver that she knew how to use and had made uncouth threats pertaining to his manhood, and the extermination of such, after finding out he had not been true. Not once, but eight times, to be exact, with a Miss Delilah Woods, her sworn enemy, who had also left town in a hurry.

As Artis stood there today in the doorway, he was hurting so bad, he thought he would die. He missed Birmingham and he wanted to go back.

Every afternoon, before his hasty exit from Birmingham, he had driven his blue two-toned Chevrolet with the whitewall tires up Red Mountain and had parked to watch the sunset. From up there he could look down and see the iron and steel mills, with their towering smokestacks billowing orange smoke all the way up to Tennessee. There had been nothing more beautiful to him than the city at that hour, when the sky was washed with a red-and-purple glow from the mills and neon lights would start coming on all over town, twinkling and dancing throughout the downtown streets and over to Slagtown.

Birmingham, the town that during the Depression had been named by FDR "the hardest hit city in the U.S." . . . where people had been so poor that Artis had known a man that would let you shoot at him for money and a girl that had soaked her feet in brine and vinegar for three days, trying to win a dance marathon . . . the place that had the lowest income per capita of any American city and yet was known as the best circus town in the South . . .

Birmingham, which at one time had the highest illiteracy rate, more venereal disease than any other city in America, and at the same time proudly held the record for having the highest number of Sunday School students of any city in the U.S. . . . where Imperial Laundry trucks had once driven around town with WE WASH FOR WHITE PEOPLE ONLY written on the side, and where darker citizens still sat behind wooden boards on streetcars that said COLORED and rode freight elevators in department stores.

Birmingham, Murder Capital of the South, where 131 people had been killed in 1931 alone . . .

All this, and yet Artis loved his Birmingham with an insatiable passion, from the south side to the north side, in the freezing-cold rainy winter, when the red clay would slide down the sides of hills and run into the streets, and in the lush green summers, when the green kudzu vine covered the sides of the mountains and grew up trees and telephone poles and the air was moist and heavy with the smell of gardenias and barbecue. He had traveled all over the country, from Chicago to Detroit, from Savannah to Charleston and on up to New York, but there was never a time when he wasn't happy to get back to Birmingham. If there is such a thing as complete happiness, it is knowing that you are in the right place, and Artis had been completely happy from the moment he hit Birmingham.

So today he made up his mind to head on home, because he knew he would rather be dead than be away any longer. He missed Birmingham like most men miss their wives.

And that's just what Miss Electra Greene intended to become . . . if she let him live, that is.

As he walked by the Fife and Drum Bar, somebody played a song on the jukebox:

Way down South, in Birmingham, I mean South, in Alabam',
An old place where people go to dance the night away,
They all drive or walk for miles to jive
That Southern style, slow jive, that makes you want
To dance 'til break of day.
At each junction where the town folks meet
At each function, in their tux they greet you.
Come on down, forget your care. Come on down
You'll find me there. So long town!
I'm headin' for Tuxedo Junction now.

NOVEMBER 25, 1950

## Popular Birmingham Bachelor Marries

Miss Electra Greene, daughter of Mr. and Mrs. R. C. Greene, became the charming bride of Mr. Artis O. Peavey, son of Mr. and Mrs. George Peavey, of Whistle Stop, Alabama.

Officiating at the colorful wedding rites was Dr. John W. Nixon, pastor of the First Congregational Church, while nuptial music was provided by the accomplished Mr. Lewis Jones.

*Radiant Bride*

The lovely bride was fetching in a forest-green ensemble, with amber accessories, mink trimmed off the face. She wore a brown felt hat, gloves and shoes to match, with a corsage of valley lillies.

Miss Naughty Bird Peavey, sister of the groom, was arresting in a grape-colored woolen crepe with draped front, multicolored beaded necklace, and cerise gloves and shoes.

*Colorful Reception*

Immediately following the nuptials, a colorful wedding reception took place at the home of Mrs. Lulu Butterfork, who is prominent in the city's leading beauticians' circles, being both a beautician and a hairpiece specialist.

Several well-known Birminghamians who attended the colorful reception were served punch, ice cream, and individual cakes, and were busy registering awe at the brilliant display of countless bridal gifts.

Monday night, October 5, at 11 o'clock, the bridal party was honored at a spicy after-supper dance, with Mrs. Toncille Robinson as hostess.

Glamour marked the occasion, which saw the Little Savoy Cafe, scene of the select occasion, given a festive appearance by brilliantly embellished yuletide effects and a long, heavily laden table of choice foods and viands. A hot seven-course chicken supper was served, featuring wine as an appetizer and topped off with hot coffee and dessert.

The couple will reside in the bride's home on Fountain Avenue.

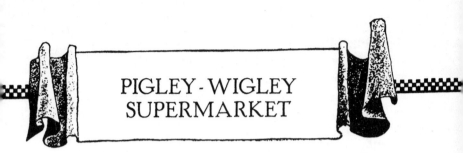

# PIGLEY-WIGLEY SUPERMARKET

BIRMINGHAM, ALABAMA

MAY 19, 1986

It had been nine long, hard days since Evelyn Couch had been on her diet, and today she woke up with a feeling of euphoria. She seemed in complete control of her life, tall and thin, and when she moved, she felt willowy and graceful. Those nine days had been like climbing a mountain, and now she knew she had reached the top. Somehow, today, she knew in her heart that she would never eat anything as long as she lived unless it was crisp and fresh; just like she was at this very moment.

When she went into the supermarket, she sprinted past the cookies and cakes and white breads and aisle three, canned goods, where she had spent most of her shopping life, and went straight to the meat department, where she ordered chicken breasts without the skin. Then she headed over to the produce section, a place she had only visited on occasions to buy potatoes for mashing, and bought fresh broccoli and lemons and limes to cut up in her Perrier water. She stopped briefly at the magazine section to buy a *Town and Country* magazine, featuring an article on Palm Beach, and then went to the express checkout counter, where the checkout girl greeted her.

"Hey, Miz Couch, how are you doing today?"

"Just great, Mozell, how are you?"

"I'm fine."

"Is this gonna be all for you today, hon?"

"That's it."

Mozell punched up the amount.

"You look awful pretty today, Miz Couch."

"Well, thank you, I feel good."

"Well, bye-bye, now. You have a nice day."

"Thank you. You too."

As Evelyn was going out, a beady-eyed, mean-mouthed boy in greasy pants and a T-shirt slammed through the EXIT ONLY door and knocked Evelyn back. He brushed past and, Evelyn, still in a good mood, mumbled to herself, "Well, there's a nice gentleman."

The boy turned and with a surly look said, "Fuck you, bitch!" and went on.

Evelyn was stunned. The hatred in his eyes took her breath away. She felt herself getting all shaky and started to cry. It was as if someone had hit her. She closed her eyes and told herself not to lose control. He was just a stranger. It didn't matter. Don't let it upset you.

But the more she thought about it, she knew she had to make it all right. She would go on outside and wait for him and tell him that she had just been trying to make light of the situation and had not meant to hurt his feelings and that she was sure he had come in the wrong door by mistake and hadn't realized that he had run into her.

She was sure, as soon as she explained it to him, he would probably feel bad and the whole thing would be over and she could go home feeling better.

The boy burst out of the door carrying his six-pack and walked past her. She walked faster and caught up with him.

"Excuse me. I just wanted you to know that there was no reason for you to be so mad at me in there. I was only trying to . . ."

He shot a disgusted look at her. "Get the hell away from me, you stupid cow!"

Evelyn was breathless.

"Excuse me. What did you call me?"

He continued on, ignoring her. Now she was running after him, in tears.

"What did you call me? Why are you being so mean to me? What did I ever do to you? You don't even know me!"

He opened the door to his truck, and Evelyn, hysterical, grabbed his arm.

"Why? Why are you being so mean to me?"

He slammed her arm away from him and stuck his fist in her face, his eyes and face twisted with rage. "Don't fool with me, bitch, or I'll knock your fucking head off—you fat, stupid cunt!"

And with that, he pushed her in the chest and knocked her down.

Evelyn couldn't believe what was happening. Her groceries spilled everywhere.

The stringy-haired girl with the elastic halter top who had been waiting for the boy looked down at Evelyn and laughed. He got in the truck, threw it in reverse, and squealed out of the parking lot, yelling names back at Evelyn.

She sat there on the ground, her elbow bleeding, old and fat and worthless all over again.

DECEMBER 12, 1941

## War Starts

Grady Kilgore is in charge of the Whistle Stop draft board, and he says for all you boys to come on in and sign up and get it over with.

It seems like lately there's nothing but troop trains and tanks passing through. It makes you wonder where they are all from and where they are going.

Wilbur says the war won't last more than six months. I hope he's right for once.

The Jolly Belles Ladies' Barber Shop Quartet has been invited to attend the National Convention of Ladies' Barber Shop Quartets in Memphis, Tennessee, this spring, to perform their most popular rendition of "Dip Your Brush in Sunshine and Keep On Painting Away."

Reverend Scroggins asks, would the individual or individuals who are giving out his address and phone number to people looking for whiskey please stop, as his wife, Arna, is in the middle of a nervous condition and has broken out several times this week. Bobby Lee Scroggins joined the navy. By the way, that service star in the window over at the cafe is for Willie Boy Peavey, Onzell's and Big George's boy, who is the first colored soldier in Troutville to join up.

... Dot Weems ...

P.S. Everybody is getting ready for the annual Christmas pageant and because of the shortage of men in our town, Opal, myself and Ninny Threadgoode have been cast as the three wise men.

# 212 RHODES CIRCLE

BIRMINGHAM, ALABAMA

### AUGUST 8, 1986

After the boy at the supermarket had called her those names, Evelyn Couch had felt violated. Raped by words. Stripped of everything. She had always tried to keep this from happening to her, always been terrified of displeasing men, terrified of the names she would be called if she did. She had spent her life tiptoeing around them like someone lifting her skirt stepping through a cow pasture. She had always suspected that if provoked, those names were always close to the surface, ready to lash out and destroy her.

It had finally happened. But she was still alive. So she began to wonder. It was as if that boy's act of violence toward her had shocked her into finally looking at herself and asking the questions she had avoided for fear of the answers.

What was this power, this insidious threat, this invisible gun to her head that controlled her life . . . *this terror of being called names?*

She had stayed a virgin so she wouldn't be called a tramp or a slut; had married so she wouldn't be called an old maid; faked orgasms so she wouldn't be called frigid; had children so she wouldn't be called barren; had not been a feminist because she didn't want to be called queer and a man hater; never nagged or raised her voice so she wouldn't be called a bitch . . .

She had done all that and yet, still, this stranger had dragged her into the gutter with the names that men call women when they are angry.

Evelyn wondered; why always sexual names? And why, when men wanted to degrade other men, did they call them pussies? As if that was the worst thing in the world. What have we done to be thought of that way? To be called *cunt*? People didn't call blacks names anymore, at least not to their faces. Italians weren't wops or dagos, and there were no more kikes, Japs, chinks, or spics in polite conversation. Everybody had a group to protest and stick up for them. But women were still being called names by men. Why? Where was our group? It's not fair. She was getting more upset by the minute. Evelyn thought, I wish Idgie had been with me. She would not have let that boy call *her* names. I'll bet she would have knocked *him* down.

Then she made herself stop thinking because, all of a sudden, she was experiencing a feeling that she had never felt before, and it scared her. And so, twenty years later than most women, *Evelyn Couch was angry.*

She was angry at herself for being so scared. Soon, all that belated anger began to express itself in a strange and peculiar way.

For the first time in her life, she wished she were a man. Not for the privilege of having the particular set of equipment that men hold so dear. No. She wanted a man's strength, so at the supermarket she could have beaten that name-calling punk to a pulp. Of course, she realized, had she been a man, she would not have been called those names in the first place. In her fantasies, she began to look like herself but with the strength of ten men. She became Superwoman. And in her mind, she beat that bad-mouthed boy over and over again, until he lay in the parking lot, broken and bleeding, begging for mercy. Ha!

Thus, in her forty-eighth year, the incredible secret life of Mrs. Evelyn Couch of Birmingham, Alabama, began.

. . .

Few people who saw this plump, pleasant-looking middle-aged, middle-class housewife out shopping or doing other menial everyday chores could guess that, in her imagination, she was machine-gunning the genitals of rapers and stomping abusive husbands to death in her specially designed wife-beater boots.

Evelyn had even made up a secret code name for herself ... a name feared around the world: TOWANDA THE AVENGER!

And while Evelyn went about her business with a smile, Towanda was busy poking child molesters with electric cattle prods until their hair stood on end. She placed tiny bombs inside *Playboy* and *Penthouse* magazines that would explode when they were opened. She gave dope dealers overdoses and left them in the streets to die; forced that doctor, who had told her mother she had cancer, to walk down the street naked while the entire medical profession, including dentists and oral hygienists, jeered and threw rocks. A merciful avenger, she always waited until he finished his walk and then beat his brains out with a sledgehammer.

Towanda was able to do anything she wanted. She went back in time and punched out Paul for writing that women should remain silent. Towanda went to Rome and kicked the pope off the throne and put a nun there, with the priests cooking and cleaning for her, for a change.

Towanda appeared on *Meet the Press,* and with a calm voice, a cool eye, and a wry smile, debated everyone who disagreed with her until they became so defeated by her brilliance that they burst into tears and ran off the show. She went to Hollywood and ordered all the leading men to act opposite women of their own age, not twenty-year-old girls with perfect bodies. She allowed rats to chew all slumlords to death, and sent food and birth control methods, for men as well as women, to the poor people of the world.

And because of her vision and insight, she became known the world over as Towanda the Magnanimous, Righter of Wrongs and Queen without Compare.

Towanda ordained that: an equal number of men and

women would be in the government and sit in on peace talks; she and her staff of crack chemical scientists would find a cure for cancer and invent a pill that would let you eat all you want and not gain weight; people would be forced to get a license to have children and must be found fit, financially and emotionally—*no more starving or battered children.* Jerry Falwell would be responsible for the raising of all illegitimate children who had no homes; no kittens or puppies would be put to sleep, and they would be given a state of their own, maybe New Mexico or Wyoming; teachers and nurses would receive the same salary as professional football players.

She would stop the construction of all condos, especially ones with red tile roofs; and Van Johnson would be given a show of his own . . . he was one of Towanda's favorites.

Graffiti offenders were to be dipped in a vat of indelible ink. No more children of famous parents could write books. And she'd personally see to it that all the sweet men and daddies, who had worked so hard, would each receive a trip to Hawaii and an outboard motor to go with it.

Towanda went to Madison Avenue and took control of all the fashion magazines; all models weighing under 135 were fired, and wrinkles suddenly became sexually desirable. Low-fat cottage cheese was banned from the land forever. Ditto, carrot sticks.

Why, just yesterday, Towanda had marched into the Pentagon, taken all the bombs and missiles away, and had given them toys to play with instead, while her sisters in Russia were doing the same thing. Then she went on the six o'clock nightly news and gave the entire military budget to all the people in the United States over sixty-five. Towanda would be so busy all day that Evelyn was exhausted by bedtime.

No wonder. Tonight, while Evelyn was cooking dinner, Towanda had just put a roomful of porno and child exploitation film producers to death. And later, as Evelyn was washing the dishes, Towanda was in the process of single-handedly blowing up the entire Middle East to prevent the Third World War. And so, when Ed yelled from the den for another beer, somehow, before Evelyn could stop her, Towanda yelled back, "SCREW YOU, ED!"

He very quietly got up from his recliner and came into the kitchen.

"Evelyn, are you all right?"

FEBRUARY 9, 1943

## War Speeds Up

My other half is working two shifts, along with just about everyone else over at the railroad, since the iron and steel industry is working overtime, and I'm one lonesome gal these days. But if he's helping out Uncle Sam and our boys, I guess I can take it.

Tommy Glass and Ray Limeway write from camp to say hello.

By the way, has anybody seen Idgie's and Ruth's victory garden, by the old Threadgoode place? Idgie said that Sipsey grew butterbeans the size of silver dollars. I can't get anything but a few sweet potatoes, over at my place.

Three of the members of the Jolly Belles Ladies' Barber Shop Quartet, me and Biddie Louise Otis and Ninny Threadgoode, went to Birmingham and had dinner at Brittling's Cafeteria, and then went to see our own Essie Rue Limeway. The picture playing was not half as good as the show in between. We are mighty proud. We wanted to tell everyone in the theater that she was our friend. Ninny did turn to the person next to her and inform him that Essie Rue was her sister-in-law.

By the way, don't forget to save rubber.

. . . Dot Weems . . .

P.S. Who says we are the weaker sex? Poor Dwane Glass fainted at his own wedding last Sunday and had to be held up by his bride-to-be throughout the entire ceremony. He said he felt much better after it was over though. He leaves for the army right after his honeymoon.

# WHISTLE STOP, ALABAMA

JANUARY 12, 1944

In Birmingham, at the big L & N Terminal train station, a brass band and a crowd of five hundred people had gathered to welcome home the returning sons, husbands, and brothers; war heroes, all. The flags were waving already, waiting for the six-twenty from Washington, D.C.

But tonight, the train made its first stop twenty minutes outside of Birmingham, and down at the end of the platform was a black family, waiting for their son. Quietly, the wooden box was lifted off the baggage coach and placed on the cart that would take him over the tracks to Troutville.

Artis, Jasper, and Naughty Bird walked behind Onzell, Sipsey, and Big George. As they walked by, Grady Kilgore, Jack Butts, and all the railroad boys took their hats off and stood at attention.

There were no flags or bands or any medals, just a cardboard name tag on the box, with P.F.C. W. C. PEAVEY written on it. But across the street, in the window of the cafe, there was a flag and a service star in the window and a sign that read: WELCOME HOME, WILLIE BOY . . .

Ruth and Idgie and Stump had already gone over to Troutville to wait with the others.

Sweet Willie Boy, Wonderful Counselor Peavey, the boy
who had been accepted at Tuskegee Institute . . . the smart
one, the one who was going to be a lawyer, a leader of his
people, a shining light from the back roads of Alabama to
Washington, D.C. Willie Boy, the one who had the chance to
make it, had gotten himself killed after a bar fight by a black
soldier named Winston Lewis from Newark, New Jersey.

Willie Boy had been talking about his daddy, Big George,
who, whenever his name was mentioned down home, blacks
and whites alike would always say, "Now, there's a man."

But Winston Lewis had said that *any* man working for
whites, especially in Alabama, was nothing but a low-down,
ignorant, stupid shuffling Uncle Tom.

In order to survive, Willie Boy had been trained not to react
to insults and to disguise even the tiniest glimmer of aggres-
siveness or anger. But tonight, when Winston spoke, he
thought of his daddy and crashed a beer bottle into the soldier's face and sent him sprawling on the floor, out like a light.

The next night, while he was asleep, Willie Boy's throat had
been cut from ear to ear; Winston Lewis then went A.W.O.L.
The army didn't much care; they had pretty much had it with
the knife fights among the colored troops, and Willie Boy was
sent home in a box.

At the funeral, Ruth and Smokey and all the Threadgoodes
were in the front row of the church, and Idgie spoke on behalf
of the family. The preacher preached about Jesus taking only
His precious children home early to be with Him, and talked
about the will of the Almighty Father Who sits on the golden
throne in heaven. The congregation swayed and responded
with, "Yes sir, His will be done."

Artis answered the preacher along with the rest of them, and
he swayed in his seat while he watched his mother scream in
agony; but after the service, he did not go to the graveyard.
While Willie Boy was being lowered into that cold Alabama

red-clay grave, Artis had hopped a train and was on his way to Newark, New Jersey. He was looking for someone named Mr. Winston Lewis to cut.

. . . And the congregation was singing, "Lord, don't move my mountain, just give me the strength to climb . . ."

Three days later, Winston Lewis's heart was found in a paper sack several blocks from his residence.

FEBRUARY 24, 1944

## Icebox Follies a Sidesplitter

The Dill Pickle Club put on its annual "Icebox Follies," and this one was the best yet.

Grady Kilgore was cast as Shirley Temple, who sang "On the Good Ship Lollipop." I wonder if everyone knew what pretty legs our sheriff has?

And my own other half, Wilbur Weems, sang "Red Sails in the Sunset." I thought it was good, but then, I'm no judge. I hear him every day in the shower. Ha. Ha.

The most hilarious skit was a skit depicting Reverend Scroggins, played by Idgie Threadgoode, and Vesta Adcock, played by Pete Tidwell.

Opal did all the hair and makeup, and Ninny Threadgoode, Biddie Louise Otis, and yours truly made all the costumes.

The so-called "dangerous animal" in the Mutt and

Jeff skit was none other than Dr. and Mrs. Hadley's bulldog, Ring, in a gas mask.

All the proceeds go to the Christmas fund to aid all the needy here in Whistle Stop and in Troutville.

I wish this old war would hurry up and be over with; we sure do miss all our boys.

By the way, Wilbur tried to join the army the other day. Thank God, he's too old and has flat feet, or we'd really be in trouble.

... Dot Weems ...

# ROSE TERRACE NURSING HOME

OLD MONTGOMERY HIGHWAY
BIRMINGHAM, ALABAMA

## JULY 28, 1986

Evelyn had gained back all the weight she had lost on her diet, plus eight more pounds. She was so upset, she did not notice that Mrs. Threadgoode had her dress on inside out again.

They were busy eating a five-pound box of Divinity Fudge when Mrs. Threadgoode said, "I'd kill for a pat of butter. This margarine they serve out here tastes like lard. We had to eat so much of that stuff in the Depression, I don't want to ever have to eat it again. So I just do without, and I have my toast dry, with plain apple butter.

"Come to think of it, Idgie and Ruth bought the cafe in 1929, right in the height of the Depression, but I don't think we ever had margarine there. Leastways, I cain't recall if we did. It's odd, here the whole world was suffering so, but at the cafe, those Depression years come back to me now as the happy times, even though we were all struggling. We were happy and didn't know it.

"A lot of nights we'd all sit around up at the cafe and just listen to the radio. We'd listen to Fibber McGee and Molly, Amos and Andy, Fred Allen . . . oh, I cain't remember what all we'd listen to, but they were all good. I cain't look at any of these programs they put on the TV today. Just people shootin' their guns and shoutin' insults at each other. Fibber McGee and Molly didn't shout at each other. Amos and Andy used to shout a little, but that was funny. And the colored people on the TV now are not near as sweet as they used to be. Sipsey would have Big George's hide if he talked as smart aleck as some of them do.

"It's not just TV. Mrs. Otis was over at the supermarket one day and she told this little colored boy that was passing by that she would give him a nickel if he'd lift her groceries in her car for her, and she said that he cut his eyes at her, mean-like, and just walked away. Oh, and it's not just the colored people, either. Back when Mrs. Otis was driving, before she hit that stack of grocery carts, people would run up behind us and blow their horns something awful, and when they passed us, some of them would give us the finger. I never saw such behavior. There's no call to be that ugly.

"I don't even want to look at the news anymore. Everybody fighting each other. They ought to give those boys some tranquilizers and quiet them down for a while. That's what they gave Mr. Dunaway. I think all the bad news affects people, makes them so mean. So whenever the news comes on, I just cut it off.

"Lately, for the past ten years or so, I have just taken to looking at my religious programs. I like the P.T.L. Club. They have a lot of smart men on that program. I send money every once in a while, if I have any. And I listen to *Camp Meeting U.S.A.*, from seven to eight, every night. And I like Oral Roberts and the Seven Hundred Club. I like just about all of them, except that woman with the makeup, and she'd be all right if she just didn't cry all the time. Oh, she cries if she's happy and she cries when she's sad. I'm telling you, she can cry at the drop of a hat. Now, there's one that needs her hormones. And I don't like preachers that yell all the time. I don't know why they want to yell when they have a microphone right in their hands. When they get to yelling like that, we just switch them over.

"And I'll tell you another thing, the funnies in the paper are not funny anymore. I remember when you could always get a laugh out of Gasoline Alley or Wee Willie Winkle. And I *loved* that Little Henry . . . oh, the scrapes Little Henry could get himself in.

"I just don't believe people are happy anymore, not like they used to be. You never see a happy face, at least I don't. I said to Mrs. Otis when Frances carried us out to the mall, I said, 'Look at all these people pulling such dried-up, sour little faces, even the youngsters.' "

Evelyn sighed. "I wonder why people have gotten so mean, anymore . . ."

"Oh, it's all over the world, honey. The end of times are coming. Now, we may go to the year two thousand, but I doubt it. You know, I listen to a lot of good preachers and they're all saying we're in our last time. They say it's in the Bible in Revelations. . . . Of course, they don't know. Nobody knows but the good Lord.

"I don't know how long the good Lord is going to let me live, but I'm in the jumping-off years, you know that. That's why I live every day like it could be my last. I want to be ready. And that's why I don't say anything about Mr. Dunaway and Vesta Adcock. We have to live and let live."

Evelyn felt she had to ask. "What about them?"

"Oh, they think they're in love. That's what they say. Oh, you should have seen them holding hands and smooching all over the place. Mr. Dunaway's daughter found out about it and came out here and threatened to sue the nursing home. Called Mrs. Adcock a hussy!"

"Oh no."

"Oh yes, honey . . . said she was trying to steal their daddy away from them. It was a big mess, and they took Mr. Dunaway back home. They were afraid he and Mrs. Adcock would try to have relations, I guess. I think that's a dream long dead, myself. Geneene said he lost his activities years ago and couldn't possibly harm a fly . . . so what would a little hugging and kissing hurt? Vesta is heartbroken. No telling what she'll do next.

"But I'll tell you one thing, they don't give you much slack out here."

Evelyn said, "I guess not."

AUGUST 1, 1945

## Man Falls in Lacquer

If I hadn't been married to him, I would have never believed it. . . . My other half was out at the railroad yards, hanging out where they've been painting all the troop trains, and he fell into a 250-gallon vat of lacquer. He was able to climb out, but the lacquer dried so fast, he was completely encrusted before setting foot on the ground and we had to get Opal to come over to the house and cut the lacquer out of what's left of his hair. It's a good thing we didn't have any children. I don't have time to worry about any other kids.

Does anybody know a good baby-sitter for a husband . . . ?

We are all so happy the war is finally over. Bobby Scroggins came home yesterday, and Tommy Glass and Ray Limeway got home last Thursday. Hooray!

Nothing but good news. Ninny Threadgoode came in and brought me a four-leaf clover. She said she and Albert had found three of them in her front yard. Thanks, Ninny.

... Dot Weems ...

# ROSE TERRACE
# NURSING HOME

OLD MONTGOMERY HIGHWAY
BIRMINGHAM, ALABAMA

### AUGUST 15, 1986

Geneene, the black nurse who prided herself on being as tough as nails, but really wasn't, said she was tired. She was working a double shift today, and she had come in their room to sit down for a minute and have a cigarette. Mrs. Otis was down the hall in her arts and crafts class, so Mrs. Threadgoode was happy for the company.

"You know that woman I talk to on Sundays?"

Geneene said, "What woman?"

"Evelyn."

"Who?"

"She's that little plump gray-haired woman. Evelyn . . . Evelyn Couch . . . Mrs. Couch's daughter-in-law."

"Oh. Yes."

"She told me ever since that man called her names at the Pigley-Wigley, she just hates people. I told her, I said, 'Oh honey, it does no good to hate. It'll do nothing but turn your heart into a bitter root. People cain't help being what they are any more than a skunk can help being a skunk. Don't you think if they had their choice they would rather be something else? Sure they would. People are just weak.'

"Evelyn said there are times when she is even beginning to hate her husband. He'll be sitting around doing nothing, looking at his football games or talking on the phone, and she has this terrible desire to hit him in the head with a baseball bat, for no reason. Poor little Evelyn, she thinks she's the only person in the world that ever had an ugly thought. I told her, her problem is just a natural thing that happens with couples after they've been together so long.

"I remember when Cleo got his first set of dentures he was so proud of. They'd make this clicking sound every time he'd take a bite of food, and it just grated on my nerves so bad that there'd be some nights I'd just have to get up from the table to keep myself from saying something . . . and I loved that man better than anything in the world. But you go through a period when you start to get on one another's nerves. And then, one day—now, I don't know if his teeth stopped clicking on their own or if I just got used to it or what—but it never bothered me another time. You have that kind of thing happen in the best of families.

"You take Idgie and Ruth. Now, you never saw two people more devoted to each other than they were, but even the two of them went through a period when they had their little problems. Ruth moved in with us once. I never knew what it was about, nor did I ask, because it was none of my business, but I think it was because she didn't like Idgie goin' over to the river, where Eva Bates lived. Said she felt that maybe Eva encouraged Idgie to drink too much for her own good. And it was true.

"But like I told Evelyn, everybody has their little quirks.

"Poor little Evelyn, I worry about her. That menapause has hit her with a vengeance! She said, not only does she want to hit Ed in the head, but lately, she's having fantasies in her mind where she dresses up in black clothes and goes out at night and kills all the bad people with a machine gun. Can you imagine?

"I said, 'Honey, you been looking at too many TV shows. You just get those thoughts out of your mind right now! Besides, it's not up to us to judge other people. It says right there in the

Bible, as plain as the nose on your face, that on Judgment Day Jesus is going to come down with a host of angels to judge the quick and the dead.'

"Evelyn asked me who the quick were, and do you know, for the life of me, I couldn't tell her!"

JUNE 3, 1946

The blue lights were on and you could hear the people inside carrying on, and the jukebox blaring all the way across the river. Idgie was sitting right in the middle of it, drinking Pabst Blue Ribbon beer and chasing it with more Pabst Blue Ribbon beer. She was off whiskey for that night, because the night before had been enough to last her for a while.

Her friend Eva was whooping it up with some country boys that were supposed to be at an Elks Club meeting that night over in Gate City. She passed by Idgie and looked at her.

"Good God, girl, what's the matter with you? You look like a lizard with a hangover!"

Hank Williams was singing his heart out about how he was so lonesome he could die.

Idgie said, "Ruth moved out."

Eva's mood changed. "What?"

"Moved out. Went over to Cleo and Ninny's house."

Eva sat down. "Well, good Lord, Idgie, why did she do that?"

"She's mad at me."

"I figured that. But what did you do?"

"I lied to her."

"Uh-oh. What did you say?"

"I told her I was going to Atlanta to see my sister Leona and John."

"Didn't you go?"

"No."

"Where did you go?"

"Out in the woods."

"With who?"

"By myself. I just wanted to be by myself, that's all."

"Why didn't you tell her?"

"I don't know. I guess I just kinda got mad at having to tell somebody where I am all the time. I don't know. I was beginning to feel kinda trapped, like I needed to get out for a while. So I lied. That's all. What's the big deal? Grady lies to Gladys, and Jack lies to Mozell."

"Yeah, but now, honey, you ain't Grady or Jack . . . and Ruth ain't Gladys or Mozell, either. Oh Lord, girl, I hate to see this happen, don't you remember the fits you was having until she came over here?"

"Yeah, but sometimes I just need to take off for a while. I feel like I need my freedom. You know."

"Course I know, Idgie, but you got to look at this thing from her point of view. That girl give up everything she had to come over here. She left her hometown and all her friends she grew up with—gave up all that just to be here and make a life for you. You and Stump are all she has. You've got all your friends and your family . . ."

"Yeah, well, sometimes I think they like her better than they do me."

"You listen, Idgie, I'm gonna tell you something. Don't you think she couldn't have anybody that she wanted around here? All she'd have to do is snap her fingers. So I'd think long and hard before I'd go flying off."

At that moment, Helen Claypoole, a woman of about fifty, who'd been hanging around the River Club for years, picking up men and drinking with anything that moved and would buy her drinks, came out of the bathroom so drunk that she had stuffed the back of her dress in her panties and was staggering to her table, where the men were waiting for her.

Eva pointed toward her. "Now, there's a woman who's got her freedom. Nobody gives a shit where she is and ain't nobody checkin' up on her, you can be damn sure of that."

Idgie watched Helen, with her lipstick smeared and her hair falling in her face, sitting there, looking at the men with her boozy eyes, not seeing them.

Pretty soon Idgie said, "I gotta go. Gotta think this thing out."

"Yeah, well, I thought you might."

Two days later, Ruth received a neatly typed note that said, "If you cage a wild thing, you can be sure it will die, but if you let it run free, nine times out of ten it will run back home."

Ruth called Idgie for the first time in three weeks. "I got your note and I've been thinking, maybe we should at least talk."

Idgie was thrilled. "I think that would be great. I'll be right over," and started out the door, planning to swear on a Bible in front of Reverend Scroggins's house, if she had to, that she would never lie to Ruth again.

As she turned the corner and saw Cleo and Ninny's house, something Ruth said dawned on her. What note? She hadn't sent any note.

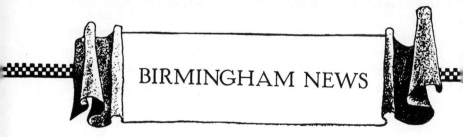

# BIRMINGHAM NEWS

OCTOBER 15, 1947

## One-Armed Quarterback Leads Team to Fifth Straight Victory

In a 27 to 20 win over Edgewood, with the score tied 20–20 throughout the fourth quarter, victory for Whistle Stop came in the thrilling 43-yard pass made by Whistle Stop's one-armed quarterback, Buddy (Stump) Threadgoode, a senior.

"Stump is our most valuable player," said Coach Delbert Naves in an interview earlier today. "His winning attitude and team spirit has made the difference. Despite his handicap, he has been able to complete 33 out of 37 attempted passes this year. He is able to take the snap from center and hug the ball to his chest, get the correct grip, and throw the ball in less than two seconds, and his speed and accuracy are outstanding."

This B-average student is also on the first string

baseball and basketball team. He is the son of Mrs. Ruth Jamison, of Whistle Stop, and when asked how he became so proficient in sports, he said that his Aunt Idgie, who helped raise him, taught him everything he knows about football.

# WHISTLE STOP CAFE

OCTOBER 28, 1947

Stump had just come in from practice and got himself a Coke. Idgie was behind the counter fixing Smokey Lonesome a second cup of coffee, and she said to him as he passed by, "I want to talk to you, young man."

Uh-oh, thought Smokey, and buried his head in his pie.

Stump said, "What'd I do? I didn't do anything . . ."

"That's what you think, little fella," she said to Stump, who at the time was six feet tall and shaving. "Let's go in the back room."

He followed her slowly and sat down at the table. "Where's Momma?"

"She's over at the school at a meeting. Now, young man, what did you say to Peggy this afternoon?"

He looked innocent. "Peggy? Peggy who?"

"You know Peggy who. Peggy Hadley."

"I didn't say anything."

"You didn't say anything."

"No."

"Then why do you suppose she came in the cafe, no more than an hour ago, just crying her eyes out?"

"I don't know. How should I know?"

"Didn't she ask you to go to the Sadie Hawkins Dance with her this afternoon?"

"Yeah, I guess she may have. I don't remember."

"And what did you say?"

"Aw, Aunt Idgie, I don't want to go to any dance with her. She's just a kid."

"What did you say?"

"I told her I was busy or something. She's crazy, anyhow."

"Mister, I am asking you what you said to that girl."

"Aw, I was just kidding."

"You were just kidding, huh? What you were doing is standing around, trying to be a big shot in front of all your friends, is what you were doing."

He shifted uncomfortably in his chair.

"You told her to come back when she had grown some tits and ask you again. Isn't that right?"

He didn't answer.

"Isn't that right?"

"Aunt Idgie, I was just *kidding.*"

"Well, you're lucky you didn't get your face popped."

"Her brother was standing right there with me."

"Well, he ought to have his butt kicked, too."

"She's just making a big thing out of nothing."

"A big thing out of nothing? Do you have any idea how much nerve it took for that poor little thing to ask you to the dance, and then for you to say something like that in front of all those boys? Now, you listen, buddy boy. Your mother and I didn't raise you to be an ignorant, knothead redneck. How would you feel if somebody talked like that to your mother? What if some girl told you to come back when you grew a penis?"

Stump turned red. "Don't talk like that, Aunt Idgie."

"Yes I will talk like that. I will not have you acting like white trash. Now, if you don't want to go to the dance, that's one thing, but you are not going to talk to Peggy or any other girl like that. Do you hear me?"

"Yes'm."

"I want you to go down to her house right now and apologize to her. And I don't mean maybe. Do you hear me?"

"Yes ma'am."

He got up.

"Sit down. I'm not through with you!"

Stump sighed and slumped back down in his chair. "What now?"

"I need to talk to you about something. I wanna know what's going on with you and the girls."

Stump looked uncomfortable. "What do you mean?"

"I've never pried into your personal life. You're seventeen years old and big enough to be a man, but your mother and I are worried about you."

"Why?"

"We thought you might outgrow this stage you're in, but you're too old to keep hanging around the boys like you do."

"What's the matter with my friends?"

"Nothing, it's just that they're all boys."

"So?"

"There are a whole bunch of girls that are just crazy about you, and you never even give them the time of day."

No answer.

"You act like a horse's ass whenever one of them tries to talk to you. I've seen you."

Stump started picking a hole in the checked oilcloth on the table.

"Look at me when I talk to you . . . your cousin Buster is already married, with a baby on the way, and he's only a year older than you."

"So?"

"So you've never even asked a girl out to a picture show, and every time there's a dance over at the school, you decide to go hunting."

"I like to hunt."

"So do I. But you know, there's more to life than hunting and sports."

Stump sighed again and closed his eyes. "I don't like to do anything else."

"I bought you that car and had it fixed up for you because I thought you might want to take Peggy somewhere, but all you do is run it up and down the road with the boys."

"Why Peggy?"

"Well, Peggy or anybody—I don't want you winding up all alone like poor Smokey in there."

"Smokey's all right."

"I know he's all right, but he'd be a whole lot better if he had a wife and a family. What's gonna happen to you if something happens to me or your mother?"

"I'll get by. I'm not stupid."

"I know you'd get by, but I'd like to think you'd have some-body to love and take care of you. Before you know it, all the best girls are gonna be taken. And what's the matter with Peggy?"

"She's all right."

"I know you like her. You used to send her valentines before you got to be so high and mighty."

No answer.

"Well, is there anybody else you like?"

"Naw."

"Why not?"

Stump began to squirm and yelled, "I JUST DON'T, THAT'S ALL. NOW LEAVE ME ALONE!"

"Listen, bub," Idgie said, "you may be a big deal on that football field, but I changed your diapers and I'll knock you to hell and back! Now what is it?"

Stump didn't answer.

"What is it, son?"

"I don't know what you're talking about. I gotta go."

"Sit down. You don't have to go anywhere."

He sighed and sat back down.

Idgie quietly asked, "Stump, don't you like girls?"

Stump looked away. "Yeah, I like 'em all right."

"Then why don't you go out with them?"

"Well, I'm not weird or anything, if that's what you're wor-ried about. It's just—" Stump was wiping his sweaty palm on his khaki pants.

"Come on, Stump, tell me what it is, son. You and I have always been able to talk things out."

"I know that. I just don't want to talk to anybody about this."

"I know you don't, but I want you to. Now, what is it?"

"Well, it's just that . . . oh Jesus!" Then he mumbled, "It's just that what if one of them wanted to do it . . ."

"You mean, wanted to have sex?"

Stump nodded and looked at the floor.

Idgie said, "Well then, I'd consider myself a lucky boy, wouldn't you? I think it would be a compliment."

Stump wiped the perspiration off his upper lip.

"Son, are you having some kind of physical trouble, you know, getting yourself up? Because if you are, we can take you to the doctor and have you checked out."

Stump shook his head. "No. It's not that. Nothing's the matter with me, I've done it a thousand times."

Idgie was amazed at the number, but remained calm and said, "Well then, at least we know you're all right."

"Yeah, I'm all right, it's just that, well, I haven't done it with anybody . . . you know . . . I've just done it by myself."

"That's not gonna hurt you, but don't you think you should try it out with some girl? I cain't believe you haven't had the chance, a good-looking boy like you."

"Yeah, I had the chance. It's not that—it's just—" Idgie heard his voice crack. "It's just . . ."

"Just what, son?"

All of a sudden he couldn't stop the hot tears from running down his face. He looked up at her. "It's just that I'm scared, Aunt Idgie. I'm just plain scared."

The one thing Idgie had never suspected was that Stump, who had been so brave all of his life, could be scared of anything.

"What are you afraid of, son?"

"Well, I'm kinda afraid I'll fall on her or lose my balance because of my arm and maybe I just won't know how to do it right. You know, I might hurt her or something . . . I don't know."

He was avoiding her eyes.

"Stump, look at me. What are you really afraid of?"

"I told you."

"You're afraid some girl might laugh, aren't you?"

Finally, after a moment, he blurted out, "Yes. I guess that's it," and he put his hand over his face, ashamed to be crying.

At that moment, Idgie's heart went out to him and she did something she very rarely did; she got up and put her arms around him and rocked him like a baby.

"Oh, honey, don't you cry. Everything's gonna be all right, angel. Nothing's gonna happen to you. Aunt Idgie's not gonna let anything bad ever happen. No I'm not. Have I ever let you down?"

"No ma'am."

"Nothing bad's gonna happen to my boy. I won't have it." The whole time she was rocking Stump back and forth, she was feeling helpless and was trying to think if she knew someone who might be able to help him.

Early Saturday morning, Idgie drove Stump over to the river, as she had so many years ago, and through the white wagon-wheel gate and up to a cabin with a screened-in porch; and let him out.

The door of the cabin opened, and a freshly bathed, powdered, and perfumed woman with rust-colored hair and apple-green eyes said, "Come on in, sugar," as Idgie drove away.

# THE WEEMS WEEKLY

(WHISTLE STOP, ALABAMA'S WEEKLY BULLETIN)

OCTOBER 30, 1947

## Stump Threadgoode Makes Good

Stump Threadgoode, son of Idgie Threadgoode and Ruth Jamison, got a big write-up in the *Birmingham News*. Congratulations. We're all mighty proud of him, but don't go in the cafe unless you're willing to spend an hour having Idgie tell you all about the game. Never saw a prouder parent. And after the game, the whole team and the band and the cheerleaders were treated to free hamburgers at the cafe.

My other half has no fashion sense. I came home the other afternoon looking so smart in my new snood that I got over at Opal's beauty shop, and he said my snood looked like a goat's udder with a fly net on it. . . . Then, on our anniversary, he carries me over to Birmingham to a spaghetti restaurant, when he knows I'm on a diet. . . . Men! Can't live with them, and can't live without them.

By the way, we were sorry to hear about Artis O. Peavey's bad luck.

. . . Dot Weems . . .

# SLAGTOWN,
# ALABAMA

## OCTOBER 17, 1949

Artis O. Peavey had been staying with his second wife, the former Miss Madeline Poole, who was employed as a first-class domestic. She worked for a family on the exclusive Highland Avenue. They were living at her house at No. 6 Tin Top Alley, over on the south side of town. Tin Top Alley was nothing more than six rows of wooden shack houses with tin roofs and dirt yards, most of which had been decorated with washtubs planted with colorful flowers to offset the drab gray wood of the shacks.

It was a step up from their last address. That had been the old servants' quarters in the back of a house, whose address was simply No. 2 Alley G.

Artis found the neighborhood extremely pleasant. One block away was Magnolia Point, where he could hang out in front of stores and visit with other husbands of domestics. In early evenings, after a supper, usually of white folks' leftovers, they would all sit on the porches, and many a night one family would start to sing, and one by one the others would join in. Recreation was plentiful because the walls were so thin that you could enjoy your neighbor's radio or phonograph along with them; when Bessie Smith sang on somebody's Victrola, "I ain't got nobody," everybody in Tin Top Alley felt sorry for her.

The area was certainly not lacking in other social activities, and Artis was invited to all of them; he was the most popular man in the alley, with men and women alike. Every night there would be at least one or two chitlin fryings or barbecuing . . . or if the weather was bad, you could just sit under the yellow light on your front porch and enjoy the sound of the rain hitting the tin roofs.

This fall afternoon, Artis had been sitting on the porch watching a thin trail of blue smoke rise up from his cigarette, happy because Joe Louis was the champion of the world and the Birmingham Black Barons baseball team had won all their games that year. Just then, a skinny, mangy yellow dog came loping around the alley, scrounging for something to eat; he belonged to After John, a friend of Artis's, named such because he had been born after his brother John. The dog wigwagged his way up the porch steps to Artis and got his daily pat on the head.

"I ain't got nuthin' for you today, boy."

The yellow dog was mildly disappointed, and wandered off in search of leftover cornbread or even a few greens. The Depression had never ended here, and dogs were in it too, for better or for worse; and most times for the worse.

Artis saw the dogcatchers' truck drive up and the man in the white uniform got out with his net. The back was already loaded with yelping dogs unfortunate enough to have been caught that afternoon.

The man who got out whistled for the yellow dog, who was up the street.

"Here, boy . . . here, boy . . . Come on, boy . . ."

The friendly, unsuspecting dog ran over to him and in a second was in the net, flipped over on his back, and was being carried to the truck.

Artis came off the porch. "Hey, whoa, mister. That dog belongs to somebody."

The man stopped. "Is he yours?"

"Naw, he ain't mine. He belong to After John, so you cain't be carrying him off, no suh."

"I don't care who it belongs to, it don't have a license and we're taking him in."

The other man in the truck got out and just stood there.

Artis began to plead, because he knew that once that dog got down to the city pound, there wasn't a chance in hell of ever getting him back; particularly if you were black.

"Please, mister, let me go and call him. He works over at Five Points, fo' Mr. Fred Jones, making ice cream. Jes' let me call him."

"Do you have a phone?"

"No suh, but I can run up to the grocery store. Won't take but a minute." Artis pleaded harder with the man. "Oh please, suh, After John is jes' a simpleminded boy no woman would marry and that dog is all he's got. I don't know what he'd do if anything happened to that dog of his. He's liable to kill hisself."

The two men looked at each other, and the larger one said, "Okay, but if you ain't back in five minutes, we're leaving. You hear me?"

Artis starting moving. "Yes suh, I'll be right back."

As he ran, he realized that he didn't have a nickel, and prayed that Mr. Leo, the Italian man that ran the grocery store, would loan him one. He ran in the store, out of breath, and saw Mr. Leo.

"MR. LEO, MR. LEO, I GOTS TO HAVE A NICKEL . . . THEY GONNA CARRY AFTER JOHN'S DOG OFF . . . AND THEY'S WAITING FOR ME. PLEASE, MR. LEO . . ."

Mr. Leo, who hadn't understood a word that Artis had said, made him calm down and explain to him all over again, but by the time he got his nickel, there was a white boy on the phone.

Artis was sweating, moving from one foot to another, knowing he couldn't make that fellow get off that phone. One minute . . . two . . .

Artis moaned.

"Oh Lord."

Finally, Mr. Leo passed by and knocked on the glass booth. "Get off!"

The young man begrudgingly said goodbye to his party for the next sixty seconds and hung up.

After he left, Artis jumped in the booth and realized he did not know the number.

His hands were wet and shaking as he searched through the telephone directory, hanging from a small chain. "Jones . . . Jones . . . Oh Lord . . . Jones . . . Jones . . . four pages full . . . Fred B. . . . Oh man, that's his residence . . ."

He had to start all over in the Yellow Pages. "What do I look under . . . Ice Cream? Drugstore?" And he couldn't find it. He dialed information.

"Information," a crisp white voice answered. "Yes, please, may I help you?"

"Uh, yes ma'am. Uh, I's looking for the number of Fred B. Jones."

"I'm sorry, could your repeat that name, please?"

"Yes ma'am, Mr. Fred Jones in Five Points." His heart was pounding.

"I have about fifty Fred Joneses, sir. Do you have a street address?"

"No ma'am, but he's over in Five Points."

"I have three Fred Joneses in the Five Points area . . . would you like all three numbers?"

"Yes ma'am."

He searched his pockets for a pencil—and she started . . . "Mr. Fred Jones, 18th South, 68799; and Mr. Fred Jones, 141 Magnolia Point, 68745; and Fred C. Jones, 15th Street, that number is 68721 . . ."

He never found a pencil and the operator hung up. Back to the book.

He could hardly breathe. The sweat was running down his eyes, blurring his vision. Drugstore . . . Pharmacy . . . Ice Cream . . . Food . . . Catering . . . THAT'S IT! Here it was, Fred B. Jones Catering, 68715 . . .

He mashed the nickel in the slot and dialed the number. Busy. Tried again. Busy . . . busy . . .

"Oh Lord."

After trying eight times, Artis didn't know what to do, so he just ran back to the men. He turned the corner and, Thank God, they were still there, leaning up against the truck. They had the dog tied to the door handle with a rope.

"You get him?" the big one asked.

"No suh," he said, gasping. "I wasn't able to reach him, but if you could just ride me over to Five Points, I could get him . . ."

"Naw, we're not gonna do that. We already wasted enough time with you, boy," and he began to untie the dog and put him in the back.

Artis was desperate. "Naw suh, I jes' cain't let you do it."

He reached in his pocket, and before either one of the men knew what had happened, he had sliced the rope holding the dog in half with the four-inch switchblade, and yelled, "Scat!"

Artis turned around and watched the grateful dog scamper around the corner, and was smiling when the blackjack hit him behind his left ear.

TEN YEARS FOR THE ATTEMPTED MURDER OF A CITY OFFI-
CIAL WITH A DEADLY WEAPON. It would have been thirty if those two men had been white.

# BIRMINGHAM, ALABAMA

SEPTEMBER 1, 1986

Ed Couch came home Thursday night and said that he was having trouble with a woman down at the office who was "a real ball breaker," and that none of the men wanted to work with her because of it.

The next day, Evelyn went out to the mall to shop for a bed jacket for Big Momma and while she was having lunch at the Pioneer Cafeteria, a thought popped into her head, unannounced:

What is a ball breaker?

She'd heard Ed use that term a lot, along with *She's out to get my balls* and *I had to hold on to my balls for dear life.*

Why was Ed so scared that someone was out to get his balls? What were they, anyway? Just little pouches that carried sperm; but the way men carried on about them, you'd think they were the most important thing in the world. My God, Ed had just about died when one of their son's hadn't dropped properly. The doctor said that it wouldn't affect his ability to have children, but Ed had acted like it was a tragedy and wanted to send him to a psychiatrist, so he wouldn't feel less of a man. She remembered thinking at the time, how silly

. . . her breasts had never developed, and nobody ever sent her for help.

But Ed had won out, because he told her she didn't understand about being a man and what it meant. Ed had even pitched a fit when she wanted to have their cat, Valentine, who had impregnated the thoroughbred Siamese cat across the street, fixed.

He said, "If you're gonna cut his balls off, you might as well just go on and put him to sleep!"

No doubt about it, he was peculiar where balls were concerned.

She remembered how Ed had once complimented that same woman at the office when she had stood up to the boss. He had bragged on her, saying what a ballsy dame she was.

But now that she thought about it, she wondered: What did that woman's strength have to do with Ed's anatomy? He hadn't said, "Boy, she's got some ovaries"; he had definitely said what *balls* she had. Ovaries have eggs in them, she thought: Shouldn't they be as important as sperm?

And when had that woman stepped over the line of having just enough balls to having too much?

That poor woman. She would have to spend her whole life balancing imaginary balls if she wanted to get along. Balance was everything. But what about size? she wondered. She never heard Ed mention size before. It was the other thing's size they were so concerned about, so she guessed it didn't matter all that much. All that mattered in this world was the fact that you *had* balls. Then all at once, the simple and pure truth of that conclusion hit her. She felt as if someone had run a pencil up her spine and dotted an *i* on her head. She sat up straight in her chair, shocked that she, Evelyn Couch, of Birmingham, Alabama, had stumbled on the answer. She suddenly knew what Edison must have felt like when he discovered electricity. Of course! That was it . . . having balls was the most important thing in this world. No wonder she had always felt like a car in traffic without a horn.

It was true. Those two little balls opened the door to everything. They were the credit cards she needed to get ahead, to be listened to, to be taken seriously. No wonder Ed had wanted a boy.

Then another truth occurred to her. Another sad, irrevocable truth: She had no balls and never would or could have balls. She was doomed. Ball-less forever. Unless, she thought, if maybe the balls in your immediate family counted. There were four in hers . . . Ed's and Tommy's . . . No, wait . . . six, if she counted the cat. No, wait just another minute, if Ed loved her so much, why couldn't he give her one of his? A ball transplant. . . . That's right. Or, maybe she could get two from an anonymous donor. That's it, she'd buy some off a dead man and she could put them in a box and take them to important meetings and bang them on the table to get her way. Maybe she'd buy four . . .

No wonder Christianity had been such a big hit. Think of Jesus and the Apostles . . . And if you counted John the Baptist, why that was 14 pairs and 28 singles, right there!

Oh, it was all so simple to her now. How had she been so blind and not seen it before?

Yes, by heavens, she'd done it. She'd hit upon the secret that women have been searching for through the centuries . . .

THIS WAS THE ANSWER . . .

Hadn't Lucille Ball been the biggest star on television?

She banged her iced tea on the table in triumph and shouted, "YES! THAT'S IT!"

Everyone in the cafeteria turned and looked at her.

Evelyn quietly finished her lunch and thought, *Lucille Ball?* Ed might be right. I probably am going crazy.

## THE WEEMS WEEKLY

(WHISTLE STOP, ALABAMA'S WEEKLY BULLETIN)

JUNE 10, 1948

## Benefit for New Balls

The Dill Pickle Club will hold a womanless wedding to benefit the high school so they can get a new set of balls for the football, basketball, and baseball teams this year. This should be quite an evening, with our own Sheriff Grady Kilgore as the lovely bride and Idgie as the groom. Julian Threadgoode, Jack Butts, Harold Vick, Pete Tidwell, and Charlie Fowler will be bridesmaids.

This affair will be at the high school on June 14, at seven o'clock. Admission is 20¢ for adults and 5¢ for children.

Essie Rue Limeway will play the organ for the wedding.

Come one, come all! I intend to be there, as my other half, Wilbur, will be the flower girl.

My other half and I went to the picture show and

saw *The Gracie Allen Murder Mystery.* It was funny, but go before the prices change at seven.

By the way, Rev. Scroggins said someone put his lawn furniture on top of his house.

. . . Dot Weems . . .

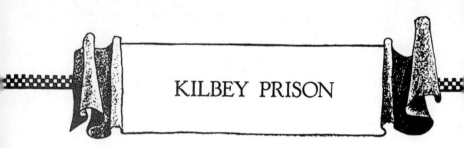

# KILBEY PRISON

JULY 11, 1948

Artis O. Peavey had been sent down to Kilbey Prison, better known as the Murder Farm, for pulling a knife on those two dogcatchers, and it had taken Idgie and Grady six months of trying before they could get him out.

On the way down, Grady said to Idgie, "It's a damn good thing he's coming out now. He might not of lasted in that place for another month."

Grady knew what he was talking about, having once been a guard there.

"Hell, if the guards don't get him, then the other niggers will. I've seen decent men turn into animals inside. Men, with a wife and children at home, will turn around and kill one another over some gal-boy . . . every night in the cell blocks was bad—but whenever there was a full moon, look out. They all go crazy and stick each other. We'd go in the next morning and there'd be about twenty-five stiffs we'd have to bring out. And after a while down there, the only difference between the men and the guards is the gun. Most of those guards are pretty simpleminded old boys . . . they'll go to a picture show and see Tom Mix or Hoot Gibson and then they come back and ride around the farm, pulling their guns, trying to be cowboys. Sometimes they get meaner than the prisoners. That's why I quit. I've seen men that would beat a nigger to death, just to have something to do. I'm telling you, that place gets to you after a while, and I hear now that they've got those Scotts-borough boys down here, things is worse than ever."

Now Idgie was really worried and she wished he would drive faster.

When they turned in the gate that led down the road to the main building, they saw hundreds of prisoners in coarse striped uniforms out in the yard digging or hoeing, and they saw the guards, just like Grady had said, showing off as the car passed by, running their horses in circles and peering at the car as it drove by. Idgie thought that most of them did look a little retarded, so when they brought Artis out, she was relieved to see that he was still alive and well.

Although his clothes were wrinkled, his hair was nappy. Artis was never so happy to see anybody in his whole life. The scars on his back from the whip didn't show, and they could not see the lumps on his head. He grinned from ear to ear as they walked out to the car. He was going home . . .

On the way back, Grady said, "Now, Artis, I'm in charge of you, so don't be going and getting in any more trouble. You hear?"

"No suh. I don't ever want to go back to that place, no suh."

Grady looked at him in the rearview mirror. "Pretty rough in there, huh?"

Artis laughed. "Yes suh, it be pretty rough, all right . . . yes suh, pretty rough."

When they first caught sight of the steel mills in Birmingham about four hours later, Artis became so excited he was like a child, and wanted to get out of the car.

Idgie tried to get him to come home to Whistle Stop first. "Your momma and daddy and Sipsey are all waiting to see you."

But he pleaded to get out in Birmingham for just a few hours, so they drove him over to 8th Avenue North, where he wanted to be let out.

Idgie said, "Please try and get on home soon, 'cause they really want to see you . . . promise?"

Artis said, "Yes ma'am, I promise," and ran down the street, laughing so happy to be back where he belonged.

About a week later, he showed up at the cafe, his hair smooth as glass, looking spectacular in his brand-new Revel hat, designed in Harlem, with the extra-wide brim, a gift from Madeline, happy to have him home.

## ROSE TERRACE NURSING HOME

OLD MONTGOMERY HIGHWAY
BIRMINGHAM, ALABAMA

SEPTEMBER 7, 1986

This week, for Evelyn and Ninny, the bill of fare was Corn Curls and Cokes and homemade brownies.

"Honey, you should have been out here this morning, you missed a *show*. We were all having our breakfast and we looked up and there was Vesta Adcock with a bran muffin on her head, doing a hula dance right in front of us in the dining room. It was a sight! Poor old Mr. Dunaway got so excited they had to give him his pill and take him to his room. Geneene, that little colored nurse, made her sit down and eat her muffin. They want us to have one of those every day, so we won't get constipated. When you get up in years, your digestive system goes off."

She leaned over and whispered. "Some of these old people out here pass gas and they don't even know they've done it."

Ninny took a swig of her Coke. "You know, a lot of these people resent having colored nurses out here. One of them said that deep down, all colored people hate white people and if those nurses got a chance, they'd kill us off in our sleep."

Evelyn said that was the stupidest thing she'd ever heard.

"That's what I thought at the time, but it was your mother-in-law that said it, so I shut my trap."

"Well, I'm not surprised."

"Oh, it's not just her. You'd be surprised how many of them out here think that way. But I don't believe it for one minute. I've been around colored people all my life. Why, when Momma Threadgoode died and was laid out in the parlor, that afternoon we looked out the window and, one by one, every colored woman from Troutville had gathered out in the side yard, there by the window, and they started singing one of their old Negra spirituals, 'When I Get to Heaven, I'm Gonna Sit Down and Rest Awhile' . . . Oh, I never will forget it. You've never heard singing like that, it still gives me goose bumps just to think about it.

"And take Idgie, for instance. She had as many friends over in Troutville as she did in Whistle Stop. She was always over there preaching at some funeral if a friend of hers died. She told me one time that she preferred them to some of the whites she knew. I remember one time she said to me, 'Ninny, a no-good nigger is just no good, but a low-down white man is lower than a dog.'

"Of course, I cain't speak for all of them, but I never saw anybody more devoted to a person than Onzell was to Ruth. Ruth was her special pet, and she let you know it, too. She wouldn't allow anybody to bother Ruth.

"I remember one time when Idgie was acting up, drinking and carrying on and she didn't come home all night, she told her, right in the kitchen the next day, she said, 'Now, Miz Idgie, I'm gonna tell you something . . . Miz Ruth's done left one no-account, and it'd be jest as easy to leave two, an' I's jest the one to help her pack.'

"Idgie just walked out of the kitchen and didn't say a word. She knew not to cross Onzell where Ruth was concerned.

"As sweet as she was, Onzell could be tough. She had to be, raising all those kids and working all day at the cafe. When Artis or Naughty Bird would get to pestering her, I've seen her backslap them out the door and never miss cutting a biscuit.

"But she was gentle as a lamb where Ruth was concerned.

And when Ruth got that terrible cancer in her female organs and had to go over to Birmingham and have an operation, Onzell went right along with Idgie and me. We were all three sitting in the waiting room when the doctor came in. He hadn't even taken off his cap and gown and he said, 'I'm sorry to have to tell you this, but I cain't do a thing for her.' It had spread to her pancreas, and once it hits you in your pancreas, you're a goner. So he said he just sewed her back up and left a tube in her to drain.

"We took her home to the Threadgoode house and put her upstairs in one of the bedrooms so she would be more comfortable, and from the moment she got there, Onzell moved into the room with her and never left her side.

"Idgie wanted to hire a nurse, but Onzell wouldn't hear of it. All of her children were grown by then, but Big George had to cook for himself.

"Poor Idgie and Stump, they just sorta fell apart. They'd just sit downstairs in a daze. Ruth went down so fast and, oh, she was in so much pain. She'd tried not to let on she was, but you could tell. Onzell was right there with her medicine, twenty-four hours a day, and during the last week, Onzell wouldn't let anybody in to see her but Idgie and Stump. She said that Ruth had begged her not to let anyone see her looking so terrible.

"I never will forget what she said, standing there in front of that door. She said, Miss Ruth is a lady and always knew when to leave a party, and this wasn't going to be any exception as long as she was around.

"She kept her word. Big George and Stump and Idgie were way out in the woods looking for pinecones for her room when Ruth died, and by the time they got back home she had been taken away.

"Onzell had called Dr. Hadley, and he had sent an ambulance over to pick up Ruth's body and take her over to the funeral home in Birmingham. Cleo and I went down there with her, waiting, and after they put her in the ambulance, Dr. Hadley said, 'You go on home now, Onzell, and I'll ride over with her and make all the arrangements.'

"Well, honey, Onzell pulled herself up tall and told Dr. Hadley, 'No suh, that's my place!' and marched right by him and got in the back of the ambulance and closed the door. She had packed Ruth's gown and makeup and did not leave the funeral parlor that night until she thought Ruth looked like she wanted her to look.

"So there's not a person alive that can tell me that colored people hate white people. No sir! I've seen too many sweet ones in my life to believe that.

"I told Cleo just the other day, I'd like for us to ride the train to Memphis and back so I could see Jasper and see what he's up to. He works on the dining car."

Evelyn looked at her friend and realized that she was confused about time again.

# WHISTLE STOP, ALABAMA

FEBRUARY 7, 1947

That rainy morning, Onzell had asked Stump and Idgie to go down to the woods by the river and get some pinecones for Miss Ruth's sickroom. She was wiping Ruth's face with a damp cloth.

"Hold on, Miz Ruth, it's gonna be over soon. It's gonna be over soon, baby."

Ruth looked back up at her and tried to smile, but the pain in her eyes was terrible. There was no rest from it now; no sleep, no relief.

Onzell, a charter member of the Mount Zion Primitive Baptist Church and the lead singer in the Halleluiah Choir, who believed with all her heart and soul in a merciful God, had made a decision.

No God, anywhere, certainly not her sweet, precious Jesus, Who died for our sins and loved us above all things, had *ever* meant anyone to suffer like this.

So it was with perfect joy and a pure heart that she gave Ruth the morphine that she'd been saving, bit by bit, day by day. Onzell watched Ruth's body relax for the first time in weeks, and then she sat down by the bed and held her little skeleton of a hand and began to rock and sing.

In the sweet by and by . . . there's a land that's fairer by day
And by faith we can see it afar . . .
For the Father waits over the way
To prepare us in a dwelling place
There in the sweet by and by . . . we shall meet on the beautiful shore
In the sweet by and by . . .

Onzell had her eyes closed as she was singing, but she felt the room fill up with sunlight that had broken through the clouds. The warmth of the sun made her cry tears of joy. As she covered the mirror and stopped the clock by the bed, she thanked her sweet Jesus for taking Miss Ruth home.

FEBRUARY 10, 1947

## Beloved Citizen Passes

The cafe will be closed tomorrow, due to the death of Mrs. Ruth Jamison, who passed away over the weekend.

Funeral services will be held tomorrow at the Baptist church. Call Reverend Scroggins for the time. She will be at John Rideout's Funeral Home in Birmingham until then.

We will miss her sweet ways and smiling face, and everyone who knew "Miss Ruth" will be at a loss. Our special love and sympathy goes out to Idgie and Stump.

. . . Dot Weems . . .

# PIGLEY-WIGLEY
# SUPERMARKET

BIRMINGHAM, ALABAMA

SEPTEMBER 13, 1986

On Saturdays, when Evelyn Couch went shopping, she always drove Ed's big Ford LTD, because there was more room, but it was hard to park; so she had been sitting waiting for the parking place on the end for five minutes while the old man loaded the groceries into his car, took another three minutes to get in, find his keys, and finally backed out. Just as she was about to pull in, a slightly battered red Volkswagen came around the corner and shot right in the space she had been waiting for.

Two skinny, gum-chewing teenage girls, wearing cut-off jeans and rubber flip-flops, got out and slammed the door and started to walk right past her.

Evelyn rolled down her window and said to the one in the ELVIS IS NOT DEAD T-shirt, "Excuse me, but I was waiting for that space and you pulled right in front of me."

The girl looked at her with a smirk and said, "Let's face it, lady, I'm younger and faster than you are," and she and her friend flip-flopped into the store in their rubber-thonged shoes.

Evelyn was left sitting there, staring at the Volkswagen with the I BRAKE FOR REDNECKS bumper sticker on the back.

Twelve minutes later, the girl and her friend came out, just in time to see all four of their hubcaps fly across the parking lot as Evelyn crashed into the Volkswagen, backed up, and slammed into it again. By the time the two hysterical girls had reached the car, Evelyn had almost demolished it. The tall one went berserk, screaming and pulling her hair. "My God! Look what you've done! Are you crazy?"

Evelyn leaned out her window and calmly said, "Let's face it, honey, I'm older than you are and have more insurance than you do" and drove away.

Ed, who worked for an insurance agency, did have plenty of insurance, as it turned out, but he could not understand how she could have run into someone six times by mistake.

Evelyn told him to calm down and not to make a big thing out of it; accidents happen all the time. The truth was, she had enjoyed wrecking that girl's car too much. Lately, the only time she wasn't angry and the only time she could find peace was when she was with Mrs. Threadgoode and when she would visit Whistle Stop at night in her mind. Towanda was taking over her life, and somewhere, deep down, a tiny alarm bell sounded and she knew she was in sure danger of going over the edge and never coming back.

# WHISTLE STOP CAFE

MAY 9, 1949

Tonight, Grady Kilgore, Jack Butts, and Smokey Lonesome were in the cafe, giggling. This was the seventh week in a row that they had managed to put a whiz bomb in Reverend Scroggins's car. But when Stump came out of the back room, all dressed up in his blue suit and blue bow tie, they stopped and decided to razz him for a while.

Grady waved at him. "Oh, usher, where's my seat?"

Idgie said, "Come on, boys, let him alone. I think he looks handsome. He's got a date with Peggy Hadley, Doc's girl."

Jack called out in a silly voice, "Oh, Doctor . . ."

Stump got himself a Coca-Cola and gave Idgie a dirty look. If it hadn't been for her, he would not be stuck having to go to the Sweetheart Banquet with Peggy Hadley, a little girl he once had a crush on but had now outgrown. Peggy was two years younger than he was and wore glasses, and he had ignored her his entire high school career. But the minute she found out he was back from Georgia Tech for the summer, she went over and asked Idgie if she thought Stump would go to her Senior Sweetheart Banquet with her, and Idgie had graciously accepted.

Being a gentleman, he had figured that one night wouldn't kill him—although at the moment he was not sure.

Idgie went over to the icebox in the kitchen and handed him a bouquet of tiny sweetheart roses. "Here, I went up to the big house today and cut some out in the backyard. Take these to her. Your mother loved those little things."

He rolled his eyes. "Oh God! Aunt Idgie, why don't you just go instead of me? You've planned the entire evening anyway."

Stump turned to the gang at the table. "Hey, Grady! You wanna go?"

Grady shook his head. "Wish I could, but Gladys'd kill me if she ever caught me with a younger woman. But then, you don't know anything about that. Just wait till you're an old married man, like I am, boy. Besides, I ain't the man I used to be."

"Or ever was, for that matter," Jack interjected.

They laughed, and Stump went out the door. "Well, I'm off. Guess I'll see you afterwards."

Every year, after the banquet, all the kids wound up at the cafe; and tonight was no exception. When Peggy came in, looking so pretty in her white eyelet dress, with her pink sweetheart roses pinned at the shoulder, Idgie said, "Thank God you're all right. I've been worried to death about you."

Peggy asked her why in the world would she be so worried.

"Didn't you hear about that girl over in Birmingham, last week?" Idgie said. "She was so excited at her Sweetheart Banquet that while she was posing for her picture, all of a sudden she burned right up. A case of spontaneous combustion. In seconds she was gone. Nothing was left of her but her high heels. Her date had to take her home in a Dixie cup."

Peggy, who had believed the story up to a point, said, "Oh, Idgie, you're playing with me!"

Stump was glad when the evening was over and they were headed home. The fact that he had been a football hero the year before made him still subject to a lot of younger boys standing around staring at him and girls squealing and giggling when he said hello, or anything, for that matter.

He stopped the car in front of Peggy's house and was getting ready to get out and go around and open her door when she took her glasses off, leaned over, and looked up at him with those big brown myopic Susan Hayward eyes of hers and said, "Well, good night."

He looked down into those eyes, realizing that he had never seen them before: pools of velvet brown that he could have dived into and had a swim in. Her face was now a quarter of an inch from his, and he smelled the intoxicating scent of her White Shoulders perfume; in that moment she became Rita Hayworth in *Gilda;* no, Lana Turner in *The Postman Always Rings Twice.* And when he kissed her, it was the most passionate moment he had ever known.

That summer, the blue suit was trotted out regularly, and that fall it wound up in Columbus, Georgia, when they went over to the courthouse to get married. All Idgie ever said to him was "I told you so."

After that, all Peggy ever had to do was take off her glasses and look up at him, and he was a goner.

# BIRMINGHAM,
# ALABAMA

MAY 24, 1949

Birmingham's black middle- and upper-class society was at its peak, and the *Slagtown News* was kept busy reporting on the doings of over a hundred social clubs; the lighter the skin, the better the club.

Mrs. Blanche Peavey, Jasper's wife, who was as light in color as he was, had just been named president of the famous Royal Saxon Society Belles Social and Saving Club, an organization whose members were of such fair coloring that the club's annual group picture had wound up in the white newspaper by mistake.

Jasper had just been reelected as Grand Vice Chancellor of the prestigous Knights of Pythias, so it was only natural that his oldest daughter, Clarissa, was a leading debutante that year and was being presented to the Carnation Coalition.

With her red-gold, silky hair, her peaches-and-cream complexion, and her green eyes, she was considered the deb you would most want to be with.

On the day of the Debutante Ball, Clarissa went downtown to buy some special perfume for the affair. She had ridden up to the second floor on the main white elevator, as she had done a few times before when she had been downtown alone, knowing that other members of her race rode the freight elevator.

She knew her mother and daddy would kill her if they knew she was downtown passing, for although she was encouraged to mingle only with the lighter-skinned people, passing for a white was an unpardonable sin. But she was tired of the stares of the other blacks when she rode the freight elevator before; and besides, she was in a hurry.

The beautiful woman in the royal blue wool dress behind the counter was so considerate and polite to Clarissa. "Have you ever tried White Shoulders?"

"No ma'am, I don't think so."

She bent down under the counter for the display bottle. "Try a little of this. Shalimar is very popular, but I think it's going to be a little too heavy for you, with your fair skin and all."

Clarissa smelled it on her wrist. "Oh, this is wonderful. How much is it?"

"It's on special, eight ounces for two ninety-eight. That should last you at least six months.

"I'll just get this, then."

The lady was pleased. "I think it suits you perfectly. Cash or charge?"

"Cash."

The woman took the money and went off to wrap the box.

A black man wearing a checked hat and coat had been staring at Clarissa. He remembered a picture in the paper. He walked over.

" 'Scuse me, ain't you Jasper's baby?"

Terror-struck, Clarissa pretended not to hear him.

"I'm your Uncle Artis, your daddy's brother."

Artis, who had had a few drinks and didn't know Clarissa was passing for white that day, put his hand on her arm. "It's me, your Uncle Artis, honey . . . don't you know me?"

The perfume saleslady came around the corner, saw Artis and shrieked, "YOU GET AWAY FROM HER!" She ran to Clarissa and held her. "YOU GET AWAY FROM HER . . . HARRY! HARRY!"

The floor manager came running. "What's the matter?"

Still holding on to Clarissa to protect her, she shouted for the entire floor to hear, "THIS NIGGER WAS PAWING MY CUSTOMER! HE WAS GRABBING AT HER! I SAW HIM!"

Harry yelled, "GUARD!" and turned on Artis with slits for eyes. "Did you touch this white woman, boy?"

Artis was shocked. "Naw suh, that's my niece."

Artis tried to explain, but by that time, the guard had spun him around like a top and had his arm behind him and he was on his way out the back door.

The saleswoman comforted Clarissa. "It's okay, honey, that nigger's either drunk or crazy."

The group of lady shoppers who had gathered around offered sympathy. "Just another drunk Negro . . . See what happens when you're nice to them?"

Artis, who had skinned his hands and knees when he was thrown out in the concrete alley behind the store, caught the south-side streetcar and walked back behind the wooden sign that said COLORED. He sat down, wondering if that girl had been Clarissa, after all.

Years later, after Clarissa was married and had children, she came into Brittling's Cafeteria, where he was working carrying trays, and tipped him a quarter; but she didn't recognize him, and he didn't recognize her.

# THE WEEMS WEEKLY

(WHISTLE STOP, ALABAMA'S WEEKLY BULLETIN)

AUGUST 10, 1954

## Mishaps Galore

Must be getting old or crazy . . . my other half, Wilbur, came home three days in a row, complaining of a headache . . . and is there anything worse than a man who has a little pain? Guess that's why we have the babies . . .

I, myself, was having a terrible time reading the paper, so yesterday morning, I went to Birmingham to get my eyes checked, and, lo and behold, I had on Wilbur's glasses and he had on mine. We are getting different colored ones next time.

I don't feel too bad. I heard there was a fire the other day over at Opal's beauty shop, and Biddie Louise Otis, who was hooked up to the permanent wave machine at the time, started screaming bloody murder because she thought it was her head that was on fire. But it was just some old hair in the wastepaper basket that was burning. Naughty Bird,

Opal's shampoo girl, put out the fire and it was fine.

Don't forget to vote. Nobody is running against Grady Kilgore, but it makes him feel good, so do it anyway.

By the way, Jasper Peavey got another write-up in the *Railroad News,* and we know Big George and Onzell must be proud.

. . . Dot Weems . . .

P.S. The Dill Pickle Club had its annual Icebox Follies again and it was hilarious as usual. My other half sang "Red Sails in the Sunset" again. Sorry, folks . . . I just cain't get him to learn a new one.

# ROSE TERRACE NURSING HOME

OLD MONTGOMERY HIGHWAY
BIRMINGHAM, ALABAMA

### SEPTEMBER 14, 1986

Evelyn and Mrs. Threadgoode were taking a walk out behind the nursing home when a flock of Canada geese flew over, honking happily through the fall sky.

"Oh Evelyn, wouldn't you love to be going with them? Wonder where they're going?"

"Oh, Florida or Cuba, maybe."

"You think so?"

"Probably."

"Well, I wouldn't mind going to Florida, but I don't care a thing in the world about going to Cuba. Smokey used to say those geese were his pals, and when we'd ask him where it was that he'd go off to, he'd say, 'Oh, I just go where the wild geese goes . . .' "

They watched them fly out of sight, and continued on their walk.

"Don't you love ducks?"

"They're pretty, all right."

"I just love ducks. I guess you could say that I was always partial to fowl."

"What?"

"Fowl. You know—poultry, things with feathers, birds, chickens, roosters."

"Oh."

"Cleo and I would have our coffee out on the back porch every morning and watch the sun come up and listen to the birds . . . we'd always have about three or four good old hot cups of Red Diamond coffee and toast with peach or green pepper jelly, and we'd talk—well, I'd talk and he'd listen. We had so many pretty birds come to the house: redbirds, robins, and the prettiest doves . . . you don't see birds like you used to, anymore.

"One day, Cleo was going out the door and he pointed up to where all the old blackbirds were sitting on a telephone wire in front of our house, and he'd say, 'Be careful what you say on the phone today, Ninny, you know they're up there listening to what you say. They can hear through their feet.' " She looked at Evelyn. "Do you believe that's true?"

"No. I'm sure he was just kidding you, Mrs. Threadgoode."

"Well, he probably was, but whenever I had a secret to tell, I'd look out the door and make sure they weren't sitting up there. He should have never told me that, knowing how much I love to jaw on the phone. I used to talk to everybody in town.

"I guess at one time we had upwards to two hundred fifty people living in Whistle Stop. But after they stopped most of the trains coming through, people just scattered all over like birds to the wind . . . went to Birmingham, or wherever, and never came back.

"Where the cafe was, they've put a Big Mac, and they've got some supermarket out on the highway that Mrs. Otis liked to go to because she clipped coupons. But I never could find anything I was looking for in there, and the lights hurt my eyes so bad, so I just walk over to Troutville to Ocie's grocery store to pick up whatever little bit I need."

Mrs. Threadgoode stopped. "Oh Evelyn, smell that . . . somebody's cooking barbecue!"

Evelyn said, "No honey, I think that's somebody just burning leaves."

"Well, it smells like barbecue to me. You like barbecue, don't you? I love it. I'd pay a million dollars for a barbecue like Big George used to make, and a piece of Sipsey's lemon icebox pie. He made the best barbecue.

"He cooked it in a big old iron drum, out in the back of the cafe, and you could smell it for miles around, especially on a fall day. I could smell it all the way over to my house. Smokey said he was coming in on the train one time and he smelled it ten miles up the tracks from Whistle Stop. People drove all the way from Birmingham to get it. Where do you and Ed get your barbecue?"

"We get it over at the Golden Rule or Ollie's, mostly."

"Well, they're all right, but I don't care what you say, colored people can make barbecue better than anybody in the whole world."

Evelyn said, "They can do most everything better. I wish I was black."

"You mean colored?"

"Yes."

Mrs. Threadgoode was completely baffled. "Lord, honey, why? Most of them want to be white; they're always trying to bleach their skin and straighten their hair."

"Not anymore."

"Well, maybe not now, but they used to. Just thank the good Lord He made you white. I just cain't imagine why anybody would want to be colored when they don't hafta be."

"Oh, I don't know, they just seem to fit in with each other . . . have more of a good time, or something. I've always felt . . . well . . . stiff, I guess, and they always look like they're having so much fun."

Mrs. Threadgoode thought about it for a minute. "Well now, that may be true, they do have a lot of fun, and they can let go when they want to, but they have their sorrows, just like the rest of us. Why, you've never heard anything sadder than a colored funeral. They scream and carry on just like somebody was tearing the very heart out of them. I think pain hurts them more than it does us. It took three men to hold Onzell when Willie Boy was buried. She went crazy and tried to jump in the grave with him. I don't ever want to go to another one of those for as long as I live."

"I know there's good and bad in everything," Evelyn said, "but I still can't help but envy them, somehow. I just wish I could be free and open like they are."

"Well, I don't know about that," Mrs. Threadgoode said. "I just wish I had me a barbecue and a piece of pie, and I'd be happy."

# WHISTLE STOP, ALABAMA

OCTOBER 15, 1949

Naughty Bird Peavey was sixteen when she first laid eyes on Le Roy Grooms. She knew immediately that he was her man; and she told him so. He was employed as a cook on *The Crescent,* which passed through Whistle Stop on its way to New York, via Atlanta. One year later, a little girl was born, whom Le Roy named Almondine, after the trout dish featured on the pullman dining car menu.

Le Roy was a handsome, good-natured boy who traveled a lot and made many stops along the route; and when Naughty Bird found out that he had moved in with an almost white, but not quite, high yellow octoroon woman in New Orleans, it just about killed her.

She was desperate when she saw the ads in the *Slagtown News:*

SKIN TOO DARK? WANT TO HAVE A COMPLEXION
THAT CHARMS?
*Then try Dr. Fred Palmer's Skin Whitener*

CLEAR LIGHT SKIN WINS KISSES
*Men admire a lovely, smooth skin. Use*
SUCCESS OINTMENT, *to have a lighter, more*
*beautiful skin in 5 days.*


BEAUTY BEGINS WITH A FAIR FACE
*So bring out all your natural beauty that*
*you can with White's Specific Face Cream (Bleach)*


HAIR TOO KINKY?
*Let modern science quickly end tight, scalp-clinging*
*twisty curls. Have gloriously beautiful, straight silky*
*hair with Genuine Black and White Pluko Hair*
*Dressing*
*Try Relaxa . . . and have straight hair in 7 days.*


*Say*
GOODBYE TO HAIR KINKS
*If your hair is short and kinky, just get NO-KINK*
*today. Temporarily makes hair lie down.*


Naughty Bird tried them all, and more, but after a month she was still the coal-black, nappy-headed shampoo girl from Whistle Stop, and Le Roy was still in New Orleans with his high yellow girl friend.

So she took her little girl over to Sipsey's, went back home, got in the bed, and was dying of love.

There was nothing anybody could do. Opal came over to see her and begged her to come back to work at the beauty shop, but Naughty Bird lay there, day after day, drinking Turkey gin and playing the same song over and over. Sipsey said it would have been better for Naughty Bird if Le Roy had died instead of living with another woman, because after drinking Turkey gin for two months straight, Naughty Bird was not getting any relief.

Fortunately, Sipsey's words turned out to be prophetic, because Mr. Le Roy Grooms left this world for another when he was hit hard in the temple with a toy iron dump truck, belonging to one of the high yellow's little male children.

When Naughty Bird got the tragic news, she got up out of bed, went into the bathroom and washed her face, and fixed herself a breakfast of eggs, ham, grits and red-eye gravy, biscuits covered with butter and Eagle Brand table syrup, and had three cups of steaming coffee. She took a bath, got dressed, applied a little Dixie Peach hair oil, leaned into the mirror to apply a triple coat of tangerine-orange rouge and lipstick to match, and headed out the door and over to Birmingham, on the rove.

Within a week she was back with a surprised-looking young man in a plaid hat with a green feather, and a brown gabardine suit.

# THE MARTIN LUTHER KING MEMORIAL BAPTIST CHURCH

1049 4TH AVENUE NORTH
BIRMINGHAM, ALABAMA

## SEPTEMBER 21, 1986

Evelyn had promised Mrs. Threadgoode that she would take her troubles to the Lord and ask the Lord to help her through these bad times. Unfortunately, she didn't know where the Lord was. She and Ed had not been to church since the children were grown, but today she felt desperate for help, for something to hold on to; so she got dressed and drove over to the Highland Avenue Presbyterian Church, where they used to be members.

But when she got there, for some reason she just drove on by and, all of a sudden, found herself across town, sitting in the parking lot of the Martin Luther King Memorial Baptist Church—the largest black church in Birmingham—wondering what in the hell she was doing there. Maybe it had been all these months of hearing about Sipsey and Onzell. She didn't know.

All her life she had considered herself to be a liberal. She had never used the word *nigger*. But her contact with blacks had been the same as for the majority of middle-class whites before the sixties—mostly just getting to know the maid or the maids of friends.

When she was little, she would sometimes go with her father when he would drive their maid to the south side, where she lived. It was just ten minutes away, but seemed to her like going to another country: the music, the clothes, the houses . . . everything was different.

On Easter they would drive over to the south side to see the brand-new Easter outfits: pinks and purples and yellows, with plumed hats to match.

Of course, it was the black women who worked inside the homes. Whenever a black man was anywhere nearby, her mother would get hysterical and scream at her to run put on a robe because, *"there's a colored man in the neighborhood!"* To this day, Evelyn was not comfortable with black men around.

Other than that, her parents' attitude about blacks had been like most back then; they thought most were amusing and wonderful, childlike people, to be taken care of. Everyone had a funny story to tell about what this maid said or did, or would shake their heads with amusement about how many children they kept having. Most would give them all their old clothes and leftovers to take home, and help them if they got in trouble. But as Evelyn got a little older, she didn't go to the south side anymore and thought little about them; she had been too busy with her own life.

So, in the sixties, when the troubles began, she, along with the majority of whites in Birmingham, had been shocked. And everyone agreed that it was not "our colored people" causing all the trouble, it was outside agitators who had been sent down from the North.

It was generally agreed too that "our colored people are happy the way they are." Years later, Evelyn wondered where her mind had been and why she hadn't realized what had been going on just across town.

After Birmingham suffered so badly in the press and on TV, people were confused and upset. Not one of the thousands of kindnesses that had taken place between the races was ever mentioned.

But twenty-five years later Birmingham had a black mayor,

and in 1975, Birmingham, once known as the City of Hate and Fear, had been named the All-American City by *Look* magazine. They said that a lot of bridges had been mended, and blacks, who had once gone north, were coming back home. They had all come a long way.

Evelyn knew this, but nevertheless, as she sat in the church parking lot, she was amazed at all the Cadillacs and Mercedeses driving up and parking all around her. She had heard that there were rich blacks in Birmingham, but she had never seen them before.

As she watched the congregation arrive, all of a sudden that old fear of black men came back.

She glanced around the car to make sure that all her doors were locked, and was getting ready to drive away when a father and mother with two children walked by her car, laughing; then she snapped back to reality and calmed down. After a few minutes, she mustered up all her courage and went inside the church.

But even after the usher with the carnation smiled at her and said, "Good morning," and led her down the aisle, she was still shaking. Her heart pounded all the way to her seat, and her knees were weak. She had hoped to sit in the back, but he had escorted her to the middle of the church.

In moments, sweat was pouring off Evelyn and she was short of breath. Few people seemed to look at her. A couple of children turned around in their seats and stared; she smiled, but they did not smile back. She had just decided to leave when a man and a woman came into the pew and sat down beside her. So there she was, stuck in the middle, just like always. This was the first time in her life she had ever been surrounded by only blacks.

All at once, she was the belly of a snake, the Pillsbury Doughboy, a page in a coloring book left uncolored, a pale flower in the garden indeed.

The young wife beside her was stunning, and dressed like someone Evelyn had seen only in magazines. She could have been a high-fashion model from New York, in her pearl-gray silk outfit, with snakeskin shoes and a purse to match. As she looked around the room, Evelyn realized that she had never seen so many beautifully dressed people in one place in her life. She was still uneasy about the men—their pants fit too tight to suit her—so she concentrated on the women.

But then, she had always admired them, their strength and compassion. She had always wondered how they could love and care for white children and nurse old white men and women with such gentleness and care. She didn't think she could have.

She watched the way they greeted each other, their wonderful and complete easiness with themselves, the way they moved with that smooth and natural grace, even the heavyset ones. She didn't ever want one of them to get mad at her, but she'd love to see somebody call one of *them* a fat cow.

She realized that all of her life she had looked at blacks but she had never really seen them. These women were good-looking; thin brown girls with cheekbones like Egyptian queens, and those big, magnificent-looking, balloon-breasted women.

Imagine all those people in the past trying to look white; they must be laughing from their graves at all the middle-class white-boy singers trying so hard to sound black, and the white girls in their corn rows and Afros. The tables have turned . . .

Evelyn began to relax and feel a little more comfortable. Somehow, she had expected the inside of the church to look much different. As she looked around, Evelyn was convinced it could have been any one of the dozens of white churches all over Birmingham; then, all of a sudden, the organ struck a chord and the 250 members of the choir, in bright red and maroon robes, stood up and sang out with a power and a force that almost knocked her off her seat:

> "Oh happy day . . .
> Oh happy day . . .
> When Jesus washed my sins away . . .
> He taught me how to sing and pray . . .
> And live rejoicing every day . . .

Oh happy day . . .
Oh happy day . . .
When Jesus washed my sins away . . .
Oh happy, happy day . . ."

After they sat back down, the Reverend Portor, a huge man with a voice that filled the church, rose from his chair and began his sermon, entitled "The Joy of a Loving God." And he meant it. Evelyn felt it all through the church. As he preached, he would throw his massive head back and shout and laugh with happiness. And the congregation and the organ that accompanied him would answer back with the same.

She had been wrong; this was not just like the white churches, certainly not the dried-up, bloodless sermons she was used to.

His enthusiasm for the Lord was contagious and spread like wildfire throughout the room. He assured them, with a great and mighty authority, that his God was not a vengeful God, but one of goodness . . . love . . . forgiveness . . . and *joy*. And he began to dance and strut and sing out his sermon to the rafters, sweat sparkling on his shining face, which he would mop off occasionally with the white handkerchief he kept in his right hand.

As he sang out, he was answered from all over the church:
"YOU CANNOT HAVE JOY UNLESS YOU LOVE YOUR NEIGHBOR . . ."
*"That's right, sir."*
"LOVE YOUR ENEMIES . . ."
*"Yes sir."*
"LET GO OF THOSE OLD GRUDGES . . ."
*"Yes sir, let go."*
"SHAKE LOOSE OF THAT OLD DEVIL, ENVY . . ."
*"Yes sir."*
"GOD CAN FORGIVE . . ."
*"Yes He can."*
"WHY CAN'T YOU? . . ."
*"You're right, sir."*
"TO ERR IS HUMAN . . . TO FORGIVE, DIVINE . . ."

*"Yes sir."*

"THERE IS NO RESURRECTION FOR BODIES GNAWED BY THE MAGGOTS OF SIN . . .

*"No sir."*

"BUT GOD CAN LIFT YOU UP . . ."

*"Yes He can."*

"OH! GOD IS GOOD . . ."

*"Yes sir."*

"OH! HOW GOOD IS OUR GOD . . ."

*"You're right, sir."*

"WHAT A FRIEND WE HAVE IN JESUS . . ."

*"Oh yes sir."*

"YOU CAN BE BAPTIZED, CIRCUMCISED, GALVAN-IZED, AND SIMONIZED, BUT IT DON'T MEAN A THING IF YOU AIN'T A CITIZEN OF GLORY . . ."

*"No sir."*

"THANK YOU, JESUS! THANK YOU, JESUS! GOOD GOD ALMIGHTY! WE PRAISE YOUR NAME THIS MORNING AND THANK YOU, JESUS! HALLELUIAH! HALLELUIAH JESUS!"

When he had finished, the whole church exploded in "Amens!" and "Halleluiahs!" and the choir started again, until the room began to throb with . . .

"ARE YOU WASHED IN THE BLOOD . . . THE SOUL-CLEANSING BLOOD OF THE LAMB . . . OH TELL ME, SWEET CHILDREN . . . ARE YOU WASHED IN THE BLOOD . . ."

Evelyn had never been a religious person, but this day she was lifted from her seat and rose high above the fear that had been holding her down.

She felt her heart open and fill with the pure wonder of being alive and making it through.

She floated up to the altar, where a white Jesus, wan and thin, wearing a crown of thorns, looked down from the crucifix at her and said, "Forgive them, my child, they know not what they do . . ."

Mrs. Threadgoode had been right. She had taken her troubles to the Lord, and she had been relieved of them.

Evelyn took a deep breath and the heavy burden of resentment and hate released itself into thin air, taking Towanda along with them. She was free! And in that moment she forgave the boy at the supermarket, her mother's doctor, and the girls in the parking lot . . . and she forgave herself. She was free. *Free;* just like these people here today, who had come through all that suffering and had not let hate and fear kill their spirit of love.

At which point Reverend Portor called for the congregation to shake hands with their neighbors. The beautiful young woman sitting next to her shook her hand and said, "God bless you." Evelyn squeezed the woman's hand and said, "Thank you. Thank you so much."

As she left the church, she turned at the door and looked back one last time. Maybe she had come today hoping she could find out what it was like to be black. Now she realized she could never know, any more than her friends here could know what it felt like to be white. She knew she would never come back. This was their place. But for the first time in her life, she had felt joy. Real joy. It had been joy that she had seen in Mrs. Threadgoode's eyes, but she hadn't recognized it at the time. She knew that she might never feel it again. But she had felt it once, and now she would never forget the sensation as long as she lived. It would have been wonderful if she could have told everyone in the church how much that day had meant to her.

It would have been wonderful, too, if Evelyn had known that the young woman who shook her hand had been the eldest daughter of Jasper Peavey, pullman porter, who, like herself, had made it through.

JUNE 1, 1950

## Railroad Employee of the Month

"His only aim is to see people happy and to make their trip more pleasant. Please don't overlook this outstanding railroad man when passing out the pats on the back to the Railroad Man of the Month."

That's how *Silver Crescent* passenger Cecil Laney described pullman porter Jasper Q. Peavey.

This genial porter has been receiving commendations since he started working for the railways at age 17, as a redcap at the Terminal station in Birmingham, Alabama. Since then, he has been cook, freight trucker, station porter, dining car waiter, parlor car porter, and was promoted to pullman porter in 1935. He became president of the Birmingham branch of the Brotherhood of Sleeping Car Porters in 1947.

Mr. Laney goes on to say, "Jasper's little courtesies begin the minute a passenger boards the train. He makes a special effort to see that all the passengers have their luggage properly boarded, and through the trip, he looks for those little unexpected things he can do to make the ride more comfortable, with his big, always-present smile and happy laugh.

"A few minutes before arrival at the station, he always announces, 'In about five minutes we will be arriving at . . . If I can help you with your baggage, it will be a pleasure to do so.'

"To us, he is a trusted friend, an attentive host, a watchful guardian, a dispenser of comforts, and a doer of favors. He chaperones the children and helps mothers in distress; he is most courteous, helpful and efficient, for which the passengers are deeply grateful. It is unusual to find such a man in the times through we which we are now passing."

Jasper is a lay pastor at the Sixteenth Street Baptist Church in Birmingham, and is the father of four daughters: Two of them are teachers, one of them is studying to be a nurse, and the youngest is planning to go to New York and study music.

Congratulations to Jasper Q. Peavey, our Outstanding Railroad Employee of the Month.

AUGUST 27, 1955

## Railroad Yard Closing

Of course, we are all so sad to hear that the railroad yard is closing. Now that we have lost most of our trains, we seem to be losing a lot of our old friends, who are moving on to other places. We can only hope that the trains will start running again. It will not seem right with just a few trains passing through.

Grady Kilgore, retired official of L & N Railroad, says that the country cannot exist without its trains, and that it is just a matter of time before the government realizes it. I say the L & N Co. will come to its senses and put them back on the line soon.

Georgia Pacific Seaboard, and now L & N. Only Southern Railroad has held out . . . it seems they just don't want passengers anymore.

Also, we hear that the cafe may be closing. Idgie says that her business is way down.

By the way—

My other half claims he has had the eight-day pneumonia for ten days . . . Men!

... Dot Weems ...

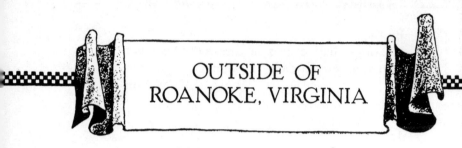

# OUTSIDE OF ROANOKE, VIRGINIA

DECEMBER 23, 1958

Jasper Peavey sat up all through the quiet night while the train glided through the snow-laden landscape and the moon sparkled on the passing fields of white.

It was freezing outside the ice-cold window, but warm and cozy inside the car. This was when he felt safest, and at ease. No more smiling for the day . . . just quiet.

The red and green railroad crossing lights slid by at each stop, and early in the dawn, the lights began to come on, one by one, in the small towns.

He was a month away from retiring, with a nice pension, from the Southern Railroad. Jasper had come to Birmingham a year later than his brother Artis, and although they were twins and both classified as Negro under the law, they had lived two entirely different lives.

Jasper had loved his brother, but hardly ever saw him.

Artis had quickly found a place among the fast, racy set down on 4th Avenue North, where the jazz was hot and dice rolled night and day. Jasper had taken up residence at a Christian boardinghouse four blocks away and had attended church at the 16th Street Baptist Church the first Sunday he was in

Birmingham. It was there that Miss Blanch Maybury had caught the eye of and took a shine to this creamy boy with his mother's freckles. Blanch was the only daughter of Mr. Charles Maybury, a respected citizen, well-known educator, and principal of the Negro high school, so it was through her that Jasper was automatically admitted to the exclusive, upper-middle-class black society.

When they married, if Blanch's father had been disappointed in Jasper's lack of formal education and background, Jasper's color and manners more than made up for it.

After he married, Jasper worked hard; and while Artis was spending his money on clothes and women, Jasper was staying in the cold, rat-infested dormitories that the company provided for porters when they were out of town. He saved until he and Blanch could go down to the piano company and buy one for cash. A *piano* in the home meant something. He gave ten percent to the church and started a savings account for the children's college education at the all-black Penny Saving Bank. He'd never touched a drop of whiskey, never borrowed a dime, and never been in debt. He had been one of the first blacks in Birmingham to move into white Enon Ridge, later known as Dynamite Hill. After the Klan had blown up Jasper's and several of his neighbors' red brick homes, some had left, but he had stayed. He had endured years of "Hey, Sambo," "Hey, boy," "Hey, George," emptied cuspidors, cleaned bathrooms, shined shoes, and lifted so much luggage that he couldn't sleep from the pain in his back and shoulders. He had often cried in humiliation when something was stolen and the railroad officials searched the pullman porters' lockers first.

He had "yes sirred" and "yes ma'amed" and smiled and brought loud-mouthed salesmen liquor in the middle of the night, had taken abuse from arrogant white women and been called nigger by children, had been treated like dirt by some of the white conductors, and had had his tips stolen by other porters. He had cleaned up after sick strangers and passed through Cullman County a hundred times, with the sign that warned, NIGGER . . . DON'T LET THE SUN SET ON YOUR HEAD.

He had endured all this. But . . .

The burial policy for his family was paid off, he had sent all four of his children through college, and not one of them would ever have to live off tips. That was the one thought that had kept him going all the long, hard, back-breaking years.

That, and trains. If his brother Artis had been in love with a town, Jasper was in love with trains. *Trains,* with dark, polished, mahogany wood-paneled club cars and plush, red velvet seats. *Trains,* with the poetry of their names . . . *The Sunset Limited . . . The Royal Palm . . . The City of New Orleans . . . The Dixie Flyer . . . The Fire Fly . . . The Twilight Limited . . . The Palmetto . . . The Black Diamond . . . The Southern Belle . . . The Silver Star . . .*

And tonight, he was riding on *The Great Silver Comet,* as slender and streamlined as a silver tube . . . from New Orleans to New York and back, one of the last of the great ones still running. He had mourned each of those great trains as, one by one, they were pulled off the lines and left to rust in some yard, like old aristocrats, fading away; antique relics of times gone by. And tonight he felt like one of the old trains . . . off the track . . . out of date . . . past the prime . . . useless.

Just yesterday, he overheard his grandson Mohammed Abdul Peavey telling his mother that he didn't want to go anywhere with his grandaddy because he was embarrassed by the way he bowed and scraped to white people and the way he acted in church, still singing that old coon-shine, ragtime gospel music of his.

It was clear to Jasper that his time was over now, just like his old friends rusting out in the yards. He wished it could have been different; he had gotten through the only way he had known how. But he had gotten through.

# HOTEL ST. CLAIR

(BIRMINGHAM'S UP-TO-THE-MINUTE HOTEL)

411 2ND AVE. NORTH

BIRMINGHAM, ALABAMA

## DECEMBER 23, 1965

Smokey was across the street from the boarded-up terminal L & N station downtown, in a hotel room that may have been up to the minute thirty-five years ago but now consisted only of a bed, a chair, and a forty-watt light bulb on a string. The room was pitch black, except for the pale yellow light that spilled through the glass transom at the top of the tall, thickly enameled, brown door.

Smokey Lonesome sat alone, smoking his cigarette and looking out the window onto the cold wet street below, thinking back to a time when there had been little stars in the ring around the moon and all the rivers and the whiskey had been sweet. When he had been able to take a breath of fresh air without coughing his guts up. When Idgie and Ruth and Stump still lived in the back of the cafe, and all the trains were still running. That time, special time, so long ago . . . just an instant away in his mind . . .

Those memories were still there, and tonight, he sat searching for them, just like always, grabbing at moonbeams. Every once in a while he would catch one and take a ride, and it was like magic. An old song played over and over in his head:

Smoke rings
Where do they go?
Those smoke rings I blow?
Those circles of blue, that
Keep reminding me of you . . .

# ROSE TERRACE
# NURSING HOME

OLD MONTGOMERY HIGHWAY
BIRMINGHAM, ALABAMA

## SEPTEMBER 22, 1986

When Evelyn Couch came into the lounge, Mrs. Threadgoode was asleep, and suddenly looked her age. Evelyn realized how old her friend really was, and it scared her. She shook her.

"Mrs. Threadgoode!"

Mrs. Threadgoode opened her eyes and patted her hair, and began talking at once. "Oh Evelyn. Have you been here long?"

"No, I just got here."

"Well, don't you ever let me sleep through visitors' day. You promise?"

Evelyn sat down and handed her friend a paper plate with a barbecue sandwich and a piece of lemon icebox pie, a fork and napkin.

"Oh Evelyn!" Mrs. Threadgoode sat up. "Where'd you get this? Over at the cafe?"

"No. I made it especially for you."

"You did? Well, bless your heart."

Evelyn had noticed that for the past couple of months, her friend seemed to be getting more and more mixed up about time, past and present, and sometimes called her Cleo. Sometimes she would catch herself and laugh; but more and more, lately, she didn't.

"Sorry I drifted off like that. But it's not only me; everybody out here is exhausted."

"Why, can't you sleep at night?"

"Honey, nobody's been able to sleep out here for weeks. Vesta Adcock has taken to making phone calls all night long. She calls everybody, from the president to the mayor. She called the queen of England to complain about something the other night. She gets herself all fussed up like an old cat and carries on all night long."

"Why in the world doesn't she close her door?"

"She does."

"Well, why don't they take the phone out of her room?"

"Honey, they did, only she don't know it, she just keeps on making calls."

"My God! Is she . . . crazy?"

"Well, let's put it this way," Mrs. Threadgoode said kindly. "She's of this world, but not in it."

"Yes. I think you're right."

"Honey, I sure would love a cold drink to go with my pie. You think you could get me one? I'd go, but I cain't see well enough to find the slot."

"Oh, of course. I'm sorry, I should have asked."

"Here's my nickel."

"Oh Mrs. Threadgoode, now don't be silly. Let me buy you a drink. My heavens."

Mrs. Threadgoode said, "No. Now Evelyn, you take this money . . . you don't need to be spending your cash on me," she insisted. "I won't drink it if you don't let me pay for it."

Finally, Evelyn took the nickel and bought the seventy-five-cent drink with it, as she always did.

"Thank you, honey . . . Evelyn, did I ever tell you I hated brussels sprouts?"

"No. Why don't you like brussels sprouts?"

"I cain't say. I just don't. But I love anything else in the vegetable family. I don't like them frozen, though, or in a can.

I like fresh, sweet corn, lima beans, and good ol' black-eyed peas, and fried green tomatoes . . ."

Evelyn said, "Did you know that a tomato is a fruit?"

Mrs. Threadgoode, surprised, said, "It is?"

"It sure is."

Mrs. Threadgoode sat there, bewildered, "Oh no. Here all these years, throughout my whole life, I've been thinking they were a vegetable . . . served them as a vegetable. A tomato is a *fruit*?"

"Yes."

"Are you sure?"

"Oh yes. I remember that from home economics."

"Well, I just cain't think about it, so I'm gonna pretend I never even got that piece of information. Now, a brussels sprout is a vegetable, isn't it?"

"Oh yes."

"Well, good. Now I feel better. . . . What about a snap bean? You're not gonna tell me that's a fruit, too?"

"No, that's a vegetable."

"Well, good." She ate the last bit of pie and remembered something and smiled.

"You know, Evelyn, last night I had the loveliest dream. It seemed so real. I dreamed Momma and Poppa Threadgoode were standing on the front porch of the old house, waving for me to come over . . . and pretty soon, Cleo and Albert and all the Threadgoodes came out on the porch, and they all started calling to me. I wanted to go so bad, but I knew I couldn't. I told them I couldn't come now, not until Mrs. Otis got better, and Momma said, in that sweet little voice of hers, 'Well, hurry up, Ninny, 'cause we're all here waiting.' "

Mrs. Threadgoode turned to Evelyn, "Sometimes I just cain't wait to get to heaven. I just cain't wait. The first thing I'm gonna do is look up old Railroad Bill—they never did find out who he was. Of course, he was colored, but I'm sure he'll be in heaven. Don't you think he'll be there, Evelyn?"

"I'm sure he will be."

"Well, if anyone deserves to be there, it's him—I just hope I know when I see him."

## WHISTLE STOP CAFE

WHISTLE STOP, ALABAMA

FEBRUARY 3, 1939

The place was jam-packed full of railroad men at lunchtime, so Grady Kilgore went to the kitchen door and hollered in, "Fix me a mess of them fried green tomatoes and some ice tea, will ya, Sipsey? I'm in a hurry." Sipsey handed Grady his plate and he walked back in the cafe with his lunch.

Nineteen thirty-nine marked the fifth winter in a row that Railroad Bill had been hitting the trains. As Kilgore passed, Charlie Fowler, an engineer for the Southern Railroad, said, "Hey, Grady, I hear old Railroad Bill hit himself another train last night. Ain't you railroad dicks ever gonna catch that boy?"

All the men laughed as Grady sat down at the counter to eat. "You boys can laugh if you want to, but it ain't funny. That makes five trains that son of a bitch has hit in the past two weeks."

Jack Butts sniggered. "That nigger boy's got ya'll jumping every which way, ain't he?"

Wilbur Weems, next to him, smiled and chewed on a toothpick. "I heard tell he threw a whole boxcar full of canned goods off between here and Anniston, and the niggers got 'em before sunup."

"Yeah, and not only that," Grady said. "That black bastard threw seventeen hams that belonged to the United States government right off the damn train, in broad daylight."

Sipsey giggled as she put his iced tea down in front of him.

Grady reached for the sugar. "Now, that ain't *funny*, Sipsey. We got a government inspector coming down from Chicago that's on my tail. I've got to go over to Birmingham and meet him, right now. Hell, we've already put on six extra men, over at the yard. That son of a bitch is liable to get me fired."

Jack said, "I hear nobody can figure out how he's getting on the trains and how he knows which ones have food on 'em. Or how he gets off before you boys can catch him."

"Grady," Wilbur added, "they say you ain't ever come close to catching him."

"Yeah, well, Art Bevins almost had him the other night, outside Gate City. Just missed getting him by two minutes, so his days are numbered . . . you mark my words."

Idgie was walking by. "Hey, Grady, why don't I send Stump over to the yard to help you boys out? Maybe he can catch him."

Grady said, "Idgie, just shut up and get me some more of these damn things," and handed his plate to her.

Ruth was behind the counter making change for Wilbur. "Really, Grady, I cain't see what harm it can be. These poor people are almost starving to death, and if it hadn't been for him throwing coal off, a lot of them would have frozen to death."

"I agree with you in a way, Ruth. Nobody cares about a few cans of beans, now and then, and a little coal. But this thing is getting out of hand. So far, between here and the state line, the company has already put on twelve new men, and I'm working a double shift at night."

Smokey Lonesome was down at the end of the counter having his coffee, and piped up, "Twelve men for one little old nigger boy? That's kinda like shooting a fly with a cannon, ain't it?"

"Don't feel bad." Idgie patted Grady on the back. "Sipsey told me the reason you boys cain't catch him is because he can turn himself into a fox or rabbit whenever he wants to. What do you think? Do you reckon that's true, Grady?"

Wilbur wanted to know how much the reward was up to.

Grady answered, "As of this morning, it was two hundred fifty dollars. Probably go up to five hundred before this thing is over."

Wilbur shook his head. "*Damn,* that's a lot of money. . . . What's he supposed to look like?"

"Well, according to our people that saw him, they say he was just a plain old nigger boy in a stocking cap."

"One smart nigger boy, I'd say," Smokey added.

"Yeah, maybe so. But I'll tell you one thing, when I do catch that black son of a bitch, he's gonna be one sorry nigger. Hell, I ain't been home to sleep in my own bed in weeks."

Wilbur said, "Well hell, Grady, from what I hear, that ain't nothing new."

Everybody laughed.

Then, when Jack Butts, who was also a member of the Dill Pickle Club, said, "Yeah, it must be pretty bad . . . I hear Eva Bates's been complaining, too," the whole place exploded with laughter.

"Why, Jack, you ought to be ashamed of yourself," Charlie said. "You ought not to insult poor Eva that way."

Grady got up and looked around the room. "You know, every one of you boys in this cafe is as ignorant as hell. Just plain ignorant!"

He went to the hat rack and got his hat, and then turned around. "They ought to call this place the Ignorant Cafe. I think I'll just take my business elsewhere."

Everybody, including Grady, laughed at that one, because there wasn't anyplace else. He went out the door and headed for Birmingham.

# 1520 WILLINA LANE

ATLANTA, GEORGIA

NOVEMBER 27, 1986

Stump Threadgoode, still a good-looking man at fifty-seven, was at his daughter Norma's house for Thanksgiving dinner. He had just finished watching the Alabama-Tennessee football game and was sitting at the table with Norma's husband, Macky, their daughter, Linda, and her skinny boyfriend with the glasses, who was studying to be a chiropractor. They were having their coffee and pecan pie.

Stump turned to the boyfriend. "I had an uncle, Cleo, that was a chiropractor. Course, he never made a dime at it . . . treated everybody in town free. But that was during the Depression, and nobody had any money, anyhow.

"My momma and Aunt Idgie ran a cafe. It wasn't nothing more than a little pine-knot affair, but I'll tell you one thing: We always ate and so did everybody else who ever came around there asking for food . . . and that was black and white. I never saw Aunt Idgie turn down a soul, and she was known to give a man a little drink if he needed it . . .

"She kept a bottle in her apron, and Momma would say, 'Idgie, you're just encouraging people into bad habits.' But

Aunt Idgie, who liked a drink herself, would say, 'Ruth, man does not live by bread alone.'

"There must have been ten or fifteen hoboes a day that showed up. But these boys weren't afraid to do a little work for their grub. Not like the ones they've got today. They'd rake the yard or sweep the sidewalk. Aunt Idgie always let them do a little something, so as not to hurt their pride. Sometimes she'd let them come sit in the back room and baby-sit with me, just so they'd think they were working. They were mostly good guys, just fellows down on their luck. Aunt Idgie's best friend was this old hobo named Smokey Lonesome. God, you could trust him with your life. Never took a thing that didn't belong to him.

"Those hoboes had an honor system. Smokey told me he heard they caught one that had stolen some silverware out of a house, and they killed him on the spot and took the silverware back to the people he had stolen it from . . . back then, we didn't even have to turn a key. These new ones on the road and riding what's left of the rails are a different breed. Just bums and dope addicts that will steal you blind.

"But Aunt Idgie never had one thing taken." He laughed. "Of course, that may have been because of that shotgun she kept by the bed . . . she was as tough as pig iron, wasn't she, Peggy?"

Peggy called back from the kitchen, "Tougher."

"Of course, most of that was just an act, but she could be a hellion if she didn't like you. She had this running feud with this old preacher at the Baptist church, where Momma taught Sunday School, and she would give him fits. He was a teetotaler, and one Sunday he preached against her friend Eva Bates, and it made her so mad she never did forgive him. Every time a stranger came to town looking to buy some whiskey, she'd take him outside the cafe and point to old Reverend Scroggins's house and she'd say, 'See that green house, down there? Just go over and knock on the door. That man's got the best liquor in the state.' She'd point out his house when some of those old boys was looking for something else, too."

Peggy came out of the kitchen and sat down. "Stump, don't be telling them that."

He laughed. "Well, she did. Always doing something mean to that man. But, like I say, she just liked for people to *think* she was mean . . . inside, she was as soft as a marshmallow. Just like that time the preacher's son, Bobby Lee, got arrested . . . she was the one he called to come get him.

"He'd gone over to Birmingham with two or three boys and gotten himself all liquored up and was running down the halls in his underwear, throwing water balloons out of the seventh-floor window; only Bobby Lee had them filled with ink and had dropped one on some big city councilman's wife when they were going into the hotel for some shindig.

"It cost Aunt Idgie two hundred dollars to get him out of jail and another two hundred dollars to take Bobby's name off the books, so he wouldn't have a police record and his daddy wouldn't find out . . . I went over there with her to get him, and coming home, she told him that if he ever let anybody know she had done it, she would shoot his you-know-whats off. She couldn't stand anybody knowing she had done a good deed, especially for the preacher's son.

"All that bunch in the Dill Pickle Club were like that. They did a lot of good works that nobody knew about. But the best part of the story is that old Bobby Lee went on to become a big-time lawyer, and wound up as an attorney general for Governor Folsom."

His daughter, Norma, came in to get the rest of the dishes. "Daddy, tell him about Railroad Bill."

Linda shot her mother an exasperated look.

Stump said, "Railroad Bill? Oh Lord, you don't really want to hear about Bill, do you?"

The boyfriend, who really wanted to take Linda out parking somewhere, said, "Yes sir, I'd love to hear about it."

Macky smiled at his wife. They had heard this story a hundred times and knew Stump loved to tell it.

"Well, it was during the Depression and, somehow, this person called Railroad Bill would sneak on the government supply trains and throw stuff off for the colored people. Then he'd jump off before they could catch him. This went on for years, and pretty soon the colored started telling stories about him. They claimed that someone saw him turn into a fox and run twenty miles on top of a barbed-wire fence. People that did see him said he wore a long black coat, with a black stocking cap on his head. They even made up a song about him. . . . Sipsey said, every Sunday in church, they'd pray for Railroad Bill, to keep him safe.

"The railroad put a huge reward up, but there wasn't a person in Whistle Stop that would have ever turned him in, even if they had known who he was. Everybody wondered and made guesses.

"I got in my head that Railroad Bill was Artis Peavey, our cook's son. He was about the right size and as fast as lightning. I followed him around night and day, but I could never catch him. I must have been around nine or ten at the time, and I would have given anything to have seen him in action, so I would have known for sure.

"Then, one morning, right around daybreak, I had to go to the toilet. I was about half asleep and when I got to the bathroom, there was Momma and Aunt Idgie in there, with the sink running. Momma looked at me, surprised, and said, 'Wait a minute, honey,' and closed the door.

"I said, 'Hurry up, Momma, I cain't wait!' You know how a kid'll do. I heard them talking and pretty soon they came out, and Aunt Idgie was drying her hands and face. When I got in there, the sink was still full of coal dust. And on the floor, behind the door, was a black stocking hat.

"I suddenly figured out why I'd seen her and old Grady Kilgore, the railroad detective, always whispering. He'd been the one who was tipping her off about the train schedules . . . it had been my Aunt Idgie jumping them trains, all along."

Linda said, "Oh Granddaddy, are you sure that's true?"

"Of course it's true. Your Aunt Idgie did all kinds of crazy things." He asked Macky, "Did I ever tell you what she did that time old Wilbur and Dot Weems got married and went on their honeymoon at a big hotel in Birmingham?"

"No, I don't think so."

Peggy said, "Stump, don't be telling that story in front of the children."

"It'll be all right, don't worry. Well anyway, old Wilbur was a member of the Dill Pickle Club, and right after the wedding, Aunt Idgie and that bunch got in a car and drove over to Birmingham as fast as they could, and bribed the hotel clerk into letting them into the honeymoon suite, and they put all kinds of funny stuff all over the bed . . . God knows what all . . ."

Peggy warned him, "Stump . . ."

He laughed. "Hell, I don't know what it was. Anyway, they got in the car and came back home, and when Wilbur and Dot got back, they asked Wilbur how he liked his honeymoon suite at the Redmont, only to find out that they had been at the wrong hotel, and some poor honeymoon couple had gotten the shock of their lives."

Peggy shook her head. "Can you imagine such a thing?"

Norma stuck her head under the serving counter. "Daddy, tell them about the catfish you used to catch down at the Warrior River."

Stump's face lit up. "Oh well. You wouldn't believe how big those catfish were. I remember one day, it was raining and I got a bite so hard, it slid me right down the bank and I had to fight to not be pulled into the water. Lightning was striking and I was fighting for my life, but after about four hours, I pulled that grandaddy mud cat out of the water and, I tell you, he must have weighed twenty pounds or more, and he was this long . . ."

Stump held out his one arm.

The skinny would-be chiropractor sat there with a stupid look on his face, seriously trying to figure out how long the catfish was.

Linda, exasperated, put her hand on her hip. "Oh Granddaddy."

Norma just cackled from the kitchen.

# ROSE TERRACE
# NURSING HOME

OLD MONTGOMERY HIGHWAY
BIRMINGHAM, ALABAMA

### SEPTEMBER 28, 1986

Today, they were enjoying a combination of things: Cokes and Golden Flake potato chips, and for dessert—another request from Mrs. Threadgoode—Fig Newtons. She told Evelyn that Mrs. Otis had eaten three Fig Newtons a day for the past thirty years, to keep her regular. "Personally, I eat 'em just 'cause I like the taste. But I'll tell you something that's good. When I was at home and didn't feel like cooking, I'd walk over to Ocie's store and pick up a package of those little brown-and-serve rolls and pour Log Cabin Syrup on them and have that for my dinner. They don't cost all that much. You ought to try it sometime."

"I'll tell you what's good, Mrs. Threadgoode, are those frozen honey-buns."

"Honey-buns?"

"Yes. They're like cinnamon buns. You know."

"Oh, I love cinnamon buns. Let's have some sometime, want to?"

"All right."

"You know, Evelyn, I'm so glad you're not on that diet of yours anymore. That raw food will kill you. I hadn't wanted to tell you this before, but Mrs. Adcock nearly killed herself on one of those slimming diets. She ate so much raw food that she was rushed to the hospital with severe stomach pains and they had to do exploratory surgery on her. And she said that while the doctor was examining all her insides, he picked up her liver to get a close look at it, and dropped it right on the floor, and it bounced four or five times before they got it. Mrs. Adcock said that she has suffered with terrible backaches ever since, because of it."

"Oh Mrs. Threadgoode, you don't believe her, do you?"

"Well, that's what she said at the dinner table the other night."

"Honey, she's just making that up. Your liver is attached to your body."

"Well, maybe she got mixed up and it was a kidney or something else, but if I were you, I wouldn't eat any more of that raw food."

"Well okay, Mrs. Threadgoode, if you say so." Evelyn took a bite of her potato chip. "Mrs. Threadgoode, there's something I've been meaning to ask you. Didn't you tell me one time that some people thought Idgie had killed a man? Or did I just think you said that?"

"Oh no, honey, a lot of people thought she had done it. Yes indeed, 'specially when she stood trial for murder with Big George over in Georgia . . ."

Evelyn was shocked. "She did?"

"Haven't I ever told you about that before?"

"No. Never."

"Oh . . . Well, it was awful! I remember the very morning. I was doing my dishes, listening to *The Breakfast Club*, when Grady Kilgore came up to the house and got Cleo. He looked like someone had died. He said, 'Cleo, I'd rather cut off my right arm than to do what I'm about to do, but I've got to go take Idgie and Big George in on charges, and I want you to go with me.'

"You know, Idgie was one of his best friends, and it liked to of killed him to do it. He told Cleo that he would have resigned from office, but he said the thought of a stranger arresting Idgie was even worse.

"Cleo said, 'My God, Grady, what's she done?'

"Grady said that she and Big George were suspected of murdering Frank Bennett back in 'thirty. Here, I didn't even know he'd been dead or missing or anything."

Evelyn said, "What made them think that Idgie and Big George did it?"

"Well, it seems that Idgie and Big George had threatened to kill him a couple of times, and the Georgia police had that on record, so when they found his truck, they had to bring them in . . ."

"What truck?"

"Frank Bennett's truck. They were looking for a drowned body and found that truck in the river, not far from Eva Bates's place, so they knew he'd been around Whistle Stop in nineteen thirty.

"Grady was furious that some damn fool had been stupid enough to call over to Georgia and give them the tag number . . . Ruth had been dead about eight years, and Stump and Peggy had already married and moved over to Atlanta, so it must have been around nineteen fifty-five or 'fifty-six.

"The next day, Grady took Idgie and Big George over to Georgia, and Sipsey went with them; nobody could talk her out of going. But Idgie wouldn't let anybody else go with her, so we all had to stay home and wait.

"Grady tried to keep it quiet. Nobody in town talked about it if they knew . . . Dot Weems knew, but she never printed anything in the paper.

"I remember the week of the trial, Albert and I went over to Troutville to be with Onzell, who was terrified because she knew if Big George was found guilty of killing a white man, he'd wind up in the electric chair, just like Mr. Pinto."

Just then, Geneene, the nurse, came in and sat down to have a cigarette and relax.

Mrs. Threadgoode said, "Oh Geneene, this is my friend Evelyn, the one I told you about who's having such a bad menapause."

"How do you do."

"Hello."

Then Mrs. Threadgoode went on and on to Geneene about how pretty she thought Evelyn was and didn't Geneene think that Evelyn should sell Mary Kay cosmetics?

Evelyn was hoping that Geneene would leave so Mrs. Threadgoode would finish her story, but she never did. And when Ed came to get her, she was frustrated because now she would have to wait a whole week to hear how the trial came out. As she left, Evelyn said, "Don't forget where you left off."

Mrs. Threadgoode looked at her blankly. "Left off? You mean about Mary Kay?"

"No. About the trial."

"Oh yes. Oh, that was something, all right . . ."

# COUNTY COURTHOUSE

VALDOSTA, GEORGIA

JULY 24, 1955

It was just before a thunderstorm; the air in the courtroom was hot and thick.

Idgie turned and looked around the courtroom, the sweat running down her back. Her lawyer, Ralph Root, a friend of Grady's, loosened his tie and tried to get a breath of air.

This was the third day of the trial and all the men who had been in the barbershop in Valdosta, the day Idgie had threatened to kill Frank Bennett, had already testified. Jake Box had just taken the stand.

She turned around again and looked for Smokey Lonesome. Where the hell was he? Grady had sent word that she was in trouble and needed him. Something was wrong. He should have been here. She began to wonder if he was dead.

At that moment, Jake Box pointed to Big George and said, "That's him. That's the one that come after Frank with the knife, and that's the woman that was with him."

The entire Loundes County Courthouse murmured with uneasiness over a black man threatening a white man. Grady Kilgore shifted in his seat. Sipsey, the only other black in the room, was up in the balcony, moaning and praying for her baby boy, even though he was almost sixty at the time.

Not even bothering to question Big George, the prosecuting attorney moved right on along to Idgie, who took the stand.

"Did you know Frank Bennett?"

"No sir."

"Are you sure?"

"Yes sir."

"You mean to sit here and tell me you never met the man whose wife, Ruth Bennett, was your business partner for eighteen years?"

"That's right."

He twirled around, with his thumbs in his vest, to face the jury. "You mean to say you never came into the Valdosta barbershop in August of nineteen twenty-eight and had a heated conversation in which you threatened to kill Frank Bennett, a man you did not know?"

"That was me, all right. I thought you wanted to know if we had ever met, and the answer is no. I threatened to kill him, but we were never, what you might say, properly introduced."

Some of the men in the room, who hated the pompous lawyer, laughed. "So, in other words, you admit that you threatened Frank Bennett's life."

"Yes sir."

"Is it not true that you also came to Georgia with your colored man in September of nineteen twenty-eight and left, taking Frank Bennett's wife and child with you?"

"Just his wife, the child came later."

"How much later?"

"The usual time; nine months."

The courtroom broke out in laughter again. Frank's brother, Gerald, glared at her from the front row.

"Is it true that you spoke against Frank Bennett's character to his wife and made her believe that he was not of good moral fiber? Did you convince her that he was not fit as a husband?"

"No sir, she already knew that for a fact."

More laughter.

The lawyer was getting heated. "Did you or did you not force her to go to Alabama with you at knifepoint?"

"Didn't have to. She was already packed and ready when we got there."

He ignored this last statement. "Is it not true that Frank Bennett came over to Whistle Stop, Alabama, trying to retrieve what was rightly his—his wife and his tiny baby son—and that you and your colored man killed him to prevent her from returning to her happy home and giving the child back to its father?"

"No sir."

The large, pigeon-breasted man was picking up steam. "Are you aware that you broke up the most sacred thing on this earth—a Christian home with a loving father and mother and child? That you defiled the sacred and holy marriage between a man and a woman, a marriage sanctioned by God in the Morning Dove Baptist Church, right here in Valdosta, on November first, nineteen twenty-four? That you have caused a good Christian woman to break God's laws and her marriage vows?!"

"No sir."

"I suggest that you bribed this poor weak woman with promises of money and liquor, and that she lost control of her senses, momentarily, and when her husband came back to get her and take her home, didn't you and your colored man murder him in cold blood to prevent her from returning?"

He then turned on her and screamed, "WHERE *WERE* YOU ON THE NIGHT OF DECEMBER THIRTEENTH, NINETEEN THIRTY?"

Idgie really began to sweat. "Well, sir, I was over at my mother's house, in Whistle Stop."

"Who was with you?"

"Ruth Jamison and Big George. He went over there with us that night."

"Can Ruth Jamison testify to that?"

"No sir."

"Why not?"

"She died eight years ago."

"What about your mother?"

"She's dead, too."

He was coming down the mountain now, and stood up on his tiptoes for a second and then twirled toward the jury again. "So, Miss Threadgoode, you expect twelve intelligent men to believe that, although two witnesses are dead and the other is a colored man who works for you and was with you the day you abducted Ruth Bennett from her happy home, and is known to be a worthless, no-good lying nigger, you are asking these men to take your word for it, just because you say so?" Although she was nervous, the lawyer should not have called Big George those names.

"That's right, you gump-faced, blowed-up, baboon-assed bastard."

The room exploded as the judge banged his gavel in vain.

This time, Big George moaned. He had begged her not to stand trial, but she was determined to give him an alibi for that night. She knew she was his only chance. The odds of a white woman's getting off were much higher than his; especially if his alibi depended on the words of another Negro. She was not going to let Big George go to jail if her life depended on it; and it very well might.

The trial was going badly for Idgie, and when the surprise witness was rushed into the courtroom on that last day, Idgie knew it had just gone from bad to worse. He came sweeping through the courtroom as pious and holier-than-thou-looking than ever . . . her old sworn enemy, the man she had tormented for years.

This is it, she thought.

"State your name, please."

"Reverend Herbert Scroggins."

"Occupation?"

"Pastor of the Whistle Stop Baptist Church."

"Place your right hand on the Bible."

Reverend Scroggins informed him that he had brought his own, thank you, and placed his hand on his Bible and swore to tell the truth, the whole truth, and nothing but the truth, so help him God.

Idgie became confused. She realized it had been her own lawyer who had brought him in. Why had he not asked her first? She could have told him that this man would have nothing good to say about her.

But it was too late, he was already on the stand.

"Reverend Scroggins, could you tell the court why you called me long distance and what you told me last evening?"

The reverend cleared his throat. "Yes. I called to tell you that I have information about the whereabouts of Idgie Threadgoode and George Pullman Peavey on the night of December thirteenth, nineteen thirty."

"Were she and her colored man not over at her mother's house that evening, as has been suggested here earlier in the trial?"

"No, they were not."

*Oh, shit,* thought Idgie.

Her lawyer persisted. "Are you saying, Reverend Scroggins, that she was lying as to her whereabouts on that evening?"

The reverend pursed his lips. "Well, sir, as a Christian, I couldn't say for sure if she was lying or not. I think it is a question of being mixed up about the dates." He then opened the Bible he had and turned to the back and began looking at a particular page. "It has been my habit through the years to write down all the dates of the activities of the church in my Bible, and while going through it the other evening, I show that the night of December thirteenth was the start of our church's yearly tent revival, down at the Baptist campgrounds. And Sister Threadgoode was there, along with her hired man, George Peavey, who was in charge of refreshments—just as he has been every year for the past twenty years."

The prosecuting attorney jumped up. "I object! This doesn't mean anything. The murder could have taken place anytime during the next couple of days."

Reverend Scroggins looked fiercely at him, then turned to the judge. "That's just it, Your Honor: Our revival always lasts for three days and three nights."

The lawyer said, "And you're *sure* Miss Threadgoode was there?"

Reverend Scroggins seemed offended that anyone would doubt his word. "Of course she was." He addressed the jury. "Sister Threadgoode holds a perfect attendance record at all our church activities and is the lead singer in our church choir."

For the first time in her life, Idgie was speechless, dumb, mute, without a comeback. All these years the Dill Pickle Club had spent lying and telling tall tales, thinking they were so good at it, and in five minutes Scroggins had put them all to shame. He was so convincing, she almost believed him, herself.

"In fact, we think so much of Sister Threadgoode at our church, the entire congregation has come over in a bus to testify on her behalf." With which the doors of the courtroom opened and in filed the oddest lot that God had ever put together on this earth: Smokey Lonesome, Jimmy Knot-Head Harris, Splinter-Belly Al, Crackshot Sackett, Inky Pardue, BoWeevil Jake, Elmo Williams, Warthog Willy, and so on . . . all with fresh haircuts from Opal's Beauty Shop and wearing borrowed clothes . . . just a few of the many hoboes Idgie and Ruth had fed throughout the years and Smokey had been able to round up in time.

One by one, they took the stand and testified solidly, remembering in great detail the river revival that December, back in 1930. And last, but not least, came Sister Eva Bates, wearing a flowered hat and carrying a purse. She took the stand and almost broke the jury's heart as she recalled how Sister Threadgoode had leaned over to her during the first night of the revival meeting and had remarked how God had touched her heart that night, due to Reverend Scroggins's *inspired* preaching on the evils of whiskey and the lusts of the flesh.

The skinny little judge, with a neck like an arm, didn't even bother to ask the jury for a verdict. He banged his gavel and said to the prosecuting attorney, "Percy, it don't look to me like you've got a case at all. First of all, there ain't no body been found. Second, we've got sworn witnesses ain't nobody gonna dispute. What we got is a whole lot of nothing. I say this Frank

Bennett got himself drunk and drove himself into the river and has long been ate up. We're gonna call this thing, here, accidental death. That's what we've got ourselves a case of."

He banged his gavel once more, saying, "Case dismissed."

Sipsey did a dance in the balcony, Grady let out a sigh of relief.

The judge, the Honorable Curtis Smoote, knew damn well that there had not been any three-day tent revival in the middle of December. And from where he was sitting, he had also seen that the preacher did not have a Bible between the covers of the book he had sworn on. He had seldom seen such a scrubbed-up lot of down and dirty characters. And besides, the judge's daughter had just died a couple of weeks ago, old before her time and living a dog's life on the outskirts of town, because of Frank Bennett; so he really didn't care who had killed the son of a bitch.

After it was all over, Reverend Scroggins came over and shook Idgie's hand. "I'll see you in church Sunday, Sister Threadgoode." He winked at her and left.

His son, Bobby, had heard about the trial and had called and told him about that time Idgie had gotten him out of jail. So Scroggins, the one she had bedeviled all these years, had come through for her.

Idgie was floored by the whole thing for quite a time. But, driving home, she did manage to say, "You know, I've been thinking. I don't know what's worse—going to jail or having to be nice to the preacher for the rest of my life."

## OCTOBER 9, 1986

Evelyn had been in a hurry to get to the nursing home today. She had badgered Ed to drive faster all the way there. She stopped, as she always did, in Big Momma's room and offered her a honey-bun, but as usual, Big Momma declined, saying, "If I ate that I'd be sick as a dog. How you can eat that sticky, gooey stuff is beyond me."

Evelyn excused herself and rushed down the hall to the visitors' lounge.

Mrs. Threadgoode, who had on her bright green flowered dress today, greeted Evelyn with a cheery "Happy New Year!"

Evelyn sat down, concerned. "Honey, that's not till three months from now. We haven't had Christmas yet."

Mrs. Threadgoode laughed. "I know that, I just thought I'd move it up a bit. Have some fun. All these old people out here are so gloomy, moping around the place something awful."

Evelyn handed Mrs. Threadgoode her treat.

"Oh Evelyn, are these honey-buns?"

"They sure are. Remember I told you about them?"

"Well, don't they look good?" She held one up. "Why, they're just like a Dixie Cream Donut. Thank you, honey

. . . have you ever had a Dixie Cream Donut? They're as light as a feather. I used to say to Cleo, I'd say, 'Cleo, if you're going anywhere near the Dixie Cream Donut place, bring me and Albert home a dozen. Bring me six glazed and six jelly ones.' I like the ones that are twisted, too. You know, like a French braid. I forget what they're called . . ."

Evelyn couldn't wait any longer.

"Mrs. Threadgoode, tell me what happened at the trial."

"You mean Idgie and Big George's trial?"

"That's right."

"Well, that was something, all right. We were all worried to death. We thought they never were coming home, but they finally got a not-guilty verdict. Cleo said that they proved beyond the shadow of a doubt where they had been at the time the murder was to have taken place, so they couldn't possibly have done it. He said the only reason that Idgie would have stood trial like that was to protect someone else."

Evelyn thought for a minute. "Who *else* would want to kill him?"

"Well, honey, it isn't a matter of who wanted to, but who *would* have. That's the question. Some say it could have been Smokey Lonesome. Some say it could have been Eva Bates and that gang out at the river—Lord knows it was a rough enough bunch, and those folks in the Dill Pickle Club stuck together . . . it's hard to say. And then, of course"—Mrs. Threadgoode paused—"there's Ruth, herself."

Evelyn was surprised. "Ruth? But where was Ruth the night of the murder? Surely someone knows."

Mrs. Threadgoode shook her head. "That's just it, honey. Nobody knows for sure. Idgie says that she and Ruth were over at the big house visiting Momma Threadgoode, who had been sick. And I believe her. But there are some who wonder. All I know is that Idgie would go to her grave willingly before she would let Ruth's name be involved with murder."

"Did they ever find out who did it?"

"No, they never did."

"Well, if Idgie and Big George didn't kill him, who do you think did it?"

"Well, that's the sixty-four-dollar question, isn't it?"

"Wouldn't you like to know?"

"Well sure I would, who wouldn't? It's one of the great mysteries of the world. But, honey, nobody's ever gonna know that one except the one that did it, and Frank Bennett. And you know what they say . . . dead men tell no tales."

## THE JIMMY HATCHER
## DOWNTOWN
## RESCUE MISSION

345 23RD AVENUE SOUTH
BIRMINGHAM, ALABAMA

### JANUARY 23, 1969

Smokey Lonesome sat on the side of his iron bed at the mission, coughing through the first cigarette of the day. After the cafe closed, Smokey had wandered around the country for a while. Then, he got a job as a short-order cook at the Streetcar Diner No. 1, in Birmingham, but his drinking got the best of him and he was fired.

Two weeks later, Brother Jimmy found him, passed out cold under the viaduct on 16th Street, and had brought him over to the mission. He was too old to tramp anymore, his health was bad, and his teeth were almost all gone. But Brother Jimmy and his wife had cleaned him up and fed him, and the Downtown Mission had been his home now, more or less, for the past fifteen years.

Brother Jimmy was a good man, having been a drunk himself, once, but as he told it, he had made the long trip "from Jack Daniel's to Jesus" and was determined to devote his life to helping other unfortunates.

He put Smokey in charge of the kitchen. The food was mostly leftover frozen stuff that had been donated; fish sticks and mashed potatoes out of a box were the staple. But there were no complaints.

When he wasn't in the kitchen or drunk, Smokey would spend his day upstairs, drinking coffee and playing cards with the other men. He had seen a lot happen at the mission . . . seen a man with one thumb meet up with his boy there, who he hadn't seen since the day he was born. Father and son, both down on their luck, winding up in the same place at the same time. He had seen men come through that had been rich doctors and lawyers, and one man who had been a state senator for Maryland.

Smokey asked Jimmy what caused men like that to sink so low. "I'd have to say the main reason is that most of them have been disappointed in some way," Jimmy said, "usually over a woman. They had one and lost her, or never had the one they wanted . . . and so they just get lost and wander around. And, of course, old man whiskey plays a role. But in all the years I've been seeing men come in and out, I'd say disappointment is number one on the list."

Six months ago, Jimmy died and they were renovating downtown Birmingham and the rescue mission was to be torn down. Smokey would have to be moving on soon. Where to, he didn't know as yet . . .

He walked down the stairs, and outside, it was a cold clear day and the sky was blue, so he decided to take a walk.

He walked by Gus's hot dog joint and down around 16th Street, past the old terminal station and under the Rainbow Viaduct, down the railroad tracks until he found himself headed in the direction of Whistle Stop.

He had never been anything more than just a tomato-can vagabond, hobo, knight of the road, down-and-outer. A free spirit who had seen shooting stars from many a boxcar rolling through the night. His idea of how the country was doing had been determined by the size of the butts he picked up off the sidewalks. He had smelled fresh air from Alabama to Oregon. He had seen it all, done it all, belonged to no one. Just another bum, another drunk. But he, Smokey Jim Phillips, perpetually down on his luck, had loved only one woman, and he had been faithful to her all his life.

It was true he had slept around with a bunch of sorry women in sleazy hotels, in the woods, in railroad yards; but he could never love any of those. It had always been just the one woman.

He had loved her from the first moment he saw her standing there in the cafe, wearing that organdy dotted-swiss dress; and he had never stopped.

He had loved her when he'd been sick, puking in an alley behind some bar, or lying up half dead in some flophouse, surrounded by men with open sores having crazy alcoholic delusions, screaming and fighting imaginary insects or rats. He had loved her in those nights he'd been caught in a hard, cold winter rain with nothing but a thin hat and leather shoes, wet and hard as iron. Or that time he had landed at the veterans' hospital and lost a lung, or when the dog had torn off half his leg, or sitting in the Salvation Army in San Francisco that Christmas Eve, while strangers patted him on the back, giving him a dried-out turkey dinner and cigarettes.

He had loved her every night, lying in his bed at the mission, on the thin used mattress from some closed-down hospital, watching the green neon JESUS SAVES signs blink on and off, and listening to the sounds of the drunks downstairs, crashing bottles and yelling to come in out of the cold. All those bad times, he would just close his eyes and walk into the cafe again and see her standing there, smiling at him.

Scenes of her would occur . . . Ruth laughing at Idgie . . . standing at the counter, hugging Stump to her . . . pushing her hair off her forehead . . . Ruth looking concerned when he had hurt himself.

*Smokey, don't you think you ought to have another blanket tonight? It's gonna freeze, they say. Smokey, I wish you wouldn't take off like you do, we worry about you when you're gone . . .*

He had never touched her, except to shake her hand. He had never held or kissed her, but he had been true to her alone. He would have killed for her. She was the kind of woman you could kill for; the thought of anything or anybody hurting her made him sick to his stomach.

He had stolen only one thing in his entire life. The photograph of Ruth had been made the day the cafe opened. She was standing out in front, holding the baby and shielding her eyes from the sun with her other hand. That picture had traveled far and wide. In an envelope, pinned to the inside of his shirt, so he wouldn't lose it.

And even after she had died, she was still alive in his heart. She could never die for him. Funny. All those years, and she had never known. Idgie knew, but never said anything. She wasn't the kind to make you feel ashamed of loving, but she knew.

She had tried so hard to find him when Ruth had become ill, but he had been off somewhere, riding the rails. When he did come back, Idgie took him to the place. They each understood what the other was feeling. It was as if, from then on, the two of them mourned together. Not that they ever talked about it. The ones that hurt the most always say the least.

RUTH JAMISON
1898–1946
GOD SAW FIT TO CALL HER HOME

# THE BIRMINGHAM NEWS

THURSDAY, JANUARY 26, 1969
PAGE 38

## Man Freezes to Death

The body of an as yet unidentified white male of about 75 was discovered early Wednesday morning beside the railroad tracks, one mile south of Whistle Stop. The victim, clad only in overalls and a thin jacket, apparently froze to death during the night. There was no identification found on the body other than a photograph of a woman. He is thought to be a transient.

## THE WEEMS WEEKLY

(WHISTLE STOP, ALABAMA'S WEEKLY BULLETIN)

DECEMBER 9, 1956

## Post Office to Close

Now that the cafe and the beauty shop have closed, I should have known I'd be next. Got my notice in the mail. The post office will be closing down and all mail will be sent over to the Gate City Post Office. It's gonna be a sad old day for me. But I'm still keeping up with the news, so just call me or bring your news on by the house, or tell my other half if you see him around town.

Since Essie Rue has gotten that job playing the organ at the Dreamland Roller Rink over in North Birmingham, she and her husband, Billy, are talking about moving over there. I'm hoping she won't . . . with Julian and Opal gone, me, Ninny Thread-goode, and Biddie Louise Otis will be all that's left of the old gang.

This week I am sorry to report that someone broke into Vesta Adcock's home and stole all her bird figurines out of her china cabinet, and some change she had in a drawer.

Not only that, I was over at the cemetery Christmas Day, putting flowers on my mother's grave, and someone stole my purse right out of the car. Times have changed. What kind of a person would do that, is what I wonder.

By the way, is there anything sadder than toys on a grave?

... Dot Weems ...

## ROSE TERRACE
## NURSING HOME

OLD MONTGOMERY HIGHWAY
BIRMINGHAM, ALABAMA

### OCTOBER 12, 1986

Evelyn got up early, went into the kitchen, and started preparing her treat for Mrs. Threadgoode. She heated up the plate right before they started for the nursing home, wrapped it in aluminum foil, and placed that in a thermo-bag, so it would be good and hot. Again, she made Ed rush across town as fast as he could.

· The old woman was waiting, and Evelyn made her close her eyes while she unwrapped the plate and undid the lid on the jar of iced tea with mint.

"Okay. You can look now."

When Mrs. Threadgoode saw what she had on her plate, she clapped her hands, as excited as a child on Christmas. There before her was a plate of perfectly fried green tomatoes and fresh cream-white corn, six slices of bacon, with a bowl of baby lima beans on the side and four huge light and fluffy buttermilk biscuits.

Evelyn almost started to cry when she saw how happy her friend was. She told Mrs. Threadgoode to eat her food while it was still warm and excused herself for minute and went down the hall to find Geneene. She gave her a hundred dollars in an envelope, and twenty-five dollars for herself, and asked if she wouldn't please make sure that Mrs. Threadgoode got whatever she wanted to eat and anything else she wanted while Evelyn was gone.

Geneene said, "No money for me, honey, she's one of my sweet ones. Don't worry, Mrs. Couch. I'll take care of her for you."

When she came back, her friend's plate was empty.

"Oh Evelyn. I don't know what I've done to deserve you spoiling me like you do. That was the best meal I've had since the cafe closed."

"You deserve to be spoiled."

"Well, I don't know about that. I don't know why you're so good to me, but I appreciate it. You know I do. I thank the Lord every night and ask Him to watch out for you every day."

"I know you do."

Evelyn sat there with her and held her hand and eventually told her that she was going out of town for a while, but that she'd be back and would have a surprise for her.

"Oh, I love a surprise. Is it bigger than a breadbox?"

"Can't tell you that. Then it wouldn't be a surprise, would it?"

"I guess not . . . well hurry up, now, and get back, 'cause you know how I'm gonna be wondering. Is it a shell? You going to Florida? Opal and Julian sent me a shell from Florida."

Evelyn shook her head. "No, it's not a shell. Now, don't ask me. You're just going to have to wait and see."

She gave her a piece of paper and said, "This is the phone number and address of where I'll be, and you let me know if you need me, okay?"

Mrs. Threadgoode said she would and held her hand until it was time for her to go. Then the women walked to the front door, where Ed was waiting.

He asked, "How are you today, Mrs. Threadgoode?"

"Oh, I'm just fine, honey . . . full of fried green tomatoes and lima beans that our girl, here, brought me."

Evelyn was hugging her goodbye when a bird-breasted woman in a nightgown and fox furs marched up to them and announced in a loud voice, "You people will have to move along now. My husband and I have just purchased this place and everyone must leave by six o'clock!"

She continued on down the hall, terrorizing all the other old ladies at Rose Terrace.

Evelyn looked at Mrs. Threadgoode. "Vesta Adcock?"

Mrs. Threadgoode nodded. "That's her, all right. What did I tell you? That poor thing doesn't have a full string of fish."

Evelyn laughed and waved goodbye. Her friend waved and called out, "You hurry back, now . . . oh, and listen. . . . Send an old lady a picture postcard sometime, will you?"

# UNITED AIRLINES, FLIGHT 763

BIRMINGHAM TO L.A.X.

OCTOBER 14, 1986

Seven years before, Evelyn Couch had been shopping out at the mall and had walked by Goldboro's Radio and TV Center when she saw a fat woman on one of the TV sets in the window who looked vaguely familiar. She tried to place who that woman was, and what show she was on. The woman seemed to be staring right back at her. Then it hit her: *My God, that's me.* She had been looking at herself on the TV monitor. She was horrified.

It was the first time she had realized how heavy she was. It had happened so gradually over the years, and now, there she was, looking exactly like her mother.

After that she had tried every diet known to man, but she just could not seem to stick to any of them. She had even failed the Last Chance Diet. Twice.

She had joined a health club, once, but was so exhausted by the time she'd pulled herself into those awful leotards, she went home to bed.

An article she'd read in *Cosmopolitan* said that doctors were now able to suck the fat right out of you, and she would have done that, too, if she had not been so afraid of doctors and hospitals.

So she had just done all her shopping at the Stout Shop and was always pleased when she saw women there who were fatter than she was. To celebrate that fact, she would usually go and treat herself at the Pancake House, two blocks away.

Food had become the only thing she looked forward to, and candy, cakes, and pies were the only sweetness in her life . . .

But now, after all these months of being with Mrs. Threadgoode each week, things had begun to change. Ninny Threadgoode made her feel young. She began to see herself as a woman with half her life still ahead of her. Her friend really believed that she was capable of selling Mary Kay cosmetics. Nobody had ever believed she could do anything before, or had faith in her; least of all, Evelyn herself. The more Mrs. Threadgoode talked about it and the more she thought about it, the less Towanda ran rampant in her mind, beating up on the world, and she began to see herself as thin and happy—behind the wheel of a pink Cadillac.

And then, that Sunday she had gone to the Martin Luther King Memorial Baptist Church, a miraculous thing had happened: For the first time in months, she stopped thinking about killing herself or others and realized that she wanted to live. So, still feeling high from the church, she had screwed her courage to the wall and, with the help of two five-milligram tablets of Valium, had actually gone to see a doctor. He turned out to be a charming young man who gave her an examination she didn't remember much about, except that he found nothing seriously wrong. Her estrogen level was low, just as Mrs. Threadgoode had suspected. That very afternoon, she had her first prescription for Premarin, .625 mg., and began to feel better almost immediately.

One month later, she had an enormous orgasm that nearly scared poor Ed to death.

Ten days after that, Ed was on an exercise program down at the Y.M.C.A.

And within two weeks of receiving her Mary Kay Beauty Showcase, she had studied and completed her *Perfect Start Workbook,* signed the Mary Kay Beauty Consultant Agreement, and was holding skin-care classes. Soon, in a special ceremony, her Mary Kay district director presented her with a special Perfect Start pin, which she wore with pride. She had even forgotten to eat lunch, once . . .

Things were happening fast. But not fast enough to suit Evelyn; so she took five thousand dollars out of their savings, packed her bags, and today she was sitting on a plane headed to a fat farm in California, reading the brochure they had sent her, as excited as she had been on the first day of school.

### A DAY IN THE LIFE OF A SPA GUEST

| | |
|---|---|
| 7 AM: | *One hour brisk walk, alternating walk in town and nature walk* |
| 8 AM: | *Coffee and 3 oz. of salt-free tomato juice* |
| 8:30 AM: | *Wake-up exercises, done to the recording of "I'm So Excited," by the Pointer Sisters* |
| 9 AM: | *Stretch and flex exercise class, using balls, wands, and hoops as aids* |
| 11 AM: | *Water fun, using balls and water wings as aids* |
| 12 NOON: | *Lunch . . . 250 calories* |
| 1 PM: | *Free time for massage and facials . . . offering Boots and Mitties, a hot oil treatment for the hands and feet* |
| 6 PM: | *Dinner . . . 275 calories* |
| 7:30 PM: | *Arts and crafts . . . Mrs. Jamie Higdon teaching painting, with still life (using artificial fruit only)* |
| FRIDAY ONLY | *Mrs. Alexander Bagge teaches us how to make basket pots out of dough (nonedible)* |

# WHISTLE STOP, ALABAMA

NOVEMBER 7, 1967

Hank Roberts had just turned twenty-seven and owned his own construction company. This morning, he and his buddy Travis, with the long hair, had just started a new job. The big yellow bulldozer grumbled and whined as he dug up the vacant lot alongside the old Threadgoode place on First Street. They were getting ready to put a red brick annex to the Baptist church.

Travis, who had smoked two joints already this morning, was walking around, kicking at the ground with his boot, and began mumbling to himself.

"Hey, man, look at this shit. This is heavy, gross stuff, man . . ."

Pretty soon Hank stopped for lunch, and Travis called over to him, "Hey, man, *look* at all this shit!"

Hank came over and looked at the ground he had just dug up. It was full of fish heads, now mostly just rows of little sharp teeth, along with dried-up skulls of hogs and chickens eaten for supper by people long forgotten.

Hank was a country boy and used to such sights, so he just looked and said, "Yeah, look a-there."

He walked back over and sat down, opened his black tin lunch pail, and began eating one of his four sandwiches. Travis was still struck by what they had uncovered, and continued to poke around. He began to trip out on the bones and skulls and teeth. "Jesus Christ! There must be hundreds of these things! What are they doing here?"

"How the hell do I know?"

"Shit, man, this is bizarre as hell."

Hank, who was getting disgusted, called out, "It's just a bunch of hogs' heads, dammit! Don't go getting weird on me!"

Travis kicked at something and stopped dead in his tracks. After a minute, he said in an odd voice, "Hey, Hank."

"What?"

"You ever heard of a hog with a glass eye?"

Hank got up and walked over and looked. "Well," he said, "I'll be damned."

# WHISTLE STOP CAFE

## DECEMBER 13, 1930

Ruth and Idgie had left the cafe and gone over to the big house to see Momma Threadgoode, who was sick. Sipsey had come down to stay with the baby, as she often did. Tonight, she had brought along Artis, the eleven-year-old blue-gummed twin, so he could walk her home. He was a devil, but she couldn't resist him.

It was eight o'clock and Artis was asleep on the bed. Sipsey was listening to the radio and eating what was left of the skillet bread and molasses.

". . . And now, the makers of the new Rinso Blue, with sodium, bring you . . ."

Outside, there was nothing but the sound of leaves cracking as the black pickup truck with the Georgia license plate drove up to the back of the cafe with its lights off.

Two minutes later, a drunken Frank Bennett kicked the back door open and came through the kitchen into the back room. He pointed his gun at Sipsey and headed toward the crib. She got up and tried to reach the baby, but he grabbed her by the back of the dress and threw her across the room.

She jumped back up again and lunged at him. "You leave dat baby alone! Dat's Miz Ruth's baby!"

"Get away from me, nigger." He slammed her with the broad side of his gun, hitting her with so much force that she was knocked cold and blood began to trickle from her ear.

Artis woke up and yelled, "Grandma!" and ran over to her while Frank Bennett picked the baby up and headed out the back door.

There was a new moon that night. Just enough light for Frank to make his way back to the truck. He opened the door and put the baby—who had not made a sound—into the front seat, and was climbing in when all of a sudden he heard a sound behind him . . . as if something heavy had hit a tree stump that had been covered with a quilt. The sound he had heard was that of a five-pound skillet hitting his own thick Irish hair, a fraction of a second before his skull split open. He was dead before he hit the ground, and Sipsey was headed back inside with the baby.

"Ain't nobody gonna get dis baby, no suh, not while I's alive."

Frank Bennett had not figured that she would get back up off the floor. He also hadn't figured that the skinny little black woman had been handling five-pound skillets, two at a time, since she was eleven. He had figured dead wrong.

As Sipsey passed by Artis, frozen in his tracks, he could see that she was wild-eyed. She said, "Go get Big George. I done kilt me a white man, I done kilt him daid."

Artis slowly tiptoed over to where Frank was lying beside the truck, and as he leaned over to get a good look, he saw that glass eye shining in the moonlight.

He ran so fast over the railroad tracks he forgot to breathe and nearly passed out before he made it home. Big George was asleep, but he could see Onzell was still up, back in the kitchen.

He flew in the door, holding his side in pain and panting, "I gotta see Daddy!"

Onzell said, "You better not wake yo daddy up, boy, he'll whup you within an inch of your life . . ." but Artis was already in the bedroom, shaking the big man.

"Daddy! Daddy! Get up! You' gots to come wit me!"

Big George woke with a start. "Whut? Whut's da matter witch you, boy?"

"I cain't tell you. Grandma wants you over to the cafe!"

"Grandma?"

"Yes! Right *now*! She say ax you to come right now!"

Big George was putting on his pants. "This better not be no joke, boy, or I'll have yo butt."

Onzell, who had been standing in the door, listening, went over to get her sweater to go with them, but Big George said for her to stay home.

"She ain't sick, is she?" Onzell said.

Big George said, "Naw, baby, naw, she ain't sick. You just stay here."

Jasper came into the living room, half asleep. "What . . . ?"

Onzell said, "Nothin', honey, go on back to bed . . . and don't wake up Willie Boy."

When they got away from the house, Artis said, "Daddy, Grandma done kilt a white man."

The moon was gone behind the clouds and Big George couldn't see his son's face. He said, "You're the one gonna be daid, boy, when I find out what you is up to."

Sipsey was standing in the yard when they got there. Big George leaned down and felt Frank's cold arm, sticking out from the sheet Sipsey had covered him with, and he stood back up and put his hands on hips. He looked back down at the body and shook his head. "Mmmm, mmmm. You done did it this time, Momma."

But even as he was shaking his head, Big George was making a decision. There was no defense for a black who killed a white man in Alabama, so it never occurred to him to do anything but what he had to do.

He picked up Frank's body and threw it over his shoulder and said, "Come on, boy," and took it all the way in the back of the yard and put it in the wooden shed. He laid it down on the dirt floor, and said to Artis, "You stay here till I get back, boy, and don't you move. I's got to get rid of dat truck."

About an hour later, when Idgie and Ruth got home, the

baby was back in his bed and sound asleep. Idgie drove Sipsey home and told her how worried she was about Momma Threadgoode being so sick; Sipsey never told her how close they had come to losing the baby.

Artis stayed in the shed all night, nervous and excited, rocking back and forth on his haunches. Along around four o'clock, he couldn't resist; he opened his knife and, in the pitch dark, struck the body under the sheet—once, twice, three, four times—and on and on.

About sunup, the door creaked open and Artis peed on himself. It was his daddy. He had driven the truck into the river, out by the Wagon Wheel, and had walked all the way back; about ten miles.

When Big George pulled off the sheet and said, "We got to burn his clothes," they both stopped and stared.

The sun had just cracked through the wooden slats. Artis looked at Big George, his eyes as big as platters, with his mouth open, and said, "Daddy, dat white man don't have no head."

Big George shook his head again. "Mmmm, mmmm, mmmm . . ." His mother had chopped that man's head off and buried it somewhere.

Stopping only long enough to take in that horrendous fact, he said, "Boy, help me wid dese clothes."

Artis had never seen a white man naked before. He was all white and pink, just like those hogs after they'd been boiled and all their hair had come off.

Big George handed him the sheet and the bloody clothes and told him to go way out in the woods and bury them, deep, and then to go home and say nothing. To nobody. Anywhere. Ever.

While Artis was digging the hole, he couldn't help but smile. He had a secret. A powerful secret that he would have as long as he lived. Something that would give him power when he was feeling weak. Something that only he and the devil knew. The thought of it made him smile with pleasure. He would never have to feel the anger, the hurt, the humiliation of the others, ever again. He was different. He would always be set apart. He had stabbed himself a white man . . .

And whenever any white folks gave him any grief, he could smile inside. *I stabbed me one of you, already* . . .

At seven-thirty, Big George had already started slaughtering the hogs and started the water boiling in the big black iron pot—a little early in the year, but not too soon.

Later that afternoon, when Grady and the two detectives from Georgia were questioning his daddy about the missing white man, Artis had nearly fainted when one of them came over and looked right in the pot. He was sure the man had seen Frank Bennett's arm bobbing up and down among the boiling hogs. But evidently, he hadn't, because two days later, the fat Georgia man told Big George that it was the best barbecue he had ever eaten, and asked him what his secret was.

Big George smiled and said, "Thank you, suh, I'd hafto say the secret's in the sauce."

## THE WEEMS WEEKLY

(WHISTLE STOP, ALABAMA'S WEEKLY BULLETIN)

NOVEMBER 10, 1967

## Skull Found in Garden

Congratulations to our new lady governor, Mrs. Lurleen Wallace, who won in a landslide victory over the other fellow. She looked darling at inauguration, and promised to pay her husband, George, a dollar a year to be her number one adviser. . . . Good luck, Lurleen.

Almost as exciting as our new governor is the discovery Thursday morning of a human skull over in the vacant lot by the old Threadgoode place.

It is not an Indian, said the coroner in Birmingham. It is not old enough, and it has a glass eye, and whoever it was had their head chopped off. Foul play is suspected, said the coroner. Anyone missing a person with a glass eye is asked to contact the *Birmingham News.* Or call me, I will do it for you. It is a blue eye.

My other half went and did a silly thing on me last Saturday. He went and had a heart attack, and about scared his poor wife to death. The doctor said it wasn't all that serious but that he was going to have to give up smoking. So I've got me a big grumbly bear at home, but I'm babying him along and Mr. Wilbur Weems has gotten his breakfast in bed for the past week. Any of you old galoots out there who want to help me cheer him up, come on over . . . but don't bring any cigarettes, because he will try to get them off of you. I know, he stole a pack of mine. Guess I'm going to have to give them up, myself.

I'm taking him on a vacation when he gets better.

. . . Dot Weems . . .

## HOTEL DE LUXE
## ROOMS FOR GENTLEMEN

8TH AVENUE NORTH
BIRMINGHAM, ALABAMA

JULY 2, 1979

A gentleman of color inquired about another gentleman of color, who was sitting in the lobby, laughing.

"Is that nigger crazy, or what? What's he laughing about? There ain't nobody talking to him."

The brown, pockmarked man behind the desk answered, "Oh, he don't have to have nobody to talk to. His mind done went addlebrained a long time ago."

"What he doin' here?"

"Some woman brought him over two years ago."

"Who's springing for the bill?"

"She is."

"Hummmmm . . ."

"She comes over and dresses him every morning and puts him to bed every night."

"Some easy life."

"I'd say."

Artis O. Peavey, the subject of this discussion, was sitting on a red Naugahyde sofa, with a good deal of cotton stuffing escaping through the various tears and cuts it had acquired over the years. His cloudy brown eyes seemed to be fixed on the wall clock with the pink neon ring around it. The only other object on the wall was a cigarette ad showing an attractive black couple enjoying a Salem cigarette, remarking that the smoke was as cool as a mountain spring. Artis threw back his head and laughed again, revealing a perfect set of blue gums where once had flashed a number of gold teeth.

To the world, Mr. Peavey was sitting in a run-down flophouse hotel lobby, on a towel supplied by the management, since he was often known to pee through the rubber pants the woman put on him every morning. However, for Mr. Artis O. Peavey himself, it was 1936 again . . . and at the moment, he was walking down 8th Avenue North, dressed in a purple sharkskin suit, wearing a fifty-dollar pair of lime-green brogans, his hair freshly straightened and pomaded down like black ice. And on his arm, this Saturday night, was Miss Betty Simmons, who was, according to the social columns of the *Slagtown News*, the toast of Birmingham's ebony glitter set.

They had just passed by the Masonic Hall and were, no doubt, headed on over to Ensley to the Tuxedo Junction Ballroom on the midnight streetcar, where Count Basie—or was it Cab Calloway?—would be playing.

No wonder he was laughing. And God bless God for not letting him remember the bad times, when it was no fun to be a "nigger" on a Saturday night. Those long, hard nights when he had been in Kilbey, beaten and kicked and stabbed by guards and prisoners alike, where a man had to sleep with one eye open and be ready to kill or be killed in an instant. Lately, Artis's mind had become just like the Frolic Theater; it chose only to run light comedies and romances, starring himself and a number of brown, tan, and cinnamon-colored beauties with swishing hips and flashing eyes . . .

He banged on the once shiny, now dull, chrome arm of the sofa, and laughed again. The movie in his mind, this time, was starring himself when his stay in Chicago had made him an important figure for telling and retelling about the famous performers he had seen—Ethel "Momma Stringbean" Waters, the Inkspots, Lena, Louis. . . . He had been able to forget the insults, and the way his manhood had been cut off in the minds of the whites. But somehow, it was that very dismissal that made it go at it with a vengeance, just to prove that he as a man did exist.

*Want a white woman?*

*I never hankered after no white woman! High yellow was as high as I cared to go.*

He liked them, in fact, big and black . . . the blacker the berry, the sweeter the juice. And more could call him Daddy than he cared to admit. He could smile and shuffle, but it never bothered him; because he had a secret . . .

Yes, life was sweet; women, important talk, Knights of Pythias, High Potentate, strutting rights, setting on porches rights, the finest men's colognes, women in peach satin gowns and multijeweled dresses to the floor, brown derbies and coats with collars puffed with purple, maroon, and green fur, midnight-colored women to kiss you good night, cigars that traveled from Cuba, a gold timepiece that could be pulled out for the hour or for impressing . . . Shake That Thing . . . good times at the Black Shadow Lounge. Bleach that skin, make us a little closer skin. If you are white, all right! If you's brown, you be around. Yellow? You're a nice fellow. But if you black, jump back . . . jump back.

Now the movie flipped to the fifties. He was standing in front of the Masonic Temple Drugstore, jingling change in his pockets. The feel and sound of folding money never appealed to him; he was not cursed with a driving desire to break his back earning the green stuff. He was just as happy with a pocket full of shiny dimes and quarters, won in the elusive game, known in the back alleys as the Galloping Dots, Seven-Come-Eleven, Snake-Eyes. But more times than not, the change was a gift from some grateful partner in passion.

When he finally lost his activities at age eighty, due to the natural deterioration and the normal wear and tear, there was many a disappointed lady in Slagtown. He was that rare and precious commodity: a woman's man.

The movie speeds up, and sights and sounds start coming faster. *Three-hundred-pound women, shaking and screaming*

*in church . . . and in bed . . . "OH JESUS, I'M COMING!"*
*. . . Mr. Artis O. Peavey and a number of women exchange*
*nuptial vows . . . sitting in the Agate Cafe, talking to his friend*
*Baby Shephard . . . "That woman done busted my head"*
*. . . "I heard tell it was the husband" . . . "I would have fought*
*for you, Odetta, but when a man's got the difference in his*
*hand, loaded and cocked, there ain't no use in being a fool"*
*. . . "Give me a pig's foot and a bottle of beer" . . . "I've got the*
*world in a jug and the stopper in my hand" . . . "You're not*
*the only oyster in the stew!". . . . Blue Shadows and White*
*Gardenias . . . amber-colored plastic cigar-holders . . . Professor*
*Fess Whatley's Jazz Demons. . . . Got the miseries? Feena-Mint.*
*. . . Princess Pee Wee Sam and Scram . . . Fairyland Park*
*Ballroom . . . Hartley Toots Killed in Bus. . . . I married her*
*without my consent, so to speak . . . "That woman domineered*
*over me". . . . Nobody knows you when you're down and out*
*. . . Watch out . . . Don't be coming down here . . . Oh no, you*
*gonna get them white folks all mad . . . all riled up. . . . No,*
*no, I ain't one of 'em, boss, they's just troublemakers . . . Yes*
*suh . . . "Get off that bus!"*

Artis tapped his foot on the floor three times and, magically,
the movie changed. He is a little boy now, and his momma is
cooking in the back of the cafe . . . *Oh, don't get in Momma's*
*way, she slap you out the door . . .* There's Naughty Bird and
Willie Boy . . . and sweet Jasper . . . Grandma Sipsey's there,
dipping her cornbread in honey . . . Miss Idgie and Miss Ruth
. . . *they treat you white* . . . And Stump . . . and Smokey
Lonesome . . .

Then, the old man, who had been agitated just a moment
before, begins to smile and relax. He is out in the back of the
cafe, helping his daddy barbecue . . . and he is happy . . . we
know a secret.

His daddy gives him a barbecue and a Grapico, and he runs
way back up in the woods to eat it, where it's cool and green
and the pine needles are soft . . .

. . .

The pockmarked man in the hotel lobby walked over and shook the smiling Artis O. Peavey, who was now quiet and still. "What's the matter with you?"

The man jumped back. "Jesus Christ! This nigger is dead!" He turned to his friend at the counter. "Not only that, but he's done peed all over the floor!"

. . . But Artis was still way up in the woods, with his barbecue.

# THE FOREVER
# SLIM LODGE

MONTECITO, CALIFORNIA

DECEMBER 5, 1986

Evelyn had been at the lodge almost two months now, and had already lost twenty-three pounds. But she had gained in another area. She had found her group, the group she had been looking for all of her life. Here they were, the candy snatchers: chubby housewives, divorcees, single teachers and librarians, each hoping for a new start in life as a slimmer, healthier person.

She had not known how much fun it would be. To Evelyn Couch and her cronies in poundage, the most important thing on their minds was what exciting low-cal dessert would the cooks come up with tonight? Would it be Chiffon Pumpkin Pie, 55 calories per serving? Or Nonfat Fruit Whip, only 50 calories? Or, maybe tonight they would have her favorite, Fitness Flan, 80 calories per serving.

It had never dawned on Evelyn that just knowing it was Boots and Mitties Day could make her heart sing, nor that she would be the one who was always early for Water Fun.

But something else had happened here that she could never have dreamed of. She had become a much sought-after, popular person! When new people arrived at the lodge, they were soon asked, "Have you met that darling woman from Alabama? Wait till you hear her talk, she has the most adorable accent, and is she a character!"

Evelyn had never thought of herself as being funny or having a cute accent, but it seemed that every time she said anything, the other women would scream with laughter. Evelyn enjoyed her newfound celebrity and played it for all it was worth, holding court at night by the fireplace. Her special friends were three housewives from Thousand Oaks, one named Dorothy and two named Stella. They formed their own, private fat club, and vowed to meet once a year for the rest of their lives; and Evelyn knew they would.

After stretch and flex class, she changed into her new royal-blue jogging outfit and stopped by the desk to get her mail. Ed dutifully forwarded all the junk mail, and usually there was nothing important; but today she saw a letter postmarked Whistle Stop, Alabama. She opened the letter and wondered who could be writing her from there?

Dear Mrs. Couch,

I am sorry to tell you that on last Sunday, around 6:30 A.M., your friend Mrs. Cleo Threadgoode passed away at her home. I have several things she wanted you to have. My husband and I will be happy to bring them to Birmingham, or you may pick them up at your convenience. Please call me at 555-7760. I am here all day. ·

Sincerely,

Mrs. Jonnie Hartman

Neighbor

Suddenly, Evelyn didn't feel cute anymore, and she wanted to go home.

# WHISTLE STOP, ALABAMA

## APRIL 8, 1987

Evelyn waited until the first warm day of spring before she called Mrs. Hartman. Somehow she could not stand the thought of seeing Whistle Stop for the first time in the dead of winter. Evelyn rang the doorbell and a pleasant-looking brown-haired woman came to the door.

"Oh Mrs. Couch, come on in. I'm so happy to meet you. Mrs. Threadgoode told me so much about you, I feel as if I know you already."

She took Evelyn back into a spotless kitchen, where she had set two places with coffee cups and placed a freshly baked pound cake on her green Formica dinette set.

"I was so sorry to have to write you that letter, but I knew that you would want to know."

"I appreciate that you did. I had no idea she had left Rose Terrace."

"I know you didn't. Her friend Mrs. Otis died about a week after you left."

"Oh no. I didn't know . . . I wonder why she didn't tell me."

"Well, I told her she ought to, but she said you were on your vacation and she didn't want you to worry. That's how she was, always looking out for the other fellow . . .

"We moved next door right after her husband died, so I guess I've been knowing her for over thirty years, and I never heard her complain, not once, and she didn't have an easy life. Her son, Albert, was like a child. But every day, she'd get up, and shave and bathe and powder him, and put on his hernia belt—treated him just like he was a baby, even after he was a grown man. . . . There was never a child more loved than Albert Threadgoode. Bless her heart, I miss her so much, and I know you do, too."

"Yes, I do, and I just feel terrible I wasn't there. Maybe I could have done something, gotten her to a doctor or something."

"No honey. There wasn't a thing you could have done. She wasn't sick. We always carried her with us to church on Sunday, and usually she would be all dressed and waiting, sitting on her front porch. But that Sunday morning, when we got ready to leave, she wasn't there, which was very unusual. So Ray, my husband, walked over and knocked on her door, but she didn't answer, so he went on in, and in a few minutes he came back out by himself. I said, 'Ray, where's Mrs. Threadgoode?' And he said, 'Honey, Mrs. Threadgoode's dead,' and then he sat down on the steps and cried. She died in her sleep, just as peaceful. I really think she knew her time was near, because whenever I went over there, she would say, 'Now, Jonnie, if anything ever happens to me, I want Evelyn to have these things.' She thought the world of you. She'd brag on you all the time and said that she was sure you'd come riding up here one day and take her for a ride in your new Cadillac. Poor old thing, when she died, she didn't have hardly anything to her name but a few knickknacks. That reminds me, let me get your things."

Mrs. Hartman came back with a picture of a naked girl swinging on a swing, with blue bubbles in the background; a shoe box; and a Mason jar with what looked like gravel in it.

Evelyn took the jar. "What in the world?"

Mrs. Hartman laughed. "That's her gallstones. Why she thought you'd want them, the Lord only knows."

Evelyn opened the shoe box. Inside, she found Albert's birth certificate, Cleo's graduation diploma from the Palmer School of Chiropractic, in Davenport, Iowa, in 1927, and about fifteen funeral programs. Then she found an envelope full of photographs. The first was a picture of a man and a little boy in a sailor suit, sitting on a half-moon. Next was a 1939 school picture of a little blond boy; on the back it said, *Stump Threadgoode—10 years old.* Then she picked up a family portrait of the Threadgoode family, taken in 1919; Evelyn felt as if they were old friends. She recognized Buddy immediately, with those flashing eyes and big smile. There was Essie Rue and the twins, and Leona, posing like a queen . . . and little Idgie, with her toy rooster. And there, way in the back, in a long white apron, was Sispey, taking picture posing very seriously.

Right underneath, she found a picture of a young woman in a white dress, standing in the same yard, shading her eyes from the sun and smiling at the person taking the picture. Evelyn thought that she was probably one of the loveliest-looking creatures she had ever seen, with those long eyelashes and that sweet smile. But she didn't recognize her. She asked Mrs. Hartman if she knew who it was.

Mrs. Hartman put on the glasses she had hanging on a chain around her neck and studied that picture for a while, puzzled. "Oh, I'll tell you who that is! That's that friend of hers who lived here for a time. She was from Georgia . . . Ruth somebody."

My God, thought Evelyn; Ruth Jamison. It must have been taken that first summer she had come to Whistle Stop. She looked at it again. It had never occurred to her that Ruth had been so beautiful.

The next picture was of a gray-haired woman wearing a hunting cap and sitting on Santa Claus's knee, with *Season's Greetings, 1956* written on the backdrop.

Mrs. Hartman took it and laughed. "Oh, that's that fool Idgie Threadgoode. She used to run the cafe out here."

"Did you know her?"

"Who didn't! Oh, she was a *mess*, there was no telling what that one would do next."

"Look, Mrs. Hartman, here's a picture of Mrs. Threadgoode." The photograph had been taken downtown at Loveman's department store, about twenty years before; Mrs. Threadgoode was already gray and looked very much like she did the last time Evelyn had seen her.

Mrs. Hartman took the picture in hand. "Bless her heart, I remember that dress. It was dark navy blue with white polka dots. She must have worn that dress for thirty years. After she died, she said she wanted all her clothes to go to the Goodwill. She really didn't have anything worth saving, poor soul, just an old coat and a few housedresses. They picked up what little furniture there was, all except for the glider on the front porch. I just couldn't bear to give them that. She used to sit in that thing all day and night, waiting for the trains to go by. It just wouldn't seem right to let strangers have it. She left her house to our daughter, Terry."

Evelyn was still taking things out of the box. "Look, Mrs. Hartman, here's an old menu from the Whistle Stop Cafe. It must be from the thirties. Can you believe those prices? A barbecue for ten cents . . . and you could get a complete dinner for thirty-five cents! And pie was a nickel!"

"Isn't that something. It costs at least five or six dollars to get a decent meal nowadays, even out at the cafeteria, and they charge you extra for your beverage and your pie, at that."

Before she was through, Evelyn found a photograph of Idgie wearing a pair of those glasses with the fake nose, standing with four goofy-looking guys dressed up in crazy outfits, with *Dill Pickle Club . . . Icebox Follies, 1942* written underneath . . . and an Easter card from Cleo, the postcards Evelyn had sent her from California, a Southern Railroad pullman car menu from the fifties, a half-used lipstick, a mimeographed copy of Psalm 90, and a hospital armband that said:

Mrs. Cleo Threadgoode
An eighty-six-year-old woman

And down at the very bottom of the box, Evelyn found the envelope addressed to *Mrs. Evelyn Couch.*

"Look, she must have written me a letter." She opened it and read the note:

Evelyn,
   Here are some of Sipsey's original recipes I wrote down. They have given me so much pleasure, I thought I'd pass them on to you, especially the one for Fried Green Tomatoes.
   I love you, dear little Evelyn. Be happy. I am happy.
   Your Friend,
   Mrs. Cleo Threadgoode

Mrs. Hartman said, "Well, bless her heart, she wanted you to have those."

Evelyn was sad as she carefully folded the note and put everything back. She thought, My God, a living, breathing person was on this earth for eighty-six years, and this is all that's left, just a shoe box full of old papers.

Evelyn asked Mrs. Hartman if she could tell her how to get to where the cafe had been.

"It's just a couple of blocks up the road. I'll be happy to go with you and show you if you want me to."

"That would be wonderful, if you could."

"Oh sure. Just let me turn off my beans and throw my roast in the oven, and I'll be right there."

Evelyn put the picture and the shoe box in the car, and while she was waiting, she walked over to Mrs. Threadgoode's yard. She looked up and started to laugh; still stuck up, high in the silver birch tree, was Mrs. Threadgoode's broom she had thrown at the bluejays over a year ago, and sitting on the telephone wires were those blackbirds Mrs. Threadgoode thought had been listening to her on the phone. The house was just as Mrs. Threadgoode had described it, with her pots of geraniums, right down to the dog-eared snowball bushes in the front.

When Mrs. Hartman came out, they drove a few blocks from the house and she showed her where the cafe used to be, sitting not twenty feet from the railroad tracks. Right beside it was a little brick building, also abandoned, but Evelyn could just make out a faded sign in the window: OPAL'S BEAUTY SHOP. Everything was just as she had imagined.

Mrs. Hartman showed her the spot where Poppa Threadgoode's store used to be, now a Rexall Drug Store with an Elks Club on the second story.

Evelyn asked if it would be possible to see Troutville.

"Sure, honey, it's right across the tracks."

When they drove through the little black section, Evelyn was surprised at how small it was—just a few blocks of tiny, run-down shacks. Mrs. Hartman pointed out one little house with faded green tin chairs on the front porch and told her that's where Big George and Onzell had lived until they went over to Birmingham to stay with their son Jasper.

As they drove out, she saw Ocie's grocery store, attached to the side of a falling-down, wooden shotgun house that had once been painted baby blue. The front of the store was plastered with faded old signs from the thirties, urging you to DRINK BUFFALO ROCK GINGER ALE . . . MELLOWED A MILLION MINUTES OR MORE . . .

Evelyn suddenly remembered something from her childhood.

"Mrs. Hartman, do you think they might have a strawberry soda in there?"

"I'll bet he does."

"Would it be all right if we went in?"

"Oh sure, a lot of white people shop over here."

Evelyn parked and they went in. Mrs. Hartman went to the old man in the white shirt and suspenders and began shouting in his ear. "Ocie, this is Mrs. Couch. She was a friend of Ninny Threadgoode's!"

The minute Ocie heard Mrs. Threadgoode's name, his eyes lit up and he got up and ran over and hugged Evelyn. Evelyn, who had never been hugged by a black man in her life, was caught off guard. Ocie started talking to her a mile a minute, but she couldn't understand a word he was saying because he had no teeth.

Mrs. Hartman shouted at him again, "No honey, this isn't her daughter! This is her friend Mrs. Couch, from Birmingham . . ."

Ocie kept grinning and smiling at her.

Mrs. Hartman was rooting around in the cold drink box and pulled out a strawberry soda. "Look! Here you are."

Evelyn tried to pay for it, but Ocie kept saying something to her that she still could not understand.

"He says put your money away, Mrs. Couch. He wants you to have that cold drink on him."

Evelyn was flustered, but thanked Ocie, and he followed them out to the car, still talking and grinning.

Mrs. Hartman shouted, "BYE-BYE!" She turned to Evelyn. "He's as deaf as a post."

"I figured that. I just can't get over him hugging me like that."

"Well, you know, he thought the world of Mrs. Threadgoode. He's been knowing her since he was a little boy."

They drove back over the tracks, and Mrs. Hartman said, "Honey, if you take a right on the next street, I'll show you where the old Threadgoode place is."

The minute they turned the corner, she saw it: a big, two-story white wooden house with the front porch that went all around. She recognized it from the pictures.

Evelyn pulled up in front, and they got out.

The windows were mostly broken and boarded up, and the wood on the front porch was caved in and rotten, so they couldn't go up. It looked like the whole house was ready to fall down. They walked around to the back.

Evelyn said, "What a shame they let this place go. I'll bet it was beautiful at one time."

Mrs. Hartman agreed. "At one time, this was the prettiest house in Whistle Stop. But all the Threadgoodes are gone now, so I guess they're just gonna tear it down one of these days."

When they got to the backyard, Evelyn and Mrs. Hartman were surprised at what they saw. The old trellis, leaning on the back of the house, was entirely covered with thousands of little pink sweetheart roses, blooming like they had no idea that the people inside had left long ago.

Evelyn peeked in the broken window and saw a cracked, white enamel table. She wondered how many biscuits had been cut on that table throughout the years.

When she took Mrs. Hartman home, she thanked her for going along.

"Oh, my pleasure, we almost never get anybody out here to visit anymore, not since the trains stopped running. I'm sorry that we had to meet under such sad circumstances, but I've enjoyed meeting you so much, and please come back just anytime you want to."

Although it was late, Evelyn decided to drive by the old house one more time. It was just getting dark, and as she came down the street, her lights hit the windows in such a way that it looked to her like there were people inside, moving around . . . and all of a sudden, she could have sworn that she heard Essie Rue pounding away at the old piano in the parlor . . .

"Buffalo gals, won't you come out tonight, come out tonight . . ."

Evelyn stopped the car and sat there, sobbing like her heart would break, wondering why people had to get old and die.

THE WEEMS WEEKLY

(WHISTLE STOP, ALABAMA'S WEEKLY BULLETIN)

JUNE 25, 1969

## Hard to Say Goodbye

I am sorry to report that this will be the last issue. Ever since I took my other half to south Alabama for a vacation, he has been having a fit to live there. We found ourselves a place right on the bay, so we are going to move down in a couple of weeks. Now the old coot can fish night and day if he wants to. I know I spoil him, but with all his orneriness, he's still a pretty good old guy. Don't know what to say about leaving, so I won't say much. Both of us were raised right here in Whistle Stop, and had so many wonderful times and friends. But most of them have gone somewhere else. The place doesn't seem the same, and now, with all these new super highways they got, you can hardly tell where Birmingham ends and Whistle Stop begins.

Now that I look back, it seems to me that after the cafe closed, the heart of the town just stopped beating. Funny how a little knockabout like that brought so many people together.

At least we all have our memories, and I've still got my old sweetheart with me.

                    . . . Dot Weems . . .

P.S. If any of you ever get to Fairhope, Alabama, look us up. I'll be the one sitting on the back porch, cleaning all the fish.

                . . .                 . . .

APRIL 19, 1988

The second Easter after Mrs. Threadgoode died, Evelyn was determined to make it to the cemetery. She bought a beautiful spray of white Easter lilies and drove out in her new pink Cadillac, wearing her fourteen-karat studded bumblebee pin with the emerald eyes, another award.

Earlier today, she'd been to brunch with her Mary Kay group, so it was late afternoon. Most of the people had been there and gone already, but the cemetery was filled with spectacular Easter arrangements of every color.

Evelyn had to drive around for a while before she finally found the Threadgoode family plot. The first grave she found was Ruth Jamison's. She walked on down the row and found the big double headstone with the angel:

WILLIAM JAMES      ALICE LEE CLOUD
THREADGOODE      THREADGOODE
1850–1929      1856–1932

BELOVED PARENTS
NOT LOST
BUT GONE BEFORE
WHERE WE SHALL MEET AGAIN

Next to them was:

JAMES LEE (BUDDY) THREADGOODE
1898–1919
A YOUTH CUT DOWN BEFORE HIS TIME
WHO LIVES ON IN OUR HEARTS

She found Edward's, Cleo's, and Mildred's graves; but she couldn't find her friend's, and she began to panic. Where was Mrs. Threadgoode?

Finally, one row down on the right, she saw:

ALBERT THREADGOODE
1930–1978
OUR ANGEL ON THIS EARTH
SAFE AT LAST IN THE ARMS OF JESUS

She looked beside Albert's grave, and there it was:

MRS. VIRGINIA (NINNY) THREADGOODE
1899–1986
GONE HOME

The memory and sweetness of the old woman flooded back in an instant, and she realized just how much she missed her. Tears ran down her face while she placed the flowers, and then she went about the business of pulling up all the little weeds that had grown up around the tombstone. She consoled herself by thinking that one thing was for sure; if there really was a heaven, Mrs. Threadgoode was certainly there. She wondered if there would ever be a pure, untouched soul like her on this earth again. . . . She doubted it.

It's funny, Evelyn thought. Because of knowing Mrs. Threadgoode, she was not as scared of getting old or dying as she had once been, and death did not seem all that far away. Even today, it was as if Mrs. Threadgoode was just standing behind a door.

Evelyn began quietly speaking to her friend. "I'm sorry I

haven't gotten out here sooner, Mrs. Threadgoode. You'll never know how many times I've thought about you and wished I could speak to you. I felt so bad I didn't get to see you before you died. I just never dreamed in a million years that I would never see you again. I never did get a chance to thank you. If it hadn't been for you talking to me like you did every week, I don't know what I would have done."

She paused for a moment, and then went on, "I got that pink Cadillac for us, Mrs. Threadgoode. I thought it would make me happy, but you know, it didn't mean half as much without you to go for a ride in it with me. I've often wished I could come and pick you up and we could go on a Sunday drive, or over to Ollie's for some barbecue."

She moved to the other side of the headstone and continued pulling the weeds and talking. "I've been asked to do some work with the mental health group, over at the university hospital . . . and I might do it." She laughed. "I told Ed, I might as well work for a disease I've had.

"And you're not going to believe this, Mrs. Threadgoode, but I'm a grandmother now. Twice. Janice had twin girls. And you remember Ed's mother, Big Momma? Well, we put her over at Meadowlark Manor, and she likes it much better, and I was just as glad. . . . I hated going out to Rose Terrace after you died. The last time I went, Geneene told me that Vesta Adcock is crazy as ever, still upset over Mr. Dunaway leaving.

"Everybody misses you: Geneene, your neighbors the Hartmans . . . I went out there and got the things you left me, and I use those recipes all the time. Oh, by the way, I've lost forty-three pounds since the last time you saw me. I still have five more to go.

"And, let's see, your friend Ocie died last month, but then, I guess you know that. Oh, I knew there was another thing I had to tell you:

"Remember that picture of you in the blue polka-dotted dress, you made down at Loveman's? I have it framed and sitting on my occasional table in the living room, and when one of my customers saw it, she said, 'Evelyn, you look exactly like your mother! . . . Isn't that something, Mrs. Threadgoode?"

Evelyn told her friend everything she could think of that had happened in the last year, and she didn't leave until she felt sure in her heart that Mrs. Threadgoode knew she was really okay.

Evelyn was smiling and happy as she walked back to the car; but as she passed Ruth's grave, she stopped.

Something was there that hadn't been there before. Sitting on the headstone was a glass jar filled with freshly cut little pink sweetheart roses. Beside the jar was an envelope addressed in thin, scratchy handwriting:

FOR RUTH JAMISON

Surprised, Evelyn picked up the envelope. Inside was an old-fashioned Easter card, with a picture of a little girl holding a basket of multicolored eggs. She opened the card:

FOR A SPECIAL PERSON AS NICE AS YOU,
WHO'S KIND AND CONSIDERATE IN ALL YOU DO,
THE FAIREST, THE SQUAREST,
MOST LOVING AND TRUE,
THAT ALL ADDS UP TO
WONDERFUL YOU!

And the card was signed:

*I'll always remember.*
*Your friend,*
*The Bee Charmer*

Evelyn stood with the card in her hand and looked all around the cemetery; but no one was there.

MARCH 17, 1988

## Elderly Woman Reported Missing

Mrs. Vesta Adcock, an 83-year-old resident of the Rose Terrace Nursing Home, apparently walked off the premises yesterday, after announcing that she needed a breath of fresh air, and has not returned.

When last seen, she was wearing a pink chenille robe with fox furs, royal-blue fuzzy-type slippers, and may have been wearing a red stocking cap and carrying a black beaded purse.

A bus driver remembered someone answering to that description getting on his bus near the home late yesterday and asking for a transfer.

If you have seen anyone fitting that description, you are asked to call Mrs. Virginia Mae Schmitt, director of the nursing home, at 555-7760.

The woman's son, Mr. Earl Adcock, Jr., of New Orleans, said that his mother may have become disoriented.

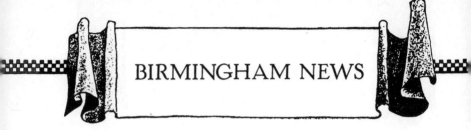

# BIRMINGHAM NEWS

MARCH 20, 1988

## Elderly Woman Found in Love Nest

Mrs. Vesta Adcock, an 83-year-old woman who had been reported missing from the Rose Terrace Nursing Home four days ago, has been found residing at the Bama Motel in East Lake. Her male companion, Mr. Walter Dunaway, 80, of Birmingham, suffered a mild stroke and was admitted to the university hospital for observation early today.

Mrs. Adcock asked to be returned to the nursing home and was very despondent, because, as she said, "Walter is not the man I thought he was."

Mr. Dunaway is listed in satisfactory condition.

# HIGHWAY 90

MARIANNA, FLORIDA

MAY 22, 1988

Bill and Marion Neal and their eight-year-old daughter Patsy had been driving all day when they passed the roadside stand that advertised: FRESH EGGS, HONEY, FRESH FRUIT AND VEGE-TABLES, FRESH CATFISH, COLD DRINKS.

They were thirsty, so Bill turned around and went back. When they got out, nobody was there; but they saw two old men in overalls sitting under a huge water oak tree, out behind the stand. One of the men got up and started walking toward them.

"Hi there, folks. What can I do for you today?"

When she heard the voice, Marion realized it was not an old man but an old woman with snow-white hair and brown, weatherbeaten skin. "We'd like three Coca-Colas, please."

Patsy was staring at the jars of honey lined up on the shelf.

While the old woman was opening the three frosty Cokes, Patsy pointed to one of the jars of honey and asked, "What's in that jar?"

"Why, that's honeycomb, right out of the hive. Haven't you ever seen that before?"

Patsy was fascinated. "No ma'am."

"Where are you folks from?"

Marion said, "Birmingham."

"Well, I'll be. I used to live in a little town just on the other side. You've probably never heard of it: little place called Whistle Stop."

Bill said, "Oh sure. Where the railroad yards used to be. They had a barbecue joint out there, as I remember."

The old woman smiled. "That's right."

Bill pointed to her sign. "Didn't know you got catfish down this far."

"Sure we do, saltwater cat, but I don't have any today."

She looked at the little blond girl to see if she was listening. "Last week I caught one, but it was so big we couldn't pull it out of the water."

Patsy said, *"Really?"*

The old woman's blue eyes sparkled. "Oh, yes indeed. As a matter of fact, that catfish was so big, we took a picture of it, and the picture alone weighed forty pounds."

The little girl cocked her head to one side, trying to figure it out. "Are you *sure?*"

"Sure I'm sure. But if you don't believe me . . ." She turned around and called up to the old man in the yard, "Hey, Julian! Go in the house and bring me that picture of the catfish we caught last week."

He called back lazily, "Cain't do it . . . it's too heavy for me to carry. Might hurt my back . . ."

"See, I told you."

Bill laughed and Marion paid for the drinks. They were about to go when Patsy pulled at her mother's dress. "Momma, can we please get a jar of honey?"

"Sweetheart, we've got plenty of honey at home."

"Please, Momma, we don't have any with honeycomb. Please?"

Marion looked at her for a moment and then gave in. "How much is the honey?"

"The honey? Well, let's see." The old woman started counting on her fingers, and then said, "You're not gonna believe this, but you hit it lucky, because today . . . it's absolutely free."

Patsy's eyes got wide. *"Really?"*

"That's right."

Marion said, "Oh, I feel terrible about not paying you anything. Won't you let me give you a little something, at least?"

The old woman shook her head. "No, it's free. You won it, fair and square. You don't know this, but your little girl, here, just happens to be my one millionth customer this month."

"I AM?"

"That's right, my one millionth."

Marion smiled at the old woman. "Well, if you insist. Patsy, what do you say?"

"Thank you."

"You're welcome. And listen, Patsy, if you ever get anywhere around these parts again, you be sure and look me up, y'hear?"

"Yes ma'am, I will."

As they pulled out, Bill tooted his horn and the little girl waved goodbye.

The old woman stood on the side of the road and waved back until the car was out of sight.


The end.

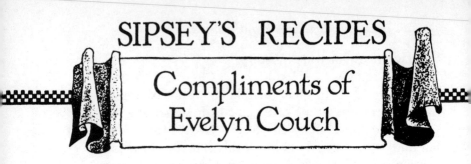

# SIPSEY'S RECIPES

## Compliments of Evelyn Couch

### BUTTERMILK BISCUITS

2 cups flour
2 teaspoons baking powder
2 teaspoons salt

¼ teaspoon soda
½ cup Crisco
1 cup buttermilk

Sift dry ingredients together. Add Crisco and blend well until like fine meal. Add buttermilk and mix. Roll out thin and cut into desired size biscuit. Bake in greased pan at 450 degrees until golden brown.

Naughty Bird's favorite!

### SKILLET CORNBREAD

¾ teaspoon baking soda
1 ½ cups buttermilk
2 cups cornmeal, sifted

1 teaspoon salt
1 egg
1 tablespoon melted bacon fat

Dissolve soda in buttermilk. Mix the cornmeal with salt, egg, and buttermilk. Add hot, melted bacon fat. Pour into greased iron skillet and bake at 375 degrees until done.

So good, it will kill you.

## COCONUT CREAM PIE

3 egg yolks  
⅓ cup sugar  
¼ teaspoon salt  
2 ½ tablespoons cornstarch  
1 tablespoon melted butter  

2 cups scalded milk  
1 cup grated coconut  
1 teaspoon vanilla or rum  
¼ teaspoon nutmeg  
9-inch pie shell, baked  

Beat egg yolks. Beat in sugar, salt, cornstarch, and butter gradually. Pour in milk and blend. Cook over boiling water, stirring constantly until thick. Add coconut, and cool. Add flavoring and nutmeg and pour into shell. Cover with meringue and bake 15 to 20 minutes in 300-degree oven.

Yum, yum.

## PECAN PIE

9-inch pie shell, unbaked  
2 cups pecans, chopped  
1 cup sugar, brown or white  
1 cup light corn syrup  
1 tablespoon flour  

1 teaspoon vanilla  
¼ teaspoon salt  
3 eggs  
2 tablespoons butter  

Line the pie shell with chopped pecans. Combine the sugar, corn syrup, flour, vanilla, and salt and mix until blended. Beat in the eggs one at a time, mixing well each time. Pour into the nut-lined pie shell, and dot with butter. Bake at 350 degrees until firm—about 1 hour.

Sinful stuff—Stump's favorite.

## SIPSEY'S SOUTHERN-FRIED CHICKEN

1 good-sized fryer          Milk
Salt and pepper             1 ½ cups sifted flour

Cut chicken into serving pieces. Rub well with salt and pepper. Let
stand awhile. Then soak in milk about 1/2 hour. Put flour, a little salt
and pepper, and chicken into a bag, and shake well until every piece
is coated. Fry in hot, deep fat at 400 degrees, until golden brown.
Leave heavy pieces in fat a little longer than the smaller ones.

So long, Mr. Chicken.

## CHICKEN AND DUMPLINGS

2 cups white flour          ⅔ cup milk
3 teaspoons baking soda     ⅓ cup Crisco oil
1 teaspoon salt             1 pot of chicken stew

Mix flour, baking soda, and salt together. Then add milk and oil.
Spoon-drop into boiling stew, cook for 15 minutes, turning dumplings
often.

Should float off the fork.

## FRIED HAM WITH RED-EYE GRAVY

Slice ham about 1/4 inch thick. Cook slowly in a heavy frying pan
until evenly browned on both sides. Sprinkle each side lightly with
sugar during cooking. Remove the ham and keep it warm, then add
about 1/2 cup of cold water or a cup of coffee. Let it boil until gravy
turns red. Blend and pour over the ham.

Good eats!

## GRITS

2 tablespoons butter            5 cups boiling water
1 teaspoon salt                 1 cup hominy grits

Add lots of butter and salt to the boiling water. Slowly stir in the grits. Cover and cook slowly for about 30 to 40 minutes, and stir till you like it.

Keeps you regular.

## FRIED CATFISH

2 pounds catfish, cleaned and       Salt and pepper to taste
  skinned                           ½ cup yellow cornmeal
½ cup sifted flour                  3 tablespoons bacon fat or
                                      Crisco

Wipe the fish with a damp cloth. Mix the flour, salt, pepper and cornmeal. Roll Mr. Catfish in the mixture and fry in hot bacon fat until golden brown on one side. Then turn and brown the other side. Total cooking time about 8 to 10 minutes.

Thank God for catfish!

## MILK GRAVY

Use hot drippings from chicken or pork chops. For each 3 tablespoons of drippings, stir in 3 tablespoons of flour and blend well. Cook and stir until lightly browned. Gradually add 1 ½ to 2 cups hot milk. Cook and stir until thickened.

Goes with everything.

## PORK CHOPS & GRAVY

*4 slices bacon*
*4 large thick pork chops*
*⅓ cup flour*

*Salt and pepper*
*1 ½ cups milk*

Fry the bacon first, then dip the chops in flour, with salt and pepper. Save what's left of the flour. Fry your chops in the hot bacon drippings until brown on both sides. Turn down heat, cover, and cook till chops are tender and thoroughly cooked—about 30 minutes. Stir your leftover flour into the fat and cook until browned. Pour the milk over the chops and simmer until gravy is thickened.

Big George could eat eight at a time.

## SNAP BEANS

*1 hambone, cooked*
*2 pounds snap beans*
*1 teaspoon sugar, brown or*
  *granulated*

*A few hot red pepper flakes*
*Salt to taste*

Place hambone in pot and add water to cover beans. Bring to a boil. String the beans and snap or cut into desired lengths. Add to the pot along with the sugar and pepper flakes. Cook over medium heat for 1 hour.

Happy beans . . . fun to eat.

## SIPSEY'S BLACK-EYED PEAS

1 ¼ cups dried black-eyed peas
4 cups water
1 onion, chopped

1 piece salt pork or 8 pieces
    bacon
A little red pepper

Put all the ingredients together in a pot and cook slowly until tender—about 3 hours.

Even better the next day!

## CREAMED CORN

6 ears sweet white corn
2 tablespoons butter

½–1 cup milk and water
Salt and pepper

Cut corn off cob, then scrape the cob down with the back of a knife to get what's left. Cook with butter over low heat and slowly add milk and water and salt and pepper till you like it. Stir for 10 minutes till just right.

Good for you.

## LIMA BEANS & BUTTER BEANS

1 quart fresh beans
Salt and pepper to taste

1 piece salt pork or 6 pieces
    bacon

Add water just up to the top of the beans. Let it come to a boil, then simmer until tender. Add salt and pepper till you like it.

Right out of the Victory garden.

## CANDIED YAMS

⅓ cup butter
⅔ cup brown sugar, packed
6 medium-sized sweet
   potatoes, cooked, peeled,
   and sliced

½ teaspoon salt
⅓ cup water
2 pinches cinnamon

In a heavy frying pan or skillet, heat together butter and brown sugar until melted and blended. Add the sliced sweet potatoes and turn until coated in the syrup and brown. Add salt, water, and cinnamon, cover, and cook slowly until potatoes are tender.

*Sweeter than candy.*

## FRIED OKRA

Wash your okra well and cut off the stems. Cut pods into sections about ½ inch long. Roll in cornmeal and fry in hot bacon drippings and deep hot fat until a nice crisp brown. Drain on paper towel, sprinkle with salt and pepper, and serve hot.

*Better than popcorn.*

## TURNIP & COLLARD GREENS

Wash greens well and take the leaves, roots, and stems off from the collards. Boil a hambone or some fatback or bacon. Add greens, a red pepper pod, and salt, pepper, and sugar to taste. Cover tightly and cook until greens are tender. Drain and place on serving platter; reserve the liquid. Serve the liquid as "pot likker" to dunk your cornbread in.

*Will cure what ails you!*

# FRIED GREEN TOMATOES

1 medium green tomato (per
   person)
Salt

Pepper
White cornmeal
Bacon drippings

Slice tomatoes about 1/4 inch thick, season with salt and pepper and then coat both sides with cornmeal. In a large skillet, heat enough bacon drippings to coat the bottom of the pan and fry tomatoes until lightly browned on both sides.

You'll think you died and gone to heaven!

# FRIED GREEN TOMATOES WITH MILK GRAVY

3 tablespoons bacon fat
4 firm green tomatoes, sliced
   ½ inch thick
Beaten eggs
Dry bread crumbs

Flour
Milk
Salt
Pepper

Heat your bacon fat in a heavy frying pan. Dip tomatoes in eggs, then in bread crumbs. Slowly fry them in the bacon fat until golden brown on both sides. Put your tomatoes on a plate. For *each tablespoon* of fat left in the pan, stir in 1 tablespoon of flour and blend well; then stir in 1 cup warm milk and cook until thickened, stirring constantly. Add salt and pepper till you like it. Pour over the tomatoes and serve hot.

The best there is.

FANNIE FLAGG began writing and producing television specials at age nineteen and went on to distinguish herself as an actress and writer in television, films, and the theater. She is the author of the *New York Times* bestsellers *Daisy Fay and the Miracle Man; Fried Green Tomatoes at the Whistle Stop Cafe* (which was produced by Universal Pictures as *Fried Green Tomatoes*); *Welcome to the World, Baby Girl!; Standing in the Rainbow;* and *A Redbird Christmas*. Flagg's script for *Fried Green Tomatoes* was nominated for both the Academy and Writers Guild of America awards and won the highly regarded Scripters Award. Flagg lives in California and in Alabama.